AN AUDACIOUS WOMAN

A Tabitha & Wolf Mystery: Book 5

Sarah F. Noel

Copyright © 2024 Sarah F. Noel

All rights reserved

The characters and events portrayed in this book are fictitious. Any similarity to real persons, living or dead, is coincidental and not intended by the author.

No part of this book may be reproduced, or stored in a retrieval system, or transmitted in any form or by any means, electronic, mechanical, photocopying, recording, or otherwise, without express written permission of the publisher.

ISBN: 9798875694295
Cover design by: HelloBriie Creative
Printed in the United States of America

To my Grandma Helen, whose chicken soup was the quintessential Jewish penicillin and who taught me most of the Yiddish I know.

CONTENTS

Title Page
Copyright
Dedication
Foreword
Prologue   1
Chapter 1   2
Chapter 2   9
Chapter 3   18
Chapter 4   25
Chapter 5   36
Chapter 6   46
Chapter 7   52
Chapter 8   59
Chapter 9   69
Chapter 10   75
Chapter 11   81
Chapter 12   91
Chapter 13   100
Chapter 14   106
Chapter 15   115

Chapter 16	125
Chapter 17	136
Chapter 18	144
Chapter 19	149
Chapter 20	158
Chapter 21	162
Chapter 22	169
Chapter 23	174
Chapter 24	179
Chapter 25	190
Chapter 26	196
Chapter 27	202
Chapter 28	211
Chapter 29	217
Chapter 30	222
Chapter 31	230
Chapter 32	237
Chapter 33	244
Chapter 34	252
Chapter 35	257
Epilogue	263
Afterword	271
Acknowledgement	273
About The Author	275
Books By This Author	277

FOREWORD

This book is written using British English spelling. e.g. dishonour instead of dishonor, realise instead of realize.

British spelling aside, while every effort has been made to proofread this thoroughly, typos do creep in. If you find any, I'd greatly appreciate a quick email to report them at sarahfnoelauthor@gmail.com

PROLOGUE

The woman heard footsteps behind her, but thought nothing of it. As she turned onto the Victoria Embankment, which suddenly seemed very dark and quiet, the footsteps continued, perhaps even getting closer. Not normally faint of heart, she suddenly realised she was being followed. There was only one person she had cause to fear, but she thought she had successfully neutralised that danger. She had never considered before how dark this street was. The woman was fully alert to her shadowy companion, but still was not unduly worried; this was nothing more than an attempt to scare her into compliance. Those were the last words she thought before a hand grasped her around the waist, and another slammed across her mouth, muffling any screams.

CHAPTER 1

Monday, October 30, 1897: Tabitha & Wolf

What was the protocol for receiving an urgent afternoon visit from your mother-in-law's butler? When she was younger, Tabitha's mother, Lady Jameson, had drilled her in the appropriate etiquette for every conceivable situation, or so she had thought. But this one had escaped the attention of even the ever-vigilant Dowager Marchioness of Cambridgeshire.

Earlier that morning, Tabitha and Wolf had received a telephone call. The Dowager Countess of Pembroke, Tabitha's erstwhile mother-in-law, was one of the few people they knew with a telephone, installing it without permission at Chesterton House. Given this, Tabitha had assumed that it was the dowager calling. Indeed, the call had come from the dowager's household, but instead of being from the woman herself, it had come from her butler, Manning.

Undoubtedly, the dowager and Manning shared a closer bond than might be expected of an aristocrat and one of her household staff. This bond had been evident when Manning was arrested for murder, and the dowager had begged Wolf, and Tabitha by extension, to prove the man's innocence. Manning's devotion and loyalty to the dowager was beyond dispute – the man was willing to go to the gallows to protect his employer's reputation. However, Tabitha had wondered at the time if the dowager reciprocated his feelings or was merely unwilling to lose a well-trained servant. Nevertheless, even this recent evidence of their bond, whatever its motivation, had not prepared Tabitha to hear her butler, Talbot, intone, "That was Mr Manning, the dowager countess' butler, on the telephone. He is worried about the dowager countess and believes she might be in imminent danger. He has asked if he might call to speak with you and Lord Pembroke after luncheon."

Unlike the dowager countess herself, Manning had never struck Tabitha as being given to melodrama and hyperbole, and she couldn't imagine what imminent danger an aged aristocrat could have managed to get herself into, such that it would drive her butler to inform on her. Yet, as she sat in the drawing room waiting for Wolf to join her for Manning's arrival, Tabitha also reflected on what it would take for the famously discreet and normally stoic butler to break ranks and tattle on his mistress: was the dowager truly in peril?

Tabitha's worried reflections were interrupted by Wolf's appearance. Even though they shared a home and ate most dinners and many breakfasts together, the sight of her deceased husband's cousin and heir caused Tabitha a brief flicker of discomfort; ever since they had shared a passionate but unexpected kiss in Brighton two weeks before, there had been an awkwardness between the pair. Tabitha knew they had to talk about their feelings towards each other. She had even promised that they would on their return to London. Yet, as the days slipped by, she found herself postponing this conversation. It was evident that Wolf, while trying to be patient and respectful of Tabitha's pace, nevertheless would prefer to have this conversation sooner rather than later. Every time they were together, he positively thrummed with an uncharacteristic nervous energy.

She looked at the tall, broad-shouldered, handsome man as he entered the drawing room: his dark, curly hair, as always, a little too long, his blue, heavily lashed eyes so kind and gentle, and Tabitha asked herself yet again, what was she so worried about? Before their unexpected detour to Brighton, Tabitha had been convinced of her determination never to marry again. Her deceased husband had been a cruel and violent man, and she had believed that it was only as a wealthy widow that she would have the freedom and independence to protect herself in the future. If she remarried, her husband would have total control over her fortune and person, and Tabitha never wanted to be that powerless again. As much as she knew that Wolf was not his cousin Jonathan, that the two men couldn't be less alike, she had been sure that she could never again willingly put herself in thrall to another man.

Knowing that she never intended to marry, Tabitha had also convinced herself that she was at peace with the idea that Wolf would someday marry someone else. But having come face-to-face with Wolf's first love, Lady Arlene Archibald, in Brighton, Tabitha had found that this hypothetical acceptance shattered in the face of reality. Confronted with the very real possibility that Lady Archibald might be able to reignite the embers of her youthful passion with Wolf, Tabitha had realised the truth behind her attempts at indifference.

Yet acknowledging her feelings to herself and saying them out loud were two very different propositions. It wasn't that she doubted that Wolf felt something for her in return, even if she wasn't as confident about the nature of those feelings. Rather, it was the knowledge that the moment those feelings were spoken, things would never be the same again. Of course, they might be better; they almost certainly would be. But they wouldn't be the same.

The last few months, sharing a home with Wolf, managing his household, raising her ward Melody, and being part of four investigations, had been the happiest of Tabitha's life. She had felt a lightness of spirit that she certainly hadn't experienced since before her wedding night to Jonathan. But even as a child and then a young woman, she had felt constrained by her mother and society's expectations of her. In the first few months of her widowhood, Tabitha was cast out of aristocratic circles because of suspicions, mostly voiced by the dowager, that she had a hand in Jonathan's death. As those suspicions died down, they were supplanted by other society gossip as Tabitha had outraged society all over again by continuing to share a house with Wolf, the new earl.

Rather than lamenting her status as an outcast, Tabitha had felt liberated by it; after twenty-two years of being forced to kowtow to society's judgement, now that she had fallen foul of it, she realised that it wasn't so awful not to be invited to the soirees of the inner circle. Not having to sit through boring formal dinners and constantly entertain matrons and debutantes for excruciating tea parties was wonderful.

But were she and Wolf to marry, society would inevitably forget its disdain for her and welcome – no, force – the earl's new wife back into the fold. As much as she would miss the freedom her black sheep status afforded her, there was more to Tabitha's doubts. There had always been a small part of her that wondered if she had been the cause of Jonathan's outbursts. The dowager had come right out and accused Tabitha of failing to be a sufficiently docile wife and driving Jonathan to his violent behaviour. This nagging self-doubt was persistent enough that Tabitha questioned her ability to be a good wife, even to a man like Wolf.

Wolf had no idea of the troubled thoughts running through Tabitha's head. At that moment, he was also worried about what Manning might have to tell them. As much as he railed against the dowager's injection of herself in his past four investigations and often found the woman high-handed and interfering, he had become quite fond of her and was genuinely worried about what trouble she might have gotten herself in. He walked over to where Tabitha sat and pulled up an armchair beside her.

"So, Manning gave no more information as to what this is all about?" Wolf asked.

Tabitha shook her head, "You know as much as I do. But he has always struck me as a reticent man, even for a butler. It's hard to imagine he would use the words 'imminent danger' lightly." She paused and cocked her head to one side in thought, "Remember when we first arrived in Brighton, and we were discussing your desire for that to be your last investigation?" Wolf nodded in acknowledgement, and Tabitha continued, "Mama was unhappy at this pronouncement, and was very insistent that you should continue to take on cases and that she would be an integral part of your investigative team."

"I remember that conversation well," Wolf answered. "I

believe the phrase she used was 'I'm not sure that it is for you to decide that our investigative collaboration is at an end.'"

"Indeed. And while I'm unsure if you've made a final determination around the issue, I'm assuming that you haven't shared with Lady Pembroke your thoughts on possibly continuing to take on investigations if and when they seem appropriate."

"I haven't decided," Wolf acknowledged, "And perhaps won't until the moment such a worthy case presents itself. Assuming it ever does. But I would never share such thoughts with the dowager countess who has made clear that she feels such a determination of my activities is within her purview."

"Is it possible that the woman has decided to seek out investigations alone?" Tabitha asked. While the dowager had previously made vague threats to that end, no one had taken them seriously. But should they have?"

Whatever Wolf was going to answer, their conversation was interrupted by a light knock on the door, followed by Talbot's entry into the room. "Excuse me, milady and milord, but Mr Manning has arrived. Should I show him in?" Wolf nodded, and Talbot withdrew, only to be replaced in the doorway a few moments later by the dowager's butler, Manning. As if to compensate for her diminutive size, the dowager had hired the tallest butler she could find. Manning was easily as tall as Wolf's private secretary, once valet and previously thief-taking partner, Bear. However, unlike the enormous, muscular Bear, Manning was rail-thin.

Tabitha's first thought on seeing Manning was relief that the man seemed to have recovered from his brief but unpleasant stay in Pentonville Prison. However, the anxiety suffusing the man's face detracted from his renewed good health. Manning entered the room and then stopped, unsure what to do next. Under normal circumstances, he would never countenance the idea of sitting in the presence of his betters. But under normal circumstances, he was the butler welcoming guests. Now he was the guest, and nothing in his long career, first as a footman and then a butler, had prepared him for the correct etiquette in such circumstances. Anxiety was now replaced on the man's visage by discomfort and confusion. Given Tabitha's musings on the moment's appropriate social protocol, she was entirely sympathetic to Manning's obvious discomposure.

Finally, it was left to Wolf, who had spent most of his life giving society's expectations and rules short-shrift, to manage the awkward moment. "Mr Manning, do come in and take a seat," Wolf said with just enough aristocratic authority that Manning didn't dare argue. The butler walked to the sofa facing Tabitha and Wolf's chairs and sat, perching on the very edge of it. He might have no choice but to sit, but no one could force him to be comfortable against his will.

Before they could ask Manning to explain his urgent visit, Talbot had re-entered the room with a tea tray. Tabitha smiled at her butler, who had intuited the discomfort everyone was likely feeling and had provided the very English solution to everything: a pot of tea. Of course, as welcome as a cup of tea and a biscuit would be, they were confronted by a new quandary: who was to pour? The idea of a guest serving his host and hostess tea was absurd. The concept of one butler being expected to treat another with all the pomp and ceremony that would usually be afforded more illustrious visitors was outrageous.

Recognising the dilemma, Tabitha decided to resolve the issue and said, "Thank you, Talbot. That will be all. I will pour tea for us." From the look on Manning's face, it was clear that having a countess pour him tea was even worse than the other alternatives, but again, subservience won out, and he said nothing.

With everyone settled with a cup of tea, Wolf said kindly but firmly, "Mr Manning, your phone call this morning was quite alarming. I assume you wouldn't have worried her ladyship for anything other than a serious issue." The look on Manning's face at this made clear that the very thought was abhorrent to everything he stood for as a butler. Wolf continued, "Then please tell us why you are concerned for the dowager countess' welfare."

Manning put down his teacup and cleared his throat but paused. He was unused to having the floor with any group higher than his fellow servants. While he reigned supreme in her ladyship's household, Manning was a naturally self-effacing man, and nothing about his long career in service had prepared him for this moment. Finally, losing patience with the man's hesitation, Tabitha asked, "Manning, let us suspend the usual rules of servant-master etiquette for the purposes of this conversation. Your phone call caused a lot of consternation for Lord Pembroke and myself. I'd rather the state of worried suspense not be dragged out a moment more than necessary. Now tell us plainly, what is wrong?"

A direct order was something Manning knew how to deal with. Sitting up a little straighter, he answered, "I believe the dowager countess has taken an investigation upon herself and may now be in danger."

While Tabitha and Wolf had just been speculating about this possibility, hearing it stated as a reality was quite shocking. Tabitha was unsure of the dowager's precise age; that was not something the woman would reveal willingly. But given that Jonathan had been more than twice Tabitha's age when they'd married, and that she knew the dowager had married a little later than was normal and had feared she would never produce an heir for the first few years of her marriage, it was safe to say that she was in her seventies. While the woman could be quite ferocious, the idea of the elderly Dowager Countess of Pembroke blithely launching herself into the seedy world of criminal investigations was rather alarming.

CHAPTER 2

Saturday, October 28, 1897, two days earlier:
The dowager

It was Saturday afternoon, around two o'clock, and the dowager countess, Julia Chesterton, Lady Pembroke, taking afternoon tea alone, was irritated and bored. Truth be told, there was little she had found truly invigorating throughout her life. Marriage had been a trial to be borne as best one could. Childrearing was tedious in the extreme, and something best left to nannies and governesses whenever possible. Her role as the self-appointed doyenne of aristocratic circles could only ever provide so much entertainment; most of the members of society were dull as ditch water. Yes, there was always some excitement to be had from meddling and manipulating, but these days, even that had lost some of its charm. If she were honest with herself, the only thing that had given her life any sense of purpose recently were the investigations she had been a pivotal part of with Tabitha and Wolf.

Julia Chesterton was never given to false modesty. So she felt entirely sure of herself when she claimed, to anyone who would listen, that she had been the lynchpin in those four successfully concluded investigations. Despite the efforts to exclude her from interviews and to keep pertinent information out of her clutches, the dowager nevertheless was fully confident that all of the investigations would have come to nought without her assistance.

The dowager was even more sure of the thrill she got from the investigations' covert activities, scheming, interrogations, and, to her great surprise, from the collaboration with Wolf, Bear, Lord Langley, and even Tabitha. Prior to Wolf's ascension to the earldom and the first investigation into the death of the Duke of

Somerset, the dowager would have considered herself someone who worked best alone. However, there had been an unexpected pleasure in being part of a team. Of course, most of her pleasure was derived from the many opportunities she found to school her teammates. The only benefit of age was wisdom, and that wisdom was only valuable when one could dispense it liberally. This sat at the heart of her irritation; the rest of the team seemed unwilling to seek out more investigations and allow her the opportunity to put her unique skills to further use.

The last time she had attempted to command Jeremy, or Wolf as he insisted on being called, to continue his investigative efforts, he had made it very clear that his time was not hers to direct. This had been just one of quite a few recent rebellious retorts by the new earl that she had finally called his attention to. The Dowager Countess of Pembroke was unaccustomed to being contradicted and defied. However, even in the face of the dowager's righteous indignation, the new Earl of Pembroke has resisted changing his mind. And so, the dowager had formed the opinion that she had no choice but to conduct investigations on her own.

Never one to underestimate her abilities, the dowager did not doubt that she was eminently capable of running the mechanics of an investigation on her own – sometimes, she was unsure what the others contributed anyway. There was no doubt that Mr Bear provided some useful brawn on occasion. But she was sure that other equally imposing physical specimens could be hired. In fact, the dowager made a mental note to contact Mickey D to ask this very question. Because, at least as far as the dowager was concerned, Mickey D, the notorious Whitechapel gangster, was her secret weapon.

That afternoon, the dowager sipped her tea, considered Mickey D and realised that he was the answer she had been looking for. As unlikely a pairing as an Irish mobster and aged countess were, when Mickey D and Julia Chesterton had first met at a dinner party she had hosted, they had surprised everyone by immediately taking to each other. The dowager had called Mickey Doherty and his wife Angie, "A breath of fresh air." He, in turn, had promised that she might safely walk through Whitechapel wearing her best diamonds. This statement particularly thrilled the dowager, who had fantasised about lording it over her fellow aristocrats with her new invulnerability.

The more she thought about Mr Doherty, the more the dowager was sure that if she was assured his help, she might proceed without any need of Wolf, Tabitha, Langley or Bear. On consideration, she wasn't even sure why she had put Langley on that list; the man had merely been on hand in Brighton but had hardly made any significant contributions to the investigation. While it was true that his credentials from Whitehall opened doors, the dowager was sure these doors could be knocked down easily by force of character and will. So, with Langley and Bear's contributions assessed and accounted for, the dowager considered Tabitha and Wolf. Tabitha had her notecards and that corkboard, which could easily be procured. There was no doubt that the younger woman had a certain useful logical ability. Still, again, the dowager was sure these skills were entirely within her vast intellectual capabilities.

When she considered Wolf, Julia Chesterton was on the shakiest ground; he had been a good source of investigations based on his reputation as a thief-taker before inheriting the earldom. But then, the dowager considered, truly hadn't she been the source of two of their four investigations? She had asked Wolf to prove Manning's innocence and called him to Scotland to find her granddaughter's missing friend. So perhaps she wasn't giving herself enough credit – and this was not a regular occurrence by any means.

As it happened, the dowager had made some attempts to drum up investigations on her own some weeks before she had been called to Scotland. She had invited Lady Willis and Lady Hartley over to tea. Lady Hartley, while a shrew, was also an inveterate gossip. If anyone knew the aristocracy's dirty secrets, it was she. However, shortly after this, the dowager had left town for almost a month. Perhaps Lady Hartley had come upon a possible investigation and had been deterred by her absence. Realising her error in not having checked in on one of her minions sooner, the dowager was determined to rectify this situation immediately.

Looking at the clock on the mantle, the dowager realised that afternoon was Lady Hartley's at-home day. Usually, the dowager refused to conform to such societal niceties; she had no desire for the hoi polloi of so-called good society to believe they had an open invitation to call upon her. When she desired someone's company, she summoned them. However, on this occasion, she decided she would be the one paying the social call. Hurrying up to her bed chamber, the dowager called for her maid, Withers.

As she dressed, the dowager realised this at-home was precisely the kind of social event she'd intended to expose her granddaughter, Lily, to in preparation for her debut that season. Somehow, since their return from Brighton, the dowager had found she wasn't as motivated to parade Lily through the drawing rooms, music rooms, and ballrooms of the beau monde as she had been. As for Lily, she had no interest in being presented or making a good marriage. She had been happy to take advantage of her grandmother's social lethargy to spend her time instead visiting London's museums and libraries. Lily was a very serious botanist who wanted nothing more than to be allowed to attend university. Given the rarity of any women attending at all, let alone those from the upper echelons of society, Lily realised that this aspiration was probably out of reach. But she nevertheless intended to make the most of her visit to London to further her studies as much as possible.

"Withers, have you seen Lady Lily since luncheon?" the dowager asked. She knew she probably should be keeping a better eye on her granddaughter. But ever since the excitement of the climax of their last investigation, when the dowager had been able to use her new sword stick to subdue a criminal, ensuring her granddaughter could correctly identify every one of the royal progeny had suddenly seemed far less urgent. Or at least less interesting.

"I believe that she went out to the British Library, m'lady."

"Unaccompanied?" the dowager demanded. And then, realising the more personal ramifications, she added, "And did she take my carriage?"

Withers hadn't survived as the dowager's lady's maid for more than thirty years without knowing how to manage the woman. She knew that Lady Lily had sneaked out; the girl's maid had admitted as much after Withers caught her putting on her hat and coat. Withers had also managed to get the pertinent details out of the maid. But she'd held off informing her ladyship until she had no choice. It was likely that Lady Lily would be home long before her grandmother noticed her missing. After all, there were many afternoons Lily would hide out in the dowager's library reading a book.

Choosing her words carefully, Withers said, "I believe her maid, Mildred, accompanied Lady Lily and that she was being driven to the British Library by your godson, Viscount Tobias."

"Tobias? What on earth is he doing going to a library? I'm sure the young rapscallion hasn't cracked open a book since the day he was sent down from Cambridge. In fact, I doubt he did much reading during his time there, hence the expulsion." If the dowager had her suspicions about why Viscount Tobias might have such a resurgence of interest in the written word, she kept them to herself. As it happened, Tobias' behaviour had been significantly improved since his return from Brighton. His long-suffering parents had been persuaded to pay off his most recent debts with the promise that their rake of a son had turned over a new leaf.

If his reformation stuck, the dowager would not be unhappy to see a match between her granddaughter and Tobias. A quick engagement could save them all the trouble of ensuring Lily had a successful season. The dowager was sure the young woman herself did not care a whit about her debut and was only having a season at her parent's insistence. While Lily was the granddaughter of an earl, her mother had married beneath her

– or at least that was the dowager's assessment – Lily's father was nothing more than a Scottish laird. They would certainly be thrilled if their daughter became a viscountess and eventually a countess.

But this was all food for thought for another day. For the time being, all that mattered was that Lily couldn't accompany her grandmother and that the carriage was free. Within thirty minutes, the dowager was dressed, bejewelled and on her way.

Lady Hartley could not remember the last time Lady Pembroke had deigned to attend one of her at-homes. In fact, she couldn't remember the last time the dowager countess had lowered herself to visit anyone else's home for afternoon tea, preferring that the world come to her on command. When she thought about it, she did remember the last time, and she blushed at the memory. More than a year ago, it had been at a gathering hosted by the Dowager Duchess of Somerset. Lady Hartley had repeated some salacious gossip about Lord Willis to Lady Merton a little too loudly, and then the two women had laughed like schoolgirls. Lady Willis had been deeply embarrassed and had immediately left. The ladies of society had enjoyed the scandal for some weeks after that, until Lord Cheshire's new mistress changed the conversation. Lady Hartley and Lady Willis had not spoken since, except for the recent afternoon they were forced together by the dowager.

As it happened, the dowager countess had greatly enjoyed watching one of her so-called friend's humiliation at the hands of another so-called friend. Looking around Lady Hartley's drawing room at the assembled ladies present, she could only hope for a scene even half as amusing.

The advantage of arriving quite late for afternoon tea was that she only had to suffer the company of the assembled harpies for a short time. To a woman, they could barely contain their curiosity at what might cause the eminent Lady Pembroke to lower herself to an at-home. While she would have been equally inquisitive in their shoes, the dowager refused to acknowledge her unusual sociability and would certainly say nothing to satiate their nosiness. Instead, she sipped her tea, nibbled on one of the dry scones on offer, and listened to the gossip, making just the occasional caustic observation.

When it was clear that they were to learn nothing from the dowager and would have to wait for a debrief from their hostess, the assembled women slowly made their farewells. Finally, only the dowager countess and Lady Hartley were left.

Lady Hartley was thin to the point of looking emaciated, with lank hair, very pale skin, and an overlarge nose. As if her physical flaws weren't enough, she was always at least two seasons behind in her dress. Adding to this generally unappealing appearance, Lady Hartley was very twitchy. Even when she was not put on edge by the sudden appearance of an unexpected and unwelcome guest, the woman couldn't sit still. But now, with the dowager staring at her with unnerving intensity, the woman's twitching seemed beyond her control, and her hands flapped away at her side.

The dowager enjoyed watching the woman squirm and twitch. Someone's visible discomfort at her presence was always reassuring. But the other woman's consternation provided limited entertainment, and eventually, the dowager spoke, "You may wonder what has brought me out on such a dreary day. And to call on you of all people." If Lady Hartley wondered this, she was wise enough to stay silent and let her guest continue. "I have now been back in London for more than a week after solving not one, but two murders! And yet, you have failed to call on me to report on your assigned duties."

Had she been assigned duties? Lady Hartley wracked her memory for what task the dowager countess had assigned her and came up empty. Her hands now flapping even more in consternation and her foot tapping away, she finally admitted, "I do apologise, Lady Pembroke, but I am unable to recall any specific task you have given me."

Lady Hartley was a good twenty years younger than her guest, and it did occur to her that perhaps the aged dowager was finally entering her dotage. This thought must have revealed itself in her expression, and the dowager replied with an icy coldness that chilled even that overheated drawing room, "Do you mean to imply that I am losing my wits?"

While this had been precisely what she had been thinking, Lady Hartley was not fool enough to acknowledge it. But even so, she could not summon any appropriate guess as to what the dowager was talking about. Finally, the dowager said in irritation, "How can you not remember? We agreed that given you are very well-informed about all that goes on in and around society, you would report back to me any scandals you hear of where there might be an opportunity for me to offer my services."

Lady Hartley stared at her, then blinked quickly as her thoughts raced. Finally, she said, "You were serious about that request?"

Lady Pembroke answered in a tone that seemed to chill the room further, "Have you known me ever to speak in jest? Why on earth wouldn't I have been serious?"

Realising the predicament she seemed to be in, Lady Hartley looked down at her fluttering hands as if they were detached from her body, rather than something under her control. When she had left the dowager's home weeks before, she had been focused on the discomfort of being forced into the same room as Lady Willis, and had not given a second thought to the request made of her. But now it seemed she was being held to account and needed to come up with some answer, no matter how flimsy.

Lady Hartley mentally flicked through all the gossip she had accumulated recently. There was the matter of Baroness Arthur's latest child, born only six months after her husband had returned from a year abroad. No, that wouldn't do. There was that particularly juicy gossip about the youngest son of Viscount James, but it still didn't seem to fit what her guest was demanding.

Despite Lady Hartley's nervous disposition, it was amazing how alive she would come when she sensed a juicy piece of gossip. Nothing seemed to control her twitchiness like the opportunity to spread some salacious tale of the misdeeds of others. Just flicking through her mental catalogue of gossip calmed her flapping hands somewhat. Finally, desperate for some sufficient titbit that would satisfy the dowager, she blurted out, "Lord Felix Farthing is indisposed."

"What on earth is that a euphemism for?" the dowager asked impatiently. Clearly, Lady Hartley had failed miserably at her assigned task and was now grasping at straws. Weak tea and poor refreshments were bad enough, but she had now wasted an hour of her day for nothing, leaving the dowager disinclined to play guessing games.

CHAPTER 3

Monday, October 30, 1897: Tabitha & Wolf

Manning had left less than half an hour later, having told his tale and barely drunk his tea. Tabitha and Wolf sat silently for a few minutes, contemplating the butler's story. Finally, Wolf asked, "What do you make of it? Should we be worried?"

These words echoed Tabitha's thoughts, and she wasn't sure how to answer, "I'm not sure. That Mama has been attempting to investigate on her own probably shouldn't be surprising. That she visited Whitechapel, I assume, in search of Mickey D, seems like the kind of arrogantly foolhardy thing she would do. That she hasn't been home all night without leaving word for her staff is what is of concern."

Wolf didn't know how to phrase his next question in a sufficiently genteel manner, and after running through a few possible phrases in his head, he finally gave up and asked, "Is it possible that Lady Pembroke has a male companion we don't know about?"

"A lover?" Tabitha exclaimed, using the terminology Wolf had been trying hard to avoid. "You think Mama might have a lover?" The very thought made Tabitha laugh out loud. It wasn't the dowager's age that made such an idea preposterous but rather the thought that the old woman might find any man good enough for her to risk such scandalous behaviour.

"Surely it's possible," Wolf said, defending his question. "It is possible that her absence has nothing whatsoever to do with her attempts at investigating."

"While that is possible," Tabitha conceded, "I believe there must be a more credible explanation than a secret love affair." Tabitha paused, then added in a rather guilty tone, "How did we not realise what she's been up to and that she's been absent so long?" Then, answering her own question, she added, "Thinking back on the timeline, Melody was to visit her as usual for lunch on Saturday, but because she had taken a bit of a chill, I had Talbot use the telephone that morning to tell Manning that she would be staying home."

Tabitha continued, "Regardless, let us review the facts that Manning was able to share." Tabitha raised her hand and started counting off on the fingers of her left hand. "We know that two days ago, Lady Pembroke made an uncharacteristic visit to Lady Hartley's at-home." She then touched her index finger and continued, "We know that yesterday, she took her carriage to Whitechapel, presumably to find Mickey D." Counting her middle finger now, Tabitha said, "Finally, we know that she left her house yesterday afternoon, did not take her carriage, and has not been home since."

Tabitha wasn't sure what was more shocking, that the dowager countess deigned to use some other form of transport, presumably a hackney cab, rather than her carriage, or that she hadn't slept in her own bed the previous night. "How can it be that Lily hasn't alerted us to her grandmother's absence?" Tabitha said.

Wolf chuckled wryly, "I suspect that young Lady Lily has been too happy to be freed from her lessons in social etiquette to question why she has that freedom." Tabitha nodded in agreement. For all of Lily's intelligence and academic intellect, she could be quite scatterbrained when it came to the practicalities of life. It was credible to imagine that the young woman had been too lost in her own thoughts and reading to notice her grandmother's absence for at least a day, if not more.

"Is it even worth talking to her to see what she might know?" Tabitha said as much to herself as to Wolf.

"At some point. But she's not the priority. I think we need to divide and conquer; you need to visit Lady Hartley, and I need to go to Whitechapel to talk to Mickey D." Wolf added, "And I don't think this can wait until tomorrow. I'm sure Manning will alert us if Lady Pembroke returns home this evening. But if she doesn't, it is a second night away."

"Do you think we should be alerting the police?" Tabitha wondered.

"It is hard to imagine that they will do much on our scant evidence. Let us see what we can both find out and reconvene here later. I am going to try to catch Mickey before luncheon." He added, "It is unfortunate that the dowager's driver has been so tight-lipped and has refused to answer any of Manning's questions. We're lucky that Manning even overheard the dowager ordering the carriage to take her to Whitechapel."

Tabitha agreed, "I believe you may need to go and question the driver. However, if the dowager has sworn him to silence, it's hard to imagine that there is any threat you can make that will be greater than his fear of his mistress." Wolf nodded in agreement. Until they had proof that the dowager was in danger, he couldn't imagine what he might say to an intractable servant.

With Wolf's task agreed upon, Tabitha considered hers. It was already late morning. Would Lady Hartley even be at home, and if she was, could Tabitha drop in for a chat without sending a note first? Under normal circumstances, the answer would be no. Tabitha had no personal relationship with Lady Hartley, and a visit that ignored all the normal social niceties would be highly irregular. However, these were not normal circumstances, and so Tabitha hurried off to change out of her day dress.

For his part, Wolf went to find Bear so that they could change into more appropriate clothes for visiting Whitechapel. Both men had kept a selection of their thief-taking clothes and usually donned them when visiting their old neighbourhood. Wolf hadn't widely announced his change in fortunes when he inherited the earldom. Nevertheless, he was sure that word had spread over time. Still, he knew that Whitechapel was not a place where his earl persona and its trappings would encourage people to answer questions.

Less than thirty minutes later, Tabitha was relieved to find that Lady Hartley was at home and alone. She was shown into the drawing room, where she barely had to wait five minutes for the lady of the house to join her. Tabitha barely knew Lady Hartley. Thinking about what she did know about the woman, Tabitha recalled that she was a widow and had been for quite some time. The most well-known thing about Lady Hartley was what an inveterate gossip she was.

The thin woman with rather watery blue eyes entered her drawing room in a highly nervous state. From what Tabitha could remember from the few times they had interacted, the woman was normally rather agitated and could never be entirely still. But now, she seemed more flustered than usual. She entered the room, walked over to a chair opposite Tabitha, her hands flapping by her side, and asked in an anxious and guilt-laden voice, "Has something happened to Lady Pembroke? I swear I had no idea she would be in danger."

What on earth had this odd woman done or said that might have set off a chain of events that had led to the dowager's disappearance? "Lady Hartley, why don't you sit and then tell me everything you know." It was certainly telling that the only conjecture Lady Hartley drew from Tabitha's appearance at her house was that something had happened to the dowager.

Lady Hartley did sit, perching on the edge of the armchair, her nervous energy too great to allow her to relax. Her hands continued to twitch and flap as if they had a life of their own. "I didn't know what to do?" She began. "When Lady Pembroke put me on the spot like that, I said the first thing that came to mind. I really can't be blamed."

Tabitha could well imagine the domineering dowager countess browbeating this nervous, awkward woman and, speaking as gently as possible, said, "Lady Hartley, there is no blame to be apportioned here. But Lady Pembroke has not been home since yesterday, and I need to know whatever you know about where she might have gone."

Finally, after some facial twitching, the other woman said, "She wanted me to find her some investigations to work on. Me? Why would she think I would be able to provide her with such things?"

Tabitha had a good idea of the dowager's motivation. However, she kept this thought to herself, and instead, she asked, "And did you tell her something that you believe she may be trying to investigate now?"

"Honestly, I was just wracking my brain to think of something to tell her so she would stop asking." Lady Hartley paused, then said in a lower voice as if the dowager were in the other room and might overhear, "Of all people, you must know how she can be." Tabitha nodded in agreement. She did indeed know. Lady Hartley then continued, "I really couldn't think of anything. Then I remembered Lady Emily Farthing."

Tabitha shook her head, "I don't believe I know her."

"You may not. Her family are not titled. They are Irish gentry. But Lady Farthing, born simply Emily Harding, is a great beauty. She met Lord Farthing, the youngest son of the Duke of Albany, at a Christmas party, and apparently they fell in love at first sight. It was quite a whirlwind romance, and they were engaged before Easter, but didn't marry for over a year." Lady Hartley lowered her voice again and said conspiratorially, "I'm not one to gossip. But I did hear rumours that they had to postpone it because Lord Farthing suffers from ill health."

As she said this, Lady Hartley stopped talking and looked knowingly at Tabitha as if she was supposed to read something into this last sentence. When she said no more but continued to make a face that seemed to imply some deeper meaning, Tabitha finally said, "I feel there is more to this story that you're not saying, but I have no idea what it is."

Lady Hartley repeated, this time with greater emphasis, "Lord Farthing suffers from ill health." When Tabitha still looked mystified, Lady Hartley said, "I have heard rumours that this ill health is not the sickness of a respectable man."

If this was supposed to illuminate the issue, Lady Hartley was to be disappointed. Finally, when it became clear that Tabitha would not catch on to her euphemisms, Lady Hartley whispered, "The loathsome disease. The man has the loathsome disease." Lady Hartley's face took on a look of abject horror that she had been forced to say such a word in her own drawing room. Heavens, the younger Lady Pembroke was even less quick on the uptake than the older had been on the subject.

Tabitha had been a complete innocent before her marriage. It had fallen to one of her sisters, Petra, to tell her what to expect on her wedding night. And even then, nothing could have prepared her for conjugal relations with Jonathan. However, what Tabitha hadn't counted on was that once she was married, she would be included in the whispered, titillating conversations titled ladies amused themselves with at social functions and which she had been shooed away from by her mother as a single young woman.

Once married, she was, if not accepted into these conversations, at least tolerated on their outskirts. She had heard the odd whispered talk of the loathsome disease, and had later asked her maid Ginny what that meant. Even though she was not much older than Tabitha, Ginny had grown up in Whitechapel and had been exposed to far more of the harsh realities of life.

While she had been somewhat embarrassed to discuss such things with Tabitha, Ginny, a plain-talking woman who realised that her young, naive mistress needed to understand some of the harsher realities of life, had explained that the ladies had most likely been talking about syphilis. She had then explained, as obliquely as she could, what syphilis was and how it was transmitted. Tabitha had blushed deeply at the latter but appreciated Ginny's willingness to explain.

Even with this explanation of Lord Farthing's illness, Tabitha still couldn't imagine what there was about this story that the dowager might have seized on as a possible investigation. She asked Lady Hartley this question, and the nervous woman said, "I mentioned to Lady Pembroke that Lady Farthing is attempting to get a judicial separation from her husband on the grounds of extreme cruelty. Or at least that is what I heard. The whole thing is very hush-hush, as you might imagine. The Farthing family has connections to the royal family, and so the situation is viewed as very delicate at the very highest levels."

Tabitha couldn't help but ask, "Then how did you come to hear of this?"

Lady Hartley smiled broadly; if there was one thing she was truly proud of, it was her ability to learn about the indiscretions of the beau monde. "Let us just say that some people talk far too loudly in public." She tapped her nose with her forefinger as she said this. Given that she had caught Lady Hartley trying to listen to a conversation she had been having with Ginny in the ladies' retiring room at a ball some months before, Tabitha was well aware of how predatory the other woman could be when hunting for gossip.

However, this still left her previous question unanswered, so she asked again, "But of what interest could this possibly be to the dowager countess?"

Lady Hartley shook her head and said, "I'm not entirely sure, to be honest. All I said was that I had heard that Lady Farthing was trying to gather evidence to prove that her husband knowingly infected her so she might be granted a separation due to cruelty. I can only assume that Lady Pembroke felt that she could offer her services to help gather such information. She certainly rushed out of here on hearing this news with such a look of such determination that I was immediately worried about what action I might have precipitated."

Tabitha was utterly perplexed by what she heard. Was the Dowager Countess of Pembroke really stooping to embroiling herself in such a tawdry domestic affair? How on earth did she believe she would be able to gather the necessary information? Lady Hartley claimed to know nothing more, and the visit soon wrapped up. Tabitha was worried that the dowager's behaviour and Tabitha's visit would themselves become fodder for the compulsive gossip, but it was hard to imagine how society could be any more outraged by Tabitha, and she felt sure that the much-feared dowager was more than capable of handling herself.

CHAPTER 4

Sunday, October 29, 1897: The dowager

Julia, Lady Pembroke, had returned from her visit with Lady Hartley energised by the news the gossip had finally handed over. But by the next morning, some of her enthusiasm had dimmed. While the dowager was not given to self-doubt, indeed considered self-indulgent anything that smacked of introspection, she had experienced a restless night.

Tossing and turning, she found herself unusually unsure of her next move; could she turn up unannounced at Lady Farthing's home and offer her investigative services? What was she even offering to help do? There was no dead body? Merely a need to gather evidence of a certain sort. But what kind of evidence was needed? Legal separations were so rare in aristocratic circles that the dowager had no idea what might even be required for one. Was she out of her depth?

Waking the following morning after finally falling into a sleep of intense dreams in the wee hours, the dowager found herself on the horns of a dilemma: did she proceed alone and risk failure or, worse, social humiliation? Or did she go to Tabitha and Wolf and ask for their help? She realised that, if she did the latter, she would lose all future credibility in her claims for investigative self-sufficiency. And anyway, it was not the dowager's way to lower herself to ask for help. But in the rawness of her waking moments, she acknowledged that she would have liked the opportunity to toss possible next steps back and forth with others.

It did occur to the dowager that perhaps it was the collaborative process itself rather than any specific collaborators that were helpful. Could she swap Tabitha and Wolf out for other people? But who? For a brief moment, the dowager considered approaching Lord Langley. But the truth was that Maxwell had always been rather a fifth wheel to their investigations, happy to help where he could but always at the peripheries. The dowager had no doubt she could command his obedience, but that wasn't the same as his genuine engagement.

There was Lily, of course. As a houseguest, her granddaughter was a captive audience and would clearly do anything to get out of her lessons and obligations for the upcoming season. However, while the dowager did not question her granddaughter's intelligence, the young woman had made it very clear on multiple occasions how boring she found the investigations. The dowager's godson, Tobias, was equally uninterested in participating except to the extent that he could peacock in front of Lily. No, neither would do, at least as a first choice. Perhaps, if there were no other options and she was in need of an audience for her ideas, the dowager would have to resort to enlisting the two young people.

But who did that leave? Manning? Withers? Would she have to lower herself to confabulation with the servants about things other than the day's wine choice or selection of outfits? No! She had not sunk that low. It briefly flicked through her mind that she might draft Lady Willis. It wasn't that the woman was intelligent, or educated, or even intuitive, but she was malleable. But was that the dominant trait needed for an investigative partner? If the dowager was honest, what made Tabitha and Wolf such effective counterparts was that they didn't immediately agree with her suggestions and instead debated and weighed all ideas. While she didn't appreciate being disagreed with in the moment, the dowager did acknowledge, at least in the privacy of her boudoir, that the vigorous challenge usually led to better outcomes.

She needed someone who wasn't afraid to stand up to her but wouldn't meddle more than requested and whose intelligence she respected. That was a limited universe of people. Suddenly, the dowager sat up in bed inspired. She did know someone who matched those criteria. Rat! Yes, he was not even nine years old, but the lad had more life experience than most of her aristocratic acquaintances put together. And she knew the boy was highly intelligent and logical; Langley's decision to mentor him was clear evidence of Rat's intellect. The boy also wasn't cowed by her. Yet, he was a child and couldn't get in her way. The worst he could do was to tell tales on her. But the dowager suspected that contrary to his nickname, Rat was anything but.

Inspired to action by this idea, the dowager veritably sprang out of bed, rung for Withers, dressed, and breakfasted with an alacrity that had all her servants exchanging glances. The dowager was not known for her love of early mornings, often not leaving her bedchamber until almost noon. To have her up, about, and cheerful to boot before ten in the morning was almost worrying.

Once she was done with an unusually hearty breakfast, the dowager considered her next move. Obviously, she couldn't tell Lord Langley what she wanted Rat for. The boy might keep his counsel, but she doubted the earl would. No, she needed a good reason to invite the lad over. And it needed to be a reason that might lead to additional visits if she continued to need to use him to share her musings with. She'd given this question a lot of thought as she'd munched her way through some delicious kedgeree, accompanied by two slices of toast and marmalade.

Finally, when she was halfway through the second slice of toast and onto her third cup of coffee, inspiration hit. She had heard Wolf say on various occasions that it was always best to stick as close to the truth as possible when employing subterfuge. Lord Langley had taken Rat under his wing as an apprentice for a future role in British Intelligence. As part of this tutelage, Langley had been working to improve the boy's speech so that he sounded less like a homeless street waif from Whitechapel and more like a member of at least the upper middle class.

The dowager was sure that Langley did not have sufficient sensibility to teach the nuances of surviving in their circles; he was a man, after all. She would offer to teach Rat some of the finer details of life in the society that he had unexpectedly been thrust into. Of course, to keep up the charade, she would have actually to teach him something of use. But the dowager genuinely believed that Rat was someone worth her time, so this would be no great sacrifice. She knew that Langley had installed a telephone at his mother's insistence before she left London to return to the family pile. The dowager rang for Manning and instructed him to put a call through to Langley House.

Maxwell Sandworth, the Earl of Langley, was pleasantly surprised to receive the dowager's offer. He had been doing his best to improve Rat's table manners and overall knowledge of social etiquette. But there was no doubt that the dowager was the ultimate authority on the dos and don'ts of acceptable behaviour. There was no one more appropriate to instruct the boy. In addition, Lord Langley was aware of how much the Dowager Countess of Pembroke's approbation would do to smooth Rat's path in life. If Langley was surprised at the dowager's eagerness to begin the lessons immediately, he was a wise enough man not to say anything. Instead, he promised to send Rat to her within the hour.

The dowager waited for her guest in her cosy parlour; she felt no need to stand on ceremony and welcome him in the formal, less comfortable drawing room. It was rare for a visitor to enter this parlour, so the dowager had indulged her design whims to a far greater extent than she would ever dare in the rest of the house. In particular, this is where she kept her porcelain figurines.

The dowager had come across the first figurine quite by chance when she had admired one on the mantel at her favourite modiste. It had been of a young shepherd girl, and the dowager was quite taken with the delicate but very realistic painting that brought the statue of the young woman to life. But as much as the dowager countess had admired the figurine, she was also conscious that she was taken with an objet d'art owned by her solidly middle-class dressmaker. It was hardly appropriate that a woman of Lady Pembroke's position in life share a taste for home decor with the woman who made her clothes, even if she was

French.

However, Madame Baptiste had noticed the dowager's admiration for the shepherd girl and had mentioned where she had bought it. At the time, the dowager had thanked her rather dismissively for the information, which she insisted she would not be making use of. But no sooner had she arrived home than she had instructed Manning to seek out the shop and purchase her a shepherdess of her own.

Somehow, that first figurine had grown to a collection of twelve. It was now part of Manning's regular duties to visit the shop he had purchased the shepherdess from monthly, and it was a mark of how much trust the dowager had in the man that he had the authority to buy any new piece that caught his eye. In fact, he had purchased a new figurine just that week: a couple of young homeless orphans huddled together, trying to keep warm. The piece had touched the dowager's heart, as Manning knew it would, with its resemblance to Rat and Melody. The little girl even had red-gold ringlets that mirrored her real-life counterpart. The dowager adored this new addition to her collection and had put it in pride of place on the little table in front of the rather ugly but very comfortable sofa that she usually sat on in this room.

When Rat was announced, the dowager was busy admiring her new purchase. The artist had perfectly captured the pathos of the two porcelain waifs. Every time she contemplated the figurine, she thought about Melody and Rat's life after their parents had died and before they'd come to Chesterton House. While the dowager was generally loathed to credit Tabitha with much, she genuinely appreciated the younger woman's role in rescuing the children. The dowager felt more affection for Melody, in particular, than she did for her own children and grandchildren. It pained her to know the suffering the little girl had once endured and how close she had come to still living on the cruel streets of Whitechapel.

This was the first time that Rat and the dowager countess had ever spent together without someone else around, even if it was just Melody, a fact that seemed to strike them both at the same time. The young boy was suddenly uncharacteristically shy, and the old woman was unsure how to begin, despite her earlier enthusiasm for her plan.

"Rat, how lovely to see you. Please come in and take a seat. I'll ring for tea. I remembered that you like iced buns, and I asked my cook to be sure to make a batch."

Iced buns were definitely the way to Rat's heart, and the boy grinned and immediately relaxed. The dowager decided to wait until she was plying the lad with sweet treats to get to the heart of her request. Instead, they discussed Rat's beloved sister, Melody. How well her reading was coming on, how she would be able to beat Lord Langley at chess soon enough, and how happy Rat was that she had a safe, loving and nurturing home. It occurred to the dowager, not for the first time, what a weight it must have been on the boy's slender shoulders to care for his four-year-old sister while living on the streets. Silently, she considered the most responsibility that had ever been expected of her children at a similar age.

Finally, after three iced buns, even Rat was satiated. He sat back in his chair, patted his stomach and said, "Those were the best buns ever. Can I take one for Melly when I see her later?"

"Of course you can. In fact, we will ask Manning to wrap them all up for you to take back with you to Lord Langley's." The dowager paused, "Talking of Lord Langley, did he mention why I'd asked for you to visit this afternoon?" The dowager had decided to approach her true topic as obliquely as possible.

"Yes, m'lady. He'd said that you was, I mean were, going to help me learn how to be a gentleman."

"Indeed. I realise that Lord Langley has been working with you, particularly on your speech, which is much improved. But there is so much more to being a gentleman than merely using the correct words."

The boy interrupted and said, "I'm learning which fork to use as well."

"Good table manners are also a part of what it means to be

genteel. But I believe that Lord Langley is more than capable of working with you on that. I would like to help you with some of the more subtle skills. For example, the art of conversation."

"The art of conversation?" Rat repeated back.

"Correct. A gentleman should be able to converse on a range of topics. So, let us begin. What would you like to discuss?"

Rat considered the question, then sat up a little straighter and said, "I think that a gentleman would always let a lady choose the topic. So, what would you like to have a conversation about, Lady Pembroke?"

The dowager smiled broadly; the boy really was very quick on the uptake. Langley had made a wise decision when he decided to mentor Rat. "Very good, young man. That is precisely the right answer. Now, what would I like to discuss?" the dowager asked, making a grand show of tapping her mouth with a finger as if mentally filtering through a huge range of potential subjects. Finally, she announced, "I know what we can talk about. We can talk about an investigation I've been asked to undertake."

Rat kept to himself any questions about why the dowager countess was now investigating on her own. Instead, he answered, "I would love to hear more about that, m'lady."

Now that she had adeptly manoeuvred the conversation around to her chosen subject, the dowager realised she was unsure how to proceed. She knew that Rat had been exposed to more of life's ugliness than any child should be. Nevertheless, would he know what syphilis was, and how would she ever begin to talk to him about such a subject? However, she had the boy here now, she might as well make an effort to discuss the investigation with him.

Taking a deep breath, the dowager asked, "Rat, this not normally a topic one should talk about, particularly over tea and buns. But I have to ask, do you know what syphilis is?"

The boy, proud of his knowledge, said cheerfully, "I do, m'lady. It's the pox, isn't it? I know because I used to hear the dollymops talking about it when I did some work, sometimes, for the abbess at the nunnery."

The dowager had not heard those terms before but, given the context, could imagine what they meant. In fact, these euphemisms might come in handy as a way to talk about the rather unsavoury subjects she needed to discuss with the child.

"Indeed, that is exactly what I mean. So, in this investigation, I've been asked to undertake," – perhaps an exaggeration, but the child didn't need to be confused by irrelevant details – "my client married a gentleman who did not disclose that he had the pox, as you call it. This lady now wants to go to court to get what is called a legal separation so that she no longer has to live with her husband." The dowager glanced at the boy, who seemed to be following along well enough. She continued, "I have been asked to help provide her with the necessary evidence to take to court." The dowager paused and asked, "Do you know what evidence is?"

"Oh yes, m'lady. I remember when one-eared Jack was caught stealing from a toff, I mean from a gentleman. The bobbies dragged him away, with him screaming they had no evidence against him. Except he didn't say that; he screamed that they didn't have the dodge. But Pa explained what that meant." The boy looked wistful for a minute at this memory of his deceased father.

Glad that she didn't have to elaborate on the fundamentals, the dowager was curious, "So, when these dollymops talked about the pox, what would they say?"

"Oh, you know that they'd had a punter who had the pox and tried to pretend it was something else. One gave Cindy a real shiner when she wouldn't service him."

Normally, the dowager wouldn't stand for such vulgar conversation. But it occurred to her that despite not having lived even one full decade, Rat likely knew more about this topic than she did after more than seventy. "It's interesting to hear you say that, Rat. I wonder if my client's husband caught his disease from such a, what did you call them? A dollymop."

"Could be, your ladyship. I liked Cindy. She used to sneak me some food for Melly. When I asked her about the shiner, she told me that a lot of the dollymops in London are riddled, and that she'd rather have a punch in the eye than be killed by the pox. The abbess of that nunnery, Mother Sharpe, was very strict about that kind of thing. She checked all her girls for the pox, and they were out on the street at the first sign of it."

The dowager knew that men in her class regularly took a mistress. She was certain her husband and son had kept many over their lifetimes. Most women in her circle looked upon these mistresses as more than a necessary evil and considered them to be performing a service to them as well as their husbands. While bearing a son and heir was an obligation, in fact, normally the point of such marriages, once that was achieved and perhaps there was a spare in the nursery, just in case, most women were happy to have their husbands' baser needs taken care of elsewhere.

It had never occurred to the dowager that men of her rank might also frequent prostitutes. But then, men's carnal desires were not something she'd given much thought to until joining the investigative team over the last few months. Could Lord Farthing have caught his loathsome disease from one such dollymop? Was that something that Lady Farthing would be aware of? The dowager assumed that Lady Farthing's sensitivities were, if not as refined as her own, at least appropriate for a woman of her rank. In which case, such topics would be as foreign to her as they were to the dowager. But in Rat, the dowager had a source who knew prostitutes and had even been in a house of ill repute, which is what she assumed he meant by a nunnery.

The clock on the mantel told her that Rat had already been with her for thirty minutes. There was only so long she could drag the visit out without making Langley suspicious. Given this, the dowager decided to drop all pretence that there was anything else she wanted to talk about and said, "Rat, dear, can you tell me everything you know about dollymops, nunneries, and the pox?" Even as she said them, the dowager couldn't believe such words had come out of her mouth. But Rat seemed unaffected by the nature of the subject matter and happily told her everything he knew.

When finally Rat seemed to have exhausted the topic, Lady Pembroke said, "Well, I believe I should return you to Langley House now, or Lord Langley will begin to wonder." She attempted to affect a casual air and added, "And if Lord Langley asks you what we talked about, what will you tell him?"

Rat was an astute boy. While he didn't see anything wrong in their conversation, he sensed that the dowager felt that other people might. He answered, "I will tell him that to teach me how to have a genteel conversation, you asked me about my life in Whitechapel and that I told you about some friends of mine and about my parents." The dowager smiled; he really was a sharp lad.

Now that she was sure of Rat's discretion, she asked, "If I wanted to speak to this dollymop of yours, Cindy, I believe you said she is called, how would I go about doing that?"

Rat thought about this briefly, then suggested, "Mother Sharpe runs a pretty tight house; most of those abbesses do. I think maybe the easiest way to talk to Cindy is to pay for her time."

Whatever the dowager had been expecting Rat to say, it wasn't to suggest that she go to a brothel and pay a prostitute. For the very first time since she had first decided to conduct her own investigations, the dowager had some niggling doubts about the wisdom of her actions. While she had no fear for her reputation – she judged society, not the other way around – she did consider how she might be sullying herself and her title by taking this path. And then the dowager countess thought about the alternative: returning to her deathly dull routine of social calls and evening card parties and answered, "Rat, can you help arrange this for me? Without Lord Langley knowing, of course." This was her first overt acknowledgement that she required Rat to be less than truthful and open with his mentor.

As it happened, Rat had a lot of freedom in Lord Langley's

household. As long as he was diligent with his studies, he was free to come and go as he pleased. Lord Langley's assumption was that this freedom primarily enabled Rat to visit Chesterton House and his sister whenever he chose. And up to this point, that is what he had done. But no one would ask questions if Rat left for the afternoon to go somewhere else.

"We need to go before the evening rush but late enough that Cindy is awake; these dollymops keep late hours." Rat looked at the clock on the mantelpiece. It was almost noon. Lord Langley would be expecting him back for luncheon and at least two hours of lessons.

The dowager said, "I have an errand of my own to run after luncheon. In Whitechapel, as it happens. Are you able to find your own way there to meet me?"

"No problem, m'lady. The nunnery is on Gunthorpe Street. So, I'll meet you on the corner there at four o'clock sharp." Rat paused, then added, "And your ladyship, if you don't mind me saying, maybe don't wear your finest. That abbess will take you for everything she can if she gets an eyeful of those diamonds."

Having taken Mickey D's promise of her safety in Whitechapel, even wearing her finest diamonds, the dowager would normally have been disinclined to follow such advice. But the idea of the madam in a brothel seeing her as an easy target for extortion was one she understood. "Those are very wise words, Rat. And with that, let us get these iced buns packed up, and I will then see you later."

CHAPTER 5

Sunday, October 29, 1897: The dowager

After Rat had departed, happily clutching his bag of iced buns, the dowager rang for fresh tea. A new, steaming cup of the brew poured, she sat back on the sofa and considered her next steps. Until then, she'd done nothing more than play-act an investigation. If she never followed up on Lady Hartley's gossip, the woman would neither know nor care. And her conversation with the boy could easily remain just that. But if she took this next step and ventured into Whitechapel to consort with criminals and prostitutes, she was making an irrevocable decision. Despite what she knew to be true about her pivotal role in solving the last four investigations, she could claim that she had been a mere bystander previously. But there was no Wolf, the thief-taker turned earl, to hide behind this time. The thought was thrilling. The dowager called for her carriage. It was time to investigate!

While Wolf always eschewed his grand carriage when visiting Whitechapel, preferring to take a hackney cab or walk, such a sacrifice never occurred to the dowager. Indeed, how could Mickey D's guarantee of her safety be effective if people didn't know who she was? Such was her total confidence in the gang leader's "promise" that it also never occurred to her to take at least a footman with her for protection. Her one concession to the roughness of the neighbourhood she was visiting was to take her new walking stick with its hidden long, sharp blade; her sword stick.

Just over three hours later, the dowager left Mickey D's house and returned to her carriage. This time, she was accompanied by an enormous man named Little Ian. The dowager considered the man not only an appropriate replacement for Bear, but an improvement; his face was so much more authentically terrifying with that broken nose and long, jagged scar running from his eye all the way down his cheek. The dowager immediately realised she'd like to employ Little Ian permanently. During the first investigation, she had enjoyed the thought of how her neighbours would be thrown into a state of horrified fascination when Bear visited her Mayfair house. But how much truer would that be with Little Ian on hand?

Settling back in her carriage, the dowager considered what she had shared with Mickey D. While she had again found the irascible Mr Doherty to be charming and entertaining company, the dowager wasn't so naive as to believe the man could be trusted. Indeed, perhaps what had most charmed her the most about the gangster was her recognition of how similar the two of them were, in essence. It was also a recognition that rigid societal constraints as much prevented an Irish gangster as it did a female member of the aristocracy from rising to the military, political or industrial heights their intelligence and strategic brilliance deserved. But that didn't mean that he was an ideal confidante.

The dowager decided to tell Mickey D the bare minimum and nothing more. Though perhaps in mentioning her proposed visit to Gunthorpe Street, she had revealed more than she'd intended. The dowager debated whether to admit that she was now running an investigation independently. Ultimately, she decided she might need to call on Mr Doherty's particular skillset later, so he needed a vague idea of her intentions. And so she had informed him that she was now investigating on her own. She also admitted that she was planning to visit Mother Sharpe's brothel that afternoon as part of an investigation. While he didn't ask why, Mickey D justified her decision to confide in him at least a little by promising that if she met any resistance that some coins didn't dispel, she should feel free to use his name.

While the dowager's driver had no idea where Gunthorpe Street was, luckily, Little Ian, seated next to the driver, knew where to go. It was not even five minutes later when the dowager felt the carriage slow down. She looked out the window and saw Rat waiting on the street, leaning against a building with an air of studied nonchalance. She noticed that the boy had changed his clothing; while he was not wearing the ragged, dirty clothing that the other people walking past him were, he had changed out of the smart, new outfit he'd worn to visit her earlier.

Driving to Mickey D's, the dowager hadn't bothered to look out the window at the neighbourhood she was visiting. But now, as the carriage came to a standstill, she couldn't fail to notice how dreary and depressing everything and everyone was. As soon as her carriage stopped, children appeared out of nowhere, begging for a penny. Rat quickly shooed them away, but not before the dowager saw how hungry and desperate those children looked. She thought about her new, beloved porcelain figurine, those two young children huddled together. Any of these pauper children could have been the model for her statuette.

Beckoning Rat to her carriage window, she said, "I noticed a bakery on the corner on my way here. Ask my driver for money and get some bread rolls for these children." Rat's face showed his surprise at this request, but he did as asked, and returned a few minutes later with a large paper bag. The beggar children hadn't dispersed so far that he couldn't lure them back quickly. Each child snatched a bread roll and fell to eating the food like wild animals coming upon a carcass.

As uncharacteristically moved by the suffering of others as the dowager had momentarily been, she refused to be distracted from the task at hand. "Rat, which house is this house of ill repute?" she asked. Rat pointed across the street to a rather unassuming-looking building with a blue front door. The dowager wasn't sure what she'd expected a brothel to look like, but she'd hoped that her first foray into such a den of inequity would be less workaday.

"I'll accompany you, Lady Pembroke," Rat said chivalrously.

The dowager considered his suggestion. She felt no hesitancy about exposing Rat to such a place; that ship had sailed long ago.

But she realised that, despite the impressive strides the boy had made over the last few months in putting his old life behind him, working on his speech and manners and studying hard, this transition was still very new. Was it right or fair to thrust him back into this world? Perhaps she should have considered that before she suggested he meet her in Whitechapel. But what's done was done. However, the dowager decided she didn't need to compound her error and, instead, she asked him to wait in the carriage for her to return.

Realising that Rat was concerned for her safety, as if an eight-year-old boy was any kind of protection, the dowager assured him, "I will be taking Little Ian in with me, don't worry." The boy nodded, helped the old woman down from the carriage and then took her place inside it. Little Ian had descended by this time, and the dowager indicated he should lead the way across the street.

When she had been in Brighton a few weeks before, the dowager had accompanied Wolf to interview a witness at her daughter's lower middle-class home. That was the elderly countess's first time inside what she had called a 'proletariat residence'. At the time, she'd been curious to observe how the masses lived in their small, cramped, very plain residences, devoid of servants. Her observation at the time was that with a screaming baby and demanding toddler, the daughter's home had been very noisy. As she raised her hand to rap on this even more plebian residence's door, the dowager positively shivered with eager anticipation.

Given her expectations, the dowager was quite surprised and disappointed to have the door answered by a rather usual-looking maid. Nothing in the girl's dress or manner suggested the salacious behaviour happening in the rooms behind her.

Pulling herself up to her full, almost five feet, the dowager said imperiously, "I would like to speak to the mistress of the house."

The maid looked surprised but said nothing. It was not an everyday affair to have a diminutive yet terrifying-looking toff accompanied by an enormous, even more terrifying-looking man requesting an audience with Mother Sharpe. But you didn't keep a well-paying job in a whorehouse by asking questions.

The maid opened the door a little wider and invited the dowager and Little Ian in. She then led the way down the hallway. An opened door to the right seemed to lead into a highly decorated parlour. Glancing in quickly, the dowager was horrified to catch sight of some very suggestive paintings on the wall. She was glad she wouldn't be having her audience with Mrs Sharpe in that room!

When they finally came to a closed door at the back of the house, the maid knocked lightly, and a rather harsh voice bid her enter. The maid opened the door and bobbed a curtsey, "Excuse me, Mother Sharpe, but you have a visitor." At this, the young maid stepped aside, and the dowager moved past her into the room, Little Ian bringing up the rear. Mother Sharpe had been standing staring into the fire, and she now turned around to greet her visitor.

In the carriage ride to Whitechapel, the dowager had amused herself imagining what this madam, or abbess, Mother Sharpe, would be like. She imagined her to be a faded glory, haggard before her time, the last vestiges of her beauty barely clinging on. Of course, the woman would be dressed like a strumpet, that went without saying. And there would be makeup, far too much makeup.

Standing opposite Vicky Sharpe, known as Mother Sharpe, the dowager did a double take; the woman looked nothing like she had imagined. If the woman looked like anyone, it was like the dowager herself. Victoria Sharpe was as petite as the dowager countess and probably of a similar age. While the aristocrat's hair was a snowy white, the brothel's madame's was more silver. The dowager's steely grey eyes looked into dark blue ones, but otherwise, the women might have passed for relatives.

All of the dowager's prejudices about the other woman's attire were proven wrong. While her dress was clearly not of the same quality as the dowager's, it was as conservative and wouldn't have looked out of place on the wife of a prosperous city solicitor. Mother Sharpe wore no obvious makeup or indeed had anything about her personage that would mark her profession.

If the dowager was surprised by Mother Sharpe, the other woman seemed less startled at her unexpected visitor. She approached the dowager with an outstretched hand, saying, "You must be the investigator that Mickey D sent word of."

The dowager had told Mickey D where she was headed next, but she was still surprised that he'd had the time and inclination to send word to the brothel. But on further consideration, perhaps she shouldn't be shocked by the ever-surprising Mr Doherty's solicitousness. She replied, "Yes, I am Julia Chesterton, the Dowager Countess of Pembroke."

"The Countess of Pembroke?" The madame repeated curiously. "You're a countess and an investigator?" she asked in surprise.

This was the first time the dowager had announced herself as such, and for a moment, she paused. She realised that she needed to be more prepared in future and made a mental note to have appropriate cards made up. What the dowager lacked in experience, she made up for in unsubstantiated confidence, declaring, "I am indeed both. The former by accident of birth, the latter by rapier sharp logic paired with great insight and boldness." As she said these words of aggrandisement, the dowager decided that would be the headline on her calling cards: The Investigative Countess, Rapier Sharp Logic paired with Great Insight and Boldness. Yes, that was just what was called for. She could already imagine the headlines in the broadsheets when she solved her first high-profile investigation.

While the dowager was not what Mother Sharpe had been expecting in the promised investigator, she had known Mickey D for many years and trusted his instincts. "Please have a seat, Lady Pembroke," she said, gesturing to one of a pair of armchairs near the fireplace. Looking over at the giant man accompanying the dowager, the madame said to the maid, "Nancy, take Little Ian back with you to the kitchen and get him something to eat.

Then bring up some tea and some of whatever cake cook was baking this morning."

The dowager took one of the offered armchairs and Mother Sharpe the other. When the door closed behind Nancy and Little Ian, the madame said, "I must admit, you are not what I was expecting when Mickey D sent word over that he had just the person to help me. But now I think about it, I believe I know what he meant."

The dowager was interested to hear where this was heading; all thoughts of her original reason for visiting Gunthorpe Street wiped clean from her head. The other woman continued, "I assume you know what this establishment is?"

"I do," the dowager replied.

"I have run this business for more than twenty years. I originally ran it with my twin sister, Margery. But while it is successful and has provided a more than sufficient income over the years, my sister always wanted more. She was like that even as a child, always grasping for what was out of reach. I was the firstborn of the two, and our mother used to say that Margie was always chasing me, trying to catch up. Anyway, about fifteen years ago, she found herself a benefactor and left to start her own establishment. She had the good grace to move to another neighbourhood so that we weren't in direct competition. However, it still strained our relationship, and we've not seen much of each other over the years. Our one concession to the sisterly bond is that we always get together on our birthday, October 25th, and share a drink or two."

The dowager had been the youngest of five children. The only one of her siblings she had ever had any time for was her sister, Peggy, who had died in childbirth many decades before. The dowager counted the fact that she had easily outlived the rest of her siblings as both lucky and inevitable, given the poor life choices they had all made. Given this, she was wholly sympathetic to the notion of sibling estrangement.

Mother Sharpe continued, "The arrangement is that we alternate who hosts. This year was my turn. We have an established routine, which means we don't need to communicate beforehand to discuss our plans; the one not hosting just turns up at one o'clock. I had our favourite meal, roast beef and potatoes, ready to eat and a nice bottle of claret ready to accompany it. I then waited for her to turn up at the usual time. I waited, and I waited. Finally, irritated at her thoughtlessness, I ate my meal alone and sent around a note telling her off for her rudeness and selfishness."

As she told this story, Mother Sharpe seemed drawn back into her feelings of irritation from that day. She paused to collect herself, then continued, "I received no reply, which just increased my irritation. But the following day, I had a visitor, one of her girls, Lou. She'd been nominated to come in person to tell me that my sister hadn't been seen or heard from in two days. And that was three days ago."

The dowager wasn't sure how to put the next question delicately, "Might your sister be staying with a benefactor?" She believed she was using that euphemism appropriately.

Mother Sharpe smiled wryly, "One of the few areas that Margie and I were in complete agreement about was separating business from pleasure. It seemed neither one of us derived any enjoyment these days from the company of men." She paused and added, "Margie has a new business partner. Or at least, that is what she called him last birthday. She was quite closed-lipped about the whole business. All Margie would tell me was that she had opened a new establishment in Villiers Street and that it was a space that catered to a crowd that appreciated discretion."

"I'm sorry, but you're going to have to be a little more explicit," the dowager explained. "This world," she gestured to the room and the house around her, "is not one with which I'm familiar."

"No, of course you're not," Mother Sharpe said apologetically. "What I mean is, while men don't generally wish to broadcast that they are patrons of an establishment such as mine, some men are particularly concerned about privacy."

The dowager was curious now, "What kind of men might those be?"

Mother Sharpe trilled lightly and said, "Oh, you know, vicars, the occasional bishop, more than a few politicians. Particularly ones who have made their name spouting fire and brimstone about the evils of such vices." She paused, then said, "It has been my experience in over fifty years in this game that the louder they protest a vice, the more likely they are to indulge in it."

The dowager answered, "The lady doth protest too much, methinks." Mother Sharpe looked confused at the quote, and the dowager explained, "Just a quote from a mediocre playwright who agreed with you. So, if I understand you correctly, your sister has gone missing, and you asked Mickey D to help you find an investigator to search for her? Why didn't you just go to the police?"

Now, Mother Sharpe chuckled. She laughed so hard that she had to wipe tears from her eyes, "I'm sorry, your ladyship, you can't understand this, coming from the world you do, but it's hard enough to get the bobbies to care when one of us has her throat cut. But to ask them to look for one who has just not been seen at her nunnery for a few days, well, that isn't even worth asking them to care about. My sister and I are not close, but I am all the family she has. If I don't care enough to look for her, no one will. That's why I need your help."

All thoughts of Lord Farthing and his loathsome disease had flown out of the window; this was a real mystery worth sinking her teeth into, the dowager thought. She had intended to request a meeting with Rat's friend, Cindy. However, rather than poking around for answers in an investigation she hadn't even been asked to work on, she was now being actively engaged. Was the investigation of the pox-ridden son of a duke more or less tawdry than that of a brothel's missing madame? Julia Chesterton was not used to seeing nuance and shades of grey, in life. She had spent most of her last seven decades plus assuming little moral ambiguity in the situations she encountered. But even the dowager realised that if she took on this investigation, she would need to approach her client and the people around her with more empathy and compassion than she might normally.

All these thoughts ran through the dowager's head as she sat opposite a woman who was more refined and intelligent than the dowager could have imagined. Not that she had spent much time over the years imagining what London's prostitutes were like. But she certainly had given the topic much consideration over the past day.

However, despite her new-found regard, at least for this particular lady of the night, the dowager was unprepared for Mother Sharpe's next statement, "I believe you must reside, incognito, in my sister's establishment to discover why she is missing."

CHAPTER 6

Monday, October 30, 1897: Tabitha & Wolf

Dressed in their thief-taking clothes, Wolf and Bear had taken a hackney cab to the outskirts of Whitechapel and then walked the rest of the way. During the cab ride, Wolf had told Bear about their concerns for the dowager.

"So, we don't know for sure that anything has happened to her?" Bear asked.

"Not for sure. But the woman has been gone all night with no word to anyone. Apparently, she didn't even leave with any of her clothes. That seems out of character," Wolf answered.

Bear paused, then asked gingerly, "Is it possible that the older Lady Pembroke has a close friend she is spending time with that she doesn't want her servants gossiping about?"

Wolf chuckled, "I asked Tabitha the same question. She felt it was unlikely. But I don't believe we should rule it out. After all, her ladyship owes neither myself nor Tabitha any explanation for how and with whom she spends her time. And she is certainly not someone who would concern herself with thoughts about her servant's worries."

Wolf then spoke more seriously, "Regardless, we know that she visited Mickey D a few days ago, and that does not bode well, even if her disappearance turns out to be benign. I need to know what entanglement she may have become caught up in such that she felt the need to seek him out."

"She was rather taken with him when they met, was she not?" Bear said. "Perhaps her visit is nothing more than a social call."

Wolf looked at his old friend and said with a voice dripping with scepticism, "You have known the woman quite a few months now. Do you really believe she would take herself out to Whitechapel to take tea with Mickey and Ange? I can see her summoning them to dine with her again but not actually venturing forth outside of Mayfair and Belgravia."

"Perhaps," Bear conceded. "But remember how much she enjoyed the outing to the public house in Brighton? I get the sense that the dowager countess is rather bored with her aristocratic life, the circles she runs in, and the neighbourhoods she visits. Perhaps the thrill of a visit to Whitechapel was too alluring."

Wolf conceded the point, "True. And let us not forget how taken she was with Mickey's so-called guarantee that she could walk through Whitechapel wearing her diamonds unmolested." The memory of that particular conversation added new worries to Wolf's growing list, "I do hope she didn't take him up on this and visit him bedecked and bejewelled." Wolf remembered only too well their outing to the Cock and Bull public house in Brighton when the dowager had initially shown up for the expedition doing just that, wearing diamonds. It was only at Wolf's insistence that such a flagrant show of wealth would impede their investigation that she had begrudgingly removed her jewellery.

They had the hackney cab drop them about a fifteen-minute walk from the Doherty household; Wolf wanted to draw as little attention to himself as possible. Nevertheless, as they walked the familiar streets, they received nods of recognition and hails of greetings from various local residents. Finally, they reached the Doherty house. Wolf knocked, and Mickey's common-law wife Angie quickly opened the door.

Angie was plump and rosy-cheeked, and there was a genuine and mutual affection between her and Wolf. The woman's face lit up when she recognised her visitors, and she pulled Wolf into a motherly hug against her ample bosom. She then followed up with a similarly affectionate embrace with Bear. "Well, what a nice surprise," Angie exclaimed. "Food won't be ready for a bit, but you're welcome to stay."

"We can't stay and eat," Wolf said apologetically. "But we'd like to talk to Mickey if he's around."

Angie led the way through the house into a cosy parlour

where the gang leader was sitting smoking a pipe. When Tabitha first met Mickey D, she was surprised at how nonthreatening he looked. She hadn't been sure what she'd expected a notorious gang leader to look like, but it wasn't the rather avuncular-looking man with bright blue eyes and a charming grin. If anything, he had reminded her of her favourite, rather roguish Uncle Jack, who had a similar twinkle in his eyes.

While Mickey might not have the noticeable scars or other visible trophies of a hard life given over to crime and violence, Wolf knew better than to underestimate the man; he was a hardened criminal. But while Mickey was certainly not above roughing up someone who had crossed him and breaking a few bones, he wasn't a murderer (at least as far as Wolf knew). He was generally not only respected but held in high regard throughout Whitechapel. While Wolf wouldn't have gone as far as to call Mickey D a Robin Hood figure, robbing the rich to feed the poor, nevertheless, the man did help the impoverished people of Whitechapel. Even if that help usually came with some kind of strings.

Mickey looked up as Wolf and Bear entered the room. He didn't seem particularly surprised to see them. He gestured for the two men to sit and asked Angie, "Would you mind bringing us something to drink, love?" Turning to Wolf, he asked, "Will a splash of Irish whiskey do? I can't offer you any of that fancy French brandy you seem to like so much these days," Mickey said sardonically; he would never turn up an opportunity to mock Wolf for his new status in life. Wolf and Bear both indicated that the whiskey would be fine.

Angie returned quickly with a tray with three glasses, a bottle of whiskey and a plate of her famous ginger biscuits, which she knew were Wolf's favourites. She poured drinks for the men, then excused herself to go and finish cooking dinner.

Mickey took a sip of his drink when the door closed behind her and said, "I'm assuming you're here to find out why her ladyship visited the other day. Though I'm not sure why that is anyone's business but mine and Lady Pembroke's."

Wolf had no interest in playing games and came straight to the point, "The dowager countess has not been home since yesterday, and Tabitha, Lady Pembroke, is worried, that is, we are both worried that she is in danger. If you know anything about where she is, I insist that you tell me now."

Wolf and the gang leader had a complicated relationship. During his thief-taking days, Wolf had sometimes worked at Mickey's behest. At other times, he had been sworn off taking investigations by the man. Recently, Wolf had helped clear Mickey's nephew, Seamus, of murder and had facilitated the young man, who was still guilty of theft, escaping to a new life in America. Mickey D had then paid back that debt by helping to prove the dowager's butler, Manning, innocent. There was a certain mutual respect, but also wariness between the men.

Mickey didn't answer immediately. Instead, he took another sip of whiskey, looking at the glass in his hand, seemingly deep in thought. Finally, he answered, "Aye, she visited. I have no idea how she knew where to find me. I had assumed that perhaps you had told her."

Wolf shook his head and said, "She did send you home from dinner in her carriage, so that's probably how."

Mickey nodded in agreement and continued, "Anyway, she visited. It must have been Sunday." The gang leader looked up with a smirk, "She wishes to take on investigations, and it seems that she considers the rest of you to be dispensable or, in the case of Bear, replaceable. She wanted to hire one of my men to be her brawn."

"And what did you tell her?" Wolf asked.

"What would you have had me tell her? No? And leave an old, defenceless toff to visit the likes of Whitechapel alone?" Mickey chuckled again and continued, "She's quite something. If she wasn't such a grand lady, I might offer her a spot in the gang." He paused and said, "Maybe I will anyway. I suspect she might be inclined to take me up on the offer."

Wolf was inclined to believe she might at that. Nevertheless, Mickey's flippancy started to wear on his nerves, and he snapped, "And you didn't try to dissuade her from any investigations?"

"Lad, do you think it's my place to tell any toff what they can and can't do? Let alone that particular one. Do you think she would have listened to anything that I have to say?" Wolf realised the truth of this statement, but it didn't dilute his irritation at all. Mickey continued, "So I did the only thing I could do: make sure she had my biggest, toughest man with her. I sent Little Ian."

Wolf knew the man and the joke the name implied; Little Ian was anything but. The man had proportions to match Bear's, and an even more terrifying visage. Unlike Bear, he had some very visible trophies from his many fights over the years, including a nose that had been broken one time too many and a large, angry scar running from his right eye down to his mouth. While Little Ian was Welsh, and not of Irish heritage, he had long ago found a place in Mickey D's gang. Wolf had to admit that Mickey had sent the right man to accompany the dowager.

Whatever consolation Wolf derived from the knowledge of the dowager's companion was immediately dispelled as he considered that, regardless of her personal protector, the woman still hadn't been heard of for days. "Has Little Ian reported back on her activities? And more importantly, does he know where she is now?"

At this, Mickey D looked a little sheepish and admitted, "I have no idea. He went off with her on Sunday, and she asked if he could stay with her for the time being. The man has no wife or children and was happy enough for the pay. So, he went with her, and I haven't heard from or seen him since."

"Wolf, did Manning mention anything about Little Ian? I'm assuming that if her ladyship had him stay in her servants' quarters, her butler would have known about it," Bear said.

Bear made a good point; Manning hadn't said anything. Surely, such an enormous, terrifying-looking companion would have been something the butler would have mentioned. What was going on? While he had initially come to Whitechapel mainly to appease Tabitha rather than because he was actually worried, now Wolf was starting to be genuinely concerned.

Before they left, Wolf was determined to discover everything Mickey D knew, "Do you know anything about what she was planning to investigate and where she might have gone next?"

"I have no idea what she is planning to do or where she is," Mickey stated.

"You didn't think to ask what an elderly aristocratic gentlewoman might be planning to do such that she would need the services of Little Ian?" Wolf asked incredulously.

"Who am I to question the actions of my betters?" Mickey answered, his voice dripping with sarcasm. Wolf wasn't sure he believed him but realised he wouldn't get any more answers from the gangster.

CHAPTER 7

Sunday, October 29, 1897: The dowager

The dowager's visit to Mother Sharpe's brothel had driven out all thoughts of Lady Farthing's potential need for her assistance. Here was a genuine investigation that she was being asked to take on. The dowager couldn't be more thrilled. This case had all the elements one might desire: a missing person, the opportunity to investigate incognito, and the delicious seediness of the setting. The dowager positively thrummed with excitement as she returned to the carriage, Little Ian in tow. She was glad that Rat wasn't a talkative child; she had far too much to think about to carry on a conversation.

Rat made the sensible suggestion that the dowager carriage drop him off some streets away from Lord Langley's house. The young boy didn't know exactly what the dowager countess was up to in Whitechapel, but he realised well enough by this point that there was skulduggery afoot and that discretion was called for.

For most of the carriage ride to Langley's house, the dowager had been considering the plan Mother Sharpe had concocted: she would accompany the dowager to her sister's establishment and introduce her as a cousin who would be staying at the brothel while Margery Sharpe was missing. "In truth," Vicky had admitted, "those girls must be running wild without Margie around, and I hate to think of the liberties the patrons will be taking. Having you keep an eye on the place solves one big headache for me."

The dowager had no idea what keeping an eye on a brothel entailed, but the woman did not doubt that her battlefield skills were worthy of any theatre of warfare. Mother Sharpe had suggested that, under the guise of watching over the house, the dowager could investigate Margery Sharpe's disappearance. The entire plan was too delicious for words. The dowager considered the danger inherent in such a plan, but immediately dismissed it; that was why she had Little Ian as a protector.

Mother Sharpe had suggested that the dowager travel to Margery Sharpe's brothel in Villiers Street in a hackney cab. Even without its insignia, her carriage was far too grand for the persona the dowager needed to inhabit and, likewise, for the dowager's clothes. Vicky had packed a few of her own dresses in a carpet bag for the dowager to take with her. Julia Chesterton wasn't sure how she felt about donning someone else's dresses. Still, given the decent quality and style of Mother Sharpe's outfit, the dowager felt that the disguise would be bearable.

Mother Sharpe had suggested that the dowager send her carriage home empty and that they immediately proceed with the plan. But the dowager felt she needed at least a couple of hours to prepare herself, and they had agreed to meet at the Villiers Street address at five o'clock that evening.

As the carriage came to a stop a few streets from Lord Langley's mansion, the dowager considered what to tell Rat. The boy hadn't inquired about her visit with Mother Sharp, and the dowager appreciated that. She had no compunction about asking for the boy's discretion, so she said, "Rat, I have taken on a new case for Mother Sharpe." Rat's eyebrows raised slightly at this news, but he said nothing. The dowager continued, "I wish to be discreet about my whereabouts as I begin this investigation. Do you know what discreet means?" she asked.

"I do, your ladyship. It means that I should button my lip about your hanky panky," Rat answered proudly.

"I wouldn't put it exactly like that," the dowager said tartly, "but I believe we understand each other."

Rat nodded his head and exited the carriage. Before she knocked on the roof to indicate her driver should continue, the dowager considered what other precautions she needed to take. Manning was a fusspot and could not be entrusted with knowledge of her plans. She also realised the questions that would be raised if Little Ian accompanied her into the house.

Leaning out of the window, she called for him, and when the enormous man descended and came to the window, the dowager suggested that she leave him there and that her hackney cab stop by to pick him back up within the hour. It never occurred to the dowager to wonder what the man might do with himself while he waited. She did, however, have the forethought to leave the bag with Mother Sharpe's clothes with Little Ian. Her appearance with the serviceable but rather plain carpetbag would definitely be cause for comment amongst her staff.

The dowager also considered what to do about her maid, Withers. The woman had served her for many years, and the dowager trusted her discretion completely. While she might benefit from the woman's assistance in Villiers Street, the dowager realised that too many people already knew about her investigative activities. She felt she owed her staff no explanation for her absence, and it never occurred to her to worry herself over any concern they might feel.

On arriving home, the dowager went up to her bedchamber and, uncharacteristically, did not call for her maid. Instead, she sat at her dressing table and looked at herself in the mirror. The dowager had never fixed her hair, but she'd certainly watched it being done enough times in her seventy-plus years. Was the style appropriate for the persona she was taking on? As she considered this question, the dowager thought about Mother Sharpe's suggestion that she not take a false name but instead go by her maiden name. While the dowager hadn't been referred to as Julia Phillips for over fifty years, it was at least a name she could remember.

The dowager considered what else the madam had suggested. That she should wear nothing but the simplest jewellery was a wise idea. The dowager removed her large, diamond engagement ring from her gnarled, blue-veined finger. She had always loved that ring far more than she had the man who had given it to her.

When Queen Victoria had become engaged in 1839, just a few years before Julia herself, her snake-shaped engagement ring featuring a prominent emerald had set a trend that the young debutante was eager to emulate. Phillip Chesterton, not yet the Earl of Pembroke, had been persuaded by his father that the young woman, while fierier in personality than usually desirable for a wife, was a good enough catch that this whim should be indulged. And so, the ring had been commissioned and, when presented to the young Julia Phillips, was almost stunning enough to compensate for the lack of emotion with which it was given.

Locking the ring away in her mother-of-pearl-inlaid jewellery box, the dowager considered the rest of her outfit. She had never been a big wearer of jewellery for its own sake; it was either ostentatious diamonds or nothing. She decided her simple, elegant chignon hairstyle was perfectly acceptable. The dress she had worn to visit Whitechapel was one of her plainest, and she thought she could continue to wear it for her trip to Villiers Street. However, the white fox-trimmed coat definitely would need to be replaced. There was the rather stern, plain black coat she had worn for her first weeks of mourning. Unused to searching through her wardrobe, it took the dowager a while to locate it, but eventually, she found it boxed up at the back. There had been a rather austere hat that matched the dress that she had also discovered.

Finally, dressed in the black coat and hat, with no jewellery, the dowager assessed herself in the mirror; she'd do. Mother Sharpe hadn't suggested a full backstory for Cousin Julia, but the dowager had been considering this while she searched for the coat and hat. She wasn't sure what kind of family circumstances women such as the Sharpe sisters might come from, but decided it was plausible that they had been born of the disreputable arm of an otherwise solidly respectable, if poverty-stricken family. Cousin Julia had been thrown into further penury thanks to poor investment choices by her father. She had then taken work as the governess to the children of a wealthy mercer and had continued as such for multiple generations of the family until she could finally retire on her meagre savings a few years earlier.

The dowager was not naive. There was not enough coarse material in the world to disguise her accent and poise. She did not fool herself that she could credibly pull off a more appropriate accent for Villiers Street. But a woman who had been educated sufficiently to get work as a governess might have picked up the manners and elocution of her betters over the years.

She still struggled to come up with a credible answer for why Cousin Julia deigned to continue to acknowledge and even associate with her disreputable cousins. Finally, the dowager realised that if that question was posed to her, she would answer it with the same disdain she might have as the Dowager Countess of Pembroke. It had been her experience over many decades that few uncomfortable questions couldn't be answered with sufficient condescension.

Confident that she could take on this persona more than adequately, the dowager took one last look at herself in the mirror and walked out of her room. She had planned to sneak out of the house while there were no servants around. But as she began to creep down the stairs stealthily, it occurred to the dowager that she had never hailed a hackney cab and had no idea how it was done. She paused on the stairs and considered her dilemma. Of course, she could call for Manning and have him hail a cab. But as suitably inscrutable as her butler was, it was hard to imagine the situation not raising questions she would rather not answer.

Just as she had decided that she might not have any choice but to call for Manning, one of the maids walked into the vestibule. The young girl was new to the household, and the dowager wasn't sure of her name. Maybe it was Maude. Perhaps Mandy. Under normal circumstances, the dowager countess wouldn't have let such a trifle as not knowing her maid's name stop her from commanding the girl. But these were not normal circumstances.

The dowager screwed up her eyes and did her best to remember the girl's name. Finally, she snapped her fingers: Mindy! The maid's name was Mindy. What kind of a name was that? But relieved to have remembered it before the girl disappeared, the dowager cleared her throat, and the young maid looked up. Seeing her mistress, Mindy curtseyed.

"Mindy," the dowager countess said imperiously, "I am in need of your service."

"Yes, m'lady," the young girl said in a soft, west country accent.

"Have you ever hailed a hackney cab?"

In truth, travelling by hackney cab was beyond the means of a lowly maid. But as it happened, Mindy sometimes ran errands for cook when she ran out of supplies. Depending on how far she had to travel and how many bags she would be bringing back, the housekeeper would sometimes give her an allowance to take a cab home.

"Yes, m'lady," the girl said nervously. Was she about to be scolded for accepting the convenience of a cab on occasion?

Much to her relief, it seemed she was not to be admonished and instead was allowed to be of aid to her ladyship. She was so relieved that it didn't occur to the sixteen-year-old girl to question why the dowager countess wasn't travelling by carriage and was dressed so austerely.

Worried that Manning might be along any moment, the dowager hustled the young maid out of the front door. They went down the stairs to the street, where, to the dowager's astonishment, the young girl put two fingers in her mouth and emitted a loud, shrill whistle.

Seeing the dowager's astonishment, Mindy explained shyly, "Mr Manning taught me that's the best way to hail a cab." Any doubts the dowager might have had about the efficacy of Mindy's methods were quickly dispelled as a hackney cab pulled up next to them. Making a mental note to learn how to whistle in such a manner, the dowager thanked her maid and quickly climbed into the cab. She then gave the man the name of the street she had left Little Ian on and told him she would be travelling on further to Villiers Street.

A few minutes later, the dowager caught sight of Little Ian, the enormous man waiting patiently, her carpet bag at his feet. She poked her head out the window and directed the driver to pull over. Little Ian climbed up beside the driver and directed him to Villiers Street. Sitting back against the rather uncomfortable back of the cab's seat, the dowager smiled with great satisfaction; her adventure was going swimmingly so far.

CHAPTER 8

Sunday, October 29, 1897: The dowager

Despite having lived in London for most of her adult life, the dowager's experience of the metropolis had been quite limited. She travelled from Mayfair to Belgravia, occasionally to Kensington. But she had never had cause to travel down to the Strand or to visit Charing Cross Station at its western end. Normally quite incurious about the city she travelled through, the dowager looked out of the cab's windows in fascination. Previously, the streets of London and the rabble of people who thronged them were merely an uninteresting landscape as she travelled from one great home to another. But now, she viewed these people and their surroundings as the backdrop to her masterful performance as Julia Phillips, cousin to a whore.

Driving past Charing Cross Station, the dowager barely noticed the impressive ornate frontage with its rather fanciful reconstruction of the medieval Eleanor cross in the courtyard. The cab turned right immediately after the station onto Villiers Street, and partway down the quite narrow, cobbled street, it came to a standstill by a building on the corner of Buckingham Street. A few moments later, Little Ian appeared at the door to the hackney cab, opened it and said, "We're here, your ladyship."

"Shhh," the dowager hissed. "I'm incognito. For the purposes of our time here, you may call me Miss Phillips." Giving this direction caused the dowager to realise that she hadn't concocted a suitable back story for Little Ian and his attendance on her. Would a lowly Miss Phillips be able to afford a manservant, and would he travel with her? It also occurred to her that Little Ian was too conspicuous a character, given his size and visage, for it not to be possible that people might recognise him. One little such crack in her story and her credibility might shatter. The dowager thought quickly and said, "Little Ian, we will say that Mother Sharpe has sent you with me as a companion." The huge man nodded. He had no idea what this odd toff was up to, and he didn't care as long as he continued to get paid well.

Little Ian helped the dowager out of the cab. She looked around her. While Villiers Street was not a long road, lined with storefronts and cafes on the side opposite the station and adjacent hotel, it was bustling with activity as people went about their business. The cab had pulled up outside a building that looked a little grander than its neighbours. With a freshly painted front door and a gleaming brass knocker, this building didn't seem to have any obvious commercial purpose. However, Mother Sharpe was waiting in front of it, so it seemed this was the brothel.

Mother Sharpe hailed the dowager, who made quite the show of hurrying to her, saying, "Cousin Vicky!" The dowager quickly whispered their back story as she clasped the other woman's hand. Vicky Sharpe was amused at the effort the titled woman had put into her disguise, but was happy to play along, "Cousin Julia. Thank you for your help in this matter." With this, she turned and knocked on the front door.

The door was opened by a maid who, as at the Whitechapel brothel, was dressed almost as conservatively as a maid in Mayfair might be. Mother Sharpe swept into the house with the dowager and Little Ian in her wake. "Kitty, this is my cousin, Miss Phillips. She will be staying here and minding the establishment until my sister returns." Kitty nodded and mumbled a greeting to her new, temporary mistress.

The house was larger than the dowager had realised, seemingly comprised of two joined houses. If she wondered why a brothel needed that much space, it became obvious as Mother Sharpe led the way down a corridor; it was also a gaming establishment. To her left, the dowager could see rooms set up for various kinds of gambling. While there were no patrons currently, it was clear from the quality of the decor that the establishment catered to a reasonably well-heeled clientele. Just as at the Whitechapel brothel, the art adorning the walls was risqué at best and shockingly explicit at worst. The dowager wasn't yet sure what Cousin Julia's attitude to such things might be, but Julia Chesterton was appalled.

Under normal circumstances, the dowager would have felt no qualms about denouncing the establishment's decor and morals. However, she realised that she had walked into this situation with her eyes open – somewhat open. Unless she were willing to haul down the flag and slink home in defeat, she would do well to bite her tongue and temper her comments.

Mother Sharpe led the way to the back of the house, calling over her shoulder, "Cousin Julia, let me show you my sister's study." Given that Vicky and Margie Sharpe were identical twins, the former's right to march through the house was indisputable, and any servants they passed merely nodded their heads in acknowledgement. So far, they had seen none of the other "workers" in the brothel. The dowager had to admit to a genuine curiosity to see what a real lady of the night looked like. Mother Sharpe had been quite disappointingly bourgeois.

Stopping at a heavy oak door, Mother Sharpe turned the handle. The dowager was behind her and couldn't immediately see into the room. But she heard a male voice hail in a voice tinged with disdain, "Oi! Who do we have 'ere then?"

"You? What are you doing here?" Mother Sharpe demanded, storming into the room, the dowager close by. Now that she was in the room, the dowager could see that a slim man of perhaps middling years, with a pleasant enough thin face and a high forehead, was sitting in a chair with his feet up on the desk, assuming the attitude of lord and master.

"Ah, for a moment, you spooked me, Vicks. What on earth are you doing 'ere?" the man inquired.

"I might ask the same of you, Rascal. And what cause would you have to be so spooked, as you call it, by my appearance in my sister's establishment?" The dowager already had cause to respect Vicky Sharpe, and the imperious manner in which she spoke to the rather disreputable man in front of her only cemented that respect.

Looking more closely at the man, the dowager considered why he looked disreputable. It wasn't his clothes, which were of decent quality. His beard stubble was a contributing factor, but it was more than that. The man had an indefinable roguish air about him. His eyes sparkled with mischief, and his voice held the promise of tall tales to be told. The dowager was a big fan of Mr Dickens' writing and felt sure that the man sitting before her – because he hadn't bothered to stand at the ladies' entrance – could have been the Artful Dodger grown to a man.

The man she called Rascal chuckled, "Maybe spooked isn't the right word. But you and Marge aren't known for your sisterly closeness, are you?"

Deciding to ignore his reaction to her presence, Vicky reiterated, "Why are you here, Rascal? Since when do you and my sister have any business together? Particularly business that would justify making yourself so comfortable in her study?"

The Rascal chuckled again, "Now that would be telling, Vicks. But let's just say I represent certain interests, and while your sister is indisposed, those certain people thought I should come and keep tabs on the place." Finally, looking over at the dowager, the man asked, "And 'oo is this?"

The dowager knew the strategic importance of being the one to set the terms of engagement. She said in her most dowager countess voice, "I am Miss Julia Phillips, cousin to Victoria and Margery. I will be staying here to, as you put it, keep tabs on the place. Now that I am here, you may vacate that seat and, indeed, the establishment. I am more than capable of managing until my cousin's return." Even as she said these words, the dowager felt a rare moment of self-doubt; was she capable of running not only a brothel but a gaming establishment? Then she considered that she knew everything there was to know about running a great house and managing a large household staff. How different could this be?

Jason Bono, for that was The Rascal's real name, did look

suitably taken aback by the dowager's tone and took his feet off the desk, at least. But he was used to being the one to put people off balance rather than the other way around. He quickly gathered himself and said, if with a rather forced jocularity, "Well, Miss Julia Phillips, that's all very well and good, but the guvnor said I'm to stay, and so stay I shall."

The dowager and Vicky exchanged glances; who was this 'guvnor'? Seeing their confusion, The Rascal added, "I work for your sister's business partner."

"Of whom do you speak?" the dowager asked.

The Rascal tapped the side of his nose with his finger and said, "That's for me to know and you to find out when the guvnor chooses. If you stay, that is. You sound like quite the toff for the cousin of an abbess," he observed.

The dowager was glad she had anticipated this question and said nonchalantly, "I have worked as a governess for a wealthy family for more than forty years. I'm glad to know that their good breeding has rubbed off on me."

The Rascal looked sceptical at this explanation but accepted it for now. Instead, he returned to the first part of his statement, "As I said, if you stay. You were worried about minding your cousin's interest while she is gone and now you know you don't need to be. I'm minding them. So, you can return to your wealthy family, Miss Julia Phillips."

The dowager drew herself up to her almost five feet, sniffed, and said, "Young man, it is not for you to direct my movements. It is far from clear to me that you are the most appropriate custodian of my cousin's interests. Therefore, I will be staying here until her return. From this point on, this study will be my domain, and that will be my desk. I don't expect to see you in here unless summoned, and I never expect to see you sitting in my chair with your feet on my desk again. Is that understood?"

The Rascal had been hustling on the streets of London for most of his life. Like Mr Dickens' Artful Dodger, he had started as a pickpocket and worked his way up through the street gangs of some of London's most dangerous neighbourhoods. Jason Bono wasn't a natural fighter. Intimidation wasn't his forte. He didn't have the build or the inclination to be a thug. Instead, his various employers over the years had appreciated his natural quickness and that he had never forgotten the skills he learned as a young pickpocket. Over the years, he'd earned a certain amount of respect on the street, and he wasn't used to being dismissed in such a matter-of-fact manner and by a tiny old lady at that. The Rascal found himself uncharacteristically caught on the back foot. He was sure his employer wouldn't be happy at this Miss Phillip's presence, but The Rascal had a feeling this old battleaxe wouldn't be easily dissuaded.

Sizing up the situation, The Rascal decided that he should retreat, for now, and perhaps alert his employer to the change in circumstances later. The Rascal was an intelligent, if uneducated, man. He knew when he was out of his league, and he definitely was at that moment. Standing up, he gestured towards the chair he'd been occupying and said, his voice heavy with sarcasm, "M'lady." Given the unwitting appropriateness of the moniker, the sarcasm was entirely lost on the dowager, who traded insincere smiles with him.

Settled comfortably behind the desk and already feeling more at home, the dowager asked, "Mr Rascal, is that your real name?"

"The name is Jason Bono, but no one calls me that except my old mum. Even the bobbies call me Rascal," the man explained.

"Be that as it may, I shall be calling you Mr Bono," the dowager explained in a voice that made clear she would brook no contradiction. While The Rascal wasn't entirely persuaded by her explanation of her accent, he could believe the woman was a governess by trade. It wasn't hard to imagine her boxing the ears of naughty children and sending them to bed with no supper for minor academic infractions. He nodded, if not in agreement, at least acknowledging that he had no say in what she chose to call him.

The dowager continued, "So, Mr Bono, you may leave us. I shall call for you if I require your services; otherwise, I expect you to stay out of my way," the dowager commanded. The Rascal couldn't wait for the guvnor to meet this termagant. He could sell tickets for that show of fireworks.

Finally, alone in the study, the dowager steepled her hands and looked at Mother Sharpe, "Now what?"

"You tell me; you're the private investigator," Vicky said tartly.

That gave the dowager pause. She had indeed portrayed herself as a seasoned investigator. While she was mostly filled with unsubstantiated self-confidence, a little part of her brain tickled with the worry that she had never been the one to kick off a case. Yes, she had contributed greatly to solving them, but Tabitha and Wolf had always done the initial legwork. How did they begin? She knew they would often interview a household staff, but she wasn't installed in Villiers Street as an investigator but as a concerned cousin "keeping an eye on the place." Any questioning would have to be conducted with the utmost discretion and subtlety. While discretion and subtlety were not two words that most people would have associated with the Dowager Countess of Pembroke, she was luckily immune from the judgement and opinions of almost anybody but herself.

"Is there any more you can tell me?" the dowager asked. "In particular, about this business partner? It is clear this house is more than a mere brothel. From what I saw, significant gaming activities are going on, as well. Is that common?"

"It is something that is becoming more common," Mother Sharpe acknowledged. "When I first got into this game, running a whorehouse was a pretty standard affair; a house, some scantily clad young girls, and a steady stream of men. But over the last few years, it has become more. How can I put it? More specialised. There are now houses that cater to every taste imaginable, and many that are likely far beyond at least your imagination."

The dowager raised her eyebrows at this statement, unsure what such outrageous tastes might be. The dowager was well-read, could speak multiple foreign languages, and could have debated politics in the Lords without embarrassing herself. Still, even she had to admit that her knowledge of the carnal desires of men was narrow. Blessedly, her husband had died early in their marriage, and even up to that point, their congress had been no more than the required minimum. She had always assumed her husband, who she found generally vulgar and violent, had desires that were equally so. It had never occurred to the dowager that she might have to experience them, so she had never given them more than a passing thought.

Mother Sharpe had paused, then added, "My sister has a small coterie of women, professional acquaintances, friends you might say, who meet regularly at each other's establishments to break bread, share gossip, discuss business, and from what I've heard, drink far too much claret for that time in the afternoon. From what I understand, these women run brothels across the spectrum of tastes."

The dowager was too intrigued to be appalled, "And you are not part of such a group?"

Vicky Sharpe laughed hollowly, "My sister has never shared well." She then continued, "I don't know the schedule for these meetings, so perhaps Margie will be home before you ever have the need to encounter them. However, I know that Margie likes and trusts these women and they might also be of service to you as you investigate, so I will share their names with you." She then proceeded to rattle off a list of quite extraordinary names: Pretty Pearl, Zsa Zsa, Girl Lizzy, Spanish Gemma, Half-blind Kim, Sameera – often referred to as Spicy, and Russian Alexandra, known as Alexa, and finally, Tamara, known as Madam Tammy.

As Vicky listed the other madams, the dowager flicked through what seemed to be a diary. There were some rather cryptic entries over the past couple of weeks, and the dowager made a mental note to review them further when she was alone. Meanwhile, she glanced at the entries for that day and the following. As Vicky finished the madam recitation, the dowager looked up and remarked, "These women may be meeting tomorrow afternoon. The entry is labelled 'The Ladies of KB'. What on earth does that mean?"

Vicky laughed, "Oh yes, that's them. Apparently, when they

first started to meet some years ago, it was at Zsa Zsa's establishment in Knightsbridge, KB, you see. I believe the name just stuck, even though she moved to a place in Piccadilly some years ago."

The dowager tapped the diary entry in front of her, "Well, that seems to be where they are to meet tomorrow, apparently. What will they think if I just turn up?" It had never occurred to the dowager that she might do otherwise. The prospect was far too intriguing. Drinking claret with Zsa Zsa, Pretty Pearl, and someone known as Spicy was an opportunity the dowager couldn't forego. No one who had spent the last fifty-odd years politely sipping tea with the likes of Ladies Hartley and Willis could be expected to do otherwise.

"I will send a note with you, and Lou can accompany you."

"Who is this Lou?" the dowager enquired.

No sooner had the dowager asked this question than there was a brisk knock at the door. Before they had a chance to say enter, the door was opened. Standing in the doorway was a tall and sturdy woman of middle years with a rather voluptuous figure, shown off to rather outrageous effect by her scandalously low neckline. The woman had a friendly face, even if it was rather over-painted.

"Ah, Lou. Just the person we were talking about," Vicky exclaimed, gesturing for the woman to enter the room and join them. "Oh, and shut the door behind you," she said more quietly.

The prostitute, because that was clearly what the woman was, slipped into the room, closing the door softly behind her. Moving to Madam Sharpe, Lou came and kissed the older woman on the cheek as a devoted niece might a beloved aunt. "It's been a while, Vicks," she said.

Vicky shrugged, "You know how it is. It's never easy with Marge."

Lou nodded in seeming acknowledgement of this statement, sat in the spare chair, and cocked her head in the dowager's direction, "Who's the toff?"

If Vicky Sharpe was surprised that the dowager's identity

had been so easily exposed, and before the woman opened her mouth, she didn't show it. Instead, she said, "Don't worry, we call anyone who didn't grow up scrabbling for crumbs a toff."

That statement seemed to cause Lou to reconsider the woman before her, "You say that, Vicks, as if she might be a real toff."

Unwilling to divulge more than necessary, Vicky changed the subject and asked, "How long has The Rascal been in residence?"

"Ever since Margie disappeared. Funny, really, because none of us let the guvnor know she was missing. Yet somehow, not twenty-four hours later, The Rascal turned up saying 'e was watching the place. Curious that, isn't it?"

The other women agreed it was curious. With great emphasis, Vicky said, "This is our cousin, Julia." She may have winked as she said it. "She will be staying here until Margie returns. To 'look after the place'. Can you show her the ropes, Lou?" She told the dowager, "Lou has been with my sister for years. She's a good sort, heart of gold and all that. You can trust her. Entirely." With that, Mother Sharpe stood up and made her farewells.

In the end, Vicky had left rather suddenly, and the dowager wasn't entirely sure what she was to do next. The madam had even forgotten to write the promised note to the Ladies of KB. But she said Lou would accompany her, so the dowager mentioned the gathering the following evening.

"Ah, yes, the Ladies." She looked the dowager up and down and said, "Not being funny, ma'am, but are you sure you're up for meeting that group? They're a little rough for a well-bred lady such as you seem to be."

The dowager sat up a little straighter and said with great authority, "I'm sure there is nothing about these women that I cannot handle. Mother Sharpe assured me you would accompany me. And so there will be that." Lou smiled in agreement and said nothing more of the proposed visit. All that was left was to show the dowager to the madam's bedchamber.

CHAPTER 9

Monday, October 30, 1897: Tabitha & Wolf

Tabitha and Wolf had each returned from their assignations and met in the comfortable parlour that Tabitha preferred to sit in when they were not entertaining guests. Instead of the drawing room's more formal and stiff furniture, the parlour had comfortable armchairs and sofas dotted around the room. The colour scheme was in calming pastel shades and floral patterns. Tabitha had returned before Wolf and had been drinking tea and contemplating her conversation with Lady Hartley when Wolf returned and sat in his customary spot.

Wolf observed the tension and concern writ all over Tabitha's face and said, "I'm assuming Lady Hartley confirmed what Mickey D has: that the dowager has embarked upon investigating alone."

"Whatever is she thinking?" Tabitha bemoaned. "I know she has threatened to do as much in the past, but I always took it as just that, an idle threat. That the woman might actually take it upon herself to investigate crimes alone makes me concerned for her senses, if nothing else. Perhaps this is not the decision of a fully lucid mind."

Wolf thought about her words. For himself, he considered the dowager's actions foolhardy, dangerous, and born of petulance, but it hadn't occurred to him previously to consider them evidence of a potentially frail, older mind. In truth, it was difficult to imagine that the dowager was undergoing any dulling of her rapier-sharp intellect. On the other hand, it was one way to look at her recent actions.

Deciding that their actions must be the same regardless of their cause, Wolf said as much, "We must find the dowager countess as soon as possible, whatever her mental state. Even if this reckless behaviour is nothing more than an unfortunate, ill-judged extension of her recent exuberance towards investigating, our duty to rescue her from whatever situation she had fallen into remains unchanged."

Tabitha realised the truth of Wolf's words; worrying about the dowager's state of mind and positing age-related causes to her behaviour were not helpful. They needed to find the elderly woman, and then they could consider having a doctor observe her.

Wolf filled Tabitha in on the little Mickey D had told him. As Wolf described Little Ian, Tabitha took some comfort in the thought that the dowager was likely accompanied by such an enormous and terrifying-looking protector. She also wondered why Manning hadn't mentioned the man. When Wolf had ended his report, she took her turn and filled him in on her conversation with Lady Hartley.

"So, do you believe that this is the investigation she has thrown herself into?" Wolf asked.

"I have no idea. But at the moment, this is the only concrete piece of evidence we have gathered." As Tabitha spoke, she gestured to their trusty corkboard, now on the wall in the place of their original, improvised board constructed from an ugly family painting covered in a taut sheet. On the corkboard, one notecard highlighted the dowager's visit to Lady Hartley. There were also strips of notecards at the top of the board, each with a day of the week written on them. "I believe we need to create a timeline of the woman's movements, going back to her visit to Lady Hartley on Saturday."

Tabitha had a stack of blank notecards on the little table before her. She reached for one and began to write the outline of the dowager's visit to Mickey D in Whitechapel. "Did Mickey say what time she visited?" Tabitha asked.

"Not exactly," Wolf answered. "But he did mention that she had been lucky to catch him home and that it was only because it was a Sunday, when Angie always insisted on a family meal after church."

"Mickey D attends church every Sunday?" Tabitha asked in amazement.

"Apparently," Wolf said. "But I also know that he spends Sunday afternoons in the Cock. He uses the excuse of having a pint or two to catch up with his cronies and to put a bit of fear into the locals. Anyway, it seems as if the dowager had visited after the midday meal, but before Mickey had headed out. So, I'd guess early afternoon." Tabitha nodded and wrote these details on the notecard, which she pinned on the corkboard under the heading "Sunday".

Sitting back down, Tabitha tapped the pen she was holding against her mouth as she was wont to do when she was deep in thought. Wolf knew this mannerism well now and didn't interrupt her musings. Finally, she lowered the pen and asked, "What would she have done next? What would we have done next?"

It was a good question. Wolf thought momentarily, then answered, "Well, based on what we know, Lady Hartley had alerted Lady Pembroke to nothing more than a piece of salacious gossip. Surely, the woman wouldn't have gone off half-cocked without actually assuring herself there was a case to investigate and securing Lady Farthing's consent."

"Exactly!" Tabitha concurred. "At some point, relatively early in this timeline, Mama must have visited Lady Farthing. So, I believe this is what we must do, today if possible." She looked at the clock on the mantelpiece. As hard as it was to believe, it was only three o'clock, still an acceptable time for an afternoon visit.

Tabitha paused and considered what she had just said, "Of course, I don't know Lady Farthing. In fact, I'm not even sure where she lives. Normally, that is something I would have asked Mama to help with. She seems to have entrée to all the best drawing rooms in London. In her stead, I believe the answer is the Dowager Duchess of Somerset. She knows almost as many people as Mama." Catherine Rowley, the Dowager Duchess of Somerset, was the grandmother of the current duke, Anthony Rowley, a childhood friend of Tabitha's. She was also a woman who would forever be indebted to Tabitha and Wolf for their sensitive handling of her son's murder at her hand.

"Didn't Lady Pembroke insist that Anthony install a telephone at Rowley House?" Wolf asked.

"She did. I will ask Talbot to put a telephone call through now. If Her Grace would send a note around to Lady Farthing asking her to receive us, I believe that would be sufficient." Tabitha rang the bell for Talbot and requested he put a telephone call through to Rowley House. While the two women were no more than casual acquaintances, the dowager duchess was reasonably friendly with Lord Farthing's grandmother, the Dowager Duchess of Albany. And so, ten minutes later, Tabitha had the dowager duchess's assurance that a note would be sent to Lady Farthing immediately asking her to receive the Countess of Pembroke within the hour.

Tabitha returned to the parlour, feeling energised by having a plan of action. Entering the room, she paused in the doorway and looked at Wolf sitting comfortably in his favourite armchair, a glass of brandy in his hand, deep in thought. This is what marriage should feel like, she thought: companionable evenings in front of a roaring fire, sharing thoughts and ideas, taking pleasure in the ease of each other's company. Of course, this wasn't what marriage to Jonathan had been like. When they had dined together, the meal had been formal and the conversation, such as it was, stiff and silted. After dinner, she had retired to the parlour and Jonathan to his study or out for the evening. On reflection, Tabitha realised she had never shared one moment of pleasure or good company with Jonathan in over two years.

Would she and Wolf have developed the same rapport if they hadn't been caught up in investigations almost from the moment he inherited the earldom? That question gave her pause for a moment. There was no doubt that investigating gave them a shared purpose. If Mickey D had never dragged them into the case of the Duke of Somerset's murder, Tabitha might have never ended up staying at Chesterton House. She might well have stayed on for a few weeks to help Wolf transition to his new position, but would she have remained beyond that?

Of course, pondering these hypotheticals wasn't productive. There were so many tangents her life could have taken; what if she hadn't married Jonathan? What if he hadn't flown into a drunken fury that fateful last night and tripped and fallen down the stairs? There were so many possible directions her life could have taken. All that she could usefully consider and have some control over were her future choices and actions. And the most significant of those was whether, ultimately, she remained in this house with this man or not. And if she did remain, then at some point, she was staying as his wife.

Tabitha dragged herself out of her wool-gathering; she was getting ahead of herself. Wolf had not asked her to marry him. He hadn't even declared his feelings for her. However, Tabitha knew that before she encouraged the conversation that Wolf was clearly desirous of having, she had to be clear in her mind what she wanted and what she might say if marriage was proposed. And as drawn as she was to this man, and as sure as she was that he could not be more different to Jonathan, his cousin, a part of her still held back. It was not lost on Tabitha that the question wasn't whether she trusted Wolf but rather whether she trusted her instincts to make a wiser choice than she had with her first husband.

She wasn't sure how long she had stood in the doorway musing, but eventually, Wolf looked up and cocked an eyebrow, leading her to believe that her wool-gathering had been noticeable. Shaking her head to dispel her worried thoughts, Tabitha moved back to her place on the sofa and said, "The Dowager Duchess will send a note now asking Lady Farthing to receive me. I believe that if we leave here at four o'clock, it will have given her sufficient time to write and deliver it."

"Do you think I should accompany you?" Wolf asked.

Tabitha considered the question. It wasn't customary for men to participate in the time-honoured ritual that was the genteel social call. But this wasn't a social visit, was it? "Yes, I think that would be helpful," Tabitha acknowledged. She reviewed their notes on the board, "It's not much to go on, is it? I do hope that Lady Farthing has some insight to share. Tonight will be the second night that Mama is missing. As difficult as the woman is some of the time, well, most of the time really, I find myself truly anxious at the thought of her out there, in the streets of London, involved in who knows what. I hope that this Little Ian is still with her, at least. That is some consolation."

Wolf was equally worried, but he wanted to comfort Tabitha as best he could, "She may look frail, but we both know that few people are as able to strike fear into the hearts of men and woman as the dowager countess can. Truly, I believe that is why she and Mickey D are drawn to each other; like recognises like. In her way, the older Lady Pembroke is as ruthless as the Whitechapel gangster, maybe more so. He breaks fingers, but she can crush the soul with that lacerating tongue of hers. Rather than worrying for her safety, perhaps we should pity the local inhabitants she interacts with." Tabitha smiled; his words didn't lessen her concerns but did lighten the moment.

CHAPTER 10

Sunday, October 29, 1897: The dowager

Margery Sharpe's bedchamber was not luxurious. It certainly wasn't up to the dowager's usual standards, but it was clean and comfortable. The dowager spent quite a bit of time looking through wardrobes and drawers, trying to understand the woman she was attempting to find. If she was honest, there was also an element of prurient curiosity; Vicky Sharpe was not at all what the dowager had envisioned a madam to be. Was her twin sister also a surprising departure from the stereotype?

It was clear that the woman was tidy, everything was stored neatly. One interesting feature was a large, solid wardrobe full of dresses. The dresses themselves were unremarkable except for their unexpected conservative simplicity. But what was noteworthy was that the dresses were hung in a perfect colour spectrum from light to dark. This was the room of a careful and organised woman. Margery Sharpe certainly didn't seem to be someone who would casually disappear without a word.

When Lou had shown the dowager up to the bedchamber, she had carried the carpetbag of clothes and then had proceeded to unpack and hang the gowns. It never occurred to the dowager to wonder whether Lou did this because she also acted as a kind of maid for Margie or because it was obvious that the dowager was unused to doing such things for herself. Either way, Lou had hung the dresses up in a smaller wardrobe at the back of the room used mainly for hat boxes and shoes. Now, the dowager went to look in this wardrobe to see what she might change into for the evening. She was unsure whether the working classes followed the aristocratic norm of changing into evening wear. However, the work of a brothel and a gaming house took place in the evening, so she wanted to make a good first impression.

The dowager selected a pale grey silk dress that had the advantage of buttons down the front instead of the back. Given that she would be dressing without the aid of a maid for the first time in her life, the dowager thought it best to choose an outfit that seemed more of a one-woman job.

A small porcelain bowl with a jug of water beside it stood on a small table against the wall. The dowager poured water into the bowl and rinsed her face, gasping at how cold the water was. While the dowager's house had all the benefits of modern plumbing, even in the days before such luxuries, Julia Chesterton had always had servants to bring her hot water. It had never been something she'd given much thought to. She'd certainly never wasted a moment wondering what life might be like for people with no choice but to suffer washing in ice-cold water in the winter.

Lou had informed her that Mother Sharpe normally ate a light, informal dinner in the kitchen at a rather early hour, normally 5:30 pm. The evening was a time for business, not grand dining. Glancing at the clock on the mantelpiece, the dowager realised that time had slipped away more quickly than she'd imagined, and she only had twenty minutes to finish dressing for the evening. Her choice of gown had been wise, and she could change into it unassisted.

Looking at herself in the mirror, she decided that her hair was good enough, certainly good enough for a bunch of prostitutes and their customers. As this thought crossed her mind, the dowager did, for the first time, feel some trepidation at the situation she found herself in. It was all very well to desire adventure and wish to provide a jolt to her previously almost moribund life. But might she have not found sufficient excitement somewhere in Mayfair? Had it been necessary to move into a brothel and consort with prostitutes and the men who would hire them?

Also, for the first time, the dowager did wonder if it had been wise to travel to Villiers Street without leaving word with anyone. The only person who had even a clue what the dowager was up to was Rat, and she was quite sure he would keep her secret, even beyond the point when she might have wished him to inform someone. It wasn't too late to send a note to someone. But to whom should she send it? Telling Wolf and Tabitha seemed tantamount to an admission of dependence. Shaking her head at these thoughts, the dowager decided to see what the evening brought and then decide on the morrow whether or not she would send a note to someone.

If the dowager had been struck by the lack of activity in the house when she arrived, she was now equally struck by the noise and frenetic activity that seemed to be all around as soon as she stepped outside Margery's bedchamber. One scantily clad young woman chased another equally underdressed redhead down the corridor, the one in pursuit yelling, "I'll get you, Ginger, that's my perfume, and you know it."

The other girl laughed and yelled over her shoulder, "And what are you going to do to get it off my body and back into the bottle?"

The girls ran by the dowager with barely a glance at the stranger. Perhaps she did look enough like Mother Sharp, particularly in the woman's clothes, that they didn't notice that it was a different, small, old woman with a very disapproving look on her face watching them run past. There seemed to be noise coming from every room as the voices of young women called for a ribbon or shared a ribald joke.

As the dowager made her way downstairs, the noise changed in type, if not volume. Now servants were scurrying back and forth, carrying full decanters, some carrying the accoutrement of a gambling establishment, others giving every surface a last flick of the feather duster. The dowager wondered what, if anything, Lou had told everyone. No one seemed concerned about the stranger in their midst, and she was mostly ignored.

While the dowager didn't spend much time in the kitchen in her home, she had a general sense of how to get there. Was the kitchen in this, much less grand house, similarly placed? Deciding to make the assumption that it was, the dowager made her way to the back of the house, where she found some uncarpeted stairs. Walking down them, she arrived at the bottom to find she had been correct in her assumption; the large kitchen could be seen through a wide oak doorframe.

As she entered the kitchen, she finally received some acknowledgement; Lou was sitting at a large, well-scrubbed pine table and hailed her, "Miss Phillips, I'm glad you were able to find your way."

Hearing her greeting, a round, red-cheeked cook looked up from whatever she was stirring and said, "Welcome, Miss Phillips. I'm Mrs Brown. Lou said you're going to be keeping an eye on the place while Mother Sharpe is..." the cook paused, grasping for the right word, then said, "while she's away. I've made some Irish stew for the girls if that's alright with you?"

While she would never consider serving something as low-brow as Irish stew to guests, it was a dish the dowager was quite partial to when she was eating alone. There were quite a few dishes favoured by the working class that she secretly enjoyed. During their recent investigation, she had even acquired a taste for small beer and had instructed Wolf to find a supplier who could keep her cellars stocked with the bitter but tasty beverage. As she had suspected, it paired particularly well with her cook's cheese and onion pie. Again, not a dish she would ever serve to guests or even admit to liking, but very tasty, nonetheless. Indicating that Irish stew would be acceptable, the dowager asked, "Is small beer something you keep in the house?" The cook disappointed her when she shook her head in the negative.

The dowager sat at the table, and a large, steaming bowl of wonderful-smelling stew was put in front of her. She'd only tasted one delicious mouthful of the rich and hearty dish when girls started wandering into the kitchen looking for their evening meal. When she had seen them upstairs, running around in various undergarments, the dowager had assumed the women were in the process of dressing. But for the most part, it seemed she had been wrong; the revealing, saucy undergarments were the outfits for the evening. In some cases, the women wore flimsy robes over their corsets and bloomers, but even then, they did nothing more than cover shoulders, and nothing was left to the imagination.

Taking in the sight of all this exposed flesh and the utter lack of shame or embarrassment the young women seemed to feel at this dishabille, the dowager's first instinct was to sniff and make an acerbic comment. But, just in time, she caught herself and realised that while the Dowager Countess of Pembroke might appropriately express censure, Julia Phillips, cousin to two madams, would be less inclined to moral outrage.

As the girls settled, they finally seemed to notice that a stranger was in their midst. Lou said, "This is Miss Julia Phillips. She's Mother Sharpe's cousin and will be staying with us for a few days. You're to listen to any instructions she gives you."

While the dowager was grateful for such an introduction, she couldn't imagine what instructions she might choose to give to a prostitute. As she pondered this question, Little Ian entered the kitchen and, seemingly already feeling comfortable in the household, went to where the cook was stirring the Irish stew and received his own large bowlful. He made his way to the table where, with a brief nod of acknowledgement in the dowager's direction, he sat and ate his food.

The meal ended quickly enough, and the girls started making their way back upstairs. When she was finally alone with Lou, Mrs Brown having disappeared with the dirty bowls, the dowager asked, "What am I to do this evening?"

Lou laughed, "You're in charge. What do you want to do?"

The dowager thought about the question, then asked, "What would Mother Sharpe typically do?"

"Well, she would greet customers and make sure regulars were supplied with their favourite tipples. She'd keep the girls in line. They can get a little rowdy if they're not watched. And, of course, she always made sure the customers were happy and settled with the girl of their choosing wherever possible."

The dowager thought about how to phrase her next question, "And the gaming? What role does she play in that?"

"Not a lot. The guvnor's people take care of all of that. They run the tables and collect the brass. Honestly, the two businesses are quite separate. Punters come and go between the two businesses, but Mother Sharpe's only role was to keep the girls away from the gaming tables unless a punter asks for one. Honestly, most of the men are too interested in their gaming to want a girl. But once they're flush with winnings, then they'll often come wandering into the parlour looking for some company. Our johns will often start at the tables and then end up with a girl. Not the clergy, of course," she quickly added as if engaging a prostitute was one thing but gambling a bridge too far for a man of the cloth.

"And does this 'guvnor' ever make an appearance?" the dowager asked casually.

Lou barked a hollow laugh, "Never. But it always feels like the guvnor is here, trust me. I'm sure there are spies throughout the servants. Usually, The Rascal is watching out for things or some other men. They're usually fine; we stay out of their way, and they stay out of ours."

CHAPTER 11

Monday, October 30, 1897: Tabitha & Wolf

Lord and Lady Farthing lived in the more fashionable part of Kensington, in a townhouse that was stylish enough to be worthy of the son of a duke but of a size and location to proclaim that son was far removed from inheriting. Tabitha and Wolf weren't sure how to approach this interview. Was Lord Farthing still in residence with his estranged wife? Would they be forced into the awkward position of discussing the reason for their visit in front of the man? They discussed these possible scenarios for almost the entire carriage ride. Finally, Tabitha threw her hands up in exasperation and said, "Let us just do our best to manage whatever situation we find ourselves in. Trying to anticipate our possible reception with so little information at our disposal is giving me a headache." Wolf agreed.

The front door was answered by an elderly butler who seemed a little hard of hearing. Wolf had to repeat a few times, at increasing volumes, that the Dowager Duchess of Somerset had alerted his mistress to their visit. Finally, whether because he finally heard or gave up trying, the butler admitted them into the house and showed them into the drawing room.

The house's interior matched the exterior; not shabby, but definitely not in the height of fashion. The furniture was simple, sturdy, and well-made but lacked the elegant beauty of the pieces found in the best drawing rooms in London. As they sat and waited, Tabitha looked around the room. On closer inspection, the furnishings really were quite old-fashioned, and the room had the heavy, dreary feel of much earlier in the century. What was Lady Farthing's plan if she managed to secure her legal separation? Was it to remain in this house? Surely not. But it didn't look as if Lord Farthing's coffers were overly full, so would the man be obliged or even able to continue to support his wife if she managed to obtain the legal separation she sought?

After a few minutes of waiting, the door opened, and a beautiful young woman entered. She had dark, almost black hair and large, lustrous, equally dark eyes that shone like black obsidian out of a perfectly proportioned face. The woman's dress matched the room's furnishings: simple and slightly out of fashion. But she wore the dress with an elegance of posture that elevated the sophistication of the whole well beyond the lack of style of the parts.

Lady Farthing's face showed curiosity at their visit, but not surprise. It was evident that the dowager duchess had been as good as her word. Tabitha and Wolf both stood. "Thank you for receiving us in such an unorthodox manner." Lady Farthing nodded her head in acknowledgement. Whether of her benevolence or of the strangeness of the visit, it wasn't clear. She indicated that they should all sit and was quickly followed into the room by a maid with a tea tray.

The social niceties of tea pouring and cake plating dispensed with, the maid left the room, closing the door behind her. "How can I help you, Lord and Lady Pembroke?" Lady Farthing put just enough emphasis on the question to make clear she knew their unusual living situation.

Ignoring any intended slight, Tabitha waded in, "We believe that the Dowager Countess of Pembroke visited you a few days ago about an investigation you need help with."

Lady Farthing's face showed total incomprehension at this statement. Either the woman was an extremely good actress, or she didn't have a clue what Tabitha was talking about. "I do not know the dowager countess; she has never visited me, and, as far as I'm aware, I have need of no investigator," Lady Farthing said this in a rather tight voice that suggested she was beginning to wonder if the Dowager Duchess of Somerset had sent her lunatics.

Tabitha wasn't sure how to phrase her next question. In all the discussions she and Wolf had engaged in on the drive, the one scenario they had not accounted for was that they might need to spell out their awareness of Lady Farthing's unfortunate marital state. "I was, well, we were under the impression that your estrangement from Lord Farthing might have necessitated the investigative help of a professional."

At this, Lady Farthing's eyebrows rose in disbelief, "And is the Dowager Countess of Pembroke a professional investigator now?"

Tabitha sighed; this conversation was not going to be easy. She had no desire to impose the entire narrative of the last few months on their hostess. However, was there a concise way to explain their visit? Luckily, Wolf stepped in, "Lady Farthing, while you may not be aware of the fact, I was such an investigator before I inherited the earldom and have been drawn into some investigations since. The dowager countess has..." he paused, torn between honesty and the effectiveness of this conversation. "She has been of some aid," he landed on as a compromise. "The younger Lady Pembroke was given some intelligence that has led us to believe that the dowager countess may be attempting to set herself up as an investigator and that you are her first case."

Unsure which part of this incredible statement to address first, Lady Farthing landed on the one most personally related to her, "I am? Pray do tell, what is the case she had undertaken on my behalf?"

The sarcasm that dripped from her mouth was impossible to ignore. Unsure of the wisdom of proceeding but with no graceful exit from the conversation evident, Wolf said, "Our understanding is the dowager countess is helping you with the matter of your legal separation."

Lady Farthing's face went from an ashen shock to a heated anger, "I'm not sure who is spreading malicious gossip about me and about my marriage, but I can assure you that I consider such matters intensely personal and have not and will not be engaging any persons to manage them on my behalf except for my solicitor. I can say with one hundred percent certainty that if this dowager countess has undertaken such an investigation, she has done it without my consent, indeed without my knowledge." With this, Lady Farthing stood. The visit was clearly at an end.

Tabitha was mortified. To impose themselves on a stranger, uninvited and then to allude to such delicate and personal matters was such a breach of all social etiquette that Tabitha felt quite ashamed. She could only imagine what her mother would say if word of this ever reached her ears.

It was unclear to Tabitha what the appropriate words of apology might be; truly, no words could reduce the shame of the past fifteen minutes. However, knowing they must say something, she stuttered, "Our apologies, Lady Farthing, for interrupting your afternoon and imposing on you in what now appears to be an utterly unwarranted manner." Lady Farthing said nothing in reply, and the look on her face confirmed she was not of a mind to offer absolution.

Realising that all they could now do was to leave as quickly as possible, Tabitha and Wolf exited expeditiously. In the carriage, Tabitha let out the full force of her embarrassment, "What have we done, Wolf? I can only pray that Lady Farthing's concerns for her own privacy will prevent her from speaking of our behaviour. There really can be no excuse."

Wolf was not as encumbered by social etiquette as Tabitha, but even he realised that they had intruded on a woman's time and alluded to highly personal circumstances for no good reason, it appeared. But no, there was a good reason, even if Lady Farthing hadn't been told it. "Tabitha," he pointed out, "as much as I feel the embarrassment of the situation, there was a good excuse; an elderly woman is missing, and we fear may have put herself in harm's way. While we didn't have the chance to explain this to Lady Farthing, and given the circumstances, perhaps that was for the best. Nevertheless, our motives were pure. What else could we have done, given what Lady Hartley told you?"

In her heart, Tabitha knew Wolf was correct, but this

knowledge didn't dull the shame she felt. But his words did highlight perhaps the worst aspect of their visit, "But all we have confirmed is that, whatever Mama is doing, she is not investigating on behalf of Lady Farthing. We are no further along in tracking her down and may actually be worse off than we seemed prior to our visit. What on earth do we do next?"

Wolf wished he had a good answer for Tabitha, but he was at a loss. If the dowager hadn't gone off half-cocked on Lady Farthing's behalf, what was she investigating? Considering this question, he said, "I believe we need to talk to the dowager's household staff. Someone must know something. If nothing else, her carriage driver took her to Whitechapel. Did he observe anything that might give us some clues?" Seeing the look on her face, he added, "We will find her, Tabitha. I promise."

Even though it was past five o'clock already and had been a very busy day, Tabitha and Wolf felt there was no time to waste, and the carriage went directly from Lady Farthing's home to the dowager's. Manning answered the door, his face showing his cautious optimism when he saw it was them, "Has her ladyship been found?" the butler asked with all the concern of a loving family member.

Wolf shook his head, "I'm sorry, Manning, not yet." Manning led them into the drawing room, and Tabitha and Wolf followed; the drawing room was as good a place as any to question the servants. "Manning, we would like to talk to the entire household staff," Wolf explained.

Manning's eyebrows rose. Did the earl propose to have the gardeners traipse through the house? But of course, the alternative, that the earl and countess be inconvenienced, was even more outrageous. Tabitha, perhaps sensing the man's hesitation, said, "Manning, perhaps it would be easier if we were to use your butler's study for the interviews." Seeing Wolf glance at her, she added, "I believe the staff will be more comfortable with that arrangement than being asked to sit in their mistress' drawing room."

Manning's relief at this solution was visible, "I do believe that will encourage the staff to answer your questions as fully as possible. Would you like some tea here before I take you down?"

"Tea would be lovely, but why don't we take it downstairs. I don't believe we should waste any time."

If Manning had any doubts that there was any more information to be gleaned from his fellow servants, he certainly wasn't going to say as much to the earl and countess. Apart from the difference in status between them, Manning would be forever grateful to Tabitha and Wolf for proving his innocence when he was accused of murder recently. He had no doubt that if they felt there was more to be learned, then there very well might be. Manning led the way back out of the drawing room, through the house and into its bowels: the kitchen, laundry room, storage rooms and various other rooms that made up the domain of the household staff.

While Tabitha had never ventured below stairs in the dowager's house, she had certainly spent enough time there at Chesterton House to have a good idea of how such areas normally functioned. Even without its mistress in residence, the workings of a grand house ground on. There were still servants to be fed, rooms to be cleaned, and clothes to be laundered. The holiday season would be upon them soon enough, and some wonderful smells were coming from the kitchen. If Tabitha had to guess, she would say that Christmas cake was being baked in preparation for weeks of feeding with brandy.

While the butler's study at Chesterton House, where Talbot presided over the day-to-day smooth running of the household, was just off the kitchen, that seemed not to be the case in the dowager's home. Walking past the kitchen, Manning led them through to quite a large room that seemed to double as an office and butler's pantry. Glass-fronted cupboards full of china and silverware lined the walls, and a large, quite ornate mahogany desk dominated the far corner. As Tabitha would have expected, everything was perfectly neat, tidy and in its place. The desk had a chair behind it and two in front, ready for any stern conversations Manning might need to have with the staff members under his dominion.

They had decided they would talk to one servant at a time, beginning with the ones more likely to have interacted with the dowager in the day or so before she disappeared. Given this plan, Wolf moved one of the two chairs to join the solo one behind the desk, then indicated that Tabitha should take the more comfortable, originally placed chair, and he took the recently moved one.

Once they were settled, Wolf said to Manning, "We assume that you have already told us everything you can remember. However, if our conversations with the others turn up anything, we may call you back." Manning nodded in acknowledgement. "I think we should begin with the carriage driver. What is his name?"

"James," Manning answered. "James Green. I'll send him back. I should warn you, he is a taciturn man. Quite the loner. Spends most of his free time in the carriage house with the horses."

"Duly noted," Wolf said.

Manning left, and a few minutes later, there was a knock on the door and, on Wolf's command to enter, a small, wiry man of middle years entered the room, his cap clasped in his hands and a nervous look on his face.

"Mr Green, please take a seat," Wolf said.

The man was clearly uncomfortable sitting in the presence of his betters, but Tabitha smiled at him and said kindly, "Please do sit. There is nothing for you to be worried about. You're not in any trouble. But you may have been one of the last people to have seen the dowager countess, and we'd like to understand more about her movements on that day."

Now, the driver looked even more uncomfortable, and while he did sit, he perched on the edge of the chair with the air of a trapped rabbit, trying to find a way to escape from a snare. Realising what likely sat behind some of the man's discomfort, Tabitha continued, "Mr Green, his lordship and I realise that the dowager countess may have commanded your silence about her activities, and you may feel a very understandable sense of loyalty and perhaps fear of disobeying her." The man nodded his head slightly in agreement. Tabitha continued, "However, we are now very worried that some danger may have befallen her ladyship, and under these circumstances, any duty of silence you may feel you are under is now superseded." At his look of confusion at her words, Tabitha amended, "It is now overruled by your duty to your mistress' safety."

The man still didn't look wholly convinced, so Wolf chimed in, "I will take full responsibility when her ladyship returns safely, I assure you."

This seemed finally to quell the carriage driver's last concerns, and he said, "I will tell you whatever I know."

Relieved to have gained the man's trust, Tabitha began the questioning, "Mr Green, let's go back to the day you drove her ladyship to Lady Hartley's. That was Saturday afternoon, correct?"

The man thought about the question, then answered, "I believe so, m'lady. I remember that cook had given me some cheese scones to eat while I waited, and she usually makes those on Saturdays."

"Good. So, you drove her there and then home. Did she go anywhere else that day?" The man shook his head. Tabitha continued, "Then let's move to Sunday. You drove Lady Pembroke to Whitechapel in the afternoon? How did you know where to go?"

"Her ladyship told me to take her to the house of the gentleman and lady who had been for dinner a few weeks before and who I'd driven home," the man explained. He then continued, "Then after, we went and met the lad on Gunthorpe Street."

This was new information. Wolf interjected, "Which lad did she meet?"

"Rat," the driver explained.

"She met Rat in Whitechapel?" Tabitha asked incredulously. "By accident?" While she couldn't imagine what would have taken Rat back to Whitechapel, the boy wasn't a prisoner at

Langley House, so it was certainly possible he had chosen to go back to see friends. Unless, of course.... She glanced over at Wolf suspiciously.

Seeing her look, Wolf raised his hands up and said, "Don't look at me. I didn't send him there."

James Green hurried to explain, "I believe her ladyship had arranged to meet the boy. He stayed in the carriage and waited for her while she went into the house on Gunthorpe Street."

Wolf thought about Gunthorpe Street. He knew it well from his days in Whitechapel. It wasn't a long street. It had a few houses, a couple of shops, and a brothel. Discounting the possibility that the brothel was the dowager countess' intended destination, he asked, "Do you know which house she went into?"

The man considered the question and then answered, "It had a bright blue front door."

Wolf started at that answer. Seeing his reaction, Tabitha asked, "You know the house? Who lives there?"

Wolf quickly shook his head; this was not something he wished to discuss in front of a servant. Luckily, Tabitha understood enough about his reluctance to answer and let the topic drop. Instead, she asked, "And so she was in the house for some time and then what?"

"Then we dropped the lad off back near Lord Langley's home, though not at it, and then I drove her ladyship home. That was the last time I saw her."

Tabitha and Wolf thanked the man for his candour and let him go. As the door was closed behind him, Tabitha turned to Wolf and asked, "So what do you know of that house?"

Wolf sighed and answered, "If it is the house I believe it is, then it is a brothel run by a Mrs Sharpe, known as Mother Sharpe."

"A brothel!" Tabitha exclaimed. "What on earth is she doing visiting a Whitechapel brothel?"

At that moment, Manning re-entered the room and said, "M'lady and m'lord, not wishing to tell you what to do, but

I suggest that the next person you speak with be one of the new maids, Mindy. She hadn't mentioned anything before, but when I assembled the staff and told them that you would be speaking with them all, she became quite agitated. While you were talking to James, I took her aside and she confessed that she had helped her ladyship hail a hackney cab the afternoon she disappeared. I asked her why she hadn't mentioned this before, and she said she hadn't realised it might be important."

Seeing the look on Tabitha's face, he added, "M'lady, she is new here and very young. I'm not sure it occurred to her that there was anything extraordinary in her mistress taking a cab, or indeed doing anything she might choose to do. It was only when I told them that you wanted to talk to people who might have seen her ladyship on that day that she mentioned something."

"Well, if Mindy can really give us some clue where the dowager countess might have been headed, then given what James has already told us, we may not need to speak to all the staff. Though, I think it is worth talking with Withers," Wolf said.

"While you should of course do whatever you think is best, Withers is in bed with a terrible head cold," Manning said. "I talked with her before making the decision to come to Chesterton House the other day. Miss Withers is a very sensible woman and has worked for her ladyship for many years. She had no idea where she might have gone and why. But if you feel it is worth talking with her anyway, I will send someone up to rouse her."

"No, let the poor woman stay in her bed. But do send Mindy in," Tabitha decided.

CHAPTER 12

Monday, October 30, 1897: Tabitha & Wolf

They had left the dowager's house an hour later, having not unearthed much more information. Back in the carriage, Tabitha was the first to speak, "Villiers Street? What on earth is she doing on Villiers Street?"

Wolf shook his head, "How does she even know such a place exists?"

Tabitha agreed, "I don't know Villiers Street. Why does she? Where is it?"

"It runs by the side of Charing Cross station and down to the embankment. There are some businesses down there," Wolf paused, unsure how best to phrase what he needed to say. Finally, he said, "Given what we heard from the driver, I should add, I believe there is a brothel on that street." Seeing Tabitha's raised eyebrows, he continued, "We believe she visited one brothel that day, why not two?"

When they had entered the carriage, Wolf had told their driver, Madison, to head back to Chesterton House. But now that they were talking, he wondered whether it made sense to go home. "I believe we have three choices for possible next steps," he said slowly, thinking the options through as he spoke.

"Well, if you know which brothel she visited on Gunthorpe Street, I assume we could visit there and see what we can find out," Tabitha interjected.

"Indeed. Or we go straight to Villiers Street, though it may be like looking for a needle in a haystack. We don't even know for certain that was her final destination," Wolf pointed out. "Or," he continued, "we talk to Rat."

Tabitha shook her head, not in disagreement but in amazement that the young boy was somehow involved in, or at least knowledgeable about, whatever mess the dowager countess had managed to become embroiled in. She said, "Let's go to Langley House and talk to Rat. I want to understand the level of his involvement and, if nothing else, make sure that he doesn't involve himself any further." Wolf agreed and hit the carriage roof twice to indicate that Madison should pull over. Then, giving him new directions, they took off in the direction of the home of Maxwell Sandworth, Earl of Langley.

Tabitha and Wolf's first engagement with Lord Langley had been during their debut investigation. Then, he had been a suspect in the death of the old Duke of Somerset. In their second investigation, he had kidnapped Tabitha's ward, Melody. Even though it had turned out that he had done so in his capacity as an agent of British Intelligence, it had still taken Tabitha some time to forgive the man. But since then, he had somehow morphed into almost a friend. He was still a major presence in Melody's life, and her brother, Rat, was now living at Langley House and being mentored by Lord Langley.

During their last investigation in Brighton, Langley had shown surprising sensitivity and insight about Wolf's new life as an earl and about his complicated relationship with Tabitha. Tabitha and Wolf both trusted and liked the man now, much to their surprise. They were both sure that he knew nothing about whatever the dowager was up to. He most certainly would have alerted them if he had.

Langley was surprised to have Tabitha and Wolf turn up unannounced and his first thoughts were that something had happened to Melody. As they followed him into his drawing room, Tabitha quickly assured him that Melody was safe and sound in the nursery back at Chesterton House. She then quickly apprised him of the reason for their visit. They had dealt enough with Langley to know that the man did not quickly jump to judgment. He listened to everything they had to tell him without interrupting once.

While they talked, his butler Talbot, cousin to their Talbot, came into the room with some much-welcome tea and finger sandwiches. Tabitha realised that they hadn't eaten much since breakfast and took a break from her narrative to eat two cucumber sandwiches and take a few restorative sips of tea. Finally, with her hunger somewhat satiated, she continued with her story, ending with, "Has Rat said anything of this to you?"

Langley answered, "All I know is that on Sunday morning I received a telephone call from the dowager countess suggesting that she start meeting with Rat to help instruct him in social etiquette. This seemed like a very generous and sensible offer and so I gladly accepted. She then surprised me somewhat by suggesting that they begin that morning. While I did wonder somewhat at her eagerness, who am I to question Lady Pembroke? So, I sent the lad off. He returned just before lunch armed with iced buns. It seemed as if they had done nothing more than have tea and conversation."

"And that was it?" Wolf asked.

"Well, as far as I know, it was. Of course, Rat isn't a prisoner here and has the freedom to come and go as he pleases, as long as his lessons are done. We did do some work together after luncheon that day and then I retreated to my study to do some estate work. Honestly, I have no idea what he did between then and dinner. Why don't we fetch him and ask the boy himself?"

Rat was summoned, and five minutes later, he entered the room. They had been home from Brighton a little over two weeks, and Tabitha hadn't seen Rat since then. Watching him enter the room a little nervously, she realised he had suddenly become quite a bit taller. She recalled that children often had such growth spurts. She also recalled the boy saying something about his birthday being just before Christmas and so she realised that he was almost nine. He'd always had a rather world-weary look about him from his years living on the street and being responsible for his four-year-old sister. And while the worry that used to be etched around his young eyes was definitely gone, he still carried himself with the air of a much older boy, and his new height only added to that effect.

Rat looked nervous. Was it merely being summoned to find Tabitha and Wolf waiting for him? Or did he know something about the dowager's actions?

"Sit down, lad," Langley said kindly. "Lord and Lady Pembroke have a few questions to ask you."

The boy sat, but now his nervous look had morphed into something more like guilt. There was no doubt he knew something. Wolf and Tabitha exchanged looks, and she wordlessly indicated that she would take the lead. She spoke gently, "Rat, Lord Langley has told us that you went and had tea with the dowager countess, Lady Pembroke, on Sunday. Was that fun?"

Still on guard, Rat did relax slightly and answered, "Yes, m'lady Tabby Cat. She had these iced buns that were so good, and she let me bring the leftovers home." The boy's eyes lit up at the memory of the sweet treat.

"I love iced buns too," Tabitha said. "And what did you talk of with her ladyship?"

Rat paused, then answered with the line he and the dowager had discussed, "We talked a bit about my life in Whitechapel. Some of the people I had known. Stuff like that." For all his worldliness about some things, Rat was a child, and not yet adept in the art of obfuscation. While his words were seemingly innocuous, his eyes darted from side to side as he spoke, and he licked his lips nervously. It was abundantly clear to all the adults that he knew more than he was saying.

"What kind of people did you discuss?" Tabitha continued.

Rat licked his lips again and wiped his palms on his trouser legs, "Oh you know, just some of the people I knew and did some work for and who sometimes gave me some food for Melly."

"Anyone in particular?" Wolf asked.

Rat hesitated, then answered, "No one in particular." Seeing the look on Wolf's face, Rat then added, "I might have mentioned Cindy."

"Who is Cindy?" Tabitha asked.

"Cindy who worked for Mother Sharpe, the abbess?" Wolf asked. Given what they already knew about the dowager's visit to Gunthorpe Street, it seemed a very good guess that this was the Cindy Rat meant.

Looking like a cornered animal now, Rat didn't say anything but nodded his head.

Tabitha felt awful about interrogating the boy and decided to take another tack, "Rat, her ladyship has gone missing and hasn't been home for multiple nights now. Lord Pembroke and I are very worried about her. We need to find her and ensure she returns home safely. I know that you don't tattle, but these are special circumstances. Sometimes, even when a friend has asked you to keep a secret, they might later understand if you cannot keep that secret out of concern for their safety. Does that make sense, Rat?"

The boy nodded, "You want to know if I know where she is," he stated. "I don't, you know. I did meet her in Whitechapel, but after that, she dropped me back here, and I don't know anything about where she went after that."

Now, they were getting somewhere. Wolf decided there was no point in playing games and beating around the bush, and so stated, "We know that Lady Pembroke visited Mother Sharpe on Gunthorpe Street. You are too smart a lad to think we won't see a connection between your chat about Cindy and the dowager countess' sudden interest in visiting the house where Cindy works. So, what did you and she discuss over tea that spurred her sudden interest in visiting Whitechapel?" Confronted with these facts, Rat told them everything. Tabitha tried to control her face so as not to show how appalled she was that the dowager had discussed syphilis with anyone, let alone a child. But at least they now understood the connection between the woman's visit to Lady Hartley, her decision to investigate on Lady Farthing's behalf and then her subsequent visit to a brothel in Gunthorpe Street.

"So, her ladyship went into the Gunthorpe Street brothel to speak with Mother Sharpe while you waited in the carriage. And then afterwards, she came out, didn't say much about what they had discussed, but then dropped you home? Is that correct?" Rat nodded again. Wolf then asked, "And that is all you know? Are you sure of that, Rat?" The boy nodded yet again. Convinced that they had dragged as much out of the boy as they could, Tabitha and Wolf thanked him and sent him on his way.

When the door closed behind Rat, Langley said, "Prostitutes, brothels and syphilis; what on earth is her ladyship up to? Wolf, do you know this Cindy that the lad mentioned?"

Wolf nodded, "I have a passing acquaintance with the madam who runs that brothel, Vicky Sharpe." Seeing Tabitha's raised eyebrows and imagining what might be going through her head, he quickly added, "I did a bit of work for her once, many years ago, when I was first starting out. She was actually how I came to know Mickey D. They, how can I put it? They do business together."

"What kind of business?" Tabitha asked with genuine curiosity.

Wolf sighed; he was going to have to go into more detail about the associates from his past life than he wished. Seeing the sigh, Tabitha continued, "I'm not a child, Wolf. Nor am I a delicate bloom. And even if I was before I met you, surely the things I've seen and heard over the months since you arrived at Chesterton House have put paid to any innocence I might have had. I can't imagine that Mickey's business with a brothel is any worse."

Wolf sighed again. It wasn't so much that it was worse. After all, how much worse could anything be than the actions of the late Duke of Somerset and Tabitha had survived exposure to that sordid investigation. It was rather that Wolf wished to put his thief-taking life behind him. In particular, he wished he could disassociate himself from some of the more criminal elements he'd been forced to work with. Wolf had given great thought to Langley's suggestion when they were in Brighton that he consider continuing taking on investigations as and when they arose. Nevertheless, he had hoped that he might do so in a manner that allowed him to leave behind the moral ambiguity that tainted so much of his former life. But here he was, being sucked right back in.

Finally, realising that a situation where the dowager countess might be in danger was not the time to be precious about such things, he answered, "One of Mickey's revenue streams is to provide protection to the Whitechapel brothels. Customers know that if they hurt one of Mother Sharpe's girls or fail to pay up, they'll be answering to Mickey's thugs." Seeing the shocked look on Tabitha's face, he continued, "This is a very common practice, and I will say that Mickey's percentage is far more reasonable than is often demanded. And he is feared in Whitechapel and beyond; his protection means something."

Tabitha was shocked. She'd always viewed the Whitechapel gangster as an almost avuncular figure. She had only ever encountered his somewhat cheeky but seemingly benign side. While intellectually, she had always known he was a gangster, the word hadn't really meant anything to her. But the thought of Mickey forcing a woman to pay him for protection and reflecting on the form that protection might sometimes take cast the man in a different, far harsher light.

Trying to move beyond her initial reaction, Tabitha collected herself and asked, "So, is our next stop Whitechapel to talk to this Vicky Sharpe?" Wolf sighed once more, and Tabitha could swear she saw him and Langley exchanging glances. Correctly reading Wolf's thoughts, Tabitha said indignantly, "Are we back here yet again? I thought I'd proved my worth during our previous investigations. Why are you still attempting to exclude me?" She then added for good measure, "This will hardly be the first brothel I have been in."

This last statement was news to Lord Langley. He hadn't been part of their inner circle when Tabitha and Wolf had visited the brothel run by Old Ma Hutchins during their first investigation together. Now, it was his turn to raise his eyebrows, but he said nothing of his surprise. He did say, "You are welcome to remain here for as long as necessary to discuss your next steps. However, I have an appointment I cannot miss." Langley stood, turned towards the door and then turned back, adding, "If I can help in any way, think nothing of asking. While the older Lady Pembroke can be something of a termagant at times, I have known her my entire life and I hate to think of any danger befalling her." And with that, he gave a final nod of farewell and exited the room.

Finally, alone, Tabitha and Wolf didn't immediately launch back into their debate. Tabitha was still hungry and so availed herself of the provided refreshments. As she chewed another sandwich, the tension in the room became an almost physical presence. Finally, Wolf realised that he would have to be the one to break the silence and said, "It is not about excluding you or trying to protect you. Certainly it is not about questioning your contribution, but rather it is a matter of expediency."

When Tabitha said nothing, Wolf continued, "I have known Mother Sharpe many years, and there is a degree of trust between us. That trust is with Wolf, the thief-taker, not the Earl of Pembroke. We want the woman to open up and be candid, and I'm worried that if I appear as anyone other than the Wolf she has always known, she may be less than forthcoming. This earl persona can be remarkably effective at getting people's cooperation most of the time, but I don't believe this is one of those times."

Tabitha put down her teacup and asked very calmly, "And you cannot be Wolf, thief-taker when I am with you?"

Wolf laughed dryly, "Tabitha, whatever you wear, it is immediately obvious from the way you carry yourself and talk that you are an aristocrat. As far as I know, Mother Sharpe doesn't even know that I am now an earl. How do we explain why we are together?"

Tabitha could have continued arguing. Certainly, she had donned disguises on a couple of occasions over the last few months. Once, she dressed in some of Wolf's thief-taking clothes and had assumed the persona of a young man. Then, there was the visit to Old Ma Hutchins' brothel when Tabitha had pretended to be Lady Chalmers. However, she acknowledged to herself that pretending to be a different titled lady was not the most challenging of disguises.

Reluctantly, Tabitha did realise some truth in Wolf's words.

That didn't make her any less unhappy at being excluded, but it did make her less willing to continue to push for inclusion. "What do I do while you're off investigating?" she asked in an implicit acknowledgement that Wolf had won his point.

"It is already early evening, and the brothel will be gearing up for business, so we're unlikely to find Mother Sharpe amiable to chatting with us. I think we've done all we can today. Let us return to Chesterton House, eat and have an early night. Tomorrow morning, Bear and I will take a hackney cab to Gunthorpe Street."

Wolf then paused. Having won his point so relatively easily minutes before, he hated having to say the next words, but he knew he was being a coward, "If Mother Sharpe confirms that the dowager is at a brothel in Villiers Street and can illuminate us somewhat as to why, Bear and I will travel there afterwards to try to speak with her."

"Without me!" Tabitha finished his thought.

"Yes. Without you. If you accept, however unwillingly, how counter to the needs of the investigation it will be to have you join us in one brothel, why should the argument be any different for the one on Villiers Street?"

Again, Tabitha knew his logic was sound. But she wasn't happy and sulked the entire carriage ride back to Chesterton House.

CHAPTER 13

Sunday, October 29, 1897: The dowager

The dowager had been warned that Margie Sharpe's brothel catered to a certain kind of clientele. Nevertheless, she wasn't quite prepared for the first vicar who appeared in the brothel's parlour. It was even more shocking that the man hadn't bothered to remove his clerical collar. The dowager thought about Reverend Davis, who had the pastoral care of the congregation at St Peter's, the church that the dowager claimed to attend, even if such attendance was nothing more than Easter, Christmas and the occasional baptism.

Reverend Davis was a very mild-mannered man in his fifties. Was it possible that even he had a secret, degenerate life as some of his religious brethren seemed to? Given how boring the dowager had always found the man and his sermons, she took some comfort from the thought that perhaps there was more to him than his bizarre obsession with sparrows and dedication to stamp collecting.

A large, brutish-looking man was stationed at the door as the gatekeeper of who could and could not enter the brothel. Throughout the evening, a stream of men came through the house. For the most part, they seemed to be regulars with a preferred girl. If the men noticed that the petite, old woman greeting them was not the same one as usual, no one said a word. At some point, the possibility of coming face-to-face with someone she knew did occur to the dowager. She was acquainted with the prime minister and many of his cabinet, and of course she knew many members of the House of Lords. What would she say if and when a familiar face stumbled into the parlour? Of course, she realised, whatever they might think of seeing her in such an establishment, they could hardly be immune to the shame of being there themselves. Luckily, at least that evening, none of the clientele were familiar faces.

Seated in a comfortable, wingback armchair, the dowager loosely directed the proceedings. Although, if she were honest, there was very little that she needed to do. The girls were waiting in the parlour with her, playing cards or chatting. When a regular customer came in, their favoured girl would get up and go to greet him while the others continued with whatever they were doing. On the odd occasion a new customer entered, the girls would stand up to be viewed while they nonchalantly looked him over, judging what, the dowager could only imagine. The girls didn't seem upset at the work ahead of them, merely bored for the most part.

When the girl escorted her john down at some point later in the evening, sometimes quite quickly, sometimes after quite a while, she would tell Lou, who sat waiting with the dowager, what services she had provided, and then Lou would charge the customer accordingly. The dowager was relieved that the services were normally described in quite banal terms: twenty minutes of dairy farming, ten minutes of tipping the velvet, thirty minutes with Roger. The dowager didn't know what the terms meant and had no interest in trying to find out. But Lou clearly understood the slang and charged accordingly. None of the men questioned the charges, and all paid up promptly. Some then left, others made their way back to the gaming tables.

During the evening, the dowager had seen a steady stream of men entering the house and heading straight back to the tables. As the evening wore on, some of those men made their way to the parlour in search of some companionship. Mostly, these seemed to be men who had won at the tables that evening and arrived in high spirits. On one occasion, a very drunk and belligerent man came into the parlour using quite foul language and complaining bitterly about his losses at the tables.

The man stumbled over to one of the girls and grabbed her roughly by the arm, saying, "She'll do. And I don't expect to get charged for this after the amount of money you've had off me."

The girl, Ginger, the redhead who had run by the dowager earlier that evening, looked beseechingly at the dowager. Was this where Mother Sharpe would step in? The dowager pushed herself out of her chair and said in the booming, disdainful voice that had stopped many better men than this one over the years, "Take your hands off that young woman at once, sir!"

The man looked over at the dowager but kept a firm grasp on the girl, snarling, "The least I can do is to get an hour with one of your tarts after the losses I've had tonight."

The dowager straightened her spine and threw back her shoulders; she might be a fish out of water in many ways in her current circumstances, but she knew how to deal with a nasty bully. "Unhand that young woman immediately, or I will box your ears before throwing you out onto the street."

Under normal circumstances, the threat of having his ears boxed would hardly have been serious. But coming from the terrifying-looking little old woman, it sounded as bad as if she'd threatened to cut a limb off. The man dropped Ginger's arm, threw them all a scowl and left the parlour and then the house, slamming the front door behind him.

Once the man had gone, the dowager heard slow clapping. Looking over at the door, she saw The Rascal, Jason Bono, lounging against the doorframe. "Bravo! Very impressive, Miss Phillips. Very impressive indeed. I can't imagine even Margie being as sternly effective. Are you sure you've never done this before?"

Collecting herself, the dowager sat back in her chair, neatly folded her hands in her lap, and replied, "It seems this job has much in common with dealing with recalcitrant little boys in the schoolroom."

The Rascal laughed, "Well, whatever it was, good job. I was about to call for one of the boys to come and throw that sore loser out. But you and that governess tone of yours did the job just fine." And with that, the man disappeared back into the gaming rooms.

The dowager was used to late evenings at balls and dinners,

but even she was fading as the grandfather clock in the corner struck three. Trying to stifle a yarn and failing, she asked Lou, "How long until we close up?"

Taking pity on the elderly woman, Lou answered, "Well, we're normally up until the tables shut up. And that may not be for a while yet. But why don't you go up to bed? It's your first night, and you're unused to such hours. I can handle it from here. If there's any more trouble, I'll call The Rascal. And I saw your man, Little Ian, skulking about. One look at him will dissuade most would-be troublemakers."

The dowager would have liked to have been able to argue; she prided herself on her stoicism. But she could feel her eyelids getting heavy, and she felt that the dishonour of falling asleep on the job was greater than deserting her post.

Back in Margery Sharpe's bedchamber, the dowager was even happier about her choice of dress for the evening; it was as easy to get out of as it had been to get into without help. Normally, Withers would help the dowager into bed and bring her a hot cup of milk to soothe her off to sleep. That evening, she was so exhausted that the absence of Withers and the milk was barely felt, and she was asleep within minutes of laying her head on the pillow.

The following morning, the dowager was awakened by a young maid laying a fire in her hearth. She saw that the maid had also brought up a much-welcomed cup of tea, which sat on a tray on a small table by an armchair next to the fireplace. "Good morning, Miss," the maid said. "I've brought up some hot water for your wash." At this, she pointed in the direction of the porcelain bowl.

"What time is it?" the dowager asked.

"Past eleven, Miss. I wouldn't have woken you, but Lou said you're going to Mother Sharpe's lunch with her ladies and that I should come up. Is there anything else you need?"

Thinking about dressing herself later, the dowager said, "Please come back in fifteen minutes and help me dress." The young maid bobbed a curtsey and then left the room. The dowager got out of bed and went over to the armchair. She was happy to see that, besides the tea, the tray held a plate of buttered toast.

Sitting in the armchair before the now blazing fire, the dowager ate her toast, drank her tea and contemplated the day ahead. As interesting as the previous evening had been, she hadn't learned anything more about Margery Sharpe's disappearance. Vicky Sharpe had intimated that the Ladies of KB might have useful information to share. But even so, the dowager felt she needed to do more to move the investigation forward. She just wasn't sure what. She knew that in previous investigations, Tabitha and Wolf had often found pertinent information in private studies of suspects and victims. Should she go through Margery Sharpe's study?

The dowager was keenly aware that The Rascal was about, and she didn't want to be caught snooping by the man. But was it snooping if she was Margery's cousin? She needed someone to watch out for, but who could she trust? Vicky Sharpe seemed to trust Lou. But the only person in the house she was sure had nothing to do with Margery's disappearance was Little Ian. Yes, that is who she would ask. After all, he was there in order to keep her safe. Satisfied with her plans for her afternoon, the dowager finished her tea and toast and then washed herself in the still-warm water.

Twenty minutes later, she had dressed with the help of the young maid, whose name she discovered was Kitty. The dowager descended the stairs and made her way back to the kitchen. The house was very quiet. No girls were chattering away, and there were not even any servants to be seen. Considering what time everyone must have retired, it was no surprise they were still abed. Unsure if she would even find the cook awake, the dowager was pleasantly surprised to see the rosy-cheeked woman hard at work.

"Did you get your tea and toast?" the cook asked.

"I did. Thank you for that. Despite the tea's restorative effect, I find myself still suffering from such a late night. Is there any chance that you have coffee brewed?" the dowager asked.

"You're in luck. I'm a coffee drinker, so I always keep a pot on the stove. Sit yourself down and I'll pour you a cup." The cook went over to the stove, and while she poured the coffee, she said, "Your man was here just a few minutes ago. He asked if I'd seen you."

The cook could only mean Little Ian. The dowager hadn't really considered what his guarding of her might entail, but she was glad that the man took his duties seriously enough to check on her. Perhaps she should take him with her to this luncheon. But on second thoughts, would it arouse undue suspicion if she were to have him accompany her as if she expected to need protection?

While she was enjoying her coffee, Lou entered the kitchen. The dowager wasn't sure how many hours of sleep the woman could have enjoyed, but she looked bright-eyed enough.

"We should be leaving soon, Miss Phillips. The Ladies normally gather quite early, from what Mother Sharpe has told me," Lou said. The dowager nodded in agreement, and ten minutes later, she was wrapped in one of Margery Sharpe's cloaks and headed out onto Villiers Street with Lou. The previous day had been the first time in her life that the dowager had travelled the streets of London in anything but a private carriage. But it seemed that novelty was to be repeated that morning. Luckily, Lou was even more conversant in the mechanics of hailing a hackney cab than Mindy. With very little wait in the cold at the station, the dowager found herself in a cab and on her way to Piccadilly to Madame Zsa Zsa's establishment.

CHAPTER 14

Monday, October 30, 1897: The dowager

From the outside, Madame Zsa Zsa's brothel looked as innocuous as Vicky and Margery Sharpe's. However, inside was a kaleidoscope of colour and patterns, a riot of floral designs. The furniture had elegant silhouettes with nary a hard edge in sight; every form was curved, in many cases elaborately. Even the servants' uniforms had a modern feel to them. The dowager wasn't sure whether she approved of such home design, but she was certainly intrigued by it.

While Lou made her way through to the back of the house, presumably to the kitchen, a maid led the dowager into a large, sunlit room that shared the same design aesthetic as the vestibule. A gaggle of women filled the room, chattering far more enthusiastically than any gathering of aristocrats in a Mayfair drawing room tea party.

The maid announced the dowager; well, she announced Julia Phillips. All the conversation stopped, and every head was turned towards the newcomer. Only now did it occur to the dowager that Lou had disappeared and that without her, she was merely an uninvited stranger barging into a private gathering. As she contemplated this fact, a tall, willowy woman, perhaps in her early sixties, stood up. The woman's dress was made of a light, soft material and seemed less restrictive and more flowing than the fashion of the time. Again, the dowager didn't quite approve, but was fascinated, nevertheless.

The woman came towards the dowager with a welcoming smile on her face. It was a very kind face with gentle brown eyes that reflected the woman's curiosity as to the identity of her visitor. "Good afternoon," the woman said. "I am Madame Zsa Zsa, and you are?"

The dowager decided that her normal, imperious tone

was inappropriate for this uncomfortable social situation. So, trying to inject her voice with an unfamiliar humility, she said, "I am Miss Julia Phillips, cousin to Mothers Victoria and Margery Sharpe. I am currently residing at Margery Sharpe's establishment. My cousin Vicky suggested I join today, accompanied by Lou, who seems to have disappeared."

At this explanation, there was a visible relaxation on Madame Zsa Zsa's face, and she held out a hand and said, "Any cousin of Margery's is welcome here. But where is our friend?" As she said this, Madame Zsa Zsa indicated that the dowager should enter the room. It looked as if every spare seat was occupied by one of the women in the room.

Looking around, the dowager realised what an eclectic group they were. It looked as if Madame Zsa Zsa was the oldest of the group, with the youngest being perhaps almost twenty years younger. But the diversity of ages was hardly the most notable feature of this group. What was most distinctive about them was their melange of faces and skin tones. One woman looked decidedly oriental and was dressed very stylishly in bright, bold colours. She was talking to a small, dark-skinned woman who was perhaps from India – the dowager had never met an Indian and was unsure.

In another grouping, there was a blonde woman who, the dowager was scandalised to see, had at least one arm covered in some kind of colourful illustration. This painted lady was sitting on a sofa beside a petite woman holding a small, fluffy dog in her lap. Next to her was another woman. Well, at least the dowager thought it was a woman. Her very curly hair was cut to just below her ears, and she was wearing a man's suit. However, her size and face did indicate that this was a woman.

Finally, in a grouping of chairs next to the sofa, there was a tall, slim woman whose nationality was hard to determine, but clearly, she was of some foreign origin. Next to her was a slim, pretty woman who was the first to introduce herself. "Welcome, Cousin Julia," the woman exclaimed energetically. "I am Tamara, but everyone calls me Madame Tammy."

Madame Tammy then proceeded to go around the room and introduce all the other women. Her tall neighbour of indeterminate origins was Half-blind Kim. The woman didn't seem to have any trouble seeing, but then the dowager wasn't sure how you could be half-blind. The woman dressed in men's clothes was, rather ironically, Girly Lizzy. The woman holding the dog was Spanish Gemma. The woman with the extraordinary painted arm was Russian Alexandra. Though she interjected, "But please, call me Alexa."

Finally, the woman who might be from the Indian sub-continent was introduced as Sameera but was known to everyone as Spicy. The dowager couldn't imagine what might induce her to refer to anyone by that name, but the woman herself seemed happy to be thus called. Finally, the oriental-looking woman was introduced as Pretty Pearl. They were a very colourful group of women. Looking around the room, the dowager couldn't help drawing a comparison to a social call with Ladies Hartley, Willis and their other cronies. The latter did not hold up well in comparison. These women seemed to enjoy each other's company so much more than any group of aristocratic women the dowager had ever been a part of. The fact that there were multiple opened bottles of claret scattered around on tables probably didn't hurt the convivial atmosphere.

Pretty Pearl, who had been taking up all of a love seat, moved up and patted the space next to her. The dowager accepted the invitation and sat down. "Now, do tell us where your cousin is and why you've come in 'er place," Pretty Pearl said. Whatever the woman's foreign origins, her voice was pure cockney, which seemed rather incongruous with her looks.

During the short cab ride to Piccadilly, the dowager had considered what story she would tell. She had reflected on Vicky Sharpe's words that her sister liked and trusted these women and decided that she had to confide in someone about her investigation, why not these women? And so, she told them everything she knew about Margery Sharpe's disappearance and Vicky Sharpe's request that she, the dowager, investigate.

AN AUDACIOUS WOMAN

When the dowager had finished, the woman known as Spicey asked, "So, you're not Margery's cousin Julia?"

Now, this was a revelation the dowager hadn't considered; who would she introduce herself as? Finally, deciding that she had already entrusted these women with so much that there was no point in not being candid, she said in an almost embarrassed tone, "No, I am Julia Chesterton, the Dowager Countess of Pembroke."

It was clear that whatever the women had expected her to say wasn't that. No one spoke for a few moments, and then the incongruously named Girly Lizzy said, "A countess? A real one?"

The dowager sighed. It had never occurred to her that she might be met with disbelief. "Yes, a real countess. Well, now, a dowager countess."

"What is a dowager countess?" Spanish Gemma asked in a foreign accent that made clear why she at least had her nickname.

"It means that my husband, the former earl, is now deceased and that my son, his heir, married a woman who became the countess," the dowager explained. Thought it was clear that there was much in her explanation that was still causing confusion. Fearing that sounding like a walking, talking copy of Debrett's was distracting from her intended conversation, the dowager pivoted back to Margery Sharpe. "It seems that Mother Sharpe's disappearance was unknown to you all."

Madame Zsa Zsa had retaken her seat and answered, "We rarely see each other outside these monthly gatherings. We are all busy women with thriving businesses to run; there isn't much room for socialising. I happened to run across Margie visiting her dressmaker a couple of weeks ago, but she didn't say anything about a planned trip."

"Did she say anything out of the ordinary?" the dowager asked.

As much as the dowager wanted to keep the conversation focused on her investigation, it seemed that the curiosity of the Ladies of KB wasn't satiated. "Why is a dowager countess

109

investigating the disappearance of a madam?" Half-blind Kim asked. "In fact, why are you investigating anything? Have you lost your fortune and need to work?"

Lost her fortune! What a presumptuous thing to say, the dowager thought. As tempted as she was to articulate this outrage, she managed to stop herself in time. Instead, she answered, "My fortune is intact. However, aristocratic life rather bores me these days. Recently, by chance, I became involved in various investigations and was instrumental in solving those cases. I have now branched out independently, having been recommended to Vicky Sharpe."

The dowager wasn't sure whether or not to trumpet her connection to Mickey D. Still, she then considered that such an association could only add to her credibility in these women's eyes. "I was recommended by a Mr Doherty, known as Mickey D, of Whitechapel." It was evident that at least some of these women knew who Mickey D was, and, as she had hoped, the association seemed to earn the dowager these women's respect.

Alexa, the painted lady, said, "How long has Margie been gone?"

The dowager considered the question and answered, "At this point, six days."

"And no one has 'eard anything from 'er?" Pretty Pearl asked.

"Nothing. And there is no indication that this was a planned trip." The dowager considered her next question and then asked, "Her sister, Vicky, indicated that there is a new business partner. And since Margery has been gone, a rather disreputable man, Jason Bono, known as The Rascal, has been watching her establishment, apparently at the behest of this business partner. Do any of you know anything about this person?"

The women were strangely silent, and nervous glances passed between them. Finally, by what seemed to be some unspoken consensus, Madame Zsa Zsa said, "We don't know all the details, mind you, but we know something of this business partner. It must have been just over a year ago that Margie told us about a new partnership. Before that, she'd had a place not far from here.

She did pretty well. We all find our niches." Seeing the dowager's confusion, Madame Zsa Zsa explained, "Well, Girly Lizzy over there caters to the gentler sex."

The dowager asked, "What does that mean? Aren't the gentler sex women?"

Madame Zsa Zsa paused, then answered, "Exactly."

The dowager was shocked to her core. While it was a given that men visited brothels to have their disgusting needs taken care of, it had never occurred to her that women might also be patrons. Unable to overcome her curiosity, the dowager asked Girly Lizzy, "And so your prostitutes are men?"

The dowager couldn't imagine such a thing and had never heard of anything so outrageous. Or at least she thought she hadn't until Girly Lizzy laughed and answered, "Why would a woman ever pay for a man? No, I cater to women who enjoy the company of other women." The dowager was so shocked that she couldn't think of what to say. But she was wrong if she thought that was the most shocking thing she was to hear that afternoon. Spicy's clientele enjoyed re-enacting their nursery days, complete with a stern governess spanking them.

Pretty Pearl's brothel was staffed entirely by girls who were also oriental. Pretty Pearl's parents had come from China, but her girls were from various Far East countries. It had never occurred to the dowager that men had such specific tastes in their desires. Russian Alexa seemed to run the most traditional brothel of the bunch. Half-blind Kim ran an establishment whose activities were so shocking that she demurred when the dowager asked about her brothel.

Spanish Gemma ran a rather upscale house of the kind that the dowager's husband and son likely frequented. The dowager was tempted to ask whether Spanish Gemma had known her son, but decided she didn't really want to know. Finally, Madame Tammy didn't say much more than, "My girls are, in fact, young men. But my customers are men." The dowager didn't know what to make of this, and decided not to ask.

Feeling that she had heard enough, and that the conversation had moved off course, the dowager tried to steer it back by asking, "So, Margery Sharpe had her niche and was doing well. Then what happened?"

Madame Zsa Zsa picked the story back up, "I don't know the details, but she was approached by this now partner about going into business together. There would be funding for a new, larger house. A gaming club would run out of it, and Margie would continue with her brothel. This partner suggested that her business would benefit from the additional traffic that would come with gaming."

"And did it?" the dowager asked.

"Again, I'm not privy to the details; I'm not sure any of us are. But yes, from what we could gather, she was doing well. Certainly, her dresses were fancier, the wine she served us finer. But even so, from things she said on occasion when the two of us were alone, I always felt as if she had formed an unholy alliance."

As Madame Zsa Zsa talked, it occurred to the dowager that the woman's speech almost sounded aristocratic. Certainly, she carried herself with an air that suggested that she had been born to a different life than the one she now had. It was neither the time nor the place to delve into the madam's background. Instead, the dowager asked, "What kind of things did she say that made you think that?"

Madame Zsa Zsa thought for a moment before she answered, "It wasn't so much what she said, but how she talked about her partner; I think she was scared of him. I'm not sure that was the case when they first went into business together. But, over the last six months or so, she seemed nervous. I know that man, Jason Bono, had been hanging around a lot more."

"I've always thought The Rascal was all bluster and was mostly harmless," Girly Lizzy interjected. Some of the other women nodded their heads in agreement.

"I don't know that she felt threatened by him, per se," Madame Zsa Zsa explained. "She didn't usually speak of it. But one day, Margie was hosting, and I happened to be early. She confessed that she was disturbed that her partner had Bono essentially spying on her."

"Do you know this business partner's name?" the dowager asked. Madame Zsa Zsa shook her head, and all the other women shook theirs.

The rest of the visit was interesting but didn't yield any more information about Margery's elusive business partner or where she might have gone. The women were a little more subdued now that they knew their friend was missing, but even so, they were a convivial group. After more than two hours, the gathering finally broke up. The dowager had collected Lou and was in a hackney cab back to Villiers Street when she realised, she couldn't remember when she had last enjoyed the company of other women as much. As shocking as some of the women had been at first blush, they turned out to all be intelligent, interesting, and amusing women. And perhaps what the dowager appreciated more than anything is that they were independent businesswomen who seemed to feel no shame about how they made coin.

In the hackney cab, the dowager couldn't help but try to learn some more from Lou about the madams and the brothels they ran. As much as she tried not to, apparently, her judgement about the profession seeped into her voice, and Lou said, "You know, there aren't many options for women like me. There's factory work. But that pays so little that even women working there often 'ave to lift their skirts to make some extra coin. Being an 'ore on the streets is nasty, dangerous work. But if a girl can get into a brothel, well, there's usually plenty to eat, a warm bed, and some safety. Not all madams are as good to their girls as Margie and Vicky are. Those women you were with, too. I've 'eard some terrible stories over the years: young girls kidnapped and forced into the job. And worse."

The dowager couldn't imagine what "worse" could mean, but she said nothing. Lou continued, "Sometimes, a girl ends up on the streets because she was a maid in some fancy 'ouse, and the master 'ad 'is way with 'er. Of course, when that 'appens and she ends up with a big belly, she's always the one who is punished.

More often than not, it's the grand lady of the 'ouse who kicks the girls out without a penny. Then what is she to do but make a living lifting her skirt?"

As Lou said this, the dowager felt her cheeks heat; her husband had impregnated one of their maids many years before. She had never felt that the girl, Jenny Murphy, was an innocent victim but rather the likely instigator. Nevertheless, the outcome was the same; the dowager had driven her out of the house. She comforted herself with the thought that rather than turning Jenny out onto the streets penniless, she had paid the girl well and had ensured that she had returned to Ireland. Nevertheless, the dowager realised, with more shame than she was used to feeling, that even if she had felt that Jenny was the victim of the dowager's husband's lust, her actions would not have been so different.

CHAPTER 15

Tuesday, October 31, 1897, Tabitha & Wolf

Tabitha awoke far earlier than normal. Her sleep had been fitful, and her dreams vivid. The dowager countess had now been missing for two nights. Tabitha had very complicated feelings towards her erstwhile mother-in-law, but she certainly wished no harm to the woman.

Over the last few months, she had come to view the other Lady Pembroke with far more sympathetic eyes. Being the doyenne of aristocratic society might have satisfied a lesser female. However, activities deemed acceptable to a titled woman of her class utilised just a fraction of the woman's significant strategic intelligence. In a word, the Dowager Countess of Pembroke was bored. Or she had been until Wolf had appeared in their lives and she had been caught up in their first investigation.

It was hugely ironic that the woman who had prided herself for so many years on leading polite society was, in truth, as much a victim of its diamond-encrusted prison as anyone. If she had finally, audaciously broken free of that prison, a part of Tabitha could only applaud the woman. But Tabitha also realised that, perhaps like herself to some extent, the dowager had a naive view of the ugly, dangerous world outside of Mayfair's drawing rooms. She believed that her ability to have the whip hand over her peers translated seamlessly to quelling the common man, no matter how hungry or desperate he might otherwise be.

On her earlier-than-usual descent to the breakfast room, Tabitha found that Wolf was already on his second cup of coffee. Rather discordantly, at least for the servants, Tabitha was sure, Wolf was seated at the table dressed in his thief-taking attire. It certainly wasn't the first time the Chesterton House staff had seen him dressed thus. Still, he usually changed his clothes and was out of the house too quickly for them to consider why the new Earl of Pembroke occasionally chose to wear old, ratty clothes. For Wolf to lounge around the house in such attire was likely causing the servants to raise their eyebrows, if nothing else.

Seeing Tabitha's look of curiosity, Wolf said, "Much to my valet's shame, I saw no reason to dress this morning and then change again to visit Whitechapel." Tabitha smiled knowingly. Wolf's new valet, Thompson, was excellent at his job but also flexible enough to understand that his master did not fit easily into the aristocratic mould. Whatever sartorial standards Wolf's valet might have, a willingness to bend those on occasion was perhaps the primary job qualification.

Wolf continued, "There is no point in turning up at Gunthorpe Street too early. Brothels don't keep the same hours we do. Mother Sharpe will not look kindly on me arriving before noon."

"We have to wait until then?" Tabitha exclaimed. She felt that every hour lost lessened the likelihood of finding the dowager safe and sound. "Is it really necessary to speak to this Mother Sharpe? Surely, there can only be so many brothels on Villiers Street."

Wolf was sympathetic to Tabitha's impatience, and if the truth were told, he'd considered asking around about the other brothel's exact address. But it was more than just learning a street number; he wanted to understand what had driven the dowager to Villiers Street and so felt it important to trace back fully the time timeline of her movements.

"What about if I aim to arrive for eleven o'clock? I'm sure Mother Sharpe won't be pleased, but she may at least no longer be abed," Wolf said in an attempt to pacify Tabitha.

As impatient as she was, Tabitha did realise that pushing Wolf to go to Gunthorpe Street earlier than he felt wise would likely be counterproductive. Sighing, she conceded, "No, go for noon if you feel that is the best course of action. I just wish there was something we could be doing now. In fact, I wish there was anything I could do." Tabitha was still smarting at her exclusion from the visits to Dorset and then Villiers Streets.

"Tabitha, go to the nursery and spend time with Melody," Wolf suggested. "Today is a day the child would normally go and visit the dowager. Perhaps instead, you and she can do something."

Wolf's words made Tabitha realise that they had to tell Melody something to explain the curtailment of her visits to the dowager for the foreseeable future. Speaking her thoughts aloud, she said, "I will tell Melly that Mama has also come down with a bit of a chill, which is why there won't be any visits this week. Let us hope that there is no need to prolong this lie."

After breakfast, Tabitha spent an hour with Mrs Jenkins, the housekeeper. While the household ran smoothly under Mrs Jenkins' and Talbot's management, nevertheless, Tabitha's mother had drilled into her from a young age the importance of not neglecting her duties of domestic oversight. There was a fine line to be walked between not making her trusted servants feel anything less than that and ensuring that it was always clear that their mistress was eagle-eyed regarding the household accounts.

Sitting down with Mrs Jenkins, Tabitha realised how she had neglected this duty over the past few months. More than that was the further realisation about how mundane such a task now seemed. There had been a time, at the beginning of her marriage to Jonathan, when Tabitha had derived some satisfaction from her duty to run a well-managed house for her new husband. There had been a novelty to doing so that had belied the humdrum nature of choosing menus and approving tradesmen's bills. While Tabitha had missed the intellectual challenge she had found in the schoolroom, she had been satisfied that running a great household and ensuring Jonathan's comforts was her life's true purpose. As Mrs Jenkins ran through menus and then started detailing the household accounts, Tabitha now wondered how she had ever found this life enough. Whether or not she had as a newly married wide-eyed young woman, there was no doubt that she no longer did.

Looking at the highly efficient, eminently trustworthy Mrs Jenkins, Tabitha made a decision. Standing up, she announced to the confused housekeeper, "Mrs Jenkins, I trust in any household decision you make, whether it is about menus, tradesmen or anything else. I no longer believe such decisions need my stamp of approval. Of course, if you ever feel the need to seek my counsel, please know that I am always happy to discuss any and all aspects of the running of Chesterton House with you. However, you no longer need to feel obliged to do so."

Mrs Jenkins had been part of the household staff for many years, going back to the early days of the dowager's marriage. She felt entirely confident in her own abilities. However, such a mandate was unexpected and unheard of. Of course, there were the times, including quite a few weeks recently, when her mistress had been out of town. It was a given that Mrs Jenkins would run the house as she saw fit during such periods. But to be given such free rein permanently wasn't something the sensible older woman had ever considered.

Perhaps seeing these doubts flit across her housekeeper's face, Tabitha patted her arm lightly and said, "We are almost at a new century, Mrs Jenkins. Perhaps it is time for both of us to step fully into our potential." Whether Mrs Jenkins understood the sentiment, it was not her place to argue with the lady of the house. And so, she inclined her head in acceptance of her new authority. Whatever would Mr Talbot make of this when they chatted later over sherry in the privacy of her parlour?

Tabitha felt a lightness of spirit after this impetuous decision. While her time with Mrs Jenkins over the course of a week was not significant, ridding herself of the obligation felt transgressive, which was exhilarating. Yes, when word of her decision made its way through the servants' grapevine to the ears of society's matrons, there would be inevitable expressions of faux horror at her scandalous breach of decorum, yet again. Because this was hardly the first time society had been appalled at Tabitha's behaviour. There was the matter of her continued residence at Chesterton House with Wolf, a single man who, while technically a relative, was hardly considered an appropriate housemate. And just as with that matter, Tabitha found she cared not a whit what was said of her.

This lightness of spirit put a spring in her step, and when she entered the nursery a few minutes later, Mary, Melody's nursemaid, couldn't help but remark on how happy her mistress looked. Tabitha knew that Mr James, the tutor, would be there in less than an hour for his daily session with Melody. So, determined to have their time together that morning be nothing but fun, she suggested a doll's tea party, which she knew was one of Melody's favourite games.

Melody was an enchanting little girl. With her red-gold ringlets, bright blue eyes, and a spray of freckles across her nose, she was an adorable four-year-old. That she was a very intelligent, determined child made the time spent with her even more enjoyable. The hour flew by, and before she knew it, Mr James had entered the room, and Tabitha knew it was time for her to go.

"Can't you stay, Tabby Cat?" Melody said with a little pout, using her nickname for Tabitha.

"Melly, we've had a lovely time playing, but it's time for your lessons, and I want you to concentrate." Remembering that Melody would not be making her usual afternoon visit to the dowager, Tabitha added, "Granny isn't feeling very well today. So, why don't I return and read to you this afternoon?" This offer placated Melody sufficiently, and Tabitha was able to slip out of the room after listening to the first few minutes of the child's lesson.

By this time, she was sure that Wolf and Bear had left for Gunthorpe Street, and she found herself unsure how she wished to spend her time until they returned. Finally, realising that it had been some weeks since she had visited the girls at the Dulwich House, she determined that doing so was both overdue and would be a wonderful way to occupy herself instead of counting the hours until Wolf returned from his adventures.

Calling for the carriage, she readied herself and, within the hour, was off to visit Mrs Caruthers and her charges.

Meanwhile, Wolf and Bear had set off to visit Vicky Sharpe on Gunthorpe Street. The work he had done for Mother Sharpe had been one of the first jobs he and Bear had worked on together. They hadn't crossed paths very much over the years since then, but Wolf was sure that her gratitude at the successful conclusion of the investigation had not waned.

The Gunthorpe Street front door was opened by the same maid, Nancy, who had greeted the dowager days before. Seeing two men she didn't recognise standing at the brothel's door, she hurriedly and curtly said, "We're not open for business yet."

Realising the assumption the maid had jumped to, Wolf said, "We are not here as customers. We are old friends of Mother Sharpe's and need to talk to her. Please send Wolf and Bear's apologies for the early hour, but this cannot wait." Whatever the maid thought of their names, she kept to herself.

As it happened, Vicky Sharpe was up and eating a hearty breakfast of eggs, bacon and sausage. Nancy was unsure how her mistress would feel about having her meal interrupted. Nevertheless, the two men before her did not seem like they would be easily put off. The enormous, hairy one was intimidating, even though he'd said nothing. His very handsome companion had an air of someone used to being obeyed, despite his somewhat threadbare coat and scuffed boots. The maid invited them into the house but asked them to wait by the door while she conveyed their request to her mistress.

Unlike Villiers Street, which needed all the spare ground floor rooms for gaming, the Gunthorpe Street house had a small but comfortable dining room. The door wasn't closed all the way. Nevertheless, Nancy knocked.

Vicky Sharpe had heard the doorbell and had been mildly curious about who was visiting at such an hour. She wiped her mouth with her serviette and asked, "Who was at the door, Nancy?"

"Two men, ma'am. Said their names are Wolf and Bear, and

they're sorry to disturb you so early but then need to talk with you."

On hearing who her visitors were, Mother Sharpe smiled broadly and said, "I will come and greet them. We will talk in my study And ask cook to send up some tea and cake."

With that, Mother Sharpe rose from her breakfast and went to greet her visitors. While Vicky Sharpe had sworn off the company of men when she had first opened her own brothel, nevertheless, that didn't stop her from appreciating what a fine form of a man Wolf was. Holding out her hand to him, the madame said almost coquettishly, "Wolf, what a delightful surprise. Why, if you'd come any earlier, you might have found me still in bed." As she said this, she batted her eyelashes and smiled in a way that made Wolf blush.

Satisfied at her ability to still shock a handsome young man, Vicky turned to Bear in greeting. Indicating they should follow her, she led the way to the study she had met the dowager in just days before. She and Wolf took an armchair, and Bear pulled over her desk chair.

Finally settled, the madame asked, "As thrilled as I am to see you, Wolf, I'm also rather surprised. Word around Whitechapel is that you left town a few months ago. I even heard some vague rumours of some kind of inheritance. Did someone kick the bucket and leave you a few bob?"

At this, Wolf and Bear exchanged looks. On the trip over, they had discussed just how candid to be with the madam. While Wolf's original intentions on ascending to the earldom had been to put his Whitechapel life entirely behind him, things hadn't worked out quite as he'd intended. He'd been back to his old stomping grounds multiple times over the course of recent investigations, and had even frequented the public house, The Cock. He wasn't naive enough to think that his disappearance, gossip of which he did he best to ensure spread throughout Whitechapel, but then occasional sightings, had gone unnoticed and unremarked upon.

In addition, given Mother Sharpe's business arrangement

with Mickey D, who was fully aware of Wolf's new status and wealth, Wolf thought the woman likely knew more than she was letting on. He also knew that if he wished her to be candid with him about the dowager's visit, it would serve him well to be equally candid with her. Therefore, he answered, "Indeed, you might say that someone kicked the bucket and left me a few bob. My cousin, the Earl of Pembroke, died in an unfortunate accident. He was childless, so I was the next in line to inherit."

It was clear that whatever Mother Sharpe had heard or intuited, she hadn't realised the full extent of Wolf's recent good fortune. She whistled appreciatively and replied, "An earl? You don't say." Then, looking at his thief-taking clothes, she commented, "An earl and yet you can't afford a new coat?"

Wolf smiled and admitted, "Indeed, I can. But I would rather that my inheritance not be common knowledge in Whitechapel and so wear my old clothes on the few occasions I've had cause to visit." Wolf assumed he would not have to explain why he chose not to trumpet his new fortune to his old cronies.

"So, you're the Earl of Pembroke, are you?" the woman asked. "Are you here perhaps on the heels of my visitor the other day? I imagine that a Whitechapel brothel receiving visits from two aristocrats in one week would be cause enough for comment. Let alone two who are related."

Wolf acknowledged the truth in the woman's shrewd observation. "The dowager countess is the mother to my late cousin, the previous earl," Wolf explained. "She left her home two nights ago without explanation and has not been seen or heard from since. From what I have been able to discover, one of the last things she did before she vanished was to visit you."

Wolf had considered how much to show his hand; should he admit that he knew the dowager had last been seen taking a hackney cab to Whitechapel? But a long and successful career as a thief-taker had taught him to play his cards close to his chest, and he was curious to see how forthcoming Mother Sharpe would be when she thought he knew nothing.

Mother Sharpe was also accustomed to being careful with

what she revealed. She had no reason not to trust Wolf, quite the contrary. However, the Wolf she had known and trusted, while always clearly more educated and more well-spoken than the average Whitechapel resident, had nevertheless been part of the community. But it seemed this Wolf was an earl, and Mother Sharpe's experience of her so-called betters had rarely been positive.

Silently considering her options, Mother Sharpe reflected on the case she had asked the dowager countess to take on. Even at the time, she had been surprised that Mickey D had suggested that petite, almost fragile-looking toff. However, she'd been impressed with the woman's determination and had intuited a kindred spirit and so had entrusted the investigation of her sister's disappearance to the unlikely sleuth. But had that decision been a wise one? Had she given too much credence to Mickey D's reference? As much as she wanted to find her sister, Vicky Sharpe had no desire to endanger another woman needlessly.

Finally, she said, "Yes. She came to see me. At the time, I believed Mickey D. had sent her. But, on reflection, while he had sent me a message alerting me to her suitability to take on an investigation I had mentioned to him, I'm not entirely sure that she didn't come with another purpose."

Given that Wolf knew that purpose, he didn't pursue that comment further. Instead, he asked, "And what investigation did you need help with?"

Vicky Sharpe told him what she knew about her twin sister's disappearance. Not interrupting the woman while she talked, Wolf couldn't help asking incredulously, "And Mickey D had suggested the dowager countess investigate your sister's disappearance?" Part of his incredulity was that Mickey had withheld this vital information when Wolf asked what the man knew about the dowager's whereabouts. He and Mickey D would be having words when the dowager was returned to safety.

The madam answered coolly, "Yes, he did. And after spending a few minutes in her company, any initial scepticism I had was dispelled. She is a formidable woman."

Wolf couldn't deny the truth of that statement. Nevertheless, he still couldn't keep the amazement out of his voice when he said, "And so, at your request, the dowager countess has gone to live in a brothel in Villiers Street to try to investigate your sister's disappearance? And what story did you give to explain her presence?"

Vicky Sharpe laughed, "Why, that she is our cousin Julia Phillips, a spinster governess who intends to watch over the premises during my sister's absence."

Wolf shook his head. "And people believed that the Dowager Countess of Pembroke was a lowly governess and cousin to two madams?"

If Vicky Sharpe was offended by Wolf's allusions, she chose not to dwell on his implied insult. Instead, she said, "We said enough to explain why the dowager countess speaks like a toff. Given that she bears more than a passing resemblance to me and my twin, the familial connection was believable."

Wolf still couldn't believe what he'd been told, but it seemed that once she gave the precise location of the brothel, Vicky Sharpe had no more information to impart.

CHAPTER 16

Monday, October 30, 1897, The dowager

Arriving back at the Villiers Street house at just past two o'clock, the dowager realised that it was a perfect time to snoop in Margery's Sharpe's study. Many of the house's inhabitants hadn't yet stirred after their long night of work into the small hours of the morning. Even the ladies who were up were still in their rooms, and it seemed as if it was too early for The Rascal and the other men who worked the gaming tables to start setting up.

Remembering her plan to have Little Ian act as her lookout, the dowager was then confronted with the problem of how to find him without drawing attention to herself. She had no idea where in the house the man was sleeping, nor did she intend to traipse up and down stairs looking for him. Finally, she entered the kitchen. She'd run into him there last night, and perhaps she would be lucky enough to do so again. The kitchen was once more filled with delicious smells, but Little Ian was nowhere to be seen.

The cook was at the stove stirring something, presumably for the evening's dinner. When she heard the dowager enter, she turned and asked, "Good afternoon, Miss Phillips. Dinner won't be ready for a while, but I made some shortbread earlier if you're peckish."

As it happened, the dowager was quite partial to shortbread, but lunch with the Ladies of KB had been a rather delicious, if rich, fish pie, so she declined but asked, "By any chance, have you seen my man, Little Ian?"

"As it happens, he was just in here. I gave him a plate of shortbread and shooed him out. He's been sleeping in the carriage house around the back. Your cousin doesn't keep a carriage, but it's where the male servants sleep. Do you want me to send one of the maids to get him for you?"

The dowager considered this offer. On the one hand, she wished to be careful as she searched the study. On the other hand, there was no reason why she couldn't be in there given the fiction that she was Margery Sharpe's cousin, watching the brothel for her. Finally deciding that perhaps she should just retreat to the study and hope that she wasn't disturbed rather than calling attention to her actions by having a servant seek out Little Ian, she declined the offer.

She made her way to the study and was relieved to see that no one was about. She quickly and quietly entered the room and shut the door behind her. The dowager hadn't taken much notice of the study when she was in it the day before, but now that she looked around, she observed that, much like her bedchamber, Margery Sharpe's study was very neat and organised. Going over to the large, sturdy mahogany desk and taking a seat in the matching chair, she observed that the desk's surface contained nothing more than a small clock and an inkwell and pen.

The desk had three drawers on the left side. The dowager tried the hand handle of the top left-hand one and was relieved that it was unlocked. It also contained nothing particularly noteworthy, merely some tradesmen's bills. Glancing through them, the dowager noted that none were overdue and that there were no extravagant purchases. The next drawer down was also unlocked. It contained a ledger. The dowager had managed large households for enough years to be able quickly to scan and understand the business accounts. Again, she observed that Margery Sharpe ran her business with an iron fist and a keen eye on the money coming in and out. The ledger indicated that the brothel was a profitable enterprise.

The bottom drawer was locked. The dowager knew that Wolf counted lockpicking amongst the skills he had picked up as a thief-taker, and she made a mental note to have him teach her when this investigation was over. But meanwhile, she had no way to get into that drawer and it occurred to her yet again that Wolf had had his uses in their investigations so far. She did wonder if Little Ian might help, but it struck her that the man's talents lay more in using his fists as blunt weapons rather than the more delicate art of picking a lock.

What the dowager did know was that when two drawers were unlocked, but one was locked, that drawer held something interesting. Whether or not its contents had anything to do with Margery Sharpe's disappearance, she couldn't know, but she did know that she needed to find some way to get it open. It did occur to her to try to use brute strength to force it open, but the desk was a fine, solid piece of furniture, and she doubted that she had sufficient strength for such a task. And such an act would likely draw unwanted attention if The Rascal happened to come into the study again.

No sooner had she thought about the man than the door opened, and he stood in its doorframe. The dowager still had the ledger out before her, and The Rascal asked suspiciously, "Snooping are we, Cousin Julia?"

"I believe I told you that this study would be my domain until my cousin returned," the dowager said imperiously. "As such, I expect you to knock before you enter. I certainly don't expect you to make yourself at home here. Furthermore, as Cousin Vicky informed you, I am here in her sister's stead to manage the business while Margery is indisposed. I can hardly be expected to do that without understanding the business' finances." The dowager sniffed and added even more imperiously, "Not that this is any of your concern."

The Rascal smirked, then said in an almost taunting tone, "Be careful, old woman. Stop your snooping. In fact, why don't you just take yourself back to whatever schoolroom you came from? I don't think Cousin Margery is coming back for a while, and last night's little performance aside, I don't think you're cut out for this life."

"What do you mean she's not coming back? Where is she? Do you know where my cousin is?" the dowager demanded. "Has something happened to her?"

The Rascal smirked again and tapped the side of his nose, "Nosy, nosy, nosy. Nothing good ever comes of being too nosy. Why can't you old women learn that?"

While he didn't answer her question, the threat implied in The Rascal's words was chilling. While the dowager hadn't given as much thought to what might have befallen Margery Sharpe as she might have in her appointed role as investigator, it now occurred to her that perhaps what she was investigating was a murder. This thought did give her pause; was she sufficiently equipped for this? Then, shaking off the moment of doubt, she considered her pivotal role in uncovering three murderers to date. She would have said four, but she had never gotten the full story of the old Duke of Somerset's murder and so wasn't as confident in claiming her share of the credit in that investigation.

The Rascal continued, "The guvnor has plans for the management of this establishment in your cousin's..." The Rascal paused meaningfully, then continued, "absence."

"I very much look forward to meeting this guvnor. But as for my displacement, that will not be happening any time soon."

The Rascal chuckled, "I'll have to make sure I'm around to hear you tell that to the guvnor. You're a feisty one, I'll give you that. But let's see what match you are for the guvnor." And with that, The Rascal turned and left the room, leaving the door open behind him.

The dowager continued to sit, the ledger open before her, pondering Jason Bono's words. Who was this guvnor? Was he responsible for Margery Sharpe's disappearance? And why? Had she crossed him in some way? The question chasing all her musings: what should the next steps in her investigation be? Yet again, the dowager thought with something almost akin to regret about how much more difficult it was to investigate alone. In a moment of weakness she immediately regretted, she even thought almost nostalgically of Tabitha's role in the past provocative debates about cases. Of course, this was the very reason the dowager had sought out Rat. It did occur to her to wonder if there was anything to prevent her from continuing that collaboration. It was evident that Rat was familiar with brothels and so there was little about Villiers Street that would shock the boy. However, she knew that Tabitha and Langley wished to raise the boy out of that life and that neither would appreciate her plunging him back in any more than she already had.

As the dowager sat thinking, she heard increased noise coming from outside of the study, and she realised that the brothel was coming back to life as its inhabitants started preparing for that evening's resumption of carnal activities. Quickly replacing the ledger in the drawer where she'd found it, the dowager rose and made her way back up to Margery Sharpe's bed chamber to begin her preparations for the evening.

The dowager dressed herself, again choosing a dress from Margery's wardrobe that seemed the easiest to put on alone. She thought about the evening ahead of her. She was mindful of just how little progress she had made in the investigation in the more than twenty-four hours she had been living in the brothel. There were some vague allusions to a shadowy business partner. The Rascal, Mr Bono, was mildly threatening in an almost joking manner, such that it was hard to tell whether he was warning her off or just enjoyed making her uncomfortable. And then there was the locked drawer, which might contain real evidence but might also contain nothing more than a fine bottle of brandy that Margery Sharpe wanted to hide from her girls.

In many ways, the dowager had very much enjoyed herself over the last couple of days. Life in the brothel was a very different experience for her, and she had been fascinated by her luncheon with the Ladies of KB. However, she reminded herself, the purpose of her stay in Villiers Street was not supposed to be akin to Doctor Livingstone researching native African tribes; she was supposed to be investigating Margery Sharpe's disappearance.

The dowager considered past investigations. What had Tabitha and Wolf done to find clues? Well, there was the time at the German ambassador's ball that she had feigned illness as a distraction so that Wolf could search the embassy. Of course, she mused, this was another reason there was value in investigating as a team; who would act as a distraction so she could snoop? And where would she snoop anyway? She had no idea what she was looking for. What she was sure of was there was little to be gained by another evening sitting in the parlour lightly overseeing the coital pairings. What she needed to do was to understand more about the other activities of the house.

Sitting at the dressing table, lost in thought, the dowager considered the brothel's gaming enterprise. It seemed as if whatever nefarious activities were going on were far more likely to be connected to that than to prostitution. No one had said that she had to stay in the parlour of an evening. It had been made quite clear that she was the boss and could do whatever she wanted. Of course, there was the question of what exactly she would be looking for. The dowager had never been interested in the usual games of cards that made up so many a social evening in London's best drawing rooms, let alone gaming in any more serious sense. She had no idea what to look for. Nevertheless, the dowager had absolute confidence in her intuitions. She believed with total certainty that if something underhand were going on, she would be able to sense it.

Satisfied with her plan of attack for the evening, she finished dressing and then descended to the kitchen to sample whatever of cook's delicious-smelling creations were on the menu for dinner.

After not much more than twenty-four hours in the brothel, the dowager felt she was getting used to its rhythms and seeing patterns in its seeming chaos. Looking at the women flowing in and out of the kitchen as they grabbed some food, wolfed it down and then went back to preparing for their evening's work, the dowager observed that they didn't seem like a group needing much management. The youngest of the prostitutes was perhaps eighteen, and there were definitely a few women who were using the artificial arts of excessive makeup and costume, attempting to cover the ravages of time and a hard life.

Regardless of their age, the women seemed to go about the business of the brothel in a convivial enough manner. There was some light teasing, the odd bit of bickering over a pair of earrings or a ribbon. But, for the most part, they seemed to know what was necessary and expected of them and went about their work in an orderly and, one might say, professional manner.

Certainly, it didn't seem as if any of the women was working under duress or being kept in the brothel against her will. None of the prostitutes seemed to be underage. In fact, after some of the tales told by the Ladies of KB about their own establishments, the dowager considered that the Villiers Street brothel might be considered quite mundane in its ordinariness.

Rather than eating and quickly leaving the kitchen as she had the night before, the dowager lingered as the girls came and went, listening to their conversations. But, aside from a bawdiness that the dowager would have loudly condemned under other circumstances, the chatter was quite banal. She then observed the servants. There was no doubt that most of the household staff ignored the prostitution going on around them and were focused on the gaming activities of the house.

The dowager spotted the maid who had opened the front door to her the day before, Kitty. The girl was coming in and out of the kitchen in quite a frenetic manner, carrying trays of glasses, decanters, vases of flowers, and other paraphernalia apparently necessary to create an ambience conducive to the business of gambling.

Finally, seeing Kitty struggling with an overly loaded tray, the dowager approached her and took one of the larger decanters off it, saying, "Let me help you, my dear." If the young maid was surprised at the offer, she nevertheless nodded her thanks and led the way out of the kitchen.

The dowager had seen the gaming rooms when she had first entered the house and realised that they were the reason for combining two houses, but now she realised just how much of the downstairs space those rooms took up. There were three large rooms, each decorated opulently. Enormous crystal chandeliers sparkled in each room, and all of the furnishings were of a quality that wouldn't be out of place in any of the grand gentleman's clubs of London.

Kitty walked through two rooms, and the dowager followed her, glancing about as she walked. Her only other experience of such an establishment was the gaming house she had visited with Tabitha and Wolf in Brighton during their previous investigation in search of her godson, Viscount Tobias. Just as then, these rooms seemed set up for various gaming activities. Men dressed smartly in evening dress were busy preparing the tables for the evening's entertainment.

When they arrived in the third and largest room, Kitty indicated a highly decorative table laden with glasses and other decanters. "Just put it down here, ma'am," she said. "And thank you for the help."

Looking around, the dowager realised that this room was empty except for the two of them and said in a tone she hoped sounded casual and friendly, "How long have you worked in this house, Kitty?"

Grateful for a chance to catch her breath and convinced enough of the authority of the woman before her that she felt any questions reason enough for a break, Kitty answered, "Six months. Cook is my ma's sister and got me the position. My ma and da weren't sure to begin with and wanted me to find a position elsewhere, but the money is so good it was hard to turn down. I have a cousin who works in a grand house in Chelsea, and I make twice what she does. And I get two afternoons off a week."

Realising that she had a short window in which to question Kitty, the dowager asked, "And do you enjoy your work here, Kitty?"

The girl paused momentarily, then acknowledged, "The evenings can be hard. I'm rushed off my feet, and when the men start losing, they can get quite nasty and will take it out on whoever is nearest. I've been knocked around a bit. But usually, it's fine."

"And, is my cousin, Mother Sharpe, a fair employer?"

Kitty laughed lightly, "Well, from what I can see and what the girls say, she is. But I don't work for Mother Sharpe. I work for the guvnor. When that man, the one they call The Rascal, hired me, he made that quite clear." The girl paused and then continued, "My aunt, Mrs Brown, the cook, she came with Mother Sharpe from her other place. And maybe the scullery maid did as well. But most of us didn't."

The dowager realised that the young maid couldn't stand talking to her much longer without risking censure, and so, wanting to make the most of the time, she decided to go straight to the heart of the matter, "Kitty, do you have any idea where Mother Sharpe might be? Her sister and I are worried about her. She left with no word to either of us."

Vicky Sharpe had said that it was one of the girls, presumably the prostitutes, who had first alerted her to Margery's absence. But surely, their mistress's absence had not gone unnoticed amongst the servants. Indeed, Kitty became visibly nervous as the dowager asked this question. The girl looked around as if searching for an escape. Worried that the maid might just turn and run, the dowager stepped forward and put a gentle but firm hand on the girl's arm, "Kitty, Mother Sharpe may be in danger. If you know anything, you must tell me."

Kitty was a pretty girl with large, warm, brown doe eyes. Now those eyes were even wider and almost pleading as she looked at the dowager and said in a quiet voice, "I don't ask no questions. It's better that way. Maybe Mother Sharpe asked too many."

Before the dowager could ask what that cryptic sentence meant, there was a noise behind them. The dowager quickly took her hand off Kitty's arm and stepped away. Turning to leave the room, she came face to face with The Rascal. "Well, well, well. What do we 'ave 'err? I thought you were 'ere to mind your cousin's business, not my guvnor's."

The dowager had dealt with cocky, sure of themselves men like Jason Bono her whole life. If she didn't allow herself to be bullied by them in the best drawing rooms in London, she certainly wasn't going to kowtow here. "Mr Bono, I do not answer for my movements to anyone, certainly not to you. Now move out of my way immediately and let me pass."

The Rascal didn't answer immediately but looked her up and down. Then, with a sly grin, he said, "You are bossy enough to be a governess, and yet, I'm not sure I believe it. Whenever you talk to me, I always get the feeling that you believe you're the Queen and I am a lowly serf who should be bowing in your presence. And I'm not sure why an old biddy who's never been anything but a governess would get to act like that."

The dowager was immediately on high alert; had she exposed her true identity? But The Rascal continued, "But then, why would the Queen or even a duchess choose to live in a nunnery and manage an unruly bunch of dollymops?" This seemed to be a genuine question, and the dowager was interested in where he would go next. "And so, I'm led to the inevitable conclusion that you are just a nosy, interfering old bag with ideas above 'er station."

Over the last few days, the dowager had reined in so many of her natural impulses, holding back whenever acerbic answers were on the tip of her tongue. But in the face of this young man's insults, she threw caution to the wind, drew back her shoulders, tipped up her chin and said in a tone that caused prime ministers, dukes, and on more than one occasion, the Prince of Wales, to wither, "Mr Bono, I cannot imagine why you believe you are in a position to speak to me thus. As far as I can tell, you are nothing more than a glorified errand boy for a shadowy overlord. My cousin may tolerate being spoken to thus by a grubby guttersnipe, but I can assure you that I don't."

And with that, she swept past him and out of the room. As she left, she heard him call after her, "Stay out of the way, old woman."

Making her way to the parlour, the dowager considered her unpleasant interaction with The Rascal. She believed that the man's suspicions about her identity had been neutralised.

However, it was evident that the man still harboured suspicions about her behaviour. As much as the dowager wanted to snoop in the gaming rooms, with The Rascal on alert, she realised that this was not the evening to be caught, yet again, where she wasn't supposed to be. Frustrated at the prospect of another night doing nothing more than vaguely overseeing a bunch of prostitutes, hypocritical vicars and low-level civil servants and politicians, she reclaimed her armchair from the previous evening and sulked. This investigation was going nowhere; she needed to change tactics. She was just unsure of what or how.

CHAPTER 17

Tuesday, October 31, 1897

The following morning, the dowager rose, dressed, and went down to find some breakfast with an air of despondency. She sat at the kitchen table, eating the toast and jam the accommodating cook had made for her, considering her options. The dowager thought of Tabitha's corkboard with its notecards and wished she could employ such a mechanism now. But this wasn't her house, and she had already caused suspicion. It was too dangerous to leave any evidence of her investigation around. And so, instead, she considered what she knew so far. And the answer was: not very much.

There was no doubt that Margery Sharpe was missing. But beyond that, everything else was speculation. It was still possible that the woman had merely gone to stay in the country. There was no doubt that her relationship with her twin sister was cool enough that it was highly unlikely that Vicky Sharpe would have been alerted to such a trip.

Then, the dowager considered the Ladies of KB. Not that the dowager had much experience of such things herself, but if she had to put a label to the relationship they seemed to have with each other it would be that they were all friends. But they were also all busy businesswomen, running their own establishments. She had found no evidence that they ever met between their monthly get-togethers. Would Margery have sent word to one of them? Particularly if she suspected she would be missing one of the luncheons. Maybe. However, as the ladies had explained their meetings, they set a date and place for the following one, and then whoever was available just showed up. So, it was unlikely any of them would have been worried if Margery didn't attend one.

As far as she could tell, Lou acted as a right-hand woman and confidante, so it was suspicious that she hadn't been warned and asked to manage the brothel in Margery's absence. But then, the dowager had left her home and not bothered to alert her servants as to her whereabouts. No, as far as the dowager could see, while it was certainly possible that some harm had come to Margery Sharpe, it was far from a given.

Considering the brothel and, more to the point, its partner gaming rooms, the dowager had a strong suspicion that something questionable was taking place. But she had no proof of this. A locked drawer and some vague threats from The Rascal hardly constituted damning evidence. It was clear that he didn't like the dowager. Perhaps, The Rascal's threatening attitude towards her was nothing more than a manifestation of those two things. Even if something nefarious was going on, what did that have to do with Margery Sharpe's supposed disappearance? After all, she was a partner in this venture. Presumably, she was party to whatever might be going on there. Or was she? Perhaps Margery had become suspicious of shadier activities than gaming, asked too many questions, and finally, been permanently silenced.

The dowager sipped her coffee and nibbled on her toast, too distracted to enjoy either. How many more nights was she prepared to spend in this house of ill repute without this so-called investigation moving forward at all? What would be the consequences if she admitted failure? The only people who knew she was here investigating were Vicky Sharpe and Mickey D. While she enjoyed the Whitechapel gangster's company, she had no real concerns about his opinion of her. Falling at this first fence would make it unlikely that Mickey D would send other cases her way, but perhaps that was all for the best. As to disappointing Vicky Sharpe, her client. Well, she had been asked to stay in the brothel, pretend to be Cousin Julia, and see if she could discover what might have happened to Margery, and the dowager felt she had certainly discharged some of this to the best of her abilities. The dowager felt that she could report back with her head held high that she had done the first two in that list and made a sterling attempt at the third. She had never promised that she would find the missing madam.

Never one to admit defeat easily, the dowager decided that she would make a serious attempt that evening to infiltrate the gaming rooms and see if she could discern what was really going on there, assuming something was. She would leave the brothel the following day if she failed or found nothing.

Happy to at least have a firm plan of action, however lightweight it might be, the dowager finished her breakfast with more enthusiasm. Of course, it was only eleven o'clock in the morning. What would she do with herself for the rest of the day? It began to occur to her that the life of a madam wasn't much more exciting than the life of a countess. They both managed a household staff, well, in the madam's case, a group of prostitutes and servants. Nevertheless, there were similarities. They both kept an eye on the household accounts. And they both had to manage visits from people they'd rather not entertain if they had a choice.

No one had told the dowager that she couldn't leave the Villiers Street house. Indeed, when she and Lou had gone to the Ladies of KB luncheon, it had gone unremarked. So, perhaps she would spend a little time that day exploring this neighbourhood that she would otherwise have never set foot in. Of course, even she was not foolhardy enough to think she could wander the streets of London alone. But this was exactly why she had secured Little Ian's services. The man hadn't had to do much so far. The least he could do to earn his coin was to escort her out for a couple of hours.

Satisfied that she had a plan of action of some sort, all she had to do was send a servant to summon Little Ian and ready herself for a brisk walk on what was likely to be a chilly day. Little Ian was found easily enough, and within twenty minutes, the dowager was bundled up in one of Margery Sharpe's coats, and she and Little Ian were making their way up Villiers Street.

The dowager was not normally overly concerned about the

weather. She travelled everywhere in a carriage with heated bricks at her feet when necessary, and there was always a servant to hold an umbrella over her head when it rained. But now, looking up at the cloudy sky, it occurred to her that it would have been worthwhile seeing what the weather was like before setting out. Well, lesson learned. She would be fine if it didn't rain for the next hour or so. She had one of Margery's thick wool scarves wrapped around her neck and a hat that was more functional than any she owned on her head. She was ready to explore.

The dowager found her walk with Little Ian fascinating. She had always been quite clear on her feelings about those of her class walking the streets. A few months before, she had happened upon Wolf walking back from Whitechapel in his thief-taking clothes. Insisting that he instead get in her carriage immediately, she had admonished him, saying, "I cannot let the Earl of Pembroke continue to walk the streets, and in such attire. What will people say?" And yet here she was, choosing to walk, with no particular destination in sight, through a part of London that, while safer and cleaner than Whitechapel, was definitely not Grosvenor Square. The dowager shook her head in amazement at where she found herself. The Dowager Countess of Pembroke of a year ago would not have recognised this woman walking down the Strand in clothes borrowed from a madam, living in a brothel and consorting with prostitutes.

Unaccustomed as she was to walking, the dowager found her stamina was lacking. Little Ian had naturally long strides and would have struggled under any circumstances to keep a pace suitable for a petite, old woman. But under these circumstances, he found that the only way to manage the slow pace that was all the dowager could manage was to take a step or two and then wait for her to catch up. Even so, he had no complaints. Little Ian's size compensated for a slow mind. Mickey D found that the giant had his uses, but he was usually relegated to physical tasks or left behind when they ran jobs. This job, looking after the odd little old toff, was easy enough so far. And she was paying him more daily than he usually earned in a week. So, Little Ian had no complaints.

The dowager was fascinated by the sights and sounds around her, even if she found some of the smells a little off-putting. So, this is the average man and woman at work, she thought to herself. Of course, she was vaguely aware of the various tradesmen and women who provided much of the food and drink she consumed and sewed the clothes she wore. But she had never interacted with them. When she visited her modiste, the workers were normally kept in the back behind a curtain so as not to bother the clientele with the unpleasant view of the women slaving away in cramped, uncomfortable quarters for twelve hours a day. The tradespeople were dealt with by the housekeeper or by Manning. And that was as it should be. The dowager had always believed that the mark of a smooth-running household was that things should magically appear just as she needed them. How those things were made, transported and prepared were questions she had always felt she had a right to never have to think about.

Yet, seeing people going about their business was fascinating. There were clerks with satchels of letters, street vendors calling out the quality of their wares, street urchins sweeping the streets clean after the carriages had gone by, and so much more. Had her strength been greater, the dowager would happily have walked further and seen more. But as it was, barely thirty minutes had gone by before she was forced to admit that they would need to turn back if she was to have any chance of making it back to Villiers Street.

Wolf and Bear had left Gunthorpe Street and walked for a while. It was never easy to hail a hackney cab in Whitechapel; there were not enough potential customers to entice the average driver to mill around. Wolf had intended to hail the first hackney cab they saw. Still, as they walked through the narrow, crowded lanes lined with residential buildings and small businesses that made up Whitechapel and started walking toward the Victoria Embankment, no cab crossed their path. Eventually, they just decided to walk.

The walk took almost an hour but gave them time to consider their conversation with Vicky Sharpe. As they walked, the buildings became grander, the streets cleaner, the beggars fewer. Wolf was grateful that the missing Mother Sharpe had her establishment in a vaguely respectable part of town. At least a less dangerous, desperate one. He was sure the dowager would have untaken the investigation no matter where the brothel was, so it was a matter of luck that she had found herself just off the Strand. As they walked, mostly in companionable silence, they passed through bustling streets filled with the sounds of horse-drawn carriages, street vendors, and people going about their daily business.

Finally, and uncharacteristically, it was Bear who spoke first. The normally taciturn man made a wonderful sounding board but rarely put his thoughts forward unasked. "It is hard to imagine her ladyship living in and running a brothel," he said.

Wolf agreed, "I'd always thought that her stated desire for adventure was mostly bluster. It never occurred to me, and I'm sure it never occurred to Tabitha, that she might do something such as this."

"Do you think she might be in danger?" Bear asked.

This was the question that had been consuming most of Wolf's thoughts as they walked. "I'm not sure," he answered. "For all we know, there is a very innocuous explanation for why Margery Sharpe is missing. However, what we heard about a business partner and a gaming establishment does make me a little worried. And as we know, her ladyship is not known for her restraint and tact. What she can get away with in the drawing rooms of Mayfair is very different than what it is advisable for her to do outside of it. Let alone in the situation she seems to have planted herself."

They decided to get to Villiers Street by heading down to the Thames and walking along the Victoria Embankment. Completed just over fifteen years before, the Embankment had been developed to improve its locale's sanitation and aesthetics.

Turning down towards Blackfriars Bridge, they quickly made their way to the start of the Victoria Embankment. The riverside walkway made a pleasant respite from the noise, smells, and bustle of the London Streets. Just after they passed Waterloo Bridge, they turned into the Embankment Gardens. While it was possible to continue the rest of the way to Villiers Street on the roadway, taking the more verdant route was quicker and more pleasant.

After having their senses overwhelmed by Whitechapel and then the City of London, the gardens were a delightful respite. Even though it was too late in the year for much in the way of flowers, the greenery was well-manicured, and the paths well-swept. Wrought iron benches were placed along the paths. They were almost at Villiers Street and hadn't formulated a plan yet.

Wolf indicated that they should take a seat on one of the benches. "I'm not sure how to proceed," he confessed. "We have no idea what we might encounter. We're not even sure that her ladyship is still in residence."

They sat in silence for a few moments, contemplating their next moves. Finally, Bear said, "Well, we believe that Little Ian is still with her. He knows me well enough. Why don't I do some reconnaissance on the house and see if I can find him."

"And then what?" Wolf asked. It was a decent enough start to a plan, but he still wasn't sure what should come next.

"I believe we need to talk to her ladyship, away from that house if possible. We have no idea who might be listening or watching her. Do you know Gordon's at the bottom of Villiers Street?" Bear asked.

Wolf nodded, "It's just as we come out of these gardens, right? I've never been in, but I know of it. Are you suggesting we meet with her ladyship there?"

"Yes, it's dark with low ceilings and private nooks; a good place for a clandestine meeting. And they don't serve beer, only wine, port and sherry, so it keeps out the rowdier elements."

Wolf didn't have a better idea, so with that decision made, the two men stood and made their way to the end of the Embankment Gardens. The men could see Gordon's on the corner as soon as they exited. Wolf made his way into the establishment, down steep, narrow stairs and into the bar, which was all vaulted ceilings and dark corners lit by candlelight. If they had to meet with the dowager in public, it was as good a place as any for a discreet conversation.

Wolf realised how hungry he was and ordered a large slice of game pie and a glass of port. Then, taking his food and drink, he looked around for the most private spot he could find. Through an archway that looked too low for Bear to get under while standing straight up, he could see a table and benches in a dark corner. He told the stout, middle-aged woman behind the bar to send his friends through when they arrived. One of the many good things about Bear's size and visage was that it was very easy to describe him to strangers. As it happened, even Wolf had to stoop to get under the archway. He couldn't have gone further into the area if he'd wanted, the ceiling was so low, and so settled for the nearest table.

Meanwhile, Bear had made his way further up the street until he saw a house that matched the description given by Vicky Sharpe. The house was on the corner of another street, and Bear assumed that he could reach the back of the house and the kitchen door that way. He still wasn't sure what story he was going to give to anyone in the household he might encounter.

CHAPTER 18

As Bear stood on the street, looking at the brothel, he heard a familiar strident voice off to his left. Looking up Villiers Street, he saw the Dowager Countess of Pembroke flanked by Little Ian. At least in that rather unflattering coat and hat, he thought it was her. The woman was carrying on a monologue about something, and Little Ian looked as if he wasn't paying any attention.

Drawing closer, the dowager finally noticed Bear, who gave Little Ian a nod in silent greeting. "Well, I never…" the dowager started to say. Before she could give away his identity to anyone watching, Bear covered the ground between them and, slowing down but not stopping entirely, he said to Little Ian in a low voice, "Bring her to Gordon's. Wolf is waiting." Little Ian nodded in acknowledgement, and Bear continued up Villiers Street.

The dowager was too short to have heard what the one giant of a man said quietly to the other. But she knew that something had been said. Putting her hand on Little Ian's arm, she asked quietly, "What did he say?"

Instead of answering, Little Ian beckoned for her to follow him. Deeply curious about where they were going and why, the dowager followed with no more questions asked. Villiers Street wasn't long, and it took only a few moments more, even at the dowager's slow pace, to arrive outside of Gordon's. Ever vigilant, Little Ian went first down the narrow, steep steps, which was counter to the etiquette the dowager normally insisted all around her lived by.

Entering the dark bar, Little Ian was immediately recognised by the woman serving. Well, he was mistaken for Bear, but the result was the same; the very large man with the tiny old woman was pointed in the direction of the dark, nook.

Having just seen Bear, the dowager shouldn't have been surprised to find Wolf waiting patiently for her. But somehow, she'd imagined that encountering Bear on the street was just a coincidence. It never occurred to her that Tabitha and Wolf might have been looking for her and that, having discovered where she was, Bear had intentionally been outside of the Villiers Street brothel.

"Jeremy, dear, what on earth are you doing here?" she imperiously demanded.

Wolf wasn't sure what he'd expected from this meeting, but it certainly wasn't that the dowager might be in an immediate state of high dudgeon.

"Please lower your voice, and take a seat," he answered. "Little Ian, can you please fetch a sherry for..." he paused. Did Little Ian know who he was working for? And even if he did, Wolf would rather not announce the dowager's identity. "Please, fetch a sherry. And get something for yourself if you'd like."

With Little Ian gone, the dowager settled on the bench and asked, "Now, why don't you tell me what you're doing here, Jeremy?"

Trying to keep the exasperation out of his voice, Wolf answered, "Looking for you. What else?"

"Well, why on earth are you looking for me? As you can see, I am perfectly well."

"Tabitha and I know," Wolf answered through gritted teeth.

"Know what, dear?" the dowager answered in as innocent a tone as she could manage.

"We know about Margery Sharpe. We know that you've been living in the brothel here. We know about your investigation."

"And what of it?" she answered somewhat defensively. "I am not a child. I am the Dowager Countess of Pembroke, and if I have chosen to take on a solo investigation, I'm not sure why it is anything that you and Tabitha should concern yourselves with."

Wolf felt sure that he had just rolled his eyes. He just hoped the lighting was too dim in the dark corner for the dowager to notice. Taking a deep breath, he said, "Manning visited us yesterday beside himself with worry. Did it not occur to you that disappearing for multiple nights would cause your servants concern?"

Even in the dimness, Wolf could tell that the look on the dowager's face indicated that he might as well have said that last part in a foreign language for all his words meant to her. Confirming his intuition, she answered, "Did it occur to me that I might cause my household staff concern with my actions? Of course it didn't. What an absurd question."

Realising he would get nowhere with that argument, Wolf pivoted and asked, "Do you think a brothel is an appropriate or safe place for a woman of your station?"

Normally, the dowager was the first to make mention of what was and was not appropriate for a member of the aristocracy to be doing. She'd certainly used that particular cudgel on Tabitha and Wolf many times. But when this argument was turned on her, she said in her most high-handed of tones, "If I decide to do something, it is then a de-facto appropriate thing for one of my station to do. I thought that you realised by now that I do not follow society. It follows me."

It was evident to Wolf that any attempt to make the dowager feel at least somewhat abashed was futile. He had always wondered if the woman was capable of feeling shame, and now he was sure that she wasn't. By this time, Little Ian had returned with a sherry for the dowager, placed it on the table in front of her and then retreated to the bar. Taking a sip of her drink, the dowager wrinkled her nose at the quality of the sherry, placed her glass back down, and asked, "Aren't you curious as to how the investigation is going?" Of course, Wolf was curious. Given that this seemed to be the one topic the dowager wished to discuss, he let her tell her story uninterrupted.

Because the dowager didn't know how much Wolf already knew about her actions over the last few days, she started back at Lady Hartley's. Wolf could have interrupted her, but the woman was in full flow and never appreciated someone breaking her stride.

Finally, the dowager had told everything she had to tell. Wolf rested his wrists on his head and sat back against the cushion, contemplating all he had heard. "Do you believe you can discover anything more by staying in the brothel?" he asked.

The dowager considered this question. She had been prepared to have Wolf try to order her to leave. She hadn't been prepared to have him seemingly leave the decision up to her. If he had tried to command her, the dowager was ready with a full range of ammunition to defend her continued residence in the brothel. But in the face of a reasonable question as to the true utility of remaining, she had to pause and consider the question. Finally, she was forced to concede, "Probably not. The gaming business seems to be so separate from the actual business of the brothel that I've been unable to come up with a reason why I need to be involved in it. And this Jason Bono character is clearly suspicious of me, making it even harder to snoop."

The dowager paused, and then, because Wolf had treated her as a rational being, an equal, she let her defences down somewhat and admitted, "I have been feeling somewhat redundant there, if I'm honest. It seems as if the brothel side of it can be managed perfectly well by this woman, Lou, who seems to have been something of a right-hand-woman to Margery Sharpe."

"Do you have any possessions that you cannot leave behind?" Wolf asked.

"Nothing," the dowager acknowledged.

"Then, I suggest that you leave with me now."

"Won't they wonder where I've gone and why?" the dowager asked.

"By your account, there hasn't been much curiosity about where the actual madam has gone. I doubt that your disappearance will be questioned too deeply."

The dowager acknowledged the truth of this statement. In truth, she couldn't wait to return to her soft bed, silk gowns, and the life of comfort that her large household staff afforded her. Her time in the brothel hadn't been as entertaining as she'd imagined, and while she would never admit it, the dowager was relieved to have been discovered by Wolf and persuaded of the wisdom of leaving.

Wolf had assumed that the Little Ian would return to his employment for Mickey D. But no sooner had he suggested that than the dowager interrupted, "Little Ian, if you and Mr Doherty are amenable to it, I would like to continue employing you for the time being." Wolf raised his eyebrows but said nothing. What on earth was this about? Little Ian quickly acceded to this arrangement.

Now, all that was left was to round up Bear and hail a hackney cab to take them back to Mayfair. Ascending from Gordon's poorly lit depths, they were happy to find Bear waiting on the street. Wolf quickly informed him of their plans, and he went ahead of them up Villiers Street to find a hackney cab. Wolf assumed that some would be waiting outside of Charing Cross station.

CHAPTER 19

Manning's relief when he opened the front door and saw his mistress standing there alive and well would have been touching to a mistress who didn't take her staff's fealty for granted. As it was, she walked past him with barely an acknowledgement, saying, "I need to bathe and change out of these clothes. Send Withers to me, Manning." Turning to Wolf and Bear, she added, "Why don't you settle yourselves in the drawing room? We need to discuss our next steps. I assume you'll insist on involving Tabitha, so have Manning put in a telephone call to Chesterton House and ask her to join us."

Wolf was astounded at how blasé the woman was about her multi-day absence. It seemed to either not have occurred to the dowager, or not concern her, that the people in her life might have been truly worried or, in the case of Manning, distraught at the thought that harm might have befallen her. He caught Manning's eye. The normally appropriately inscrutable butler may have raised his eyebrows slightly and cocked his head an infinitesimally small amount to acknowledge some otherwise perfectly suppressed frustration. Or perhaps he didn't.

Wolf felt no such restraint and led the way into the dowager's drawing room, shaking his head and muttering about, "infuriating and self-absorbed people."

After two nights of washing in cold water and dressing herself, having Withers draw her a hot bath and tend to the dowager's every need was delicious. As the dowager luxuriated in her large bathtub in her elegant but comfortable bathroom with Withers buzzing around, ensuring her every need was satisfied almost before she had realised it, the dowager was tempted to be grateful for the easy, comfortable life she led. Luckily, the moment passed, and before she had descended back downstairs, the dowager had complained about the water temperature, berated Withers for some perceived tardiness, and demanded that the housemaid do a better job sweeping out the grate. For her part, Withers smiled indulgently; it was good to have her mistress back, and unchanged by whatever her adventure had been.

While the dowager washed off whatever vestiges of proletariat sympathies had survived the carriage ride back to Mayfair, Wolf and Bear waited patiently in her drawing room. Manning had put the telephone call through to Chesterton House, and once he had Talbot on the line, Wolf had taken over on one end and Tabitha on the other. Assured of the dowager's safety, Tabitha promised to change her outfit quickly and make her way over to join them. Wolf had suggested she bring the corkboard with her.

Just over an hour after the dowager countess had first re-entered her natural habitat, Wolf, Bear and Tabitha were settled in the drawing room, sipping tea and eating Madeira cake. Finally, the dowager had completed her toilette sufficiently to be sure that the stench of Villiers Street was nothing more than a faint memory.

Seated in the drawing room with Wolf and Bear, the corkboard now propped up on a sideboard, Tabitha leapt to her feet when her diminutive mother-in-law entered the room. "Mama," Tabitha exclaimed, "I was so worried about you. I am so relieved to see you home safe and well." Tabitha was tempted to rush to the old woman and embrace her with genuine affection, but any urge to do so was tempered by a look on the dowager's face, which suggested that gratuitously emotional gestures were not welcomed.

"I'm not sure what everyone is making such a fuss about," the dowager answered tersely. "I am hardly in my dotage yet. If I choose to spend a couple of nights away from my own bed, this is hardly something I am obliged to inform anyone about. Least of all, you, Tabitha. I wish everyone would stop acting as if I was off wandering the streets in some state of decrepitude." In a rare example of a rebuke being felt as sincerely and immediately as it was given, Tabitha suddenly was reminded of why she owed this terror of a woman nothing and should never have lost sleep over her disappearance.

Sitting back down, Tabitha answered her in a business-like manner, "I have brought the corkboard. However, our use of it so far has been to find you. With that now accomplished, I assume there is an actual investigation for which we have need of it."

Wolf realised that Tabitha was not up-to-date; she didn't even know about Margery Sharpe's disappearance. He quickly ran through all he had learned from Vicky Sharpe and then began to give a summary of the dowager's investigations over the previous few days. He spoke of the dowager impersonating the twin madams' cousin and residing in the brothel. Tabitha's eyebrows rose and then rose again as he spoke of the dowager's supervision of the prostitutes. However, she let him continue uninterrupted.

Well, Tabitha let Wolf continue uninterrupted. No sooner had he started the narrative of her incognito escapade than the dowager felt the unfairness of the lack of spotlight and interjected, "Yes, I was to be Cousin Julia, the governess. I was terribly adept at disguise. Which perhaps should come as a surprise to no one." As it happened, this came as a surprise to everyone; the dowager seemed far too large a personality to be effectively camouflaged.

Realising that the story would be told more efficiently, if more colourfully, if the dowager was given centre stage, Wolf said, "Lady Pembroke, perhaps you should continue from here." And so the dowager told her story. As the narrative unfurled, Tabitha was hard-pressed to keep her shock and amazement to herself. That the Dowager Countess of Pembroke, the self-proclaimed arbiter of high society's foibles and peccadillos, should have been managing the business of prostitution was far-fetched enough. That she talked of taking luncheon with a group of exotic-sounding madams as if it were no different than taking tea with Lady Willis and her cronies seemed beyond belief.

The dowager seemed unaffected by the incredible

juxtaposition of her lifelong proclamations with her recent actions. She broke off from her narrative to confide, "I had no idea of the range and types of proclivities men, and it seems even some women, might indulge in." This was said as if she were discussing people's interesting tastes in beverages rather than their carnal pleasures. Tabitha was grateful that the dowager did not delve into greater detail and instead quickly picked back up her story's main thread.

When the dowager recounted her last interaction with The Rascal, Tabitha could no longer contain herself and exclaimed, "Mama, you put yourself in great danger. These were clearly ruthless criminals that you were dealing with."

The dowager had felt much the same after the encounter and had been relieved to have been discovered by Wolf. However, the thought that this chit of a girl, whose own recent behaviour had been devoid of all regard for society's appropriately parochial strictures, was chastising her was beyond the pale. Straightening her already stiff spine and throwing her shoulders back, the dowager proclaimed, "If I am able to make the Prime Minister quake in his shoes, you can't imagine I was daunted by some ha'penny mobster's lackey."

No one had an appropriate response to this statement, and so didn't try. When the tale was finally told, Tabitha asked, "What do we do now, if anything?"

"Well, the last part of your question is the most pertinent," Wolf said. "We don't even know if there is a crime to investigate." He paused and amended his sentence, "While I'm sure there is criminal activity going on in that brothel, it is unclear if Margery Sharpe's disappearance is in any way related to it. I suggest that our first act is to try to determine if anything nefarious has befallen Mother Sharpe." Turning to Bear, he said, "Go to the nearest mortuary and see if they've been sent any unidentified bodies over the last few days matching Margery Sharpe's description. You know her twin, Vicky," Wolf pointed out. As Bear stood, ready to leave immediately, Wolf added, "Take some coin to sweeten the pot."

As Bear left on his mission, Wolf turned to Tabitha and said, "Let's redo this board with the facts of the actual case before us as opposed to the fool's errand we'd embarked on." As he said these words, he turned towards the dowager and raised his eyebrows slightly. Now that the woman was safely returned, Wolf allowed himself to feel and express how foolhardy and unnecessary her disappearance had been.

"Fool's errand?" the dowager exclaimed. "Is that what we're calling it now?" For good measure, she added one of her signature harrumphs.

Wolf, and particularly Tabitha, would have appreciated being able to spend time chastising the woman. However, not only would it fall on deaf ears, but they had more important things to do. And so, they ignored the dowager's fit of pique, and instead, Wolf moved to the little writing table against the wall while Tabitha began taking down the old notecards on the board and began writing new ones.

Before he picked up the pen to begin writing, Wolf explained, "We need to know who owns the house on Villiers Street. From everything Lady Pembroke has said, it seems clear that it isn't Margery Sharpe. Who is pulling all the strings? I'm writing to my solicitor, Anderson, to see what he can find out." This had been a tactic Wolf had used previously in their investigation into the death of Claire Murphy. Then, the solicitor had discovered that a limited liability company owned the house. He had explained that this was often done to shield the actual property owners. But even then, with Mickey D's safe-cracking help, they had pierced that shield and discovered the actual owner. Wolf hoped that it wouldn't come to that this time. He owed Mickey D enough favours as it was.

At Wolf's explanation, the dowager looked, if not chagrined, at least thoughtful. While she would never acknowledge it, not only was she relishing investigating as part of a team again, but the actions that Wolf had taken in the short time they had been back had highlighted the deficiencies of her investigative efforts over the past few days. The dowager had her own solicitor. There was no reason she could not have sent him a note asking him to look into the ownership of the brothel. However, it had never occurred to her. And as to inquiring about recent unidentified bodies, the dowager wouldn't have known where to start. While she was sure she could command the obedience of the Home Secretary, would that have been the wisest or most efficient way to gain the information? Even if it had been, she hadn't done so.

Instead of doing any of the things that now seemed so obvious, the dowager had thrown herself headlong into the "fun", cloak and dagger part of the investigation. Never one for self-flagellation, the dowager gave herself credit for making important progress. However, she silently acknowledged that she might have become too caught up in impersonating Cousin Julia and that her time undercover could have been used more effectively.

Wolf quickly dashed off a note to his solicitor, sealed the envelope, then called for Manning and asked for it to be delivered immediately. As an afterthought, he told Manning to tell whoever delivered the note to inquire whether his solicitor had a telephone installed. He'd never wanted the damned contraption, but now it had been installed, they should perhaps make the most of it.

Returning to the armchair he had been sitting in, Wolf saw the board starting to be populated with facts about Margery Sharpe's disappearance. Reading what they knew so far, he decided and said, "I believe I must visit this gaming establishment tonight."

The dowager, proud of her newly acquired specialised knowledge of such things, said, "We are not its normal patrons."

Obviously, the "we" in her statement referred to the aristocracy. It had never occurred to Wolf to attend as the Earl of Pembroke. But it also didn't sound as if this was the kind of gaming hell that Wolf, the thief-taker, might frequent either. He needed to assume a more middle-class persona.

Tabitha's first thoughts were less sartorial, "Are you a card player?" she asked.

As it happened, this was a skill that Wolf had picked up at Oxford. Unlike many of his fellow students, he had not found gambling enticing. But given his penurious situation in those days, he had found his innate skill at it to be a useful income stream at times. Not wanting to go into too many details about his old life, Wolf merely nodded and said, "I can be when I have to."

Tabitha would have loved to have delved into that somewhat cryptic answer, but she had more important things to deal with. Not the least of which was claiming her role in this investigation. She felt she had been left on the sidelines so far. Wolf and Bear had visited Mickey D, Vicky Sharpe and Villiers Street without her. In all these instances, she had reluctantly accepted the efficacy of being left behind. However, now that the investigation was less personal and her fears for the dowager's safety were no longer at stake, Tabitha was more willing to insist on her involvement. "I will be joining you," she stated as matter-of-factually as if she were planning to join Wolf at a society dinner.

"Absolutely not!" Wolf exclaimed with all the vehemence that Tabitha had expected. "What on earth are you thinking even suggesting such a thing?"

Tabitha had anticipated such a response and immediately answered, "I accompanied you to the gaming house in Brighton."

"Against my better judgement," Wolf countered. "And that was not housed in a brothel. I cannot imagine that such a place is frequented by ladies other than the prostitutes working there."

Tabitha turned to the dowager, "Were there ever female guests?"

Even as she asked, Tabitha realised that whatever the truth of the matter, the dowager was never inclined to support Tabitha. So, she was surprised when the woman quickly and decisively answered, "Actually, I did see one or two over the days I was there. I'm not sure how reputable I would say they looked. I suspect that some of the men had brought their mistresses along. After all, who else would attend such an establishment?"

Shaking his head with exasperation, Wolf turned to Tabitha and asked, "And so you plan to play the part of my mistress? Do you think that will be any more believable than that her ladyship was nothing more than a lowly governess?"

While she might not be inclined to defend Tabitha, the dowager could not let this personal dismissal stand. "Jeremy, I will have you know that my adoption of the necessary persona was masterful and entirely believable."

Given that the dowager herself had admitted earlier that this Rascal character had questioned her credibility as Cousin Julia, Wolf just shook his head. He realised that this might not be a battle he could win. Instead, he stood up and said, "I believe this to be an unwise move, but it seems my wishes are to be overruled. And so, I suggest we return to Chesterton House to see what appropriate disguises your maid and my valet can concoct."

The dowager, hating the thought of being left out of such a charade, also stood and announced, "And I will be resuming my role as Cousin Julia."

This unexpected declaration was where Wolf drew the line, "Have you lost your mind?" he challenged the dowager rather more forcefully than he intended. "We have just rescued you from that place. You can't just waltz back in."

"I did not need to be rescued, nor is that what happened," the dowager pronounced. "And I have been gone for only a few hours. As far as anyone in the brothel knows, I went for a walk with Little Ian. I did not tell them when I would return. I will merely say that we stopped in a tea house if anyone asks. Which they won't."

Seeing that Wolf was not placated, the dowager continued, "I assume that one of the goals of tonight's masquerade is to pick the lock of the drawer in the study. How will you find it without my help?"

"Lady Pembroke, with the greatest respect, I have a long career behind me sneaking through houses and picking locks. I'm more than capable of doing so without your help. Perhaps you could describe the house layout to me?" Even as he uttered these words, Wolf realised that, yet again, his arguments were futile. There was no way the dowager would agree to be left out. A stony silence was his only answer from the dowager. Sighing, Wolf said with resignation, "Fine, then I believe you also have a disguise to put back on. Meet me back in Gordons tomorrow morning at eleven o'clock," he told her. Wolf hoped that all it would take was for the dowager to return to the brothel for one more night and that the following morning, they could extract her for good.

CHAPTER 20

Before he and Tabitha had left the dowager's home, Wolf had tried once more to dissuade the old woman from returning to the Villiers Street brothel. When it became clear that his words were falling on deaf ears, Wolf then impressed on her the need to return as soon as possible if that's what she insisted on doing. The longer she was gone, the more suspicious her absence would be. "If you must do this, be sure to take Little Ian with you," was Wolf's final admonishment.

Although the dowager didn't appreciate Wolf's patronising tone, she did realise the wisdom of his words. As soon as he and Tabitha had left, the dowager had sent Manning off to find Little Ian, who had left the dowager on her return and made his way behind the house to the kitchen door. The dowager then went to her bedchamber, where Withers was still puttering around.

The dress that the dowager had returned in was still lying on the bed. The dowager presumed that Withers planned to donate it to one of the other servants. While not to the dowager's standards, it was a well-made dress made of sturdy, warm material.

Withers looked up as her mistress re-entered the bedchamber, "M'lady, can I help you?" the long-suffering woman asked in a tone that suggested that her enthusiasm for her mistress' return had waned over the time it took to bathe and dress the difficult woman.

"There has been a change of plan, Withers. I will be resuming the persona I adopted over the past few days." On her return, the dowager had felt no need to explain to any of her servants where she had been and why she was dressed in somebody else's clothes. And with the resumption of the charade, she felt no more compelled to satisfy her household staff's curiosity. The dowager was well aware of the servants' gossip mill that would spread from her household to others where her staff had relatives and friends. While the dowager felt no fear of society's censure – it wouldn't dare – she did not need to go out of her way to feed grist to this mill.

Withers had been holding some stockings that needed to be fixed, and on her mistress' words, she put them on a table next to her but still didn't jump to action. In truth, she had no idea what her ladyship meant by her words. Seeing the confusion on her maid's face and impatient to get back to the action, the dowager moved to the bed, touched Margery Sharpe's dress and said in an exasperated tone, "Get me out of my dress and back into this one. What was so hard to understand about my prior statement?"

Withers had worked for the dowager countess long enough to know she would get no more explanation than that and quickly moved to unbutton the beautiful, pale blue silk dress the dowager had changed into and to help her into the far more workaday, dark brown serge dress that Withers had considered keeping for herself.

As her maid dressed her, the dowager considered if there was anything she wished to take back to the brothel with her. She would have liked to have taken some of her fine rose-scented soap and perhaps her silk pillowcase. But on further consideration, the dowager realised that, even if she could explain how she had returned from a walk with these items, their appearance in her room at the brothel might cause suspicion and chatter amongst the servants.

Once she was dressed, the dowager removed all the jewellery she had put back on earlier and had Withers redo her hair in the simpler style she had been managing herself for the past few days. Finally, the dowager again donned Margery Sharpe's serviceable winter coat and scarf and looked at herself in the mirror. Did she look much as she had that morning when she had left the brothel to go for a walk? To her eye, any differences were negligible, and she hoped that no one in the brothel had taken sufficient notice of her to think otherwise.

Descending the stairs, she saw Manning finishing a telephone call. He relayed the details of the call to her before she left the house.

The dowager had descended to her vestibule to find Little Ian waiting patiently. Though she had spent a reasonable amount of time in the large man's company, the dowager had not heard more than a few words with the untalkative giant. This time was no different; he asked no questions about why they were heading back to the brothel she had seemingly been rescued from earlier that day. Instead, he led the way out of the grand house and hailed a hackney cab to take them back to Villiers Street.

The dowager had instructed Little Ian to tell the cab driver to take them back to where they had caught the hackney cab from earlier that day with Wolf, Charing Cross station. Making the short walk down Villiers Street back to the brothel from the station, the dowager considered what she might say if questioned by anyone. She and Little Ian had left the brothel just after eleven in the morning, and it was now almost five o'clock in the afternoon. She thought about who might have seen her leave. Just before departing, she had been in the kitchen eating breakfast. The cook hadn't paid any attention to her, and it had been too early for any of the girls to be up. The dowager couldn't be sure whether or not any of the servants had been around as she'd left the house; she'd had too many decades behind her of acting as if servants weren't in the room to have suddenly started noticing them. What she was sure of was that she hadn't spoken to anyone nor told anyone what her plans were for the day.

Arriving back at the Villiers Street house, Little Ian made his way around to the back, and the dowager used the knocker to announce her return. After a few moments, the door was answered by the same maid who had greeted the dowager when she'd first arrived. The maid barely acknowledged that the dowager had returned from somewhere and certainly didn't ask where she had spent her time.

Deciding that nonchalance was the best tactic, the dowager, in turn, said nothing and instead made her way upstairs to Margery Sharpe's bedchamber. Perhaps she would be very lucky, and no one would notice her returning, and she could pretend that she had returned to the room after breakfast and had never left. Making her way along the hallway, the noise around her indicated that the girls were awake and getting ready for their evening's work. Stealing along the hallway as quietly as possible, the dowager had almost reached safety when the door of a room down the hallway from hers opened.

The dowager froze, nervous about who she might run into, but breathed an audible sigh of relief when it turned out to be Lou. The cheery woman smiled but cocked an eyebrow, "Been out 'ave yer?" Lou asked casually.

"Yes, Little Ian and I went for a stroll and then stopped for some luncheon." As the dowager said this, she tried to remember what Vicky Sharpe had originally said about Cousin Julia's backstory. She believed not a lot had been revealed. Praying this was, in fact, the case, the dowager added, "My usual abode is in Hertfordshire, and so I was curious to see more of London. It has been quite a while since I spent any time here."

Lou nodded in acknowledgement of the credibility of this story, then asked, "Where did you end up eating?"

While the question had been asked as casually as the rest of the conversation, and Vicky Sharpe had vouched for Lou's trustworthiness, the dowager was caught off guard momentarily by the question. Just in case someone else could hear their conversation, she didn't want to be caught in an obvious lie. Instead, she answered, "I do not remember the place. Some tea house that we passed. In truth, I let my man lead the way and have no idea where we walked."

Lou seemed to accept this answer and merely smiled as she walked towards the dowager and continued to the staircase. Reaching the first step, she turned and said breezily, "See you downstairs then." The dowager nodded and hurried into the bedchamber.

CHAPTER 21

During the carriage ride back to Chesterton House, Wolf made one more attempt to dissuade Tabitha from joining him that evening, "I know you feel that you are being left out, but I see no good reason for you to thrust yourself into such a potentially dangerous, and certainly unpleasant situation."

Tabitha scowled, "How many times are we to keep having this same conversation?" she demanded. "You are neither father, brother, nor husband to me. You do not get to dictate my actions. And, if Mama is to be involved, then I see no reason why I might not be."

Wolf felt as if he had been doing a lot of sighing that afternoon, yet he found himself doing so again. "As you well know, I thoroughly disapprove of her ladyship's continued involvement. My hope is that I can conduct whatever investigation I need to this evening without involving her at all."

Tabitha silently noted his use of "I" rather than "we". Nevertheless, she would not be excluded and promised herself that her disguise and demeanour that evening would persuade Wolf that she was perfectly capable of presenting as someone other than a countess.

They had been home for less than two hours when Bear returned. He found Wolf in his study, and they quickly sent for Tabitha and reconvened in the comfortable parlour used when they didn't have guests. They had brought the corkboard back with them from the dowager's home and returned it to its normal place in the parlour.

Finally, seated in their favourite seats, Wolf asked Bear, "So, what do you have to report?"

"It's Margery Sharpe, all right. They pulled her out of the Thames the other day. I was lucky her body was even still there." Turning to Tabitha, Bear said, "Are you sure you want to listen to this?" Tabitha stiffened her spine and indicated she would not be put off by whatever gruesome details Bear might be about to relay. He continued, "After some time in the water, the body was bloated and her face unrecognisable. But the body was the right height, the hair was the same colour as Vick's, and it was clear by the clothes that the woman wasn't a beggar or a street whore."

Bear looked over at Tabitha apologetically and nodded to indicate her ability to listen to a few coarse words. He added, "The body had been caught up in some old fishing nets and other debris, which is why it hadn't floated downriver or been discovered earlier. There was no identification on the woman, so, in a few days, she likely would have been carted off to a public grave."

"Did they perform an autopsy?" Wolf asked.

"No. There were no visible signs of a struggle. It just looked as if an old lady, perhaps under the influence of something, slipped and fell into the Thames and drowned."

Wolf shook his head in frustration but wasn't terribly surprised. Autopsies cost time and money. There were just too many bodies pulled out of gutters and the river to bother investigating every single one. In almost every case, the cause of death was obvious: drink, poverty, illness. Certainly, there were deaths due to the various gangs that roamed London. But as long as they were killing their own, the authorities considered it almost a public service to rid the streets of yet another thug.

"We need to go and tell Vicky tomorrow. If nothing else, she can ensure that her sister has a proper burial," Wolf concluded.

"Yes. I already told the mortuary not to move the body and that we would be coming back to collect it. Vicky will have to confirm that the body is Margery's," Bear said.

"At least Margery's sister will know for sure," Tabitha said in a tone that suggested that she realised this might be cold comfort. "Does this mean that there is no case to investigate? If there was no sign of a struggle and no visible wounds, then perhaps this was just an accident."

Wolf thought about this conjecture. He stood up and went over to the corkboard and looked at the notecards Tabitha had written up earlier. There wasn't a lot to go on, that was certain. But his gut told him that something was going on at that brothel. Perhaps whatever it was didn't have anything to do with Margery Sharpe's body ending up in the Thames, but he wasn't certain enough of that to call off the investigation just yet.

"Perhaps it was," he agreed. "But something feels off here. We need to go to Villiers Street and see for ourselves. After all, every bit of evidence we have so far is from the dowager countess. I'm not sure I'd consider her an unassailable witness. Let us see the plan through for this evening and then regroup and consider whether we plan to continue. I won't hear back from my solicitor on the ownership of the house until tomorrow at the earliest. That may tell us something more."

Wolf went to the sideboard and poured brandies for everyone, then sat back down, cradling his glass and staring into the warm, amber depths of the liquid. When he was a thief-taker by trade and relied on cases to put bread in his mouth, he had a higher tolerance for murky cases such as this one. While he had thought seriously about Langley's advice that he might continue to take on some investigations even as an earl, this case is not one he would have willingly chosen. Of course, he hadn't chosen it, the dowager had.

One thing that they all quickly agreed upon was that the dowager needed this new information as soon as possible. They knew that she would be leaving for Villiers Street shortly, and so Wolf hurried to telephone and tell her the news. Returning to the parlour, he admitted, "I wasn't thrilled when that infernal device was installed. However, I have to admit. It has its uses. I was able to catch her ladyship before she left, and Manning said he would relay the news."

After an early dinner, Tabitha and Wolf separated to confer with her lady's maid and his valet, respectively. Thompson, who seemed never to be nonplussed by any of his master's requests no matter how unusual they might be coming from a peer of the realm, spent a few moments considering what was being asked of him. "Tell me again what persona you're aiming for," the valet asked.

Wolf mused on the question, "Well, definitely not a rich earl. From the sounds of things, this place mostly caters to a solidly middle-class crowd: solicitors, bank clerks, and maybe middling-level civil servants. Apparently, the brothel, if not the gaming house, does a lively trade in men of the cloth." Thompson raised his eyebrows at that but didn't comment. Wolf continued, "However, it seems that Lady Pembroke will be joining me." Wolf paused, "As my mistress."

At this, even the normally imperturbable Thompson exclaimed, "Surely not!"

"That was indeed my reaction. But she will not be swayed. That creates other complications, not the least of which is that I must be someone who can afford to keep a mistress. And a relatively high-end mistress at that because I don't think there's enough makeup and gaudy jewellery to persuade anyone that Lady Pembroke is anything less than that. If we're lucky."

Thompson walked around his master, considering the brief he had been given. Wolf carried himself with the assurance of someone who, despite his father's reduced circumstances, had been born the grandson of an earl. In many ways, this natural poise had served Wolf well as a thief-taker. Even when the wear and tear on his clothes might suggest otherwise, that he carried himself with a certain air enabled him to deal with a higher class of clientele and witness. But in this situation, it would work against him.

Finally, Thompson snapped his fingers, "I have it. You are the dissolute, disgraced fifth son of a baron. You grew up with some wealth and a good education, but you now spend what allowance you have bouncing between the gaming hells and the opium dens. You are, in essence slumming it."

Wolf considered Thompson's words and said, "I like it. I will be The Honourable John Carmichael. Such a man might very well keep a mistress, even if it stretches his meagre purse. Would such a man wear evening dress?"

"I doubt that evening dress is the norm in such an

establishment; certainly, it would be unlikely to be required. I think we can pull a suitable look together. I have a jacket and waistcoat that I believe will fit you, which is more appropriate for Mr John Carmichael's lack of coin."

When he'd first ascended to the earldom, Wolf had resisted having a valet and had only given Bear that title because he knew his friend had no interest in pressing his trousers and tying his cravat. Finally, he had been reluctantly persuaded to hire an actual valet. Even then, Wolf had not seen the point. But after having Thompson in his employ for less than two months, Wolf could admit that the man was a gem. It was not every valet to a peer who would casually suggest that his master don his servant's attire. While Wolf might not need some generic, stiff-collared manservant, Thompson was cut from a different cloth, and for that, Wolf was truly grateful.

In another bedchamber in the house, Ginny was similarly displaying her value as a lady's maid who did not baulk at dressing her mistress as a kept woman. She and Tabitha were also trying to attain the correct modulation in her outfit. As soon as Wolf and Thompson had crafted an appropriate persona and backstory, Thompson had slipped down the hallway to knock on Tabitha's door and, in a low voice, inform Ginny of what they were aiming for.

Ginny listened intently, then closed the door and turned back to Tabitha. Quickly apprising her mistress of the plans, she added, "At least we are not trying to put together eveningwear. I don't think anything you own would pass as middle class."

Tabitha agreed. "What about my Lady Chalmers dress?" she asked. During her first investigation with Wolf, Tabitha had pretended to be a distraught mother called Lady Chalmers. She and Ginny had chosen an old, dark plum-coloured, silk walking dress. Ginny had performed some sewing magic on the dress, and suddenly, it was a little more plunging and daring than anything Tabitha would normally have worn.

Ginny went to the large wardrobe and fished in it, finally reappearing triumphantly with said dress. Looking it over,

Ginny said hesitantly, "You may not want to hear this, m'lady. But I don't think it's daring enough."

"Not daring enough?" Tabitha repeated nervously. During her marriage to Jonathan, he had enforced an almost puritanical severity of dress on Tabitha. Since she had come out of mourning, Tabitha had been experimenting with less conservative attire. Nevertheless, the dress Ginny held had exposed far more bosom than Tabitha was comfortable showing. The idea that it might expose more caused her to blush.

Sensing her mistress' discomfort, Ginny said gently, "You don't have to, of course. I can leave it as it is. But you are a man's mistress, joining him at a gaming house in a brothel. I doubt such women have much shame."

Tabitha knew she was right. And gulping, she agreed that Ginny should again work her needlecraft magic. Not only was Ginny good with a needle, she was fast. Soon enough, she was helping Tabitha out of the dress she was wearing and into the new dress. As Lady Chalmers, she had wanted to accessorise in a way that proclaimed great wealth. That was not the case this time, so she and Ginny considered what jewellery she should wear.

Considering all her pieces, Tabitha finally said, "I have a very simple gold necklace that has two strands with small seed pearls at intervals along it. It was given to me as a sixteenth birthday present as a suitably modest necklace for a young girl not yet out. If you look through that larger jewellery box over there, Ginny, I think you'll find it."

Ginny went and fished around, opening and closing velvet-covered boxes. Finally, she came towards Tabitha, holding an open box. "Yes, that's it!" Tabitha exclaimed. "It's perfect. It's pretty but not showy."

Ginny placed the necklace around her mistress' neck and then proceeded to fix Tabitha's hair and makeup. As Lady Chalmers, Tabitha had worn far more makeup than she ever would normally: a little powder, rouge and tinted lip balm. Ginny decided that subtlety wasn't called for that evening and applied all three with a somewhat heavier hand. She pulled Tabitha's beautiful chestnut hair, with its threads of red and gold, into a topknot of curls but left one long ringlet dangling provocatively over her shoulder.

When Ginny was done, Tabitha stood up and turned towards her mirror. At her first sight of herself, she gasped and turned bright red with embarrassment. Ginny's alterations had not left much to the imagination. "Ginny, I can't..." Tabitha stammered.

"M'lady, I'm sure his lordship would understand if you don't want to accompany him," Ginny said guilelessly, nevertheless saying the exact words that would stiffen Tabitha's spine.

Tearing her eyes away from her image in the mirror, Tabitha said, "Take my cloak, Ginny. I will join his lordship downstairs."

CHAPTER 22

Much to his shame, Wolf still occasionally dreamt of Tabitha in her Lady Chalmers outfit. Seeing her enter the drawing room with an even more scandalous décolletage, Wolf barely knew where to look. Correction, he knew he wanted to look at Tabitha and to drink in every inch of her in that dress, but he also felt how inappropriate such thoughts were and ran his finger around the inside of his collar in discomfort.

Seeing how discomforted Wolf was by her outfit, Tabitha asked innocently, "Is it that bad? I told Ginny this was too much. I can change."

Wolf could barely speak. He somehow managed to choke out, "No, it isn't bad at all. Quite the opposite." When he had first met Tabitha, he had considered her a handsome woman. For a long time now, Wolf had thought her the most beautiful woman of his acquaintance. But standing before him in this dress, he felt a heat pulse through his body that was beyond his control. A few weeks before, in Brighton, they had shared a sudden and passionate kiss. Looking at Tabitha now, Wolf was unsure how he would last the evening without repeating that embrace. It was taking all his self-control not to sweep her into his arms there and then.

"So, I should keep it on then?" Tabitha asked, blithely unaware of the effect she was having on the man before her. She turned her back to him and said, "I'm not sure that Ginny closed the clasp on this necklace fully. It always was a little tricky. Would you mind checking? I'd hate to lose it."

Wolf didn't move. He wasn't sure he could trust himself to be that close to Tabitha and touch her. Finally, he realised that he had no good reason, or at least none he could admit to, for not doing as Tabitha asked. And so he crossed to where she stood. She had stray wisps of curls covering the necklace clasp, and he gently swept them away. Taking hold of the necklace, he couldn't help but touch Tabitha's smooth, silky skin. The feel of it caused him to shudder. Get a grip on yourself, man, he thought.

For her part, Tabitha perhaps wasn't quite as innocent and unaware as she seemed. She had seen the longing in Wolf's eyes and hadn't been upset. She had worried that he would be disgusted by the sight of her in this dress; Jonathan certainly would have been. But the emotions she had seen play out on Wolf's face and in his nervous movements had no relation to disgust. Quite the opposite.

Tabitha's passionate response to that kiss in Brighton had surprised her. Any kisses from Jonathan had been stiff, cold pecks on the cheek for the most part. Their activities in the marital bed had been brief and passionless. So, kissing Wolf was a revelation. And her body's reaction to him was even more of one. Now, as she felt his fingertips light flutter against the skin on the back of her neck, Tabitha shivered with pleasure.

Wolf fixed the clasp on the necklace but continued standing behind Tabitha. Slowly, she turned around to face him, no more than an inch apart. Wolf's breath became ragged, and his eyes had a look that might have frightened Tabitha if she hadn't been so sure of him. He raised his hand and gently caressed her face. Tabitha could have stopped him. She should have stopped him, but she didn't.

Wolf's hand moved down her neck, his touch as gentle as a feather. When he came to her shoulders, his fingers trailed along their mostly exposed length. With Wolf's every movement, Tabitha felt her breath becoming as laboured as his. When Wolf lowered his head and gently kissed the soft spot at the base of her neck, letting his tongue linger on her skin, Tabitha felt herself undone. She moved closer to him and put her arms around Wolf's neck. He raised his head, and their eyes locked.

Neither one was sure what might have happened next. But before they could throw all caution to the wind, there was a knock at the door. Tabitha and Wolf sprang apart just as Talbot entered the room. If the always discreet butler noticed anything out of the ordinary in how his master and mistress were standing and looking at each other, he was far too much of a professional to let it show. Instead, he said, "The carriage has been brought around, milord and milady."

Under normal circumstances, Tabitha would not have gone out for the evening with Wolf without Ginny. But these were not normal circumstances. For this evening, she was Wolf's mistress. As Tabitha put on her cloak and thought about the masquerade ahead of them, she wasn't sure if she was more terrified or excited.

As Wolf followed Tabitha into the carriage, she realised that they would be alone, in the dark, for the ride to Villiers Street. She shivered in anticipation. Wolf had also realised this and, to Tabitha's disappointment, chose not to sit next to her and instead took the bench opposite. Tabitha had no idea how much he wanted to sit close to her and take advantage of the privacy and darkness to continue what they had begun in the drawing room. But this was not the time. They had a job to do, and he knew that if they were to pick up where they had left off, he would not be able to exert the self-control needed.

They didn't speak for a few minutes, each caught up in their thoughts of their encounter. Finally, if only to say something, Tabitha asked, "How should a mistress behave in such a setting?"

Wolf quietly groaned. Whatever his feelings about Tabitha playacting his mistress had been earlier, the idea of it now was unbearable. When he didn't immediately answer, Tabitha asked again, "Would such a man as your pretend persona act with public affection towards his mistress?"

Affection wasn't the word that Wolf might use. While he was at Oxford, he'd certainly spent some evenings with men who could afford to keep a mistress. On occasion, while the men drank and gambled, those women might drape themselves over their benefactor. If the man was losing, he rarely had the patience for such things. If he was winning, he might relish the usually voluptuous flesh pressed close. Wolf was ashamed to admit that he had rarely taken much notice of these women. His memory was of faceless, nameless women who were usually no better than common light skirts.

Wolf had brought enough money with him that if he chose to lose, he could do so for a while and keep playing. Until he was at the tables, he wouldn't know how well he would choose to play that evening. He also intended to find time to investigate the brothel. Certainly, he intended to pick the lock of the drawer in the study. They would be in a brothel. If a man chose to steal away with his mistress into a dark corner, it was unlikely that it would raise any suspicions. Given this, his behaviour with his mistress had to suggest such a disappearance was a natural conclusion. Reluctantly, Wolf answered Tabitha, "For my purposes tonight, you need to be all over me. And I need to be highly receptive."

Wolf couldn't believe what he was suggesting. And yet, he was lightheaded at the thought. As nervous as Tabitha was about the part she was to play, she was also secretly titillated at the prospect of an evening with license to flirt with Wolf.

The air between them was charged with a tension that was as unbearable as it was delicious. Hoping to break this tension and return them to the task before them, Wolf informed Tabitha, "As I said earlier, I intend to avoid engaging with the dowager countess if I can possibly help it. I may not have been able to stop her from returning to the brothel, but I can control my own engagement with her. To that end, let us avoid her if we can. She had described the building layout well enough that I have no doubt I can find the study without her help." Tabitha agreed. But she also recognised Wolf's naivety in believing that the dowager would be so easily excluded.

Searching for another topic to distract them, Tabitha asked, "Are you adept at any particular card game?"

Wolf shrugged nonchalantly, "I have always had a facility for mathematics. It seems to give me a certain advantage in games that aren't based purely on chance. Any game that involves understanding odds, calculating probabilities, and being able to make strategic decisions from there, are ones I've always done best at. So Faro, Poker, definitely Vingt-et-Un."

"And will those be the games on offer?" Tabitha asked.

"Let us hope so."

Luckily, the ride to Villiers Street did not take long, and before they knew it, they were pulling up at Charing Cross station. Wolf did not want the Pembroke carriage to be seen dropping them off. He told Madison, his driver, to wait for them at the station. He jumped out of the carriage and then put his hand out to help Tabitha down. The touch of her hand caused a ripple of heat to flow through Wolf. This was going to be a long and trying evening.

CHAPTER 23

The dowager went down to the kitchen for the evening meal at her usual time. Dinner that night was a quite delicious shepherd's pie that she happily consumed two helpings of. Whatever the sacrifices of comfort she had endured during her stay at Villiers Street, they hadn't been of a culinary nature. The girls started to drift down in their normal state of dishabille. It was remarkable how quickly the dowager had become used to such things. For the most part, the girls did nothing more than nod or mumble a greeting to the dowager as they then sat and quickly scarfed down food. Certainly, no one commented on her prolonged absence that afternoon.

When there was a lull in activity, and the dowager was alone with Mrs Brown, she asked as casually as possible, "Have you seen The Rascal around this evening?"

Without turning away from the stove, the cook answered, "He came in for some lunch, then said something about having some jobs to run for the guvnor tonight. Why did you need him?" The dowager quickly assured the woman that her question had been nothing more than idle curiosity and silently gave thanks that the obnoxious and suspicious man was not something she'd have to worry about that evening.

Wolf had not been specific as to what time he and Tabitha would be arriving. As she considered their earlier conversation, he hadn't given her any real details about the plan for that evening. The more she considered the subject, the more the dowager was convinced that "Dear Jeremy" meant to exclude her from all the fun. Well, he should know better than to think she was so easily put off. The dowager decided to move the armchair in the parlour to afford her a better view of everyone who entered the brothel that evening. The harder part of her makeshift plan was deciding how she might insert herself into the investigation after that. But Julia Chesterton was never one to let uncomfortable truths and inconvenient facts stand in her way.

When she reached the parlour, Lou was already in place. As the dowager surveyed the armchair she had been using during her evenings in the brothel, she realised that she would not be able to pick it up and move it. Looking at Lou's sturdy body, the dowager asked, "Might you help me move my chair over to here?"

Lou looked up from the account book she had been writing in, "Any particular reason you want to move it?" she asked.

The dowager hadn't considered a suitable innocent reason for her request. Looking at the current location of the chair, she answered, "I find its place so near to the fire to be overly warm. I would prefer the cooler air that comes in from the hallway." Lou's face expressed her scepticism at this answer, so the dowager quickly added, "It is my time of life, dear. One day, you will also find yourself plagued by such inconveniences." As it happened, the opposite was true, the older the dowager became, the more she felt the cold. But Lou didn't have to know that.

Seemingly satisfied with this answer, the strapping woman rose from her chair and performed the requested task. Now seated with a much clearer view of the front door, the dowager took more interest in what Lou had been doing. "It seems that you can read and write," she stated, not realising how condescending such a comment might sound.

Lou shrugged off any sense of being underestimated she might feel; it wasn't an uncommon experience. Instead, she answered, "I started out young with an abbess, Mother Peters, who took a shine to me. She taught me to read, write and do me sums. Marge and Vicks was at the same nunnery for many years. When Mother Peters passed on, many years ago now, the business passed to Marge and Vicks."

The dowager remembered her conversation with Vicky Sharpe days before, "And when Cousin Margery left their joint business to start her own," the dowager paused, "nunnery, you chose to go with her?"

Lou put down the pen she had picked up and looked directly at the dowager, "I was born and raised in a whorehouse. It is the only life I've ever known, and I'm not a youngster anymore. When Marge went off on her own, she told me that, being able to read and write, I was more useful to 'er 'elping with the girls and the books than lying on me back. And I've been doing some version of that ever since."

The dowager was curious about the professional advancement open to prostitutes. "Did you never have dreams of opening your own establishment?" she asked.

Lou laughed bitterly, "It's not as easy as Marge and Vicks make it look. Most whores end their sorry days still spreading their legs. That's if they're lucky enough to find johns still willing to pay 'em for it."

Whatever Lou might have said next was interrupted by a stream of scantily clad girls coming into the parlour and settling themselves. It was not much later that there was the first knock at the front door that indicated that the business of the evening had begun.

The dowager couldn't tell if the men entering the parlour, selecting a girl and then, with nary a look of shame, retreating upstairs, were the same men as the previous evenings or new ones; there was a sameness to them that bored the dowager. She had always found the middle classes unworthy of her notice. She barely found the upper classes worthy of her time. Recently, she had begun to take some interest in the lower levels of society, delighting in Mickey D and his common-law wife, Angie. And she truly had found the Ladies of KB intelligent and entertaining. But she had yet to meet a man of the cloth, the law, or of finance who wasn't repugnant in his obsequious snivelling and tedious in the extreme at his sense of his own self-importance. If anything, her knowledge that at least some of these men had dirty little secrets about visits to places such as Villiers Street almost made them a little more interesting to her. Almost.

As the pace of visitors, both to the brothel proper and to the gambling rooms, picked up, Lou became busier, and the dowager became increasingly bored. She wished she knew what time Wolf was planning to arrive. She didn't even know what disguise he planned to assume. But what she was sure of was that she was contributing nothing to the investigation by continuing to sit in this chair, barely able to prevent herself from dozing off. Looking over at Lou, busy dealing with a rather drunken and belligerent patron, the dowager stood up and slipped out of the parlour. But where should she go?

By this time, every room seemed full and raucous. Servants ran back and forth, trying to keep up with the demand for refreshments, and girls were going up and down the stairs as they plied their trade. The dowager moved stealthily along the hallway towards the room she had been talking to Kitty in. That seemed as good a place as any to start. As she walked towards the room, she noticed one of The Rascal's associates, Johnny, she thought his name was, a burly man with an ugly, pock-marked face, leaving one of the gaming rooms and heading back towards the servants' quarters carrying a large box. Curious as to where he was going, she quietly shadowed him.

Johnny went down the backstairs towards the kitchen, and the dowager followed. If he heard her, she would merely say she was going to talk to Mrs Brown. Tiptoeing down the stairs behind him, she saw the man turn sharply to his right, take a key out of his pocket, unlock a door, and then disappear behind it. The dowager wasn't foolish enough to follow him down there and instead made her way into the kitchen.

Attempting a nonchalant air, she asked the cook, "Where does the locked door outside the kitchen lead to?"

Mrs Brown was run ragged, replenishing empty platters that kept being brought down to her with fresh hors d'oeuvres. She didn't even look up as she answered, "That's the cellar. None of us are allowed there. The guvnor keeps the booze down there."

The hallway leading to the cellar was poorly lit, and it wasn't difficult for the dowager to find a dark nook to hide in to wait for Johnny to emerge. She didn't have to linger for long before she heard the key turn in the lock and saw the door open. Johnny came out, still carrying the black box. Whatever was being kept down there, it was more than just alcohol, the dowager thought to herself.

Johnny went back upstairs, and the dowager waited a few moments and then followed him. She watched Johnny return to the gaming room and slipped in after him. She saw Johnny go over to a desk in the corner of the room. A nondescript man who could have passed as a bank clerk in dress and demeanour sat behind the desk, counting money that he withdrew from the black box. In front of him were stacks of gambling chips. A large, florid man, looking very happy with himself, held his hand out and was presented with a large stack of bank notes.

CHAPTER 24

The dowager didn't know much about how gambling houses ran, but on the surface of it, there wasn't anything particularly odd about the transaction she had witnessed. Nevertheless, she made a mental note to mention the cellar to Wolf if he ever turned up. No sooner had she thought that than she saw Wolf and Tabitha coming down the hallway towards her. Or at least she thought it was Tabitha. With a painted face and an abundance of cleavage on display worthy of a brothel, her daughter-in-law was barely recognisable as a countess. The dowager barely restrained herself from comment. She realised that they were all in disguise that evening, but even so! At least on catching sight of her mother-in-law, Tabitha had the good grace to blush deeply.

Wolf caught the dowager's eye and slightly inclined his head. She took a deep breath and decided that her beratement of Tabitha could wait for another day. Instead, she walked towards the couple, reached out her hand, and said, for the benefit of anyone listening, "Good evening, sir and madam. Welcome. Are you first-time visitors?" As Wolf took her hand in greeting, she leaned in and said, "Take a look in the cellar. Go down the back staircase behind me, and it's on the right. They keep the money down there. Maybe that's all there is to it. But none of the servants are allowed down there." Wolf nodded again.

The dowager gave one more disapproving glare in Tabitha's direction and then carried on back to the parlour, satisfied that she had made a contribution to the evening's covert activities. In the time she'd been gone, there'd been a lull in traffic in and out of the parlour. When the dowager returned to her armchair, Lou sat alone in the parlour for a change. "Where 'ave you been?" she asked.

The dowager wasn't prepared to be questioned and stammered, "I was using the facilities."

"All this time?" Lou asked sceptically. "Something you ate?" The dowager, unused to discussing such private affairs, had no desire to become more conversant now and merely nodded some vague assent. But it seemed that Lou's curiosity wasn't satiated. She cocked her overly painted face to the side and asked, "'Ow long you planning on staying, Miss Phillips? Don't you 'ave a schoolroom you're supposed to be in?"

Luckily, in preparing a backstory, this was a question the dowager was prepared to answer. "The family graciously pensioned me off a few years ago," she explained.

"And so, you're staying 'ow long?" Lou pressed.

The dowager was not used to having her actions questioned thus, particularly not by someone who was essentially a servant. A tart retort was on the tip of her tongue, but she bit it back and answered, "Let us hope that Cousin Margery returns soon and there is no further need for me to stay."

Lou smiled, but it didn't quite reach her eyes, "Marge always trusted me to run this place whenever she was away. I don't need supervising," she paused, then added, "Cousin Julia."

With the news Bear's discovery of what was almost certainly Margery Sharpe's body in the mortuary, the dowager anticipated her residence in the brothel to be almost at an end. However, she realised it was premature to reveal Mother Sharpe's demise. Apart from anything else, how would she explain her privileged knowledge? And so, she merely sniffed and answered, "Let us hope that my stay will be a short one."

Meanwhile, Tabitha and Wolf had moved into the gaming room. A cloud of cigar smoke hung over the full tables as men at various levels of either excitement or desperation shuffled cards and threw dice. A few heads came up as the couple entered. It wasn't Wolf who caught the men's attention. His beautiful, alluring companion, whose charms were on such full display, caused at least some of those heads to stay up longer than they might. While men were occasionally accompanied by their mistresses, few, if any, had the sophisticated allure that this fine specimen did.

Aware of the attention they were garnering, Wolf put his arm around Tabitha's waist and pulled her close. He lowered his head and kissed her neck, whispering as he did so, "This is the moment to dispel any doubts as to why you are with me."

Any excitement Tabitha might have normally felt at the kiss was overwhelmed by her nervousness. It had been one thing to demand in a fit of pique that she be included in the evening's plans. It was quite another to now find herself here, in public, with more of her body on display than even her husband had ever seen, stared at by a roomful of men and expected to act the bawd. But Tabitha knew that if she failed now, she would forfeit the opportunity to be involved in any future covert investigations. And so, she forced herself to giggle inanely, then turned to Wolf and pulled him into a kiss.

However taken aback Wolf was at Tabitha's assertive, seemingly uninhibited behaviour, his surprise did not compare to hers. When she had dressed as Lady Chalmers, she had felt a sense of liberation in assuming a different persona and shrugging off, at least briefly, the constrained behaviour that had always been expected of her. But then, she had at least been impersonating a member of the aristocracy. But the character she had slipped into for that evening had none of the constraints drilled into Tabitha from childhood. Gigi, for this, was the name she had decided to assume, was not only allowed to act with abandon, but she was also expected to. And, for a moment, the freedom was exhilarating.

Their kiss had caught the attention of many of the men in the room, but it couldn't compete for long with the allure of the tables, and soon, every head was again bent towards a more beguiling mistress than any mere woman could be. Reluctantly pulling out of the kiss, Wolf whispered in Tabitha's ear, "Let us go and purchase some gaming chips, then get a feel for the place." Wolf planned to flash a lot of money about, enough that he would get the attention of whoever was running the room tonight. He directed Tabitha over to the clerk and pulled a wad of notes out of his purse, and exchanged them for so many chips that the clerk gave him a velvet pouch to carry them in.

As the clerk exchanged the money, Wolf surreptitiously glanced around the room, trying to ascertain who was in charge. The dowager had described Jason Bono, the man she had referred to as The Rascal. But there didn't seem to be anyone matching his description. However, he did see a man standing at one of the tables behind the croupier, who appeared to be scanning the room constantly. Wolf wanted to be sure to get that man's attention. Taking his bag of chips, he moved to that table with Tabitha hanging on his arm.

Seeing him standing by the table, the croupier asked if he wanted to be dealt in, but Wolf shook his head. He didn't intend to play yet, he wanted to observe. Wolf was not only a good card player, but his mathematical skills enabled him to quickly spot cheating, a talent that had served him well at Oxford. He watched a round of poker, which was the game being played at that table. There was a man to his left who had accumulated a large pile of chips and a man to his right who was down to his last few. That man had an air of desperation about him as new cards were dealt.

Wolf watched the croupier carefully and became increasingly certain that cheating was happening. What was interesting was that it seemed to be cheating that was benefiting the man to his left rather than the house. Was the man a plant? Finally, Wolf decided to play to see how his presence changed the dynamics at play.

Tabitha knew nothing about cards, and once Wolf was involved in the game, she didn't feel he would appreciate Gigi's attentions. So, she stood slightly apart and merely observed. While she didn't know how the game worked, even she could tell that Wolf was suddenly accumulating a lot of the little, round, colourful chips. Even a neophyte like herself could tell that this meant he was winning.

Within the hour, the pile was three times the size he had started with. Laying down his last winning hand and drawing his winnings towards him, Wolf said to Tabitha but loudly enough to be heard by the croupier and his fellow gamblers, "Gigi, you must be my lucky charm tonight. I can't remember the last time I did so well at the tables. I may have to bring you with me every time I visit." As he said this, he pulled Tabitha close again and seductively kissed her neck. Again, any sensual excitement Tabitha might normally have felt was offset by her consciousness of the eyes on them.

As the croupier went to deal the next hand, Wolf said, "I believe I will quit while I'm ahead. At least for now." He put all his chips in the velvet and then said, again loudly enough to ensure he was overheard, "Let us partake of some of that champagne I saw circulating, and then I can show my lucky charm some appreciation. I'm sure there are many private dark nooks in a house such as this." With this, he looked around the table and winked lewdly. The croupier caught the wink and smirked back; no one had any doubt how Wolf would be showing his appreciation. It was a brothel, after all.

Whatever titillation Wolf and Tabitha had provided to the men at the table was short-lived, and all eyes returned to their cards. Wolf led Tabitha to the side of the room where a tray of champagne flutes was on offer. Wolf handed one to Tabitha and then took one for himself. Taking a sip from his glass, he pulled Tabitha into his side and leaned in as if to whisper sweet nothings into her ear, "There is no doubt there is cheating going on. I should not have won what I did."

Tabitha laughed in what she hoped was a seductive manner and turned to whisper back, "Isn't the point of cheating normally so that the gaming house wins, not a patron?"

"Indeed," Wolf answered. What was going on there?

Wolf pulled Tabitha into a poorly lit corner of the room and said in a low voice, "Now is the time when we need to persuade anyone watching that we have slipped away to find a more secluded spot." Tabitha steeled herself. As much as she had secretly fantasised about what it would be like to be held in Wolf's arms and kissed again as passionately as she had been in Brighton, nothing about this evening's embraces had been what she had in mind. Perhaps, she considered, this was more akin to actors embracing on stage. As she thought of that analogy, Tabitha relaxed somewhat. Yes, this is what this was: a performance. Nothing more.

Tabitha decided that if this was to be a performance, then she might as well give it her all. Leaning back against the wall, Tabitha pulled Wolf towards her and kissed him with a passion that she didn't have to pretend. Her arms tightened around his neck, and she pulled him even closer. As the kiss deepened, she felt all the artifice fall away, and she melted into the embrace.

Wolf was similarly affected by the kiss but more aware of the need not to get swept away by the intensity of the moment; there was a job to be done. Reluctantly, pulling his lips away from hers, he said, again more loudly than necessary, "I cannot wait for a carriage ride home. You are a saucy wench who I must have immediately." A couple of men at the nearest table turned and gave Wolf looks of envy. Wolf picked up his box, grabbed Tabitha's hand and pulled her from the room with the abrupt eagerness befitting his supposed rakish arousal.

In the hallway, Wolf was struck by a new conundrum: normally, he would demand that Tabitha wait for him while he skulked about picking locks. But the narrative was that they had sneaked away together to be alone. Realising he had no choice but to keep her by his side, Wolf glanced around to see if anyone was around, then led the way to the back of the house. If they ran into any servants, he would continue the charade that they were merely looking for an appropriately secluded dark corner.

They found the back staircase easily enough, and fairly confident that no one was around, Wolf led the way down. The dowager had said that the cellar door was to the right of the staircase. Trying the doorknob of the first door he saw and finding it locked, Wolf hoped that indicated this was the right door. Bringing out his small set of lockpicks, Wolf made quick work of opening the door, and quickly slipped into the cellar with Tabitha close behind him. Wolf was sure to lock the door behind them. If one of the servants came down, they could hopefully find a dark corner of the cellar to hide in. There was no reason to cause anyone to suspect that the door had been tampered with.

Making their way down the rickety cellar steps, Wolf was relieved to find that the cellar was lit, however dimly, by gaslight. As with his cellar, this one was comprised of what looked like a main room with other, probably smaller, chambers leading off from it. At first glance, there was nothing particularly unusual about this main room. Rack upon rack held bottles of wine and champagne.

The cellar was dank and cold, and Tabitha shivered as much from the gloom of the place as from the chill of her exposed flesh. She followed Wolf into one of the chambers. This one was no more interesting than the other. However, it did have a door whose lock proved no more difficult to pick than the one before had. The door opened to reveal a large room whose walls were covered in heavy fabric and floor with thick rugs.

In the middle of the room was what dimly appeared to be a printing press. This room wasn't lit, but Wolf was relieved to find that the lamps had automatic igniters. He turned on two lamps, and the printing press was now illuminated. On a table next to it was a stack of engraved plates.

"What are they printing here?" Tabitha asked. She had heard that dissident groups often secretly printed pamphlets promoting their extreme ideas. Was that what was happening here?

Wolf could make a good guess what was being printed. These suspicions were only confirmed when he went and looked at the intricately engraved copper printing plates. "Money," he explained. "They're forging banknotes." Wolf now had a pretty good idea what scheme the guvnor of the brothel was running. Looking around the room, he saw a stack of crates with an open one on the top. Moving over to them, he reached inside and, not to his surprise, found stacks of bank notes. He took one and slipped it into his pocket.

Turning back to Tabitha, Wolf said, "I've seen enough. Let's get out of here before we're discovered." He turned the gaslights back off and locked the door behind them. They made their way out of the cellar, relocking that door. Emerging out into the hallway, they could hear voices coming from the kitchen, and Wolf quickly pulled Tabitha up the stairs to the main level. No sooner had they emerged from the stairwell than they heard footsteps approaching them. Wolf grabbed at Tabitha's waist, pushed her against the wall and began mumbling indistinct but quite carnal-sounding noises.

The footsteps revealed themselves to be coming from the same man the dowager had seen earlier emerging from the cellar with the box of cash. He had witnessed Tabitha and Wolf's performance in the main gaming room and merely passed them, chuckling.

When the man had gone down the stairs, and it seemed the coast was clear, Wolf pulled away from Tabitha and apologised. "Are we going to find the study now?" she asked warily. As much as she had insisted on being part of the evening's clandestine activities, she felt there had been enough adventure for one evening.

As it happened, Wolf agreed. He had a good enough idea of what was happening in that house and didn't feel it was worth the risk to break into yet another room. What he did want to do was to cash out his chips. He wanted to take the notes he received back with them to compare to the one he had taken from the cellar.

Holding his hand out to Tabitha, he explained that they were leaving but needed to return to the main room first. Looking at her, he said in an apologetic tone, "We need to make you look a little more dishevelled."

"What do you mean by dishevelled?" she asked, though she was afraid she did know.

"We want to continue the ruse that you and I have been intimate out here," Wolf explained awkwardly.

"That's what they all think we were doing?" Tabitha exclaimed in horror.

"What did you think we were leading them to believe?" Wolf asked, genuinely surprised at her shock at this.

What had she thought they were doing, Tabitha wondered. In an unsure voice, she muttered, "Just kissing?"

Wolf laughed, "I'm sorry to tell you, but our characters would have come out to a dark hallway to do more than just kiss." Given Tabitha's naivety about this, Wolf felt awful saying his next words, "We need to muss your hair and perhaps pull down the shoulder of your dress."

The hair mussing was one thing, but the dress was quite another. Tabitha was already showing far more flesh than she was comfortable with. The idea that she might show more was horrifying. Even so, she realised that if she were to baulk and thereby jeopardise their investigations somehow, she would prove herself to be the delicate flower she continually denied being. Taking a deep breath, she took the sleeve of the dress that Ginny had already taken apart and resewn to be far more revealing than Tabitha was comfortable with and pulled it down further. Doing so revealed significantly more bosom, and Tabitha could feel her face heat up with embarrassment. But she left the dress as it was and moved to pull some strands of hair out from their pins.

Finally, she turned to Wolf and, in a strained tone, asked, "Is this good enough?"

Wolf was almost as embarrassed as Tabitha. For all the world, she looked as if he had ravished her in the dark corner. He felt terrible for having to ask her to do this. But he now realised they were dealing with serious criminals and couldn't afford to raise any suspicions about where they'd been. "Yes, that is good enough," he told her. "I'm sorry about this, I really am." Tabitha just shook her head in reply. As if what he had asked of her wasn't enough, he added, "As we go back into the room, you need to behave, if anything, in an even more wanton manner than before."

Again, Tabitha just nodded. She clung to his arm, and they walked back into the room. As they entered the room, Tabitha affected what sounded to her ears like a very false, tinny giggle. Multiple pairs of eyes again looked up from the gaming tables. Seeing Tabitha's state of dishabille and hair, more than one man chuckled knowingly. Again, there were a few winks sent in Wolf's direction. Now that there had been an acknowledgement of their supposed activities, Tabitha felt that it was safe for her to pretend to have only just noticed the state of her dress and attempt to fix it. In doing so, she seemed merely to attract even more knowing and lascivious looks.

Wolf led the way back over to the clerk and exchanged his chips for banknotes. As the clerk made the exchange, Wolf said, "What an excellent spot this is. I am rarely so lucky at the tables. I will be sure to return." The clerk said nothing in reply but merely nodded. Wolf quickly pocketed them, even though his stack was so large that this was no mean feat. He and Tabitha made their way out of the gaming room and back towards the front door.

As they were leaving, they saw a parlour and sitting just inside the door, looking tired and bored, was the dowager. Catching her eye, Wolf nodded his head just enough to indicate the success of their mission. He and Tabitha collected their outerwear. Wrapping her cloak tightly around her, Tabitha was relieved finally to be covered up.

They didn't say much during the carriage ride back to Chesterton House. From the moment they had kissed in the drawing room earlier to the far more outrageous behaviour she'd engaged in as the night wore on, Tabitha felt quite overwhelmed with a host of emotions. A large part of her was mortified at how she had behaved, even though it had been nothing more than a charade. But it hadn't been a charade, not really. And that was what really made her blush.

Tabitha had spent the weeks since they had returned from Brighton trying not to think about the kiss that she and Wolf had shared up on Devil's Dyke. It wasn't because the kiss had been unpleasant or unwanted. Quite the opposite. But it had stirred up feelings she didn't feel she was ready to deal with.

But if her response to Wolf in the drawing room had been any indication, she could no longer bury her head in the sand. However, she wasn't ready to have this conversation that night in the aftermath of the heated "playacting" they had been engaging in all evening.

Arriving back at Chesterton House, Wolf asked, "Would you prefer to retire for the night or discuss our findings first?"

As much as Tabitha wanted to hear what Wolf had to say about the printing presses and everything else about the gaming house, she needed to put some physical space between them, at least for a few hours. Making the excuse of exhaustion, she took her leave of him and made her way up to the safety of her bedchamber.

CHAPTER 25

The following morning, Tabitha and Wolf met at the breakfast table. In a reaction to the generous amount of bare flesh she had shown the previous evening, Tabitha had insisted on donning one of her most conservative, high-necked gowns from the days of her marriage to Jonathan. Ginny had wisely kept her counsel as her mistress insisted she pull the drab, olive-green dress out of the wardrobe. Wolf also noticed the severity of Tabitha's attire but thought better about commenting.

Feeling a little more protected by her armour of mousey modesty, Tabitha felt that she was at least able to look Wolf in the eye this morning. They talked of unimportant things while they drank their coffee and ate. As if by unspoken consensus, they moved to the parlour when they were finished eating.

Tabitha took up a stack of blank notecards and a pen and asked, "So, what do we know?"

As she asked the question, the door opened, and Bear entered. "Just the man we need," Wolf exclaimed. Tabitha looked at him inquisitively. While Bear was always a valuable member of their group, Wolf's eagerness for his company that morning was unusual. Seeing her look, Wolf explained, "Bear's father, Donny Caruthers, had some, let's say, unusual skills."

"No need to fudge it on my account, Wolf," Bear said. Turning to Tabitha, he explained, "My pa was a forger. One of the best. Was known throughout London for his skills."

Wolf picked up the narrative, "While Bear never followed in his father's footsteps professionally, he did pick up a thing or two over the years." Wolf went over to a table in the corner of the room and opened one of the drawers. He pulled out a wad of bank notes; Tabitha assumed the ones he had won the evening before. Bear had sat by this time, and Wolf walked over and handed him the money.

Bear looked closely at the notes. He took the first one off the top and scrutinised the front and back. Then he did the same with random other notes from within the stack. Finally, he looked up and announced, "They're good. Really good. But they're forged."

"How can you tell?" Tabitha asked.

"Well, over the years, the Bank of England has introduced various innovations to thwart forgeries. But one of the hardest to replicate is the watermark on every bill. The ones on these are good. But they're not perfect. Only one man could do a perfect watermark, and that was my pa."

Wolf nodded, then took a folded note out of his pocket. Tabitha assumed this was the one he had taken from the cellar. "I'm assuming this is also forged," he said, sure of the answer.

Bear took it and again looked front and back, "Definitely," he answered.

Wolf started pacing the floor as he thought through the previous evening. "We know they're forging banknotes in that brothel. And they seem to be paying out wins using them."

"That's quite clever," Bear admitted. "Beyond printing credible notes, one of the biggest problems with forging money is finding ways to use it without being detected. The people my father worked for used to use all sorts of methods to try to swap fake money for real. But doing so in a gaming house where men have had a few drinks and are all too keen to sweep up their winnings is genius. And the variety of men coming in helps distribute the money with a randomness that is often hard to achieve."

"Didn't you say that they were cheating but, in your favour, last night?" Tabitha asked Wolf.

"I'm certain of it. I haven't gambled in any serious way since I left Oxford. Still, I do remember some of the other fellows, the ones who were in deep, talking about visiting a new gaming hell, winning big the first or second time they went and then continuing to patronise the same spot. Gamblers tend to be very superstitious people. Anything that feels as if it brings luck must be repeated religiously."

"Not unlike theatre folks," Tabitha suggested. During their last case, they had encountered just how absurdly far actors might go attempting to ensure good luck for a performance.

"Indeed," Wolf agreed. "A man who felt that a particular gaming house, table, or croupier brought him good luck would be sure to try to replicate those exact circumstances on subsequent visits."

"And what about when he then loses?"

"As with the theatre company, something that seems to break the supposed lucky streak is usually not counted as evidence that luck had nothing to do with it but rather that some aspect of the lucky charm had not been suitably reproduced." Wolf asked Bear, "Do you remember that gaming scam we encountered a few years ago?"

"Yes. I think I do. Weren't they manipulating the tables so that for the first visit or two, the gamblers usually won, sometimes quite big?"

"That's it." Turning to Tabitha, Wolf explained, "We'd been hired by a London merchant to watch his son. The lad was green and had been caught up in a fast set of young men, led by the younger son of a baron, a total rake, Forthington, his name was. Anyway, our client was worried that his son was being taken advantage of. The boy had been losing a lot of money at the tables. It turned out this Forthington had a scam going whereby he would befriend young men, such as our client's son and take them to this particular gaming hell where they would be carried away by early wins. Forthington would then egg them on to continue their winning streaks, ensuring they went back to the same gaming hell, where eventually, they might lose everything but the shirt on their backs. Forthington got a cut for his part."

"Were you able to stop this, at least for your client's son?" Tabitha asked, appalled at the story.

"Well, yes and no. By the time we were employed, the boy had come to his father in desperation after a final, enormous loss. He begged his father to pay the marker the gaming house now held for him. There had been threats made about what would happen to him if the debt wasn't paid."

"What did the father think you and Bear could do about this?" Tabitha asked.

"His son had broken down and confessed everything that had happened since falling in with Forthington. Our client thought the initial wins followed by substantial losses, all egged on by Forthington, were suspicious. And it turned out he was right," Wolf explained. "As you saw last night, I'm quite adept at spotting cheating at the tables. It's easier with some games than others. This lad, Nicholson, had been playing Vingt-et-Un, which is particularly easy for me to scrutinise."

Tabitha was intrigued by this hitherto unknown aptitude that Wolf possessed. "How do you manage that?" she couldn't help but ask.

Wolf shrugged off the question. He'd always found his mathematical aptitude to be more of a hindrance than a help. In school, he'd been bullied incessantly for his ability. At Oxford, there had been a professor who was interested in mentoring him, but Wolf had no interest in a life of academic pursuits. The only place his talent had provided any real help was at the gaming tables. And even then, he derived little pleasure from gambling and was not motivated enough by money to continue merely to accumulate wealth.

Realising that Wolf was uncomfortable with this subject, she returned to the topic at hand and asked, "So what did you do for Mr Nicholson?"

Bear laughed at this, "He played them at their own game, didn't he?"

"Yes, I watched a couple of hands and quickly realised how they were cheating. Rather as I did last night, I posed as a wealthy, if doltish young man. Mr Nicholson senior gave me some money to gamble with. I turned the tables on them, appearing to know nothing of poker, counting cards, and then winning an enormous haul. Nicholson used the money to pay off the debt and hopefully learned his lesson. Oh, and Bear went and had a quiet word with Mr Forthington."

Tabitha found the story entertaining and was impressed that Wolf and Bear had been honest enough to turn all their winnings over to their client. After all, they'd lived a very hand-to-mouth existence in the days before Wolf had inherited the earldom. But she still wasn't entirely clear how this story pertained to their current investigation. "So, you think the gaming house on Villiers Street is doing something similar?" she asked.

"Well, I think they're doing various illegal things. They're forging banknotes and using them to pay out winnings. At the same time, they're using the same ruse as Forthington's friends to lure in unsuspecting men and encourage them until they finally lose a lot. So, they're taking in legal tender and paying out forged notes. It's brilliant in many ways. Either way, the house always wins."

Tabitha had been busy writing notecards as Wolf spoke and now stood and placed them on the board. Standing looking at what they had, she mused, "Are we assuming that Margery Sharpe knew the true nature of the operation? Did she demand a bigger cut, and this guvnor got rid of her? Is it as simple as that? And if it is, I can't imagine how we'd prove that."

"Or get the police to care enough to investigate," Bear added. "Dead madams killed at the hand of their criminal partners is hardly high up the list of the Metropolitan Police's priorities."

Wolf couldn't disagree. It was hard to know where to go from here. Looking at the clock on the mantelpiece, he said, "We need to meet her ladyship in Gordon's at eleven, and it's already past eight o'clock. I think we need to split up. Bear, go and talk to your mother. See if she has any ideas about who is forging these notes."

Tabitha cocked a quizzical eyebrow. Wolf explained, "Bear's father learned his trade from Mother Lizzy's father. He was his apprentice, you could say. Consequently, she also knows a thing or two about the forging game. His father and grandfather have been dead for quite a few years, so I'm not sure how much she still knows about London's current batch of forgers, but it's worth asking."

Bear rose and turned to leave when the telephone rang. There were only so many people they knew who had telephones, and so Wolf was prepared to bet that it was his solicitor calling. He indicated that Bear should wait and went to take the call.

A few minutes later, he re-entered the parlour, a thoughtful look on his face. "That was Anderson. It wasn't hard to discover who owns the house, and it wasn't Margery Sharpe. He's going to send the full papers over to me, but the name he has is M. Tuchinsky."

Anticipating Tabitha's next question, Wolf said, "I have no idea who that is. Perhaps when we visit Vicky Sharpe, she will know."

"So, I'm to be allowed to accompany you this time?" Tabitha asked in a more sarcastic tone than she intended.

Wolf sighed, "I think after last night, we can both agree that my attempts to shield you from the more sordid aspects of this case have failed miserably. And I believe your presence will be of great benefit if we're to tell Vicky Sharpe that her sister is dead." Despite an initial flush of embarrassment at the mention of the previous evening, Tabitha couldn't help but smirk at Wolf's, albeit reluctant, inclusion of her in the morning's activities.

Tabitha stood and said, "Then let me change, and I will meet you down here shortly." She retired to her bedchamber, Bear left to see his mother at the Dulwich house, and Wolf remained in the parlour, contemplating the notecards.

CHAPTER 26

It was not even a full year since Jonathan had died, and yet, Tabitha reflected, this was the third brothel she had been in since then. Well, the fourth if she counted the Holborn house of horrors where the old Duke of Somerset had installed underage girls for his pleasure. She had learned that brothels were often housed in deceptively plain buildings. The first one she had visited during their initial investigation had resembled, more than anything, a solidly prosperous middle-class home. The paintings on the wall had been a little more risqué, and the silks and velvet that seemed to cover every piece of soft furnishings were a little gaudier. She was curious to see if Vicky Sharpe's brothel was any different.

In the carriage on the way to Whitechapel, Tabitha asked, "Should we continue investigating this case?"

Wolf looked at her in surprise; Tabitha had been one of the people encouraging him to continue to take on investigations, yet here she was suggesting that they end this one. "What makes you ask that?" he asked.

Tabitha wasn't quite sure that she could find the right words. Finally struggling to articulate her thoughts perfectly, she answered, "Discovering who killed the old duke ended up uncovering a great evil and rectifying it. Our second investigation involved freeing Manning and finding Melody. Identifying who murdered Claire Murphy was merely a means to that end. In Scotland, we investigated because Peter was a friend of Lily's, and his death seemed to have something to do with the criminal infringement of workers' rights. And even in Brighton, at the end of the day, our investigation was about proving a man's innocence. A man we suspected had been targeted because of the colour of his skin."

Tabitha paused, then continued, "But this investigation that the dowager countess had dragged us into is tawdry. Margery

Sharpe may have been killed because of her involvement in a gambling hell that was cheating patrons and forging money. She is hardly the innocent victim. If her shady business partner turned on her, isn't that for the police to deal with? Or not deal with as they choose? And if her death was nothing but an accident, then the activities of the brothel concern us even less."

Wolf considered Tabitha's words. The original impetus for investigating was because the dowager countess had been missing. But that mystery had now been solved. Tabitha was right, this investigation had a moral ambiguity to it lacking in their previous cases. Well, perhaps not in the case of the Duke of Somerset's murder. But, by the time they realised how well-deserved his death was, there were bigger issues at play to resolve and children to rescue. Wolf wasn't sure that Tabitha was wrong. They seemed to be in the middle of a nasty case of criminal-on-criminal crime, if it was anything. Was that the best use of their investigative skills?

But then, Wolf realised, "What if the dowager countess refuses to stand down? Are we prepared to leave her in the middle of this situation, knowing how dangerous it could be for her?"

Tabitha sighed; therein lay the rub. They were silent for the rest of the trip, each absorbed by these thoughts.

The Gunthorpe Street brothel was as inconspicuous as the Villiers Street one, if somewhat smaller and less grand. Tabitha and Wolf were shown to the study at the back of the building. The small, grey-haired, blue-eyed old woman who greeted them looked so similar to the dowager that Tabitha did a double-take.

Vicky Sharpe came towards Wolf with a friendly, if curious, look in her eye. "Wolf, how nice to see you again so soon." Vicky sized up his clothes and those of the woman accompanying him and said, "Now I can really believe that you're a toff."

Vicky Sharpe indicated that they take the two armchairs in front of the fire, and she pulled up a chair near the bookcase.

Gesturing towards Tabitha, Wolf explained, "And this is Tabitha, Lady Pembroke. The late earl's widow."

"My, my," Mother Sharpe exclaimed. "There was a time I never expected to see any toffs in my home, and now I've had three in a matter of days. Though I didn't expect you to turn out to be one, Wolf. Or should I be calling you m'lord?"

"Wolf is fine," he promised.

"Are you helping her ladyship investigate Margie's disappearance?" Vicky asked.

Tabitha rose and approached the old lady, crouching beside her chair and taking her hand. She didn't have to say anything. This gesture and the look on Tabitha's face was enough, "Margie is dead. Is that what you've come to tell me?"

Vicky Sharpe was dry-eyed, but she croaked these words out of a throat that sounded constricted suddenly.

"Yes, Mrs Sharpe. I'm afraid that is what we've come to tell you." Tabitha stood and said to Wolf, "Can you go and see if you can find a maid to bring us tea?" Wolf stood and left the room. Tabitha raised the other woman and said, "Come sit by the fire. You'll be much more comfortable."

Mother Sharpe let herself be led like a child. She sat down in the armchair and stared into the fire. "Are you sure?"

Tabitha wished that she didn't have to be the one to break this further piece of bad news, "No, we're not one hundred percent certain. That is why you will have to go down to the mortuary to identify the body. We have ensured that they will not do anything further with the body until you have been."

The old woman still did not shed a tear, though her face was pale and drawn. New lines around her mouth indicated strong emotions being tightly controlled. Finally, Vicky Sharpe said, "We were never close, you know? People always imagine that twins are far more closely bound than other siblings. And perhaps for others, that is true. But with us, it always seemed we were competing for the same small slice of pie. I am not sure if Margie would consider being the first to be murdered a win or a loss. But that is how she would be assessing the situation if the tables were turned. Certainly, if she is looking down on us now, she must be appreciating the spotlight of attention." These words were not said bitterly but with sadness for the end of any hope of reconciliation.

Listening to the wistful melancholy in the other woman's voice, Tabitha could not help by think of her own family: three sisters she did no more than exchange the occasional letters with, a brother whose life she was entirely divorced from, and a mother who she went out of her way to avoid. But this was not the time to indulge in such reflections. Tabitha shook herself out of pensiveness and focused on the woman beside her as Vicky asked, "Do you believe that she died as a result of foul play?"

"There was no obvious sign of a struggle. The conclusion was that the death was an accident, perhaps as a result of an excess of drink," Tabitha answered.

Vicky shook her head, "My sister never lost control of herself. She would drink up until the point at which she felt her control start to slip and would immediately stop imbibing. I have never known her to be merry, let alone sauced. However she ended up in the Thames, it wasn't from drink."

Tabitha didn't want to debate the point with the grieving sister. She could imagine all sorts of ways an elderly woman, alone on a dark night, might meet with an accident. Instead, she asked, "Do you have someone to go with you to the mortuary?"

Vicky indicated that she did. Then, looking up at Tabitha, she asked plaintively, "Will Wolf find the person who did this to my sister?"

This was exactly the topic Tabitha and Wolf had discussed in the carriage: their desire to step away from this sordid case. Yet, she found herself saying, "I promise that Wolf and I will do what we can to find justice for your sister."

Wolf returned just as she said these words. He said nothing but raised his eyebrows at this pledge. He was followed into the room by a maid bearing a tea tray. Realising that Tabitha had just made a commitment on his behalf, Wolf decided it was as good a time as any to discuss what they knew so far with Vicky. "Did you know that a gaming hell was being run out of your sister's brothel?" Vicky nodded, and Wolf continued, "We've found evidence that, even by the standards of such places, there was criminal activity going on; it was being used as a way to pass false coin. Did you know that?"

The look of surprise on Vicky's face answered the question. "Do you believe Margie was caught up in this?" she asked.

"They're printing the forged money in the cellar of the Villiers Street house. While it's clear that there are attempts to muffle the sounds of the printing press, it's hard to imagine that people and supplies could be brought in and out of that house without your sister having any idea what was happening. Perhaps she didn't know the details of how the forged banknotes are being used in the gaming rooms."

Vicky laughed harshly, "My sister was many things, Wolf, but unobservant wasn't one of them. If something was going on, she was fully aware of it. She would never have caught a whiff of such activity and then turned a blind eye to it."

Tabitha had to ask, "Would she have disapproved? Or is this something she might have willingly participated in?"

"We are running houses of ill repute. In doing so, we are already living and working on the edge of criminality. Certainly, at the heart of immorality as far as most of the world is concerned. Is it such a stretch to imagine taking that criminality just a little further?" Vicky asked. This almost seemed like a rhetorical question, so neither Tabitha nor Wolf answered, and Vicky continued, "I believe what you are asking is, do I know if my sister was involved in these activities? I don't, not for a fact. But she and I were not confidants."

"Who might she have confided in?" Tabitha asked. "The dowager countess talked of a group of friends, the Ladies of KB, she called them. Might any of them know more?"

Vicky Sharpe shrugged, "I have no idea. That is a group I was never invited to be part of. The chilly relationship between me and Margie was well known; you choose one or the other, never both. When we were younger, and both dollymops ourselves, we used to work alongside the one who calls herself Madam Zsa Zsa now but was just plain old Luton Laurie back then.

In the beginning, Laurie and I were close. But Margie always wanted what I had, and so eventually, she managed to break that friendship. I believe it was Laurie who brought Margie into the group. But even then, if she's still the Luton Laurie I remember, she's not someone Margie would have confided something like this to. If anyone knows, it's Lou. They were always tight. And Lou is sharp; if something dodgy is going on in that house, it wouldn't have slipped past her."

Tabitha thought about this. The dowager had only talked about this Lou in passing, but perhaps she was someone to question more closely. It was hard to imagine how they might do that without exposing the dowager's true identity. She looked at Mother Sharpe and realised the effort it took the woman to control her emotions so tightly. They should let her grieve in peace. But one more question had to be asked, "Have you heard of a man called Tuchinsky?"

"Some foreigner, I assume. Why do you ask?"

"It appears that he owns the house on Villiers Street, and so we assume that he is your sister's elusive business partner," Wolf explained.

"If he is, I certainly know nothing of it," Vicky said.

It seemed unnecessarily harsh to question Vicky Sharpe anymore in her initial grief, so Tabitha and Wolf took their leave. Wolf had told Bear they would go straight from Whitechapel to Gordon's to meet the dowager. Depending on how long his roundtrip to Dulwich took, he would either rendezvous with them there or meet them back at Chesterton House.

CHAPTER 27

The dowager had retired early the previous evening. Once she saw Tabitha and Wolf leave the brothel, she decided there was nothing more to be gained from staying up. Lou had made it quite clear that she neither needed nor appreciated the supervision. Consequently, the dowager rose earlier than usual that morning. Opening her eyes, and grateful that it wasn't so early that the maid hadn't set the fire, the dowager pushed herself up in bed. Heavens, but she was almost getting used to not being woken by Withers with tea and toast. Not that she wouldn't be grateful to return to her pampered life.

The dowager remembered that she was to meet Wolf in Gordon's at eleven o'clock, which was a long time away. She considered the likelihood that Wolf would again endeavour to persuade her to leave the brothel. The proletariat lifestyle was beginning to lose its novelty, and she acknowledged that she hadn't added much to the investigation since returning to Villiers Street. Despite her residence at the scene of the crime, she felt as if she were again on the outside of an investigation. Her movements were too proscribed as Cousin Julia, and it was almost impossible to impose herself on Tabitha and Wolf as Julia Chesterton could. Yes, it was time to leave.

The dowager rose and dressed. She realised that to support the narrative that Cousin Julia was returning to her little cottage in the country, she needed to pack the clothes she had arrived with and take the carpetbag with her when she met Wolf.

Entering the kitchen, she found The Rascal eating a plate of eggs and bacon with gusto. "If it isn't the bossy old woman who thinks she's a duchess," he sneered.

"If it isn't the dull-witted lackey," the dowager replied. Thinking that it was as good a time as any to announce her departure, she sat down, pulled the teapot towards her, poured a cup, and said with an attempt at nonchalance, "You will be pleased to hear that I will be departing this morning."

Putting down his fork, The Rascal looked at the dowager, "Is that a fact?" he asked suspiciously. "I'm curious, duchess, wasn't your plan to stay to watch the place while Margie was gone? I don't see 'er back, yet you're suddenly legging it out of 'ere like the devil's on your tail."

The dowager thought carefully about her answer, "Not that I owe you an explanation, but I had originally told Cousin Vicky that I would only be able to stay a few days. We both hoped and expected that Cousin Margery would have returned sooner. But it is clear to me that Lou is more than capable of managing until my cousin's return, and so I feel no qualms about sticking to my original plan."

The Rascal cocked his head to the side, "Why would a tough old bird like Vicky Sharpe ask an 'igh-and-mighty busybody like you to watch a nunnery? There wasn't one single better person she could think of?"

Giving one of her signature sniffs of dismissal, the dowager replied, "Perhaps she felt a close relative was someone she could trust."

"Maybe she did. Maybe she did," the man said with a mocking tone to his voice.

As tempting as it was to continue to bicker with the insolent cur, the dowager realised that within a few hours, she would be gone and would never have to see or speak with him again. Little Ian came into the kitchen just then, and the dowager stood, turned her back on The Rascal and informed her huge protector. "Little Ian, I will be returning home today. Please meet me outside at quarter before eleven o'clock." Little Ian grunted his acknowledgement of the order and then went over to Mrs Brown to get some breakfast.

Back in Margery Sharpe's bedchamber, it occurred to the dowager how early it still was, only just past nine-thirty. What would she do with herself until it was time to leave and meet Wolf? She also pondered whether she should take her leave of anyone else. It was unlikely that the prostitutes would care if she was gone; her interaction with them had been minimal. But Lou probably deserved notice that she had left. Lou was a late riser, so it would be unlikely that a farewell could be given in person.

The bedchamber had a small writing desk in front of the window. Looking through the drawers, the dowager found some paper, an inkwell, and a pen. While the stationary was not up to her usual standards, the dowager was prepared to lower herself to inscribe upon it. Sitting down, she wrote a few brief lines explaining that she was returning to the country and would assure Cousin Vicky that the brothel was in good hands. Despite almost signing it Julia Chesterton, she caught herself in time and signed Phillips, folded it, and addressed the note to Lou. She would hand it to a maid before she left.

Writing the letter had managed to occupy fifteen minutes at best. Now, the dowager remained sitting at the writing desk, contemplating what she could spend the rest of her time doing. It would be a matter of moments to pack Vicky Sharpe's clothes back into the carpetbag. That still left a lot of time on her hands. Surely, she should spend it productively and try to get in some more investigating before she had to leave. The locked desk drawer still bothered her. Had Wolf managed to pick the lock the evening before?

As she thought about Margery Sharpe's study, the dowager wondered if she had missed anything in the drawers she had gone through. Was there anything she might take with her for Wolf to look at? Given that The Rascal was lurking around in the kitchen, the dowager decided to bide her time. Hopefully, he would eat and then go about whatever business it was he did for this guvnor. She decided to take her carpetbag downstairs at ten thirty and slip into the study for one last poke around before she left. This left her almost forty-five minutes in which to twiddle her thumbs and contemplate, with greater appreciation than she might have had before coming to Villiers Street, the resumption of her life as Julia Chesterton.

While there were things she had enjoyed during her

masquerade, particularly meeting the Ladies of KB, she decided that it was far, far better to be rich and bored than poor. Not the least of the advantages of wealth was that she would never have to pack her own bags again. The dowager had always appreciated that Withers was a dutiful and loyal servant. At least to the extent that she appreciated anyone. But as she stuffed all of Vicky Sharpe's dresses back into a carpetbag that seemed far too small to have ever held them all a few days before, the dowager reflected on what an unappreciated talent good packing was. What she had anticipated taking but a few moments took her over fifteen minutes to do adequately enough that she was able to close the bag.

Finally, the bag was packed. The dowager looked at the clock on the mantelpiece; it was ten past ten. Impatience won out, and she picked up the rather heavy bag, left her room and started along the hallway. There was no reason to hide the fact that she was leaving, and yet she found herself trying for stealth. Luckily, it was far too early for any of the girls to be out of their rooms. The dowager considered leaving the carpetbag in the hallway but, at the last minute, decided she didn't want to alert anyone that she was up and about. It made sense that discretion was the better part of skulking.

Moving down the hallway to the study, the dowager paused at the door, looking around to ensure no one else was about. Then, sure that she wouldn't be observed, she slipped into the room. She set the bag down by the door and moved into the study, doing a 360-degree turn as she considered where to spend these final minutes searching. Was there a hidden safe, perhaps? But even if she could find it, she was sure she couldn't open it. The dowager made a mental note to add safecracking and lock picking to the skills she needed to add to her repertoire. While she knew that Wolf could pick locks and she suspected he could crack a safe, she knew with certainty that he would be resistant to teaching her either of those skills. But Mr Doherty almost certainly had a coterie of lock pickers and safe crackers at his command. Yes! She would ask the gang leader for instruction.

The dowager was satisfied to have resolved this question, yet it didn't help her current situation. Moving over to the desk, she was about to sit and go back through the unlocked drawers for anything she might have missed when she heard voices outside in the hallway and saw the door handle turn. Of course, there was no reason she couldn't be in her cousin's study; she had proclaimed as much. But in the heat of the moment, the dowager panicked and took refuge in the first place she could think of: behind the heavy velvet curtains. She had secretly read enough penny dreadfuls to realise what a cliché of an amateur detective she was in doing this, but couldn't think of any alternative. She barely managed to hide before she heard the owners of the voices from the hallway enter the room and the door shut behind them.

The first voice she heard was a woman speaking with barely contained anger at an artificially low volume, "I'm telling you, we need to do something about this situation."

"I'm not sure where the 'we' is in this. This isn't my mess."

"Isn't it?" the woman said. The dowager was sure this was Lou, and if she wasn't mistaken, the man she was arguing with was The Rascal. "We wouldn't be running the gaming rooms 'ere if you 'adn't 'ad the brilliant idea to introduce Marge to the guvnor. What if someone 'as got wise to the racket that's being run 'ere?"

"It wasn't me who got into a big fight with Marge just before she disappeared, was it? I'd say that if the nosy, old 'ag is sniffing around after anything, it's Marge's disappearance."

Nosy, old hag! The dowager thought. Were they talking about her? Such was her outrage that she sniffed in high dudgeon before she could consider that she was hiding behind a curtain. The voices were immediately silenced. Realising what she had done, the dowager hoped they would ignore the sound or perhaps believe it came from the hallway.

Holding her breath as she tried to remain as still and quiet as possible, the dowager congratulated herself that she had got away with the blunder when she felt an object poke her through the curtain. "Come out, old woman, and don't make a sound, or I'll shoot you."

Slipping out from behind the curtain, the dowager was confronted by The Rascal pointing a gun at her and scowling even more than usual. In her seventy-plus years on this earth, the dowager had learned the power of swearing black was white and sticking to her position. She sniffed again, this time the sniff of royalty sneering at the peasantry, and replied, "How dare you point a gun at me. I believe that I made it quite clear that my cousin's study would be my domain and my domain only."

"And so why are you 'iding behind the curtain?" The Rascal sneered.

Why was she hiding behind the curtain? She couldn't come up with one sensible answer as to why that was where she had been found. The dowager had always believed that the best defence was a strongly asserted offence and instead answered, "Why are you and Lou sneaking around and arguing? And what did you mean by 'sort her out'? Do you know where Cousin Margery is?"

"Who are you, old woman? And don't bother telling me that you're Marge and Vicky Sharpe's cousin. I never believed that story, and I really don't now. Spill your guts, or I'll be more than 'appy to shoot you," The Rascal snarled.

From the look on his face, the dowager believed he would happily pull the trigger. Nevertheless, she baited the man, "I don't believe that even you are stupid enough to shoot me here, in a house full of people."

Turning to Lou in the hope of finding a more sympathetic ear, the dowager said, "I have no idea how you became embroiled with this scoundrel, but I'm sure you were merely caught up, unwittingly, in this man's machinations, whatever they are. My bag is behind you. I am leaving this morning. As you made clear last night, you are more than capable of running this establishment in my cousin's absence, and so I will just be on my way."

As she said this, the dowager slowly started to back away from The Rascal. "Stop where you are, old woman. If you believe

I won't shoot you, then you 'aven't learned much over the last few days, despite all your poking around. I will shoot you with pleasure. And as for everyone in this 'ouse, none of them are snitches. If they don't work for my guvnor, they know what side their bread is buttered on." Turning his head towards Lou, The Rascal said, "I've got a 'ankie in my back pocket. Take it and tie it around this crone's mouth so I don't have to 'ear 'er yack anymore."

Any thought of the danger she now found herself in was momentarily superseded by disgust, "You are not putting your dirty handkerchief anywhere near my mouth," the dowager exclaimed in horror.

"Don't worry yourself, duchess, it's clean. Though, that should be the least of your worries, as far as I can see," the man said mockingly.

Any hope that Lou would be more sympathetic to her plight or more pliable was shattered as the woman went and pulled a large, blue handkerchief out of The Rascal's back pocket and approached her. The dowager considered putting up a fight, but by the time she had thought how she might effectively do that against the much larger and younger woman, Lou had grabbed her and pinned her arms behind her back. The dowager felt her hands being tied with something that felt like a ribbon, and then the dreaded handkerchief was thrust in front of her mouth and tied behind her head. Any thought for her safety was obliterated by the indignity of being trussed up like a pig on a spit.

"What do we do with 'er now?" The Rascal asked. Realising the futility of trying to talk with the gag in her mouth, the dowager ceased trying and watched the dynamics between her captors. She was surprised to note that, despite the devil-may-care, roguish air that the man usually maintained, he wasn't the one in charge here. Everything about his demeanour and tone suggested he was in thrall to Lou. Were they lovers? It was evident that they were in league somehow.

"I don't know. I 'ave to think. Give me a minute," Lou answered him in a panicked voice. Whatever they were up to, neither seemed like hardened killers. The dowager wasn't sure how she would get out of this situation, but she stored away the knowledge of their hesitancy and uncertainty. If there was anything the redoubtable woman knew how to do, it was to take advantage of the weaknesses of others.

Lou continued in a thoughtful voice, "We need to get 'er out of 'ere. I want to question 'er and find out who she really is. But there are too many people around 'ere."

"What about the cellar?" The Rascal asked. "It's soundproofed in the printing room. She can scream all she wants, and no one will 'ear 'her."

"When's Jimbo coming by to do the next printing?"

"Not until tomorrow. So, there's no reason for anyone to come down until at least tonight when they'll fill the coffers. Go and make sure the coast is clear, and then we can shuffle 'er down there."

"We can't take the chance of walking 'er down there gagged like this," Lou worried. Turning to the dowager, she said, "I'm going to take this gag out while we walk downstairs. But the gun is going to be in your back the entire time. One squeak out of you, and we'll shoot and explain later. Do you understand?" The dowager nodded. While she wasn't sure how they might explain shooting her, she'd prefer not to take the risk.

Lou went to the door, opened it and looked up and down the hallway. She could hear one of the maids whistling in the parlour as she cleaned, but no one else was around. She gestured to The Rascal, and he grabbed the dowager, turned her around, and pushed her in front of him, all the while holding the pistol in the small of her back. As he guided her out of the room and down the hallway towards the back stairs, the dowager considered her options. Might she fake a stumble in the hopes of alerting a nearby servant? But she was unsure enough about the servants' loyalties; even if someone realised that The Rascal was holding her at gunpoint, would they do anything to stop him? Luckily, she was blissfully oblivious to the possibility of putting someone else in danger of being shot.

Before she knew it, The Rascal had hustled her down the stairs to the cellar door. He passed a key ring with a few keys on it to Lou, and she unlocked the door. The Rascal then pushed the nose of the gun into the dowager's back to encourage her to follow the other woman down. The dowager had never been in a cellar. She knew she had one, of course, but, as with various rooms in her house, it was the domain of servants and consequently of no concern to her. As she noticed the dank, mustiness of this one, the dowager couldn't help by wonder whether her cellar was similarly unpleasant. This idle musing was interrupted when they came to a closed door. Lou used another key on the ring to open this door, and before she knew it, The Rascal had pushed her into the room and shut and locked the door.

CHAPTER 28

The dowager had stumbled in the dark of the cellar until she came upon what seemed to be a chair. She might be there for a while, and so decided she might as well be as comfortable as she could be. Contemplating her situation, she couldn't decide if Lou and The Rascal were hardened criminals, perhaps even killers, or merely bumbling fools who had panicked when they had come upon her. On the whole, she was inclined to go with the latter theory, though she realised that they might be even more dangerous in that case. Professional criminals would calmly consider their strategy, or so she presumed. But if Lou and The Rascal felt backed into a corner, who knows what they might do out of desperation? She did not doubt The Rascal's claim that the servants and prostitutes in the house might turn a blind eye if she were shot.

She wasn't sure how long she had sat there in the dark when she heard the door open and suddenly gaslights, which she hadn't realised were on the walls, were turned on. With the room suddenly illuminated, she could see that a large printing press took up a lot of the room. That must have been what she'd stubbed her toe on earlier. As her eyes became accustomed to the light, she realised that The Rascal was standing in the doorway with Lou behind him.

"Come on, duchess, it's time to move," The Rascal commanded.

"Where are you taking me?" the dowager asked, trying to keep any fear out of her voice. She knew that maintaining an indomitable facade was the only way for her to get through this.

"You don't get to ask the questions here, old woman. But if you must know, we're taking you somewhere we can question you without worrying that any friends of yours might come looking for you."

The dowager's heart sank. She had hoped exactly this: that

Wolf would come to search for her in the brothel when she failed to appear at Gordon's. Her only hope of being found was to remain in this house somehow. "I'll tell you whatever you want to know now," she offered, trying to keep the desperation out of her voice.

"Oh, you'll tell us what we want to know. You just won't be telling us 'ere." The Rascal cackled nastily. He came into the room, pulled her out of her chair, and again, held her in front of him while he held the revolver in her back. They then retraced their steps from earlier, climbing up the rickety cellar steps, turning onto the back staircase, and entering the kitchen. The house was still quiet, and they didn't encounter anyone. Entering the kitchen, the only person the dowager could see was Mrs Brown, the cook, and she seemed too absorbed in whatever she was stirring on the stove.

Pushing the dowager through the kitchen while trying not to attract Mrs Brown's notice, Lou mentioned something about a hackney cab. The Rascal mumbled, "The guvnor isn't going to be 'appy." And with that, he shoved the dowager out of the kitchen door, the pistol pointed firmly at the small of her back. As they walked up the alleyway by the side of the house, she hoped against hope that Little Ian had come out early to meet her. But she was disappointed to see that her large protector was nowhere to be seen, but there was the promised hackney cab waiting. Lou and The Rascal almost pushed the dowager up the steps into the hackney cab. No words were exchanged with the driver, so the dowager assumed they had already informed the man where they were going.

They drove for a while, though the dowager couldn't have said how long. The blinds were pulled down, and they sat in semi-darkness. "Why don't we just question 'er now?" Lou asked.

The Rascal didn't answer immediately. Finally, he said, "It might be best. The guvnor doesn't like surprises. 'Oo are you, old woman? Don't bother to say, Cousin Julia, because we know that isn't true."

The dowager considered the question. She did not doubt that

life was cheap on the hardscrabble streets of London. But her life had value. And not just because she considered herself more important than other people. It had literal value. The police might not be roused to action to search for Cousin Julia, but they certainly would be for the Dowager Countess of Pembroke; that might give Lou and The Rascal pause. The dowager discounted the possibility of these two being persuaded to trade her for a ransom. It was possible, but she didn't think that either of them was capable of being that strategic. Nevertheless, she decided that it could only benefit her current situation for her captors to understand the severity of the situation they had gotten themselves into.

"I am Lady Julia Chesterton, the Dowager Countess of Pembroke," she exclaimed in a tone as imperious as any she had ever used.

Lou's first reaction was to scoff, "Right, you're a countess, and I'm the Queen of France."

The Rascal, Jason Bono, was more inclined to believe their hostage. After all, he had spent days mockingly calling her the duchess. He had used that moniker for a reason; she carried herself and spoke like a toff. Why was it so incredible if she turned out to be one? And yet, as he had said just the day before, why would a countess, or a dowager countess, whatever that was, be living in a brothel, pretending to be the cousin of a madam? So, he asked this question and was answered with the same story the dowager had given the Ladies of KB, which was essentially the truth. Or at least the dowager's version of the truth.

"So, you're a grand lady in a fancy house, with servants to wait on you, but you decided that wasn't enough and set up as a private inquiry agent?" When The Rascal said this, the dowager considered how well it sounded. Yes, that was what she was: a private inquiry agent. Momentarily distracted from her dilemma, she reconsidered the wording she would put on her calling cards. Instead of the inscription she had considered the other day, she would have them say, The Investigative Countess,

Rapier Sharp Logic paired with Great Insight and Boldness. A Private Inquiry Agent.

The dowager's wool-gathering was interrupted by the Racal asking again, "Well? Is that what you think you are?"

Making no attempt to hide the contempt she held him in, the dowager answered in an overweening voice, "I do not think I am anything. When the Dowager Countess of Pembroke makes a decision, whether it's about who to cast out of society or how long sleeves should be this season, it then becomes the new reality. Your very abduction of me is evidence enough that you find my 'snooping', as you called it, to be a threat to your criminal activities."

The Rascal shook his head in amazement at the woman's audacity; she spoke as if she were the one holding the gun on him and not vice versa. "Is this what globs of money gives you: a brass neck?"

"I have no idea what that phrase means, but if you are suggesting that my authority and confidence in it derives merely from wealth, I can assure you that I know many people who have more wealth than they know what to do with but have spines of jelly. I might even say that applies to most of the aristocracy and much of the government. My authority comes from a supreme confidence in my own intelligence, abilities, and rightful dominance."

Looking across the carriage to the diminutive yet feisty old woman who seemed unconcerned that he was training a gun on her, The Rascal had to admit that she might have a point. However, they were getting off the topic. He wanted to understand what this supposed countess was up to and what she knew before he marched her before the guvnor who he knew wouldn't be happy at this situation. When The Rascal had been charged with keeping an eye on the Villiers Street brothel, the guvnor had made very clear that the expectation was that order would be maintained at all costs. The Rascal was quite sure that a well-connected, old toff poking around the place and now held captive was not what the guvnor had in mind by order.

If The Rascal could have thought of anything to do with his prisoner other than bring her to the guvnor, he would have. He glanced at Lou and was pretty sure that she would have had him kill this countess, dispose of the body and hope that no one knew that she'd been at the brothel. But Jason Bono had never been a natural killer. Moreover, he recognised that killing some mongrel gang member in a fight in the East End was a very different proposition than killing an aristocrat in cold blood.

Attempting to get his interrogation back on track, he asked, "So let's say I believe you, and you are a self-styled private investigator. Who hired you? Vicks? And since when did an abbess from Whitechapel have connections to a toff from Mayfair?"

The dowager considered this question. In truth, this back and forth was just the kind of chess match that she most enjoyed. It would have been more enjoyable if she had believed either of her captors to be worthy opponents. As it was, she decided there was more strategic benefit in the truth and said, "Yes, I was hired by Margery Sharpe's sister, Victoria. I was recommended to her by a Michael Doherty of Whitechapel, perhaps known to you as Mickey D."

These final words were her checkmate; it was one thing potentially to bring the Peelers down on the guvnor, but a gang war with the likes of Mickey D and his boys was the last thing that any of them wanted. The dowager's words gave him such pause that The Rascal almost turned the hackney cab around. But where would they go, and what would he do with this old woman who, if she didn't suspect anything before they kidnapped her, most certainly did now? In truth, The Rascal had never felt so caught between an anvil and a hammer.

Perhaps sensing her accomplice's ambivalence about their current course of action, Lou snapped, "We'll be there in a few. Don't be getting in a two and eight now. Unless you want to kill 'er and dump 'er body in the river, we don't 'ave no choice."

These words chilled the dowager. Was that what had happened to Margery Sharpe? Until then, the dowager hadn't really believed that The Rascal had murdered the other woman. He seemed more bark than bite. Perhaps for the first time, she became genuinely concerned for her safety. The Rascal didn't have time to answer before the cab stopped. The dowager was hustled out of it as unceremoniously as she had been shoved in. Looking around her, the dowager had no idea where she was. The street was bustling with market stalls up and down it with vendors yelling over each other to advertise their wares. It was evident this was a poor part of London; the street was dirty, the buildings narrow, their paint peeling. Looking at the people thronging the streets, they appeared foreign: dark hair, swarthy skins. They certainly sounded foreign, speaking in a language that seemed related to German, which the dowager spoke fluently, yet not. Where was she?

The gun still at her back, The Rascal pushed the dowager towards a tailor's shop. As they entered, a man with a long grey beard, wearing a funny little round cap on the top of his head, looked up from a piece he was hand sewing and said, "So, the gonif is back. And what can we do for you today, Mr Gonif?"

Ignoring what he was sure was an insult, if only he understood it, The Rascal asked, "Is the guvnor here?"

The tailor didn't stop sewing but nodded towards a door behind him, "In the back."

The dowager, sandwiched between The Rascal and Lou, was pushed around the counter and through the door. At first, the room the door opened onto seemed like an ordinary shop backroom, not that the dowager had spent much time in those. But when she was measured at the modiste, she occasionally caught sight of the women sewing in the back room, and a similar sight greeted her now. There were three tables, each with a sewing machine on it, but no one at them. But as they moved through the room, the dowager could see another room off this one. The Rascal gave his gun to Lou, moved in front of the dowager, and knocked on the door to that room, answered by a curt bark of, "Enter."

CHAPTER 29

The Pembroke carriage dropped Tabitha and Wolf off on the Strand, a few streets down from Villiers Street. Walking down the street towards Gordon's, Wolf saw Little Ian waiting in front of the brothel. This was the first time that Tabitha had seen the enormous man. It was hard not to stare at the scar, so long and jagged that it seemed as if his entire cheek must have once been slashed and splayed open. Wolf didn't want to attract the attention of anyone who might be watching in the brothel, so he said loudly as he approached the other man, "Excuse me, good sir. Can you help me find an establishment called Gordon's?"

Little Ian wasn't the sharpest tool in the box; he looked at Wolf in confusion, blinking a few times as he tried to consider why Wolf was asking him a question he knew the answer to. Wolf moved closer and said in a low voice, "Just pretend that you're giving me directions. Pretend you don't know me." Understanding dawned on the man's face, and Wolf continued softly, "Why are you out here?"

Gesturing down the street as if pointing out where Gordon's was, Little Ian said in an equally low voice, "Her ladyship, I mean Miss Phillips, told me to meet her here at quarter to eleven. I've been waiting for a while now, and she ain't never come out."

Wolf wasn't unduly worried; he doubted that the dowager felt she owed her servants prompt timekeeping. "We'll be waiting for her in Gordon's. I assume you're to return with her." Little Ian nodded. "Very well then. My carriage is waiting up on the Strand. Accompany Miss Phillips down to Gordon's, and I will then drive you both back to her home." Reflecting on his earlier worries that the dowager would insist on remaining in the brothel, he asked nervously, "She is planning to leave Villiers Street, is she not?"

"When I saw her in the kitchen when I was eating my brekkie, she announced that she was going today. So, seems like it."

Wolf and Tabitha left Little Ian waiting outside the brothel and continued down the street to Gordon's. Descending into its subterranean gloominess, Tabitha couldn't help but wonder that the Dowager Countess of Pembroke, doyenne of aristocratic society, was prepared to enter such places these days. Tabitha would have liked to believe this was an indication that the other woman was becoming less rigid in her judgements and more accepting of those outside of her small social circle, but that seemed a little farfetched. Wolf wasn't sure how long they'd have to wait, but they couldn't sit in the establishment and not purchase something, so he ordered two ports. Picking up the glasses, he led Tabitha towards the dark, more private corner he had sat in previously with the dowager.

Despite the relative privacy of their nook, it still seemed unwise to discuss the investigation, so Tabitha and Wolf made small talk and eventually lapsed into silence. After some time had passed, Wolf looked at his pocket watch and said, "It is more than a quarter past the hour. What is keeping her?"

After another fifteen minutes, Tabitha started to worry, "What can be keeping Mama? And how can we possibly check? It isn't as if we can knock on the door and enquire." Wolf didn't have a good reply, but his constant checking of the time indicated that he was as worried as Tabitha.

Finally, a full thirty minutes after their planned rendezvous, Little Ian appeared. "How long do I keep standing there?" he asked.

"Why didn't you return to the house to see what was keeping her?" Tabitha asked. "We cannot do so, but it wouldn't cause comment if you did."

Little Ian was not a creative problem solver; he had been told to wait outside the brothel and then go down to Gordon's, which he had done. Nodding as if he was only now seeing how Tabitha's suggestion might be a good tactic, the large man asked, "So, should I do that now? And what do I do if I can't find her?"

Wolf couldn't imagine where the dowager might be if she

wasn't in the brothel. Nevertheless, realising that Little Ian needed to be given detailed instructions to cover every possible scenario, he said, "I want to remain as inconspicuous as possible, at least for the time being." No sooner had he said these words than Bear approached the table. "Perfect timing," Wolf exclaimed. "Bear, Miss Phillips has failed to make her planned rendezvous." As he said this, Wolf raised his eyebrows and looked meaningfully at Bear, who immediately understood the situation. "Little Ian will return to the brothel to see what may have kept Miss Phillips. Now that you're here, I think you should return with him. I wouldn't go in the house, at least for now. There may be an innocent explanation, and we don't need to raise questions unnecessarily. But hang around, maybe at the back of the house."

Turning from one giant of a man to the other, Wolf said, "Little Ian, start with her bedchamber. Then check the study, and if you still can't find her, make discreet enquiries of the servants. Again, try not to raise suspicions if you can help it. But if she's not in that house, someone must have seen her leave." Both large men nodded and then left.

Tabitha gnawed on her lip with worry, "Something is wrong, I can just feel it. As injudicious, even reckless, as Mama's recent actions have been, I don't believe she would leave us here without relaying a message. Particularly as she had so recently instructed Little Ian to wait for her. Clearly, she intended to leave that house and join us at least a couple of hours ago. What changed?" Wolf didn't have a reassuring answer for her. It was worrying. When they had first discovered where the dowager was and what she was doing and had managed to extricate her from Villiers Street, he should have insisted that she remain safely at home rather than returning. Though, even as he had this thought, Wolf wasn't sure how he would have enforced such a demand.

He and Tabitha were both so on edge that Wolf went and bought two more ports, if only to give them something to do while they waited. They sipped their port, exchanging few words, each deep in their thoughts. According to Wolf's pocket watch, Little Ian and Bear had been gone for no more than twenty minutes, but it felt like hours had passed when the men finally reappeared. Tabitha was so impatient that she didn't even give them time to sit before she blurted out, "Did you find her?" Of course, if they had, would they have left the dowager back at the brothel? Both men shook their heads.

Little Ian took a seat next to Wolf and explained, "I looked in the bedchamber, the parlour and then the study. I didn't find Miss Phillips, but I did find her carpetbag." Now Tabitha started to panic. While the clothes the dowager had taken to the brothel weren't hers, that she had bothered to pack them into a bag implied that she was planning to leave with them. Would she have abandoned the bag if she had left the house voluntarily? And anyway, where would she have gone? As self-absorbed as the woman could be, it was hard to imagine that even she would wilfully ignore the plans they'd had to meet.

It seemed Little Ian had more to tell, "So, then I asked a couple of maids, but no one had seen her that morning. Finally, I asked Mrs Brown, the cook, and she remembered seeing Miss Phillips leaving with Lou and that Jason Bono fellow they call The Rascal."

Exasperated, Wolf exclaimed, "Perhaps you should have led with that!" Little Ian looked shamefaced, even though he wasn't entirely sure what he had done wrong.

"Did she look as if she was being coerced?" Tabitha asked.

"Co... what?" the large, slow man asked.

"Forced. Did this Mrs Brown think that Miss Phillips, her ladyship, was being forced into leaving with these people?"

"She didn't say," he admitted.

"Did you ask?" Little Ian shook his head. He was used to being nothing more than the brawn, and the finer points of investigating were lost on him.

Tabitha turned to Wolf, "We have no choice but to go into the brothel and talk to Mrs Brown ourselves."

Wolf surprised her by agreeing, "At this point, we have little to lose. And we can say in all honesty that Vicky Sharpe has asked us to investigate." He stood up and held out his hand to Tabitha. "There's no time like the present." He looked at Little Ian and considered what task he was suitable for. Wolf told him, "Why don't you stay here just in case her ladyship turns up? I don't want her to think that we left without her. There may yet be a perfectly reasonable explanation for why she didn't meet us on time. If she doesn't appear in an hour, go and wait at her home."

Wolf considered what they had uncovered that morning and said to Bear, "I want you to go and find Mickey D. I want to know more about this Mr Tuchinsky. Given that he seems to be running a criminal enterprise, I'd be surprised if Mickey didn't at least know the name. I want to know where we can find him."

"How will I contact you?" Bear asked.

Wolf sighed; he was starting to get used to the convenience of the telephone and found himself wishing they were installed in more businesses and homes. How much easier it would be to make and receive telephone calls from wherever one found oneself. But, even if that day ever came, it was not the current situation. If the dowager was in danger, then time was of the essence. Nevertheless, he had learned over his decade of thief-taking that, no matter the urgency, it was better to be methodical rather than act in haste. "Before you head off, come with us to question this Mrs Brown. Depending on what we learn, we may have more of a sense of what direction we're heading in."

With a plan of sorts in place, Tabitha, Wolf, and Bear left Little Ian in Gordon's and headed back up Villiers Street towards the brothel. Arriving at the house, Wolf paused. Was it better to enter through the front door, boldly announcing their investigation, or employ a bit more subtlety and go around the back and attempt to talk to the cook discreetly? Finally, deciding that there was nothing to be gained yet by showing all their hands, he led the way around to the kitchen door.

CHAPTER 30

Mrs Brown was a good cook and a practical, no-nonsense woman. She had worked for Margery Sharpe, both in her first brothel and now in this one, for many years. She had long ago made her peace with working in a brothel; feeding people was feeding people, no matter how they made their coin. And she made very good coin cooking for Mother Sharpe. She'd seen Miss Phillips leave with Lou and The Rascal, and if she thought anything of it, she put those thoughts to the back of her mind. Now, she had two toffs and a giant almost as fearsome as Little Ian asking her questions.

Wiping her hands on her apron, Mrs Brown indicated that the three should take a seat at the kitchen table while she brewed some fresh tea. Tabitha was in no mood to sit and take tea as if she hadn't a care in the world. However, sensing her impatience, Wolf caught her eye and gave a little shake of his head. He had interviewed enough witnesses over the years to know that everyone told their stories at a different pace and that it was always best not to try to force someone to rush.

With a fresh pot of tea and a plate of freshly baked shortbread biscuits in front of them, Wolf asked again, "So, Mrs Brown, you saw Miss Phillips leave here?"

"That I did," the woman answered. Because Tabitha and Wolf hadn't realised they would be doing anything more than visiting Vicky Sharpe and meeting the dowager, they had not gone to great lengths to dress down. Mrs Brown looked at them. There was no doubt, both from their dress and voices that the handsome man and beautiful woman were quality. Mrs Brown had learned over the years to keep her opinions to herself and not to ask too many questions. However, she couldn't help by comment on the unusual situation, "Miss Phillips isn't Mother Sharpe's cousin, is she?"

Wolf wanted the woman to be honest with him, and he knew

that candour on his part was the best way to encourage that. "No, she's not." He paused, then admitted, "In fact, she is the Dowager Countess of Pembroke."

At this news, Mrs Brown sat back in her chair and said in amazement, "Well, I never. The Rascal jokingly called her the duchess, but it seemed he wasn't far wrong. And so, who would you be, the count?"

"Actually, the male counterpart to a countess is an earl. But yes, I am Lord Chesterton, the Earl of Pembroke, and this is Lady Chesterton, the Countess of Pembroke." Wolf realised that this misleading explanation would imply that he and Tabitha were man and wife. However, the complexities of their relationship were more than needed to be explained in the current situation.

Mrs Brown cocked her head and asked in a voice full of questions, "And why are a bunch of earls and countesses spending time in a place like this?" she gestured around her as she spoke.

As much as Wolf wanted to be honest with the woman, he wasn't sure how much detail he wanted to go into nor how much would be wise to reveal. Instead, he decided to tell a story that bore some passing resemblance to the truth, "Before I became an earl, my friend Bear here and I were thief-takers in Whitechapel." This seemed to be the part of the story that Mrs Brown found most unbelievable if her face was any indication. But she didn't interrupt. Wolf continued, "On occasion, I still take on investigations, some of which the dowager countess has involved herself with."

Tabitha had to smile at the thought of what the dowager would have said if she'd heard Wolf's description of her participation. Mrs Brown nodded as if she understood but then asked, "But what are you investigating here?"

Deciding to speak bluntly and try to gauge the cook's reaction, Wolf answered, "Your mistress, Margery Sharpe, is dead. She was killed a few days ago."

There seemed no doubt that Mrs Brown's reaction was genuine; she turned a ghostly shade of pale, and the shock and horror in her eyes couldn't have been faked. "Dead? Marge is dead?" Then, as if she'd just realised what Wolf had said, she added, "Killed? You think someone murdered her?"

"It was done well. But it's hard to imagine how else Margery Sharpe ended up drowned in the Thames. Her sister, Vicky, swears that Margery was never one for the bottle except socially."

"Drowned? The poor lamb. What a way to go."

There was a question that hadn't occurred to Tabitha until that moment, "Mrs Brown, is it possible that Mrs Sharpe took her own life?" Certainly, it wasn't unheard of for desperate men and women to pitch themselves into the river. While Tabitha couldn't imagine it was a pleasant death, it was probably a relatively quick and painless one. Certainly, more so than some of the poisons that might be an alternative.

But Mrs Brown shook her head so vigorously that some whisps of hair came loose from her cap, "I've known Marge a long, long time. I can't think of anyone less likely to take their own life. She's always had a fire in her, a determination to come out on top, no matter what. Nothing keeps her down for long. I've seen her have setbacks over the years. But I've never seen anyone with a better head for how to turn muck into gold." The cook crinkled her nose as if deep in thought, "Thinking back to the last time I saw her, she was in a temper, but she wasn't down."

"Do you know what she was in a temper about?" Tabitha asked.

The woman laughed, "Had the fight right here in my kitchen they did. Couldn't help but hear."

Tabitha tried to curb her impatience and asked, "Who did she fight with, and what was it about?"

"Lou. And they went at it. They've known each other even longer than I've known Marge. I've always wondered about their relationship. But I know better than to meddle in their business."

Wolf couldn't help but try to dig further into what the cook had said, "What did you wonder about their relationship?"

Mrs Brown looked a little guilty, but she admitted in a lowered voice, "Whether Marge was Lou's mother. I know Lou was born into the brothel that Marge and her twin worked in as young lasses. And they had a familiarity with each other that just made me wonder. Of course, Marge may be her mother, and Lou doesn't know. But why keep that a secret? She wouldn't be the first whore to find herself in the family way, would she?" Tabitha was worried they'd got Mrs Brown off-track, but the woman seemed to realise that and pivoted back to the original question. "They didn't fight often, but when they did, they didn't care who heard them at it. And honestly, I'd have had to be half deaf not to hear them go at it, even if I weren't in the same room."

Perhaps sensing Tabitha's patience wearing thin, Mrs Brown said, "They fought about Lou's position here. It was what they always fought about. Lou felt that no matter what she did, Marge never thought of her as more than perhaps one step above the whores. In truth, Lou has taken on much of the day-to-day running of the place over the last few years. From what she was yelling, it sounded like Marge had made her promises when we came to Villiers Street, and Lou was accusing her of being all talk and no trousers."

"So, they fought, then what happened?" Wolf asked.

"Lou stormed out of here in a huff, and Marge went back to her study. It was probably about six o'clock by this time, and the girls were starting to come down to the parlour for the evening. Usually, it's Lou who manages them and the johns. But she didn't come back all evening, so Marge had to handle it. That put her in the right mood from what the girls told me. They said that at one point, The Rascal went into the parlour and asked her a question. Marge snapped at him, said she wasn't his lackey and was done. Grabbed her coat and stormed out of the house. Never came back."

This was certainly adding vital details to the information they'd had up to now, but Tabitha had to ask, "The girls didn't think anything when Mrs Sharpe didn't come back that night?"

Mrs Brown laughed, "You think these dollymops have a thought other than getting through the night without getting a black eye? Working in a house like this is a lot better than being out on the streets, better than a lot of other whorehouses as well. But that's still what it is, and it's difficult work. I'm sure they didn't give a thought to the abbess being gone. Probably collected the money from the johns for themselves and considered it Christmas come early."

"When did Lou come back?" Wolf asked.

"I don't know for sure, but she was here for breakfast the next morning. Cheery as anything, as if nothing had happened the night before. But then, that's her way. She went about her day. I didn't think much of not seeing Marge. She often skips eating in the morning, sometimes only coming in here for dinner. But by the time she didn't appear that evening, there were rumblings. Honestly, even then, we thought she'd taken herself off to cool down. It was only when a whole other night went by with no hide nor hair of her that we thought to send to her sister. Marge has worked too hard to build this business up to step away and leave it unattended."

"Were you all worried?" Tabitha asked tentatively. She didn't want to lead the woman, but she was curious how they had all felt about their employer's absence.

"The girls didn't much care. I think it's all the same to them who's running the nunnery. Lou didn't say anything until I happened to mention it. Then she agreed that it was unlike Marge to be in a strop for this long. She did wonder if she'd taken herself off to her sister's and so offered to go and visit the other Mrs Sharpe. They went back a long way, so it made sense that she'd be the one to go. And I'm guessing you know the rest."

Having gleaned more of the backstory to Margery Sharpe's disappearance than they had anticipated, Tabitha and Wolf, as if by unspoken consensus, turned to the matter of the moment: the dowager's most recent disappearance. As they had walked up Villiers Street to the brothel, it had occurred to Tabitha that they had already panicked once that week at the dowager's disappearance, which had ended up being wholly of her own making. Was it possible that this was another instance of the woman's selfishness and lack of consideration for the feelings of others? While it seemed unlikely that she had chosen to overlook her arranged assignation with Little Ian and then with Tabitha and Wolf, surely it wasn't entirely out of the question.

With this shadow of a doubt at the forefront of her mind, Tabitha wanted to get an unvarnished opinion from Mrs Brown about what she believed she had witnessed earlier that day. "Returning to the matter of the dowager countess, she was supposed to meet with us earlier and never turned up. Now we hear that she left with Lou and this Rascal character and that you saw them leave. What can you tell us about this?"

Mrs Brown was a sensible woman and usually one to keep her head down and mind her own business. Being the centre of attention for anything but her cooking was an unfamiliar but not unpleasant experience. However, she also had food bubbling away on the stove, and it was a miracle that the kitchen wasn't already full of girls wiping the sleep out of their eyes and grumpily demanding their first meal of the day. Her dedication to her culinary arts won out over any desire to string her story and time in the spotlight out, and she answered crisply, "There is not much to tell. I was at the stove stirring the porridge, and I heard low voices behind me. I couldn't catch much of what they were saying, but as they opened the kitchen door to leave, I turned my head and caught sight of Miss Phillips, I mean her ladyship, leaving with Lou and The Rascal."

"Did it seem as if she was leaving willingly?" Wolf asked.

"At the time, I didn't think much of it. But now that you ask, there was something awkward about how they were bunched together as if The Rascal was holding her in front of him forcibly."

"I just have one more question, Mrs Brown," Wolf said, "What did you catch of what they said?"

Mrs Brown thought for a moment. She tried to block out most of the conversations she overheard in her kitchen; they were too many and, for the most part, too foolish to waste her time paying attention to. "If I think back, what I remember is less what they said and more the desperation in their voices. Not her ladyship, she didn't say anything." That alone was enough to cause Tabitha and Wolf to be suspicious; the dowager was not known for keeping her own counsel. Mrs Brown continued, "All I heard clearly was Lou saying she hoped the hackney cab was waiting out front. Then The Rascal mumbled something that I couldn't understand, though I did hear him say something about the guvnor."

That raised one more question Tabitha wanted to ask Mrs Brown, "Do you have any idea who this guvnor is that Mrs Sharpe has gone into business with?"

"No idea at all. All I know is that just over a year ago, she informed us all that we were moving to a new, fancy place. We turned up here, and it became obvious that the house would have gaming rooms as well as our girls. Then The Rascal and some of the other lads began hanging around and mentioning this guvnor. But it could be anyone, as far as I know." She paused, thinking for a few moments before she added, "One thing, and I'm not sure I ever really put this together before, but from a few comments made over time, I've always had the feeling that Lou knows this guvnor personally. Nothing I can really put my finger on, but just a general tone of familiarity whenever the guvnor comes up in conversation."

Mrs Brown had no more to share. However, they had learned far more than expected from the cook and thanked her profusely. Bear had waited for them outside the kitchen door. Wolf quickly brought him up-to-date with what they'd learned. "I believe that the dowager countess has been taken by force to a different location. I can only imagine that the people who have taken her have weapons; it's hard to imagine how else they could compel her to go with them. If we are to go after them, we must be similarly armed. There's a change of plans; I want you to return to Chesterton House and get our weapons. I will go to talk with Mickey D. The odds are that wherever they've taken her ladyship is likely nearer to Whitechapel than to Mayfair, so I will leave word with Mickey about where you should meet me. I will size up the place while we wait for you."

Tabitha heard all this and knew full well what Wolf intended for her, and as she suspected, he turned and said, "Tabitha, return to Chesterton House. This is far too dangerous a situation for you."

Would they never stop having this same debate repeatedly? "And why am I to be relegated to the sidelines?" she asked caustically.

"Because weapons are involved, and I don't need the added distraction of worrying about you," Wolf answered.

"I am an excellent markswoman," Tabitha said, thrusting her chin forward indignantly. "My father taught me how to shoot when I was young."

"Tabitha, firing at clay pigeons and ducks in the country is very different than shooting a pistol at a person."

Tabitha was as offended by the condescension in Wolf's tone as by his assumption that she could be of no use in the dowager's rescue. "I know how to shoot a pistol," she informed him. "In fact, I'm a very good shot. Again, my father taught me."

Wolf wanted to ask why Tabitha's late father had decided to teach his youngest daughter such a skill, but that was a conversation for another day. Instead, he accepted the inevitability of her inclusion in the rescue plan and said to Bear, "Bring my Bulldog for her ladyship. It's better suited for smaller hands."

CHAPTER 31

The carriage ride to Whitechapel was tortuous for Tabitha. They had already lost time waiting for the dowager in Gordon's and then talking with Mrs Brown. Even as she nervously bit at her cuticles, there was a little voice in the back of her head that kept asking why she cared so much. Even when Tabitha had been married to Jonathan, the dowager had been unkind, often cruel. The more time that had passed without Tabitha producing an heir, the more cutting and hurtful the comments had become. Because it was obvious that Jonathan did not care to defend his wife, her mother-in-law had full rein to berate Tabitha, already heartbroken about her inability to bear a child.

After Jonathan's death, Tabitha had been shunned by society at the dowager's behest, and even though that stricture seemed to have been eased, the woman never missed an opportunity to disapprove of everything from Tabitha's clothes to her continued presence at Chesterton House. Of course, she couldn't forget that the dowager was hardly an innocent victim of circumstance. She had taken on this case in secret with no thought for whom she might worry by disappearing. Then, when Wolf had found her, she had insisted on returning to the brothel against Tabitha and Wolf's better judgement. Yet, despite all of this, Tabitha worried for the woman. Perhaps it was because if she and Wolf didn't worry about her, who would? The dowager's relationship with her daughters was tenuous at best - again, mostly through fault of her own - and it was hard to imagine any of the woman's so-called friends truly caring.

All attempts to rationalisation came back to this one fact: Tabitha was worried. Very worried. Finally, the seemingly endless carriage ride came to an end. On all his prior visits back to Whitechapel, Wolf had eschewed the grand Pembroke carriage with its gold insignia and walked or taken a hackney cab. He had also always turned up in his thief-taking clothes. But time was of the essence, so he must deal with whatever fallout there might be when people from his old life saw him turning up with all the trappings of wealth and power.

Even Angie's eyes widened in surprise to see Wolf with Tabitha and the carriage behind them as she opened the door. "Wolf, this is a surprise," she admitted. Wolf didn't have to ask if the surprise was that he was there or how he was there. "I'm assuming you want Mick. You're lucky to catch him in. He'd just popped back for a bit of lunch. I made sandwiches. I can bring some through if you'd like." Wolf's first instinct was to decline, but it was well past lunchtime, and they hadn't eaten since an early breakfast, so he gratefully accepted.

Tabitha and Wolf had picked Little Ian up from Gordon's on their way from the brothel and he'd sat up on top for the carriage ride. Now, he descended and greeted Angie. "Go out to the kitchen, lad and get yourself some food," she said.

This wasn't Tabitha's first time in Mickey D's house. She'd accompanied Wolf, disguised as a young man, on their first investigation, so she knew where they were going as they followed Angie to the parlour. Mickey D was in an armchair, perusing one of the daily rags when they entered. He looked up surprised and said affably, "Wolf, I wasn't expecting to see you back so soon."

Wolf answered less affably, "Well, perhaps if you had been candid with me when I was last here, I wouldn't be."

"And you've brought the charming Lady Pembroke with you. I'd say welcome to my home, but I believe it's not your first time here," he said with a wink. Tabitha blushed a little as she took a seat. Wolf had assured her that her disguise that night had not been as good as she believed, and it seemed he had been correct.

Mickey D continued, "Now, when am I ever anything less than candid?"

Wolf barked, "Ha! Do you really want me to answer that? Let's start with the fact that you told me that you knew nothing of what her ladyship was investigating nor where she had gone when she left here. But we now know that not only did you know where she was going, but you sent a note on ahead suggesting that Vicky Sharpe hire the dowager countess to investigate her sister's disappearance."

Wolf said this last part triumphantly as if he had backed Mickey D into a corner and now expected the man to be suitably chagrined. Instead, the gang leader smiled and said in an infuriatingly unperturbed tone, "So what if I did? Lady P's not a child. If she didn't choose to tell you, why would I?"

"Because by the time we came to see you, she had been missing for two days," Wolf exclaimed.

By this point, Angie had brought in a platter of sandwiches and a plate of her famous ginger biscuits and had put them on the table in front of them. Mickey D reached for one of the biscuits, took a bite and savoured the buttery, spicy taste, then said, "Just because you didn't know where she was, didn't mean she was missing. I assumed that if she'd wanted you involved in her investigation, she would have asked you. She did tell me that she's now conducting investigations on her own, and I say, good for her!"

"Good for her? For heaven's sake, man, she's an elderly aristocrat. What on earth made you believe that this insanity on her part was something to encourage?"

Mickey sat up straight in his chair, all joviality gone from his face, "She's quick as a cricket is Lady P. I remember when a young, green toff appeared in Whitechapel about ten years ago and wanted me to give him a chance with an investigation. Remember that, Wolf?" By the look on Wolf's face, Tabitha determined that he both knew precisely what Mickey D was referring to and wasn't well pleased at the reminder. Mickey continued, "If Lady P wants to be a private investigator, I say good on her. And I happened to have been asked not long before if I could help Vicks Sharpe track down Marge."

Tabitha could see that the bickering between the two men was getting them nowhere. Instead, she said, "We found her ladyship residing in Margery Sharpe's brothel on Villiers Street.

A building that is owned by an M. Tuchinsky." Seeing Mickey D's eyebrows raise at this news, she asked, "You know the name?"

"Runs one of the Jewish gangs out of Brick Lane in Spitalfields. We've had some interactions over the years. But those gangs tend not to dabble in the same trades that I do. More counterfeiting, protection rackets, some blackmail, that sort of thing."

Wolf overlooked the fact that he knew that Mickey ran his own protection racket amongst the Irish population of Whitechapel. Instead, he asked, "Do you know where we can find this Tuchinsky?"

"Depends why you want to know. I don't need to start a gang war by ratting the Jews out to the likes of you," Mickey answered.

Tabitha replied, "One of this Tuchinsky's thugs, known as The Rascal, has kidnapped Lady Pembroke. The last they were seen, this Rascal fellow was overheard telling his accomplice, Lou, that they were going to see the guvnor. Given that we know that Tuchinsky owns that house and was running a gambling den out of it, complete with counterfeit money for the winnings, it seems safe to assume that is where they've taken her ladyship."

Mickey D whistled, "So that's the operation they are running out of Marge's place? I'd heard rumours of the gambling but was surprised to hear that Tuchinsky's band was doing something so, relatively speaking, above board." Tabitha was surprised to hear Mickey refer to the gaming hell as if it was a legitimate business. Still, relatively speaking, compared to the gang's other activities, perhaps it could be viewed that way. "And you say that low-life Bono, who likes to call himself The Rascal, has taken Lady P?"

"Yes, we don't know the details, but there seems no doubt that she was taken against her will. From what we know, she was taken some hours ago. So, time is of the essence. Anything you can tell us would be greatly appreciated," Tabitha pleaded.

Mickey stood up, "I'll do more than tell you. I'll take you. We'll settle this one gang leader to another. I swore to Lady P that she could walk these neighbourhoods without anyone touching a hair on her head, and I see no reason that promise shouldn't extend beyond Whitechapel." He stopped, "I'm surprised you're not planning to take Bear."

"We are. He's gone back to Chesterton House to get the guns. We don't know what we'll be walking into it."

Mickey D nodded his approval, but he also looked over to Tabitha inquisitively.

Seeing his look and understanding what underlay it, Wolf shrugged and said resignedly, "Apparently, she can use a pistol, and she insists on coming with."

Mickey laughed, "If there's no time to waste, let's use my guns." He went to the door and called, "Ang, can you bring your Deringer? Lady Pembroke here is going to borrow it." Returning to the room, he nodded approvingly at Tabitha, "A woman should always be able to defend herself. Whoever taught you to shoot had the right idea. Angie's pa taught her when she was a lass."

"My father taught me," Tabitha said, throwing Wolf a triumphant look.

Wolf knew he had lost this battle but couldn't help taking one last shot, "You know, it's one thing to ensure that a woman can defend herself and another to encourage her to put herself in harm's way." But he knew he was talking into the wind for all anyone paid attention.

While they waited for Angie to bring her gun, Mickey went to a drawer, unlocked it with a key on a chain at his belt, and pulled out four guns. At least Tabitha thought they were all guns. Two of them were very bizarre looking, with the handles seemingly brass knuckle-dusters. As Mickey D held one, he made a sudden action, and a knife blade sprang out. Seeing her bemusement, he explained, "It's an Apache. It doesn't have the best range, but as you can see, it's three weapons in one. Handy little thing if we suddenly find ourselves in hand-to-hand combat."

Hand-to-hand combat? Is that what they were walking into? For just a moment, Tabitha questioned whether she should be one of the rescue party.

Mickey continued, "And it's a bruiser at short range." He handed one to Wolf, folded the other back up, and put it in his pocket. Then, handing over one of the other guns, he said, "This is what the British Army uses. It's a Webley. Lovely instrument."

"Do I want to know how you have guns made for the British Army?" Wolf asked. His answer was a deep chuckle.

"I assume you know how to handle these, Wolf," Mickey said. Wolf nodded. He hadn't used a Webley before, but looking it over, there didn't seem to be anything particularly unusual about it. He placed the Webley in the waistband of his trousers and the Apache in his coat pocket.

Angie returned and handed Tabitha a compact gun with a mother-of-pearl handle. She also handed her bullets. "It's a single-shot barrel, so make the shot count," she advised, handing over additional bullets. Turning to Mickey, she asked, "Where are you going?"

"Brick Lane, the Jew, Tuchinsky, has Lady P."

"Do you need some of the boys to go with you?" she asked in a concerned voice.

"Nah, we'll be fine. Better to not storm in there with a bunch of hotheads. That's the surest way to a gang war. We'll take Little Ian with us, and Bear will be here at some point. Tell him where we've gone. It's the tailor's shop halfway up Brick Lane. Tell him we'll be in the back." Mickey stopped and thought, "Tell him not to go through the front. If memory serves me correctly, there's an alleyway running beside the store. If we get into trouble, we may need him to have the element of surprise."

There was nothing about what they were about to do that Wolf was happy exposing Tabitha to. Despite her protestations that she knew how to shoot, she was not prepared for gangs and guns in Spitalfields.

It seemed incongruent to take the Pembroke carriage to the slums of Spitalfields to ambush a gangster. Certainly, under other circumstances, Wolf could only imagine what the dowager would say about such an appalling breach of etiquette. But it was the most expedient way to travel, and they would have to deal with the inevitable curiosity they would cause when they rattled down Brick Lane.

CHAPTER 32

Since her introduction to Mickey D and their surprising mutual recognition of a kindred spirit, the dowager considered herself quite au fait with London's seedy underworld. Certainly, she prided herself on having first-hand knowledge that her society cronies of bored matrons could not even imagine. Nevertheless, even she was unprepared for what greeted them when The Rascal opened the door. There were a few swarthy men standing or sitting around, one or two wearing the same little round cap the tailor had worn. And they were all very clearly in thrall to the person who sat in a large, brown leather chair, feet up on the table, cigar in hand.

While this person was dressed quite sharply in a suit and cravat, it was evident that this was a woman, not a man. Perhaps forty or a little older, this woman had her curly hair cut in a bob just off her shoulders. Surprisingly, she was rather pretty. Like most of the men in the room, her hair was dark, but her eyes were a startling shade of blue.

The Rascal had doffed his hat on entering and now clutched it to his chest while he almost genuflected. "Rav Tuchinsky, I'm sorry to bother you, but we 'ave a bit of an issue that I could use your guidance on."

The woman took her cigar out of her mouth and waved him in. "What is it, Lobbus?" she asked mockingly. But as he entered the room and the woman caught sight of Lou with the dowager in front of her, she became very confused and asked, "Who's this alter kaker you've brought with you?"

Lou pushed the dowager into the room. Deciding she needed to take control of the situation immediately, the dowager announced, "This old woman is Lady Julia Chesterton, the Dowager Countess of Pembroke." While the dowager was still dressed in Vicky Sharpe's clothes and so hardly looked the part, her voice and her carriage made this claim less absurd than it might have been. The dowager continued, "To whom am I speaking?"

Taking another puff of her cigar, the woman said, "Miriam Tuchinsky, at your service, countess. Take a seat." Her sarcastic tone suggested she wasn't entirely sold on the dowager's identity. Thinking back to the dowager's words, Miriam asked, "How do you know Yiddish?"

"If that is what you were speaking, I don't. But I am fluent in German, and it seems there is an etymological connection between the two languages."

Miriam laughed, "I don't know what those big words are, but yes, there's a lot of overlap between German and Yiddish, or so I've been told."

"Are you of German heritage then?" the dowager asked.

"No, my bubbe and zaide emigrated from a shtetl in Poland when my papa was a young man. He was unmarried and so came with them." She swept her arm to take in the tailor shop, "All this was my zaide's and then my papa's."

"I take it you are not a tailor by trade," the dowager asked dryly.

Instead of a response, Miriam turned to The Rascal and said harshly, "I'm busy, Lobbus. What is this problem that you need the Rav to solve for you?"

The Rascal briefly explained how the dowager had shown up at the brothel claiming to be Margie and Vicky Sharpe's cousin. He then made a lot of how he was suspicious of her from the start, that she was asking a lot of questions and poking around where she did not need to be. The dowager's natural inclination was to interrupt and argue every point the man made. However, looking carefully at Miriam's face as she listened to The Rascal's story, the dowager realised that she was better off letting the man dig his own grave with his guvnor.

When The Rascal had finished, Miriam didn't say anything for a few moments. She merely puffed on her cigar and stared at her minion. Finally, she spoke in a terrifyingly calm, cold voice, "So, let me get this straight. You suspected that the countess here was not who she claimed to be, and instead of reporting this back immediately, you pair of idiots," and with this she waved her cigar towards Lou, "decided to kidnap this woman and then leave a trail that leads back to me? Is that about it?"

The Rascal stammered, "There's no trail; nothing ties this back to you."

"So, no one saw you leave the house with the countess?" Miriam shot back. Whatever lies The Rascal was about to tell, his face gave away the truth of his realisation that Mrs Brown had likely seen and perhaps overheard them. "Exactly!" Miriam said without letting him speak the falsehood.

Turning to the dowager, Miriam asked, "Let's say I believe you are who you say you are, as unbelievable as it sounds. Why were you living in a brothel pretending to be Marge's cousin?"

The dowager then quickly gave her now standard explanation; she was a private inquiry agent and had been hired by Vicky Sharpe to investigate her sister's disappearance.

"And what have you found?"

The dowager watched Miriam's reaction carefully as she said, "I have discovered that Margery Sharpe is dead. Murdered. Pushed in the Thames."

If the other woman's reaction was pretence, she was a very good actress. She seemed genuinely shocked to hear this news. "Marge is dead? Are you sure?"

"Well, an associate of mine did a preliminary identification of the body, and Margery's sister will be going to do so formally. But my associate had a high degree of certainty that he was correct." The dowager paused, "In addition, it has become clear to me that there is more going on than merely prostitution and gaming. I suspect that Margery was killed because she in some way discovered or threatened this business."

At this, Miriam took her feet off the table, leaned forward, and said in a very nasty voice, "Are you accusing me of killing her?"

The dowager realised that rather than defusing the already dangerous situation, she was throwing fuel on the fire. Nevertheless, she looked the other woman dead in the eye and answered, "Well, that was my assumption before meeting you." She added quickly, "Oh, I never thought you did the deed yourself, but I did believe that The Rascal or some other minion killed her on your command."

Miriam Tuchinsky was the daughter of poor immigrant Jews and the granddaughter of Polish peasants. She was born and raised in a quarter of a mile radius from Brick Lane. Unlike Mickey D, she didn't make her money stealing from the high and mighty, so her knowledge of and interactions with London's high society were almost non-existent. While the distance, as the crow flies, between Brick Lane and Grosvenor Square was a mere three miles, it could have been three hundred. The dowager countess and the world she lived in was a foreign country to Miriam. However, if she'd been asked what she imagined London's upper class to be like, the physically frail-looking little old lady with the nerves of steel and a ferocious glare to match her own would not have been her description.

There was a long silence after the dowager's proclamation, and everyone in the room held their breath for what would come next. Then, Miriam slapped her hand down hard on the table and laughed, "You have some pluck for a fancy alter kaker. I'm glad to hear that you no longer believe that I killed Margery. Dare I ask why?"

"I am a very good judge of character and read people well. You were clearly shocked to hear of the death. I do not doubt that if you were responsible, you would have no qualms about owning your role," the dowager explained in a calm voice. "This leads me to assume that your lackey here did so without permission."

The Rascal wasn't always the quickest on the uptake, but he immediately recognised that he was being set up as the murderer. "'Ey, guvnor, 'ang on a minute. I didn't 'ave anything to do with killing Marge. I swear."

As he said this, his eyes involuntarily shifted to look at Lou. Miriam followed his glance. Realising what he'd done, The Rascal quickly looked away, but his guvnor had seen enough in that moment. "You didn't kill her, Lobbus. But if I'm not mistaken, you know who did. And then you covered up for your sister here. How long did you think you could keep this from me?"

Sister? Did she hear that correctly, the dowager thought. Lou and The Rascal were siblings. She'd have never guessed. But what did this mean?

Realising that his eyes had given him away, The Rascal stammered, "Guvnor, she thought she was doing you a favour. Didn't you, Lou?"

Lou looked too terrified to speak. The older sibling, she was used to leading her brother Jason by his nose. She was beginning to realise the full import of what she had led him into this time. She started to stammer something, but Miriam held up a warning hand, "Before you leap into your lies, I just want to remind you, well remind you both, that you came to me, Lobbus, with the idea of working with Margery Sharpe. In fact, if I remember correctly, you told me then that the association was through your sister, and because of that, you could personally vouch for the benefits such a partnership would bring. I believe your words were," Miriam paused, then said with a rather theatrical flourish, "'My sister has my back, and I have yours.' Or am I wrong?"

The Rascal didn't look as if he would tell Miriam she was wrong if she said the sky was green; he certainly wasn't going to contradict her version of events. Miriam turned her attention back to the dowager and explained, "Margery Sharpe knew full well what our partnership entailed." It seemed she would be elucidating no further on the details of that partnership. Miriam shook her head in exasperation, "This was not what I wanted to spend my day dealing with." Gesturing to a large, meaty-looking man standing mutely in the corner of the room, she commanded, "Take the Lobbus and his trouble-maker of a sister, nebech, and lock them up for now." This command was quickly followed, and Lou and The Rascal were led away quietly. It seemed they'd decided that subservience was the best tack to take.

Turning back to the dowager, Miriam smacked her lips on her cigar as she considered the situation she found herself in. While the woman in front of her wasn't dressed as she'd expect a countess to be, and she still didn't understand why someone who had wealth and status would choose to scrabble around in the muck, playing at private investigator, nonetheless, she believed that the woman was who she claimed to be. As incredible as the claim was on its surface, the woman had an air about her that somehow made it wholly believable.

For her part, the dowager was fascinated by the female gang leader. Prior to this meeting, she had believed that the Ladies of KB were the most interesting women she'd ever met. But this Miriam Tuchinsky might be even more so. While dressed as a man, she didn't seem to be going to any great lengths to disguise herself as a man. Yet, from her cigar smoking to her posture to her command of her men, there was something, if not masculine, certainly not feminine about Tuchinsky. It was as if she had discovered a new way to move through the world as a woman. The dowager knew a thing or two about imposing her will in a world so thoroughly dominated by and set up for the benefit and ease of men. However, for the most part, she had achieved her goals as an iron fist in a silk glove. It had never occurred to her that she might swap her gowns for trousers and meet men on a more level playing field.

The dowager did not support the suffragette movement. This was not because she felt that women shouldn't have the vote, but rather because she didn't even believe all men should. Julia Chesterton had a very low opinion of most people and was horrified that most men who owned property or were tenants were deemed qualified to choose who should govern her. The idea that this privilege could be extended even further was horrifying. But for the first time in her life, a thought flitted through her mind with the fragility and lightness of a butterfly wing that perhaps women such as the one before her were more worthy of a vote than most men the dowager knew.

"So, what am I going to do about you?" Miriam asked in a

genuinely perplexed tone.

CHAPTER 33

As the Pembroke carriage arrived in Spitalfields, Wolf asked Mickey D, "Do we just pull up outside? Will the carriage hurt or help this situation?"

Mickey D considered the question. He didn't have a lot of dealings with the Tuchinsky gang professionally, and the Irish and Jewish gangs didn't mix socially. The Jews of the East End of London kept to themselves for the most part. From what he knew, they did everything they could to keep themselves apart; their meat had to be butchered by their own people in some special way, they'd only drink their own wine, even prayed on a Saturday instead of a Sunday like regular people. But he also knew that Tuchinsky was no fool and could be ruthless on occasion. Their domains of Whitechapel and Spitalfields were adjoining, and so it was inevitable that there were the occasional spats over turf. For the most part, Mickey had taken some consolation in the thought that the Jews were even more despised by Londoners than the Irish. One thing Mickey D was sure of: while there were some Irish in the police force, he doubted there were any Jews. That was an advantage he never took for granted.

Finally, making up his mind, Mickey D replied, "Let's give them the full-on toff experience and pull up outside."

During the short ride from Whitechapel, Tabitha and Wolf had filled Mickey D in on what they knew or thought they knew about the activities at the Villiers Street house. When they were done, Mickey D whistled appreciatively, "I wish I'd thought of that diddle. You win when the sports lose, and when they win. And the brothel is just another way to lure the punters in and keep them coming. Brilliant. I always knew Tuchinsky was sharp, but even so."

It had crossed Mickey D's mind to warn Tabitha and Wolf that M. Tuchinsky was, in fact, female, but he decided it would be far more amusing to let them figure that out for themselves. While he hadn't argued with the need to arm themselves for the visit, he didn't anticipate any real need. There was a certain honour amongst thieves that the various gang leaders of London informally adhered to when they weren't involved in an acknowledged inter-gang war.

Tabitha had been eagerly looking out of the carriage windows during their drive from Whitechapel to Spitalfields. While there was much that was similar about the two neighbourhoods, now they were in Brick Lane, she was fascinated by the very different feel that the immigrants of this neighbourhood had brought to their adoptive city. There were sights, sounds and some marvellous smells. Tabitha knew nothing more about Jews than she had gleaned from The Merchant of Venice. She had no idea how much of a caricature Shylock was. There were certainly men walking through the Brick Lane market with some physical characteristics usually associated with Shakespeare's famous Jew. But there were also men, women and children who wouldn't look out of place in any other part of London.

Wolf descended and then gave Tabitha his hand to guide her down. There was no doubt that their carriage had caused quite a commotion. Still, even as they stared, pointed and made their curiosity evident, people went about their business, haggling over chickens, squeezing vegetables, and trying to sniff out the day's bargains. Wolf instructed Madison, his driver, to wait. He didn't share Mickey D's confidence and wanted to be sure they could make a quick getaway if necessary.

Mickey D had considered whether they were better off ambushing Miriam Tuchinsky and her men. What would be gained by walking in the front door and announcing themselves? Still, an ambush was the easiest way to start a gunfight. While he was never one to shy away from confrontation where necessary, Mickey D hadn't lived to middle age without realising that hot headedness rarely solved anything. Leading the way, he entered the tailor's shop.

The same old man was still sewing away. Whether or not

he recognised Mickey D, the toffs with him who had descended from the fancy carriage were remarkable enough a sight that the old man put down the sleeve he was sewing and gave the unusual visitors his full attention.

"I need to speak to your guvnor," Mickey D said with quiet authority. "You can say that Mickey D needs a word."

The tailor nodded, put down his work, and disappeared into the back. In almost no time, he returned and gestured for them to follow him. He didn't lead the way to the room at the back that The Rascal and company had been taken to. Instead, Wolf, Tabitha Little Ian, and Mickey D followed him up a narrow flight of stairs to the building's next level. Mickey D didn't like it; were they walking into a trap? He'd only visited Tuchinsky in this location once or twice in the past, but all the meetings had been conducted on the ground floor in the back of the building. Nodding subtly to Wolf, Mickey D kept his hand on his Webley. Wolf easily read the gang leader's facial expression and body language and ensured that he was similarly ready. Normally, the perfect gentleman, Wolf had insisted that he ascend in front of Tabitha to keep her sheltered behind him.

As they arrived at the landing, it became evident that these were living quarters. Wonderful smells lingered in the air, and Tabitha was reminded by her grumbling stomach that, except for the few mouthfuls of sandwich at Mickey D's, she hadn't eaten since early that morning. As the tailor led the way down the hallway, they heard raised voices and laughter. As they got closer, Tabitha thought she must be imagining things; she was sure that one of the voices she could hear raised as part of the cheerful clamour was the dowager's.

The door to the room the merriment was emanating from was open. As they approached what seemed to be the kitchen, they could see a group collected around the kitchen table, bowls in front of them, happily eating a delicious-smelling soup. And indeed, looking for all the world as if there was nowhere she'd rather be than in the kitchen of a Jewish gangster in a London slum, was the Dowager Countess of Pembroke.

"Mrs Tuchinsky, you simply must send me home with the recipe for this chicken soup," the woman was gushing.

"Your ladyship, I only wish I could," said a tiny, wizened, old woman, wearing a black dress and a grey wool shawl with a scarf tied over her hair. The woman had a heavy accent that Tabitha couldn't place. "But it's not just the recipe," she continued. "You need a kosher chicken. And it needs to be killed the right way. No offence, m'lady," she said apologetically, "But the goyim chickens just don't taste the same."

"Bubbe, you always say that," said a laughing voice whose owner they couldn't immediately see. "But a chicken is a chicken."

"Shame on you, bubbelah," the old lady said. "It's a good thing your poor mother isn't alive to witness such a shanda."

The laughing voice came again, "That's a shanda, Bubbe? I thought you reserved such insults for Moishe Cohen marrying a shiksa."

"That is also a shanda," the woman conceded, but in a voice that indicated she considered the two scandals of equal magnitude. Suddenly, sensing they were not alone, the old woman looked up. "Miri, we have visitors?"

The old woman had not finished saying these words when the two large men sitting around the table had sprung up, guns in their hands.

"Miriam, it's me, Mickey D. I'm not here for a fight."

"Miri, bubbelah, my kitchen is not the place for a broyges," the old woman admonished. Talking to the two large men, she waved a wooden spoon and demanded, "Maxi, Avi, put those weapons down. I've told you, whatever else happens in the rest of this house, in this kitchen, I'm the big macher. And the worst thing that will ever happen here is that someone has heartburn from too much kugel."

Taking a cue from her grandmother, Miriam nodded to her men to put their weapons away and return to their food. Despite this, Wolf kept his hand in his pocket on his gun. There was so much to take in that Tabitha wasn't sure what to try to process first. There was the rather striking woman dressed as a man. And then there was the dowager eagerly slurping down her chicken soup and asking this poor immigrant for recipes.

Finally, seeing Wolf and Tabitha behind Mickey D, the dowager put down her spoon and said in an offended voice, "Well, it took you long enough to come and get me. Anything could have happened to me." For good measure, she added one of her signature sniffs just in case her state of high dudgeon was unclear.

If the dowager's words hadn't made clear her connection to Tabitha and Wolf, their clothes would have alerted Miriam to the presence of yet more toffs in her house. She approached them and asked Mickey D, "Aren't you going to introduce me to your friends?" She wasn't as surprised to see the Irish gang leader as she might have been; the dowager had elaborated on her story over lunch and indicated the part that Mickey D had played in introducing her to Vicky Sharpe.

"Let them come in and take seats first, bubbelah. Where are your manners?" the old woman said as she pushed the two large men out of their seats. A quick glance from their guvnor and the men retreated to the back of the kitchen but didn't leave. Mickey D didn't blame her. He would have been equally cautious if the situation was reversed.

Mickey, Tabitha and Wolf sat while Little Ian hung back just outside the kitchen door. The old woman immediately went to the stove and started ladling out bowls of the fragrant soup. Before they knew it, steaming bowls were in front of them. It was a clear chicken soup with noodles and some kind of dumplings in it. Tabitha's bowl also had what looked like small, cooked egg yolks floating in it. Seeing Tabitha eyeing the egg-like balls, Miriam said, "You get three because you're a guest. Normally, we fight over the eggs." Noticing the hesitancy on Tabitha's face, she added, "Just try them. If you don't like the taste, I'll happily have them."

Tabitha dipped her spoon into the chicken broth and brought it to her lips. She had eaten many fine meals in her life, made with extravagant, indulgent ingredients cooked by high-priced French chefs, but she didn't think she'd ever eaten anything quite as flavourful and delicious as this soup. Feeling it would be rude not to try one of the eggs, she took one with her next spoonful of soup and took a tentative bite. My, but it was delicious. It was an egg yolk, but the consistency was different to a hard-boiled egg. And it had taken on the flavour of the soup. Following that first unsure bite with a far more enthusiastic second bite, Tabitha decided she wasn't sure she wanted to know exactly what she was eating, but whatever it was, it was tasty.

Feeling more comfortable, Tabitha then took a bite of one of the dumplings. Her enjoyment must have shown on her face because the old woman said happily, "Ah, you like the kneidlach. Good. You're far too skinny. Let me feed you for a week or two, and we'll put some flesh on you. Here, let me give you more lokshen. That's how you get a tuchus like my Miriam's."

"Bubbe! Please. Can't you control yourself?"

They had sat and started eating, but introductions still hadn't been made. Mickey D hadn't touched his soup yet and finally said, "Miriam Tuchinsky, I'd like to introduce you to the Earl and Countess of Pembroke."

Turning from the stove, the old woman said to the dowager, "You're mishpocheh with these people? He's your son, the one with the handsome punim?"

Before the dowager had time to try to interpret what she was being asked, Miriam said, "Bubbe, can you perhaps go to Zaide? I'm sure he'd like some soup."

Giving a sniff that sounded not unlike the dowager's own, the old woman said, "Bubbelah, if you want me to leave, you can just tell me. I'm not a putz. I know when I'm not wanted." With a final sniff, the old woman left the kitchen.

Sighing, Miriam said, "Please excuse my grandmother. She means well. We were surprised enough to have one countess gracing Brick Street. I'm unsure what to make of two, and an earl to boot. And I certainly wouldn't have expected to have you be the cause, Mickey. I certainly didn't expect you to lead this kind of tsuris to my door. While I wouldn't have said we were friends, I certainly didn't expect this."

Mickey D opened his arms apologetically, acknowledging the situation, "I had no idea that you had gone into business with Marge. I hadn't seen or heard from her in years. It was never easy to stay friendly with her and Vicks, so I chose the one closer to home. I swear, Tuchinsky, I didn't know that you were involved until his lordship came to me today to tell me that Lady P was missing. He'd found out that you own the house on Villiers Street."

While Wolf was pleasantly surprised that rather than walking into the middle of a gun battle, they instead were sitting companionably around the gangster's table sampling her grandmother's cooking, nevertheless, he felt the need to bring the conversation back to their investigation. "Miss Tuchinsky," he began.

"Tuchinsky is fine with me. The last boy to call me miss got a shiner for his troubles," the woman informed him.

"If that is what you wish. Tuchinsky, we understand that you have a stake in the brothel and gaming den that Margery Sharpe ran." Miriam neither confirmed nor denied his statement and so Wolf continued, "While we have discovered at least some of the illegal activities happening in that house, that isn't any concern of her ladyship's or mine."

"Ha! 'Illegal activities', I have to say I love the way you phrase that. But, if you are looking for gratitude for looking the other way, I'm sorry, but you'll be waiting a long time. I'm not sure how a bunch of toffs ended up amusing themselves by mucking around in the gutter, but my business is just that, my business."

Wolf sensed the two large men stiffening somewhat as their leader became more heated. Unsure how to move the conversation back to less dangerous ground, he glanced over at Mickey D. He knew this woman. Surely, he had a sense of how to handle her. Understanding Wolf's look, Mickey D said bluntly, "Tuchinsky, Marge is dead."

"So I've heard. Do you also think that I had her killed?"

Mickey laughed, "Tuchinsky, we both know it's possible. Your bubbe isn't in the room anymore. You can drop the act."

There was silence, and Wolf instinctively put his hand back in his pocket and grabbed the gun's handle. The silence stretched on for what felt like an eternity. Then, just when Wolf was getting really worried, Miriam threw back her head and laughed a loud belly laugh. Finally, wiping her eyes, she said, "Oy vey, Mickey. You better not let Bubbe hear you talking like that, or you won't be getting any of her lokshen pudding."

Everyone breathed a sigh of relief, and Mickey asked, "So if you didn't kill her, who did? We know that your lackey grabbed Lady P and brought her here. Are you telling me he had nothing to do with this?"

"Quite the contrary. I'm just saying that whatever mishegas Bono and that sister of his have got up to wasn't at my direction."

"Sister?" Tabitha blurted out.

Before anyone else could answer, the dowager explained with great pride at her central part in the story, "Yes, I discovered that Rascal character conspiring with Lou, who is his sister. Desperate at my uncovering of their crime, they forced me at gunpoint to accompany them here." The dowager seemingly had ended her story, but then, before anyone could react, she added, "Oh, but before they brought me here, they tied me up and gagged me with a disgusting kerchief and locked me in the cellar. As objectively terrifying as this all was, I kept my head, and when they brought me here, Tuchinsky immediately recognised The Rascal and Lou for the villains they were. I have been assured they will be dealt with appropriately." She said this last sentence as if they were going to be sent to bed without dinner, which Wolf was sure was the least of the punishment that would be meted out.

CHAPTER 34

Tabitha considered the tableau they made: two East End gangsters, three aristocrats and a couple of goons in the corner of the room. It all seemed bizarrely companionable for the time being, but was it? Wolf had acknowledged that they knew about Tuchinsky's forging business. And while she claimed to have not ordered Margery Sharpe's murder, there was no doubt that one of her people had been somewhat involved, even if it was after the fact. Would she really just let them all walk out after lunch as if it had been nothing more than a charming social gathering?

Wolf had similar concerns. While it seemed as if the relationship between Mickey D and Tuchinsky was cordial enough, perhaps even professionally respectful of each other, was Mickey D's word sufficient for Tuchinsky to believe they could be trusted? Moreover, Wolf wasn't sure how he felt at the prospect of leaving Lou and The Rascal to whatever street justice Tuchinsky might or might not dispense. He wasn't sure whether it would be letting them get off easily or abandoning them to a cruel and unusual punishment. He was just wondering how best to articulate these concerns when there was a sudden and very loud commotion that seemed to be coming from downstairs.

Tuchinsky and Mickey D were immediately alert at the noise, each jumping up, weapons at the ready. A large, imposing-looking man ran into the kitchen, yelling, "They've taken Bubbe."

"What do you mean, Shlomo?" Tuchinsky asked in a panicked voice. "Who has Bubbe?"

"That goyim scum Bono and his sister. Bubbe had brought down lunch for them earlier and was coming to take the bowls away. Bono must have been lying in wait. As soon as Benny opened the door, that khlop of a sister of his hit him over the head with something, and before we knew it, she'd grabbed his gun, and Bono had grabbed Bubbe."

Tuchinsky didn't wait to hear any more and ran out of the kitchen, everyone else, including the dowager, following behind. Wolf did consider telling Tabitha and the dowager to wait back, but even as he considered saying it, he realised how little good it would do.

They ran down the stairs and were greeted by the sight of The Rascal holding a gun to Bubbe's head. "I want everyone to lay their guns down slowly," The Rascal demanded. When there was some hesitancy from the two men who had been guarding them, he squeezed Bubbe a little tighter, and she gasped.

Tuchinsky pushed past her men, "If you hurt her, I promise that not only will I kill you, but I will also cut your dirty schlang off first."

"I'm sick of your threats, Miriam," The Rascal said tauntingly. "I bet your cousins 'ere are all pretty fed up of taking orders from a woman as well. You can threaten me all you want, but I know there's no way you'll risk me 'urting your darling bubbe. Now tell your men to drop their guns and kick 'em to Lou."

"Do as he says," Tuchinsky growled.

Her men dropped their weapons and kicked them in Lou's direction. She picked up a gun in each hand. Then, looking up at Tuchinsky and the others assembled at the bottom of the stairs, The Rascal said, "You too, Miriam. And your cronies there. I want you all to put down your guns."

Tuchinsky, Wolf and Mickey D were the only ones with their guns drawn, and so Tabitha assumed The Rascal hadn't imagined that she was also armed. Deciding to take a chance on that assumption, she made no move as the rest kicked their weapons over.

"Now what?" Tuchinsky snarled. "We're no longer armed. Let her go."

The Rascal laughed nastily, "'Ow stupid do you think I am? She's our only guarantee of getting out of here safely. So, we're taking Bubbe here with us. When we're sure we're safe, I'll think about letting her go."

"She's an old woman. She's done nothing to deserve this. It's me you have an issue with. I'll go with you," Tuchinsky said pleadingly.

"You're not in charge now. You don't get to make demands 'ere."

In desperation, Tuchinsky tried another tack, "You know, Rascal, I can overlook you trying to protect your sister. But do you really want to go down for a crime she committed? I don't know why she killed Marge. But it's not too late for you to leave her to her fate."

"You don't know why?" Lou spat. "'Oo do you think runs that brothel? You think Marge was the one keeping the dollymops straight? Dealing with all those servants you 'ired? Taking the coin and hustling the johns? Yeah, she might have been your business partner, but she wasn't the one doing the work for you. I was. And what did I get for my trouble? All I got from 'er was promises. Then, when I finally tell 'er I've 'ad enough, what does she say? Tells me that if it wasn't for 'er I'd still be earning my coin on my back. That's what all these years of being as true as a copper penny got me. So yeah, when I saw 'er standing on the Embankment that night, I grabbed 'er and threw 'er in the river. And I don't regret it."

Wolf could see that their priority had to be Bubbe's safety and said, "My carriage is outside. I'll accompany you and tell my driver you will take it. Just let the old woman go." Lou and The Rascal looked at each other. It was very evident that they had acted without having any plan. Wolf knew there was nothing more dangerous than a cornered, desperate man. He put his hands up in the air and began to walk slowly towards the armed couple. "I'm coming towards you so you can take me and let Bubbe go. Then we'll go outside, and you can take the carriage."

Wolf moved very slowly, not wanting to make any sudden movements that would startle Lou and The Rascal. Just as he was almost close enough for The Rascal to make the switch, there was a sudden noise from the other side of the room. The Rascal's attention was momentarily drawn away, and Wolf took advantage of his distraction to knock the gun out of his hand and grab Bubbe. As he did so, a gunshot rang out, there was a scream, and at almost the same time, a large figure leapt out of the shadows and grabbed Lou.

As the deafening bang of the gunshot faded, the billowing gun smoke added to the chaos that ensued. The acrid smell of black powder lingered in the air as Tuchinsky and Mickey D ran to reclaim their weapons. As the smoke began to dissipate, Tabitha realised that someone was on the floor, presumably hit by the bullet. Rushing over, her breath caught in her throat as she realised that Wolf was lying on the floor, partially covering and shielding Bubbe, blood gushing from his shoulder.

Concerned for the old woman pinned under the much larger man, Tabitha's first instinct was to try to help Bubbe up without jarring Wolf's wounded shoulder. As she knelt beside the two, unsure how she would manage this, she suddenly found Bear next to her. "That was you leaping out of the shadows?" she asked in amazement.

"Angie said I was to come in through the back if I could, just in case you'd walked into an ambush. Seems it was good I did." As he said this, Bear gently picked Wolf up as if he were a young child, thereby freeing Bubbe, who seemed to be unharmed, just a little winded. As they were tending to Wolf, Tuchinsky's men were busy with Lou and The Rascal. Whatever their punishment might have been for the transgression of Margery Sharpe's murder, Tabitha had little doubt that threatening her beloved bubbe's life was a crime Tuchinsky would not be forgiving.

Wolf seemed to be unconscious. At least Tabitha hoped that was all he was. "Tell me he's alive, Bear," she pleaded with tears in her eyes.

"He must have hit his head when he fell. From what I can see, the bullet went into his shoulder. He's losing a lot of blood. He's alive, but we need to get him seen to immediately." Turning towards Tuchinsky, Bear said, "I don't think we can risk a carriage ride. Where can I put him, and is there a doctor close by you trust?"

Tuchinsky turned to one of her men, "Go and get Dr Cohen. Tell him what's happened." Turning back to Tabitha and Bear, she said, "He's the best doctor in the East End. Shlomo, show them up to my room. Then put some water on to boil and make sure Dr Cohen has all the clean linen he needs. This man saved Bubbe's life. He is mishpocheh, family now."

CHAPTER 35

Bear gently carried Wolf up the stairs to the room Shlomo led him to. Wolf had started to stir, and it was clear from the sounds he was making how much pain he was in. No matter how careful Bear tried to be, he knew that every step he took was causing his friend excruciating pain.

Tabitha followed closely behind, trying to keep her tears in check; Wolf needed her to be strong and to be calm. She was happy to see that the dowager had not attempted to follow. Instead, she seemed to have been absorbed in helping comfort Bubbe, who was in a state of shock after her ordeal. As soon as Bear had placed Wolf on the bed, Tabitha had set to work ripping his shirt as gently as she could. There was so much blood loss that she wasn't sure what she should do first. Gunshot wounds were not something Tabitha had any experience of. Looking to Bear in the hope that he had some clue, she was happy to hear voices coming down the hallway. Hopefully, the doctor had arrived.

Dr Abraham Cohen was so old and stooped over that Tabitha worried that the man was too infirm himself to be an effective medic. He had a long white beard, and on his mostly bald head, he wore one of the funny little round hats that some of Tuchinsky's men had worn. Nothing about the man inspired Tabitha's confidence. She had agreed with Bear's initial assessment that it was too dangerous to try to transport Wolf back to Chesterton House in the carriage. However, now she was second-guessing that decision. Even if they couldn't move Wolf, would the Chesterton family medical man, Dr Pauls, be prepared to travel to Spitalfields? Tabitha didn't know the man well, but she did not doubt that he would suffer the indignities of travelling to the East End if commanded to do so by the dowager.

Dr Cohen shuffled into the room and approached the bed where Wolf was laid out. Putting his black medical bag down on the chair next to the bed, he opened it up and removed a stethoscope and a magnifying glass. First, he gently pulled Wolf's shirt open and listened to his chest. Then, nodding appreciatively at the work the quick-thinking Tabitha had done to clear the site of the bullet wound, he used the magnifying glass to examine the entry point.

Tabitha hadn't even noticed the pot of boiling water and the pile of clean linen being brought into the room, but now Dr Cohen turned to Bear and indicated they should be brought to the bed. So far, the man hadn't said anything, merely muttered under his breath while he examined Wolf. He used the hot water to wash the wound gently and then took wads of the linens and pressed them on the bullet hole to try to staunch the bleeding. "You, come and put as much pressure on this as you can," he said to Bear.

Finally, turning to Tabitha, he said, "Tuchinsky told me about the tsuris here this afternoon, and about the chutzpah this young man showed in saving her bubbe." Tabitha nodded but said nothing. What was there to say? The doctor continued, "He hit his head quite hard, but I think the effects of that will be temporary. However, the bullet is lodged quite deep in his shoulder in a particularly worrying location. Often shoulder wounds can be quite superficial, but there are also major blood vessels in the shoulder and that is why this wound is bleeding so much. I can't do anything until we can slow the bleeding, or he'll die of that before anything."

Die! These weren't the consoling words Tabitha wanted to hear. As if he could read her thoughts, Dr Cohen continued, "I won't let him die. I've treated enough wounds like this for Tuchinsky and her men, and this isn't the worst I've seen by far. I'll need to take the bullet out at some point and the risk of infection is always a concern." Dr Cohen had a heavy accent, but his voice was soothing and his tone authoritative enough that some of Tabitha's concerns were allayed. While she hadn't given up the idea of calling Dr Pauls in, Tabitha realised that the Harley Street doctor was unlikely to have the first-hand experience of dealing with gunshot wounds that Dr Cohen seemed to have.

Wolf started to stir and was mumbling incoherently. Tabitha went to the other side of the bed and took his hand. "Tabitha? Tabitha?" Wolf muttered.

"I'm here, Wolf," she said. "I'm not going anywhere." And in that moment, she realised how much she meant that.

Dr Cohen began removing surgical instruments from his bag, holding them in a pair of tongs, dipping them in the boiling water, and then laying them out on a clean piece of linen. While he prepared his equipment, Bubbe and Tuchinsky entered the room, followed by the dowager. Bubbe seemed to have recovered from her ordeal and said to Tabitha in a no-nonsense but kindly tone, "Dolly, I'll help Dr Cohen. I've done it many times when those putz grandsons of mine have got themselves hurt."

Tabitha's first instinct was to insist that she be the one to assist the doctor, but a quick look at Tuchinsky, who gave a reassuring nod, and she realised the sense in the old woman's words.

Tuchinsky said gently, "Lady Pembroke, let Bubbe help. Why don't the rest of us go to the kitchen, and I'll make a pot of tea? There will be plenty for you to do to help Lord Pembroke once Dr Cohen has finished." Again, while Tabitha's first instinct was to resist, the room wasn't large, and she didn't want to be in the way. Her need to stay by Wolf's side was outweighed by her desire to do whatever was necessary to allow Dr Cohen to do all he could to save him.

Tabitha allowed herself to be led away to the kitchen, where she sat at the table, the dowager, unusually subdued, by her side. Bear had stayed behind to ensure that the doctor was sufficiently furnished with new pots of boiling water. Tabitha realised that she hadn't seen Mickey D since the gunfight. She mentioned this to Tuchinsky, who told her that the Irish gangster, not wanting to be in the way, had returned to Whitechapel.

Nursing her cup of tea, Tabitha could think of nothing else but the surgery that was taking place in the nearby bedroom. Finally, looking up, she said to Tuchinsky, "Is it possible to move an armchair into the room with Wolf? I will be staying here to nurse him." The dowager said nothing, but the expression on her face said enough. Tabitha continued in a pointed tone, "Mama if you were able to spend multiple nights in a brothel, I see no reason why I cannot remain here for as long as necessary. Assuming, of course, that is okay with the Tuchinsky family."

Whatever the dowager might have said, was forestalled by Tuchinsky saying, "As I said, Lord Pembroke risked his life to save Bubbe. He is family, and I will do whatever is necessary to aid his recovery. We have a word in Yiddish, mishpoche, that means family, but also extended family, usually by marriage. Lord Pembroke is now mishpoche, and family means everything to Jews."

More than satisfied with this answer, Tabitha replied, "Then, when the surgery is over, I will send Bear back to Chesterton House to bring back some clothes for me and for Wolf. Mama, I suggest that you accompany Bear back to Mayfair." The dowager looked as if she was about to argue but then considered her silk sheets and hot baths, and instead nodded her agreement.

Waiting for Dr Cohen and Bubbe to finish felt like an eternity. Tabitha wasn't sure how many cups of tea she had drunk as they waited. At some point, Tuchinsky put out a cake that she was said was called a babka. It looked more like a loaf of bread than a cake. Tabitha had no appetite, but out of politeness nibbled on a slice. Flavoured with cinnamon, it was very tasty, but even so, Tabitha couldn't eat more than a few crumbs.

Finally, they heard a door open and close and Dr Cohen, followed by Bubbe, entered the kitchen. The old man looked exhausted, but he smiled at Tabitha and her heart leapt. "I'm happy to say that the surgery went well. I was able to remove the bullet and staunch the bleeding. If we can manage any fever, I see no reason that Lord Pembroke won't make a complete recovery."

Tabitha realised she'd been holding her breath ever since the doctor entered the room, and she now let out an audible breath at this news. The doctor continued, "The patient shouldn't be moved for at least a few days. I'll come by twice a day to see how he is, and you should call me immediately if there is any change for the worse. Keep him cool and see if you can get him to take some of Bubbe's chicken soup at some point. There is very little that doesn't cure." Tabitha wasn't sure if the doctor was joking, but Bubbe's vigorous nodding of her head indicated her absolute faith in the healing powers of her soup.

"Can I go and see him?" Tabitha asked.

"I gave him some laudanum for the pain, and he's sleeping now. But if you wish to sit with him, that will be fine."

Tabitha needed no more encouragement and was on her feet before the doctor had finished speaking. She returned to the bedroom, entering as quietly as possible. Wolf's shoulder was bandaged up and his hand lay across his chest in a sling. His head was turned on the pillow as he slept peacefully. Bear sat in the chair next to the bed and stood when Tabitha entered. Keeping her voice low, she asked him to return the dowager to Mayfair and then collect some clothes and personal effects of hers and for Wolf.

The next three days were something of a blur for Tabitha. She insisted on sleeping in an armchair Tuchinsky had brought into the room. Bear had returned with clothes and a couple of books, and while Wolf slept, Tabitha sat beside him and read. Periodically, Bubbe would come into the room with food and insist that Tabitha eat something. Wolf would stir periodically, and when he did, Tabitha would try to feed him something. But Dr Cohen had left instructions that Wolf should be given laudanum twice a day, saying that sleep was the best healer, and so even when he was awake, Wolf was only barely conscious.

Dr Cohen had told Tabitha to taper the laudanum dosage off slowly, and by the evening of the third day, Wolf awoke in a more lucid state. Seeing Tabitha sitting in the chair by his bed, he asked drowsily, "How long have I been here?"

"Three days," she answered.

"Have you been here the entire time?" he asked.

Tabitha rose and went and sat on the edge of the bed. "Where else would I be?" she said gently.

"You've been sleeping in that armchair?" Tabitha nodded.

Wolf's eyelids were started to droop. Tabitha said, "Don't worry about me. Go back to sleep."

With his good hand, Wolf patted the space on the bed next to him, "Come and lie down with me."

She was fully clothed and Wolf was an invalid, and yet, this request stunned Tabitha. Even after the embraces they'd shared during their charade at the brothel, the thought of lying, even fully clothed, next to Wolf felt so intimate. Even so, Tabitha stood and came around to the other side of the bed and lay down. The last thing Wolf did before he fell back to sleep was to take her hand in his.

Tabitha lay there watching Wolf's eyelids finally close and listening to his breathing begin to slow. Just as she thought he was asleep, he murmured, "I love you, Tabitha."

For a moment, she wasn't sure she had heard him correctly. Then, his eyes flickered open for a moment, met hers, and he smiled. "I love you too, Wolf," she answered. His eyes closed again, and he slept finally.

EPILOGUE

On Wolf's fourth day in the Tuchinsky household, Dr Cohen pronounced him fit to travel back to Chesterton House. Tuchinsky had said nothing more about the crimes Tabitha and Wolf had uncovered during their stay in her home, and Tabitha never dared bring the subject up. Just as Wolf was about to enter the Pembroke carriage, Tuchinsky took his good hand and said, "If you ever need my help, you know where to find me. You are mishpoche now." Then, just as Wolf was about to draw his hand back, the Jewish gangster had gripped it just a little tighter, leaned in and said in a low voice that only he could hear, "I once had a second cousin killed for disloyalty."

In an equally low voice, Wolf replied, "Your business is none of my concern, Tuchinsky." The woman nodded her head and smiled at his answer.

Dr Cohen continued to visit daily for the first week Wolf was home and then every few days after that to check on the wound and change the dressing. Every time he came, he was accompanied by one of Tuchinsky's cousins with jars of Bubbe's chicken soup, which she was convinced was the main reason Wolf had recovered from his injury.

There had been no repeat of their declarations of love since that first night, but Tabitha and Wolf seemed to have an unspoken understanding now. During Wolf's first few days at home, when he was confined to his bed, she sat with him every day and read silently while he slept or to him when he was awake. They spoke of many things but never the words they had said to each other. Yet, Tabitha felt something had changed between them that Tabitha felt, even if she couldn't articulate exactly what the difference was. The tension that had hung between them after their kiss in Brighton had lifted and was replaced by a quietly joyful peace.

After three days in bed, Wolf announced, "Call Thompson. I need to get up and get dressed. I will go insane if I have to spend any longer in bed."

Dr Cohen had told Tabitha that Wolf was healing well and that he could resume some gentle activities when he felt ready. She took Wolf's words as evidence of that readiness and didn't argue. The dowager had telephoned daily for an update on Wolf's recovery, and on his first morning downstairs, she came over to inspect the improvement in his health for herself. His arm was still in a sling, and Tabitha had insisted on him sitting in the most comfortable chair in the parlour with his feet up on a footstool to receive the dowager countess.

Barrelling into the room, the dowager sat opposite Wolf and pronounced, "You look remarkably well for someone who was shot barely a week ago."

"Bubbe has been ensuring a constant supply of her miraculously healing chicken soup," he answered.

"Has she indeed? I must admit, it is a very tasty soup. I may have to send my cook down to Spitalfields to buy some of these special chickens Mrs Tuchinsky swears are necessary to get the correct flavour. She did promise to come personally to teach my cook how to make the soup and those delicious dumplings. And you probably never tried some of that babka, but I managed to get her secret recipe for that as well."

Wolf silently marvelled at the dowager countess' delight in the tasty but very unsophisticated food of the Jews in London's East End. He tried to imagine Bubbe in the dowager's Mayfair kitchen giving cooking lessons and smiled.

Just as he thought the old woman couldn't surprise him more than she had, the dowager announced, "I'm thinking of serving Bubbe's chicken soup when it's my turn to host the Ladies of KB."

At this, Tabitha and Wolf said together, "When you do what?"

"What was unclear about my statement? Was your question about my choice of menu?" the dowager asked in a completely innocent tone belied by the twinkle in her eye; she had intended her statement to have a shock value and was delighted by her success.

"You intend to have a group of madams over for lunch at your home in Mayfair?" Tabitha repeated just to be sure she had understood correctly.

"Well, it would hardly be polite to accept their hospitality and yet refuse to host myself, would it now?"

"You intend to continue to attend these luncheons?" Wolf added equally incredulously.

"Of course I do," the dowager answered as if his question was absurd. "At the conclusion of our investigation, I had felt it only right to write to Madam Zsa Zsa to inform the ladies of their friend's unfortunate demise. She then wrote back to say how delightful it had been to have me join their group that day and how welcome I was any other time. I then wrote back to inquire when and where the next gathering was and to assure her of my attendance."

"And do you not worry what people might say?" Tabitha couldn't help but ask.

The dowager shook her head, pitying Tabitha's dim-wittedness, "Tabitha, when will you learn that society says and does as I say. I can assure you that before the Season is out, the ladies of the beau monde will be fighting each other to host their own such gatherings." While Tabitha didn't doubt the dowager's ironfisted hold over aristocratic circles, she had her doubts that hosting ladies of the night for luncheon would become en vogue. However, she kept this scepticism to herself.

Two weeks passed and Wolf continued to heal, even if not as quickly as he would like. Slowly, he began to meet with his man of business and steward again, though Tabitha was ever vigilant about him over-exerting himself.

November became December. One morning, the telephone rang. The dowager had resumed her visits with Melody and their usual daily telephone calls, which is what Tabitha assumed this was. She was seated in the parlour reading when Talbot entered the room and announced that the dowager countess wished to speak with her. Such demands rarely boded well, and Tabitha couldn't suppress a sigh as she rose and left the room.

Talking into the receiver, she said, "Mama, what can I do for you this morning?"

"Tabitha, now that Wolf is almost fully recovered, we must make plans for Christmas," a booming voice said.

Christmas. Yes, that was almost upon them, wasn't it? With everything that had happened, November had slipped by without Tabitha even considering what they might do for Wolf's first Christmas and New Year as earl, to say nothing of Melody's first at Chesterton House. She admitted as much to the dowager and said, "I assume we will do what we did when Jonathan was alive." In truth, that was very little. During the two Christmases of their marriage, Tabitha and Jonathan, joined by the dowager, had eaten a Christmas meal together that was wholly lacking in festive cheer.

"Nonsense," the dowager said. "It is time for Jeremy to visit the Pembroke estate, and there is no better time than at Christmas."

Tabitha knew for a fact that the dowager greatly preferred London and had never spent much time at the country estate when she was countess. Jonathan had also preferred life in town, so Tabitha had never visited Pembrokeshire. However, she didn't disagree; Wolf needed to step into a fuller role as earl and show himself to his tenants. She worried that the train ride to Wales might be too much for him, but if they didn't leave until mid-December, he would have another two weeks to heal.

As she resigned herself to the trip, she heard the inevitable next words, "Of course, I will be accompanying you."

Tabitha sighed again and replied, "I would expect nothing less, Mama."

* * *

Wolf and Bear, the duo you've grown to love, have a friendship and business partnership spanning over a decade. Curious about the beginning of their journey? Never fear. For this short story detailing their initial meet-cute, and more, sign up for my newsletter or find the link at sarahfnoel.com

Want a sneak peek at **Book 6, A Discerning Woman?** Keep reading....

Glanwyddan Hall had originally been an abbey that Elizabeth I had gifted to the first Earl of Pembroke as a reward for services rendered to the crown. While the original building had been added to over the years, these additions did not have the jarring mismatched aesthetic that so often was the case as old estates were "improved" by aristocrats with more money than taste. Instead, the newer wings were somehow blended with the old such that the overall effect was pleasing to the eye even while it was obvious that varying eras were represented.

Clapping her hands with delight, Tabitha exclaimed, "Oh, Wolf. It's beautiful. I had no idea."

While Wolf was glad to hear Tabitha's admiration, he was unable to separate the physical structure from his unpleasant memories and could not conjure up a similar appreciation. For her part, the dowager had her own bad memories from the early years of her marriage; the first time Philip struck her had been in this house.

Sniffing, she said, "Beautiful? Is that what you think? I never saw the appeal of the place."

Looking between the two of them, Tabitha intuited her companions were plagued by demons that one merry Christmas in the house would be unlikely to banish entirely. Nevertheless, she was determined to do what she could to enable Wolf at least to turn a new page at Glanwyddan Hall. There was already much he found burdensome about the earldom; she refused to allow a house to add to that load.

Melody was riding in the carriage with them, and she slipped her little hand into Wolf's much larger one and said in a sweet, innocent voice, "Wolfie, is this your house? It's very big. I'm scared I'll get lost in it."

Looking down at the adorable little girl with her red-gold ringlets and spray of freckles across her nose, Wolf said, "Don't you worry, Miss Melly. I will show you all the best spots. There used to be a wonderful treehouse in a huge oak tree. We'll have to go and see if it's still there. And there was a swing hanging off one of the branches of the tree. I used to love playing on that swing and seeing how high I could go.""Will you push me high, Wolfie?"

"So high that you'll be able to touch the sky."

Tabitha smiled at this exchange. Initially, Wolf had been very reluctant to have Melody live at Chesterton House, harbouring serious and justified concerns about Tabitha's evident attachment to the child. However, despite his best efforts to remain detached, even he had proven unable to resist Melody. The child was not just delightful; she was very intelligent. So intelligent that Tabitha sometimes wondered how much the charm offensive the little girl directed at Wolf was guilelessness and how much calculated by an orphan who intuited that her magical new life was at his pleasure.

As the carriages drew up to the house, a line of servants waited to greet them. Despite the cold, damp weather, it looked as if the entire household staff had been shuffled outside to greet their new master. Wolf descended first and then helped the dowager, Tabitha and Melody down. Tabitha was pleased to see the familiar faces of Talbot, Mrs Jenkins and some of the other Chesterton House servants.

Talbot approached them, "Milord, milady, and milady, I hope your journey was an easy one. I won't introduce you to every member of staff, but there are a few you should meet now." He paused, then gave a conspiratorial smile in Tabitha's direction, "And one person you might remember."

With that, the sea of servants parted, and a short, very round, elderly woman wearing an apron came forward, a beaming smile on her face. "Budgie!" Wolf exclaimed. "You're still in service here? I had no idea. What a wonderful surprise."

Purchase **Book 6, A Discerning Woman**

Melody and Rat are the adorable Whitechapel street urchins Tabitha has taken under her wing. Would you love to know what they're like as young adults? Never fear, my new series, **The Continental Capers of Melody Chesterton**, will reveal all. **Book 1, A Venetian Escapade,** is available for **pre-order** now!

AFTERWORD

Thank you for reading An Audacious Woman. I hope you enjoyed it. If you'd like to see what's coming next for Tabitha & Wolf, here are some ways to stay in touch.

SarahFNoel.com
Facebook
@sarahfNoelAuthor - Twitter
Instagram

If you enjoyed this book, I'd very much appreciate a review (but, please no spoilers).

Purchase **Book 6, A Discerning Woman**

Melody and Rat are the adorable Whitechapel street urchins Tabitha has taken under her wing. Would you love to know what they're like as young adults? Never fear, my new series, **The Continental Capers of Melody Chesterton**, will reveal all. **Book 1, A Venetian Escapade,** is available for **pre-order** now!

ACKNOWLEDGEMENT

I want to thank my wonderful editor, Kieran Devaney and the eagle-eyed Patricia Goulden for doing a final check of the manuscript

ABOUT THE AUTHOR

Sarah F. Noel

Originally from London, Sarah F. Noel now spends most of her time in Grenada in the Caribbean. Sarah loves reading historical mysteries with strong female characters. The Tabitha & Wolf Mystery Series is exactly the kind of book she would love to curl up with on a lazy Sunday.

BOOKS BY THIS AUTHOR

A Proud Woman

Tabitha was used to being a social pariah. Could her standing in society get any worse?

Tabitha, Lady Chesterton, the Countess of Pembroke, is newly widowed at only 22 years of age. With no son to inherit the title, it falls to a dashing, distant cousin of her husband's, Jeremy Chesterton, known as Wolf. It quickly becomes apparent that Wolf had consorted with some of London's most dangerous citizens before inheriting the title. Can he leave this world behind, or will shadowy figures from his past follow him into his new aristocratic life in Mayfair? And can Tabitha avoid being caught up in Wolf's dubious activities?

It seems it's well and truly time for Tabitha to leave her gilded cage behind for good!

A Singular Woman

Wolf had hoped he could put his thief-taking life behind him when he unexpectedly inherited an earldom.

Wolf, the new Earl of Pembroke, against his better judgment, finds himself sucked back into another investigation. He knows better than to think he can keep Tabitha out of it. Tabitha was the wife of Wolf's deceased cousin, the previous earl, but now she's running his household and finding her way into his life and, to his surprise, his heart. He respects her intelligence and insights but can't help trying to protect her.

As the investigation suddenly becomes far more complicated and dangerous, how can Wolf save an innocent man and keep Tabitha safe?

An Independent Woman

Summoned to Edinburgh by the Dowager Countess of Pembroke, Tabitha and Wolf reluctantly board a train and head north to Scotland.

The dowager's granddaughter, Lily, refuses to participate in the preparations for her first season unless Tabitha and Wolf investigate the disappearance of her friend, Peter. Initially sceptical of the need to investigate, Tabitha and Wolf quickly realise that the idealistic Peter may have stumbled upon dark secrets. How far would someone go to cover their tracks?

Tabitha is drawn into Edinburgh's seedy underbelly as she and Wolf try to solve the case while attempting to keep the dowager in the dark about Peter's true identity.

An Inexplicable Woman

Who is this mysterious woman from Wolf's past who can so easily summon him to her side?

When Lady Arlene Archibald tracks Wolf down and begs him for help, he plans to travel to Brighton alone to see her. What was he thinking? Instead, he finds himself with an unruly entourage of lords, ladies, servants, children, and even a dog. Can and will he help Arlene prove her friend's innocence? How will he manage Tabitha coming face-to-face with his first love? And how is he to dissuade the Dowager Countess of Pembroke from insinuating herself into the investigation?

Beneath its veneer of holiday, seaside fun, Brighton may be more sinister than it seems.

A Discerning Woman

It seems Christmas will be anything but peaceful this year!

Tabitha and Wolf are hoping to spend a quiet Christmas at Glanwyddan Hall, the Pembroke estate in Wales. However, before they even leave London, they receive unsettling news of disturbing pranks happening on the estate. Is this just some local youthful mischief, or is something more sinister afoot? Moreover, why is the dowager countess so determined that they not cancel their visit? With the dowager guarding a secret, Tabitha and Wolf are thrust into a desperate quest to uncover the truth. As danger looms, they must navigate treacherous paths to safeguard their loved ones.

Will Tabitha and Wolf reveal the malevolent force lurking in the shadows before it's too late?

An Indomitable Woman

The Investigative Countess, Rapier Sharp Logic paired with Great Insight and Boldness. A Private Inquiry Agent.

When the dowager countess receives her first assignment as a private inquiry agent from Miriam Tuchinsky, an East End gangster, she immediately throws herself into the case with gusto. Meanwhile, Lord Langley hires Tabitha and Wolf for an assignment that takes them deep into London's Jewish neighbourhood. Is there a connection between the two investigations? More importantly, can the two investigative teams work together?

Wolf has made his peace with continuing to take on investigations and with having Tabitha partner with him, but how will he manage the dowager countess' continued meddling in such a dangerous case?

Printed in Great Britain
by Amazon